HUGO AND THE BIRD

HUGO
AND THE
BIRD

The Witches' Inheritance

Book Three

JEFF MILLS

Matador
9 Priory Business Park,
Wistow Road, Kibworth Beauchamp,
Leicestershire. LE8 0RX
Tel: 0116 279 2299
Email: books@troubador.co.uk
Web: www.troubador.co.uk/matador
Twitter: @matadorbooks

ISBN 978 1800460 447

British Library Cataloguing in Publication Data.
A catalogue record for this book is available from the British Library.

Printed and bound in Great Britain by 4edge Limited
Typeset in 12pt Minion Pro by Troubador Publishing Ltd, Leicester, UK

Matador is an imprint of Troubador Publishing Ltd

To Evie and Otterly

About the Author

Jeff Mills is a retired dentist who has lived with his wife, Anne, for over forty years in North Devon in the South West of England, close to the village of Westward Ho! which is the setting for much of the story.

He has two children, now both grown up, and it was to entertain these when they were small, that he started to tell them stories during the frequent long car journeys to visit their relations.

Where 'Hugo' popped up from, he does not know, but Bird was loosely based on the Big Bird character from Sesame Street, a television programme popular with children at that time. As they were driving along, Jeff would try to introduce into the stories, items or places that they were passing, giving a greater sense of reality. He has attempted to continue this theme with this book and the previous ones; *Hugo and the Bird; The Tooth Fairy*, published by AuthorHouse and *Hugo and the Bird; Gnome Wars*, published By Matador.

Periodically, as they grew up, his children would remind him of the stories he told but could not remember much of the detail, except for the main characters: Hugo, Bird and the Witch.

Nothing was done until the spring of 2014. It was a time when it never seemed to stop raining. More out of boredom, the author sat down and tried to write, what he remembered of the stories he had told his children those many years before. He admits; it was very strange writing; because the story seemed to write itself. He had no plans as to plot or characters; they just evolved from thin air. Even he was curious to know what was going to happen. What he did know was that he would like to bring the story alive by making its roots and its location, real. For this, he based the series on the historic gross miscarriage of justice with the hanging of the three Bideford witches in 1682; the last people to be legally hanged for witchcraft in England, and the places around his home in North Devon.

So sit back, put your feet up, smell the sea air coming off the Atlantic Ocean and read about the further adventures of Hugo and his strange friend, Bird, as they continue their battle against the dark forces that inhabit the North Devon village of Westward Ho!

Chapter 1

The Rescue

"Police are still searching for the young nine-year-old schoolgirl who went missing three days ago. She has been named as Emma Jones of Westward Ho! in North Devon. The girl is described as being Caucasian, about four feet five inches tall, with mid-length light brown hair. She has a slight London accent having recently moved to the area from Reading and was last seen wearing blue denim jeans, a bright red shirt, a light-blue jacket, and red trainer shoes.

She had been staying with a local dentist and his family following the death of her parents, who were tragically killed in a car accident on the A361, North Devon Link Road. The air-sea rescue helicopter and coastguard service have launched a major search along the coastline in the area but, to date, no evidence has been found as to her whereabouts. Her disappearance comes closely after that of the still missing, young freelance journalist, Sue Redwell, in the same vicinity. Police are not ruling out a connection between the two incidents and are advising people to be on their guard and to *ensure that parents are aware of their children's whereabouts at all time.*

Police are asking anyone who has seen this young girl or who has any information to contact them.

The weather forecast for tomorrow will ..."

Mr Bennett picked up the remote control of the television and switched it off. He looked at his wife, who was dabbing her eyes, which were still red from all the crying that she had done since she had returned home to find their house-guest and charge missing.

Emma had been staying with the Bennett family since her parents' death. Before this, during the summer months and the long school holiday, she had become friendly with Hugo, the Bennett's nine-year-old son. Without his parents' knowledge, Emma and Hugo had become involved in a bizarre vendetta by the daughters of the 'Three Witches of Bideford', who were hanged in 1682 for witchcraft. These three: Susanna Edwards, Mary Trembles and Temperance Lloyd, were the last people to be legally hanged for witchcraft in England. Their three offspring; Mary Edwards, Anne and Jane Trembles, had also been later hanged for witchcraft in 1697, but illegally, and using false evidence, resulting in a serious miscarriage of justice. They were made the scapegoats for the murder of their cousin, Stephen Lloyd, by a vicious and bully of a local judge, Sir Thomas Raymond, living in Bideford at that time. He had forced the young man, who was considered a local healer, to try to save his children who were seriously ill. Unfortunately, despite his best efforts, they died. The judge became angry and attacked the young man killing him and had his body thrown into the river Torridge that runs through Bideford.

The three girls had witnessed this attack, and to prevent them from accusing the judge of murder, he falsely accused them of the crime of witchcraft, plus the death of his two children, and had them hanged instead.

While in prison, awaiting execution, they had all vowed that somehow they would get their retribution on the judge and all those other false accusers, including all their descendants.

Standing on the gallows, they cursed their murderers before the lever was pulled.

***

"I'm sure that she's alright and still alive," whispered Mr Bennett sympathetically, gently stroking his wife's hair. "I just feel it somehow, and there's been no sign of a body or anything." He went on trying to reassure her, but it started her crying again.

"But what if those witches, Morgana and Putricia, or whatever their names are, didn't go away and have captured her and…?" The tearful woman did not finish her sentence. "And what about that other girl, that reporter woman, Sue Red something? She disappeared weeks ago and they never found her."

"Redwell. Sue Redwell," muttered her husband.

"Yes her." responded his wife. "Other than a few unconfirmed sightings near Hartland, nothing has been seen or heard of her. What if there's a serial killer out there preying on young girls? Who'll be next? Our Stephanie?"

"I really don't think that's the case," replied her husband. "and besides, both Hugo and Emma were convinced that

Morgana had somehow changed into Sue Redwell. Even you saw the similarity when we fought with her and the goblins at the Gnome Reserve."

Mr Bennett put his arm around his wife and hugged her. At that moment, their daughter, Stephanie, walked in through the door into the lounge. She also had been crying, as could be seen by her red, puffy eyes.

"I'm going over to Marty's," she announced.

"Not by yourself, you're not!" her mother almost screamed as she turned in the chair to face her daughter. Stephanie was about to shout back but then thought better of it and, as calmly as she could, informed both her parents that Marty's father was coming to pick her up. All three relaxed a little. Ten minutes later the doorbell rang and her boyfriend's father arrived. He came in and politely asked if they had any news, but since there was none, he expressed his and his family's sympathy, adding that if they could do anything, then they only had to ask. After further pleasantries, he and Stephanie left.

The noise of the door slamming roused Hugo, the Bennett's son, from his daydreaming. He had been replaying in his mind the events of the last few weeks, where he had found a strange stone on the beach at Westward Ho!, near to where he lived. The stone had 'hatched', revealing a peculiar magical, bird-like animal. He had also followed his pet dog into a tunnel in the cliffs, only to discover that it was the home of the witch, Kadavera. Her sole aim was to fulfil her dying vow; to destroy every descendant of the people responsible for the unlawful hanging of herself and her friends, Anne Trembles and her sister Jane in 1697.

She had captured Hugo as he tried to help rescue Puchy, the tooth fairy, who was being used as a guinea pig in the experiments Kadavera was conducting, which, if successful, would allow her to exist and roam around in daylight. The potion she had been given resurrecting her, following her execution, was rendered ineffective by sunlight. Unfortunately, Kadavera had been killed by running into it while chasing Hugo and his friends. However, her death prompted the resurrection of the two other women executed with her, now calling themselves Morgana and Putricia. They had fought and lost a battle against Hugo, his parents, Emma and ably helped by Puchy, the tooth fairy, Barguff, the leader of the gnomes from the Gnome Reserve and Bird, Hugo's magical bird-like friend.

These witches had recruited the combined forces of the Cornish goblins, to aid in killing all the gnomes that lived in a small community at the visitor attraction called the Gnome Reserve in the village of West Putford in North Devon and who had become friends of the children.

He remembered seeing how Morgana, previously called Anne Trembles, one of the women hanged in 1697, had used a special potion and had been transformed and absorbed into the body of a young girl reporter, known as Sue Redwell. She had been investigating the cave, close to where Hugo lived in Westward Ho! in North Devon. It had been the witches' home since their coffins had been placed there, centuries earlier, by person or persons unknown.

Morgana had used her skill in potion-making to revive her sister, Jane, from an inanimate condition in a coffin and resurrect her into the witch that now called herself Putricia. These two, aided by an enormous panther-like animal called Snatch, which had the head and fangs of a sabre-toothed tiger, had forced the Cornish goblins to fight and try to eliminate the peaceful gnomes that lived at the Gnome Reserve. Fortunately, Hugo, his family, who had found out what was happening, Emma, and his strange friends had been able to defeat the goblins and the witches but not before the death of many of the gnomes, including their self-proclaimed leader and friend of Hugo called Barguff.

The boy sniffed, wiped his arm across his nose and went into the bathroom to wash his face so that his parents would not see that he had been crying. Going downstairs to where they were seated, he asked if they had heard any news about the possible whereabouts of Emma. The question started his mother crying again, but his father coughed and told him that nothing had been heard so far, but he didn't sound convinced,

"No news is good news," he said, as reassuringly as he could.

"I think I'll go out and take Jake for a walk," Hugo told them, which made his mother look up in apprehension, but a nod from his father indicated that it was alright.

Slouching into the kitchen, he picked up Jake's lead from the back of the door as he went. The rattle of the chain from his leash roused the apparently sleeping dog from his stretched out position in his basket, which resulted in him overlapping both sides. His head looked up and, seeing Hugo, he jumped out of his basket, shook his head, followed by his whole body and ran up to his young owner, wagging his tail furiously.

Hugo attached the lead to his collar and opened the back door but immediately closed it again as it was pouring with rain. He was about to abandon the idea of a walk but then thought that, if he stayed in, he would only be miserable, especially as his parents had taken the disappearance of Emma so severely.

They had taken charge of her care following the death of her parents in a car accident, and both felt somehow responsible for her going missing. Was it something that they had said, or done? Had she run away, or what? They just did not know. With a sigh, Hugo searched in the cupboard by the stairs and found his anorak which, though looking old and a bit tattered, was at least waterproof. After pulling it on and fastening the zip, he grabbed the loop of Jake's lead, and together they headed outside.

At first, the young boy was unsure whether to head left into Westward Ho! to look around the shops or turn right and along the old railway track, which led to the, now sealed, entrance to the witches' cave. His previous sojourn into this cave had been the start of all the preceding's which had led to his adventures and fights with the witches Kadavera, Morgana and Putricia. He felt a small shiver go down his back as he thought of them and the havoc they had caused. He consoled himself with the thought that Emma's parents would still probably be dead, even if he had not found the witches' hideout, as they would have been driving along the same stretch of road at the same time with the same result. This realisation gave him a little comfort. Suddenly there was a strong pull on his arm and Jake shot off towards the direction of the railway track.

"Well, that decides it," thought the boy and with arm extended by the pull of the dog's lead, he set off at almost a trot, Jake tugging him forward.

The rain started to get heavier, so he pulled up the hood of his anorak and was about to continue up the path when Jake suddenly launched himself sideways. The force pulled Hugo down to the spot, where the cave's second entrance had been located which had been sealed by the police by covering it with large stones and boulders, to stop anyone getting back in.

"Oh, not again," voiced Hugo to himself. "This is how all this mess started in the first place with me following you down a hole."

He tried to pull his pet back, but the animal seemed insistent, barking and pulling at its lead. Not feeling in the mood for a battle, Hugo gave in and allowed the dog to pull him down to the entrance and the mass of debris that covered it. They both stood there looking at the rocks and the impenetrable barrier they made.

Hugo would have loved to go back inside, as he felt sure that he might discover something that might lead him to find out what had happened to his friend Emma, but there was no way he could get through the massive obstruction the rocks had created. He was lost in his thoughts when the dogs incessant barking and pawing of the stones blocking the entrance roused him from his reverie.

"We can't get in," Hugo reprimanded the dog, "and even if we could, my mum and dad would kill me if I ever went in there again. They will probably tell me off for just being here if they ever found out." He pulled at Jake's lead to try to pull him away, but the dog refused to move. It kept barking and trying to get through the obstacle in front of them. Beginning to get a little angry and frustrated with his pet, Hugo pulled hard on the lead but as he did so, the collar around Jake's neck snapped, and the dog was free. It leapt to the base of the pile of stones and frantically scratched at the gravel below, yelping and constantly barking, turning to Hugo as if to say. "Let me in."

Hugo examined the collar and realised that it was quite irreparable, but there again, it had been the same collar that they had bought when they got Jake as a puppy almost eight years previously. He tried to refashion the lead to make a temporary collar, but that did not work. He thought that if he walked away from his dog and called him to follow, the dog would respond, but Jake continued to dig and barked even louder.

At last, Hugo gave in and went up to the stones and started to pull a few away at the top. They were quite large and heavy, and despite the chilly weather, he began to sweat. He sat down on one of the larger stones to have a few moments rest when he thought he heard a very faint voice coming from the other side of the rubble. He thought at first that it was just the wind running through the tunnel and seeping through the stones, but then he heard it again. He told Jake to stop barking, which, surprisingly, he did. Hugo put his head down as far as he could to the boulders and listened... Nothing. He shouted, quietly at first, as he did not wish to bring his presence there to the attention of anyone who might be passing... Still nothing. He thought that he must have imagined the voice in the first place but decided to call out one more time. However, this time, looking around to make sure that no one was in earshot, he cupped his hands and shouted, as loudly as he could;

"Hello! Anyone there!"

There was a short pause; then a very faint, high-pitched voice trickled from between the rocks,

"Help me! Please help me."

Hugo looked at Jake, who looked at him and barked loudly, wagging his tail furiously, as if to say, "Told you so."

Hugo pulled and tugged at the stones which were very heavy for a nine-year-old boy; after all, they had been put there in the first place to stop people moving them. After several short breaks to catch his breath and pull out the sharp pieces of grit that kept getting embedded in his hands, he could make out the first signs of a space developing at the top of the pile. He put his face to the hole and shouted,

"Are you still there?" which he thought later was a bit stupid as, where could they go?

His question was answered by the same words, "Help me. Please help me."

Spurred on by the answer, he tore at the biggest boulders at the top of the heap until there was a noise of falling stones at the back of the pile. A boy-sized opening appeared. Hugo had to fight off Jake who was trying to jump in front of him to get into the hole, but he pushed him down and ordered him to stay and sit. The dog whined but eventually obeyed Hugo's instruction.

Hugo started to crawl into the darkness beyond but found that his anorak kept catching on the sharp edges of the boulders, so he eased back out and took it off. Fortunately, the rain was now abating, but his shirt soon became clammy as, what rain there was, soaked into it. With great care not to graze his knees and ankles, he manoeuvred himself through the space until he could see the other side. He moved further forward, but then the stones beneath him suddenly gave way and he fell headlong down the slope and into the tunnel. It took him several moments to recover. Rolling upright, he felt a stinging in his elbows and knees. He rubbed them to try to ease the pain and became aware that they felt sticky. He thought that he was bleeding but, after a final rub, ignored the discomfort. He listened very carefully for the noise of anyone who might have called out for help but could hear nothing, except the sound of the sea and the wind outside. He called out, but there was no reply. He called again but still nothing. Then there was a noise from the hole through which he had just fallen and Jake pushed his face through.

"Stay!" Ordered Hugo, but the dog bounded forward into the dark void. Hugo could hardly see his pet as the light coming in through the hole was very dim, but as his eyes became accustomed to the darkness, he could see the animal just to one side of him, pawing at something on the floor. At first, Hugo could see nothing; then he noticed a very faint line of glowing blue dots ahead of him extending up the tunnel for as far as he could see. The dots seemed to end where Jake was pawing, at something on the ground. The boy could not make out anything at first, but then he saw, what he thought looked like, a white piece of cloth covered by large, red polka dots. Poking from out of the white material Hugo made out a small pair of legs that looked extremely bloody. He carefully eased himself forward, so as not to make more stones fall on him or the apparent figure lying there and very gently pulled the small creature out from below the rocks that had fallen around it.

When free, he bent forward to see if the small gnome, for that, in the dim light, was what it appeared to be, was breathing. He could not feel any breath and was unsure how and where to take a pulse on a gnome, even if they had one. While he was deciding what to do, Jake came up to the figure and started to lick it enthusiastically. Hugo was about to stop him, as he thought that the dog might be considering the casualty as potential food, when it gave a little moan and moved one of its legs. He sat up and waited to see what was going to happen. Slowly and with a few more slobbering licks from Jake, the little gnome started to regain consciousness.

Hugo took off his shirt, as it was wet from the rain which was still falling outside. Carefully and as gently as he could, he wiped the dirt and grit from around the tiny creatures face and head, then started to clean it's badly bruised and bleeding legs but the gnome gave a cry of pain, which made him stop. He was trying to think of what to do next when a shaft of sunlight burst through the hole in the rocks and illuminated the individual lying there, but more importantly, its red-spotted pantaloons. Suddenly Hugo remembered about what Barguff had said about red-spotted pantaloons and how they belonged to Orleg, one of his cousins.

Hugo went back down on his knees and whispered, "Orleg. Orleg. Is that you? Are you all right?"

The little gnome groaned and opened her eyes but quickly recoiled as she saw the outline of a big person in front of her.

Hugo sensed that she was frightened. He remembered seeing her being lifted onto Morgana's table and given a potion which made her appear to die, so he leaned back a little and whispered.

"Don't worry Orleg. It's me; Hugo, Barguff's friend. Don't be afraid. I'm here to help you. Can you move?"

"Where's Barguff?" she moaned.

Hugo did not think it was the best time to tell her that he had been killed while fighting off six or seven goblins when they had been attacked at the Gnome Reserve. Ignoring the question, he told her that he was going to get her out of there and to safety.

Although very frightened and initially resisting Hugo's efforts, he eventually managed to get her wrapped up in his shirt so that he could carry her back through the hole in the rubble and take her somewhere where she could receive treatment. With Jake barking encouragement, Hugo lifted the little bundle and pushed her through the hole, wedging her between two large rocks while he and Jake extricated themselves from the tunnel. It was not a moment too soon, for just as his foot touched the beach, the stones and rocks above the hole, loosened by the now pouring rain, collapsed and fell in completely, resealing the entrance but this time for good.

Shirtless, soaked with rain and covered in mud and sand Hugo looked around to see if he could find any protection for his parcel as he did not want her to die now, after all the trouble he had taken to rescue her. It was then he saw his anorak, which he had thrown on the ground outside the entrance. As he picked it up, rainwater streamed from it, but he shook it out as best he could, covered his head and Orleg with it and raced back to his house as fast but as carefully as he could, chased by Jake, who was still barking wildly and jumping up to look at the small gnome.

Mrs Bennett was standing in the kitchen, about to pour some hot water into the teapot to make a cup of tea, when the half-naked Hugo, carrying a small bundle, followed by a soaked and bedraggled Jake, burst through the kitchen door shouting;

"Mum! Mum! Come quick!"

His mother, startled by the whirlwind entry and strange appearance of her son and pet, turned and let the hot water pour over the kitchen worktop. She was about to loudly admonish her son, when he carefully laid out the parcel he was carrying onto the kitchen table and unwrapped his sodden shirt from around it, exposing the distraught small gnome.

When she saw another 'Big Person', who was even taller than the first, she cowered and tried to pull the shirt back over herself to hide.

"This is Orleg mum," blurted out Hugo. "She is Barguff's cousin and was the one that Morgana was using in her experiments before the battle. She gave her some sort of potion, and it looked as if she had died. She was left in the cave before the witches attacked the gnomes. Everyone forgot about her in the excitement, though Barguff wanted to go back and rescue her when they all realised she was missing."

"What are you talking about?" demanded his mother.

As quickly as possible, Hugo explained how, while Bird and Barguff were trying to rescue the gnomes from the cave where Morgana had held them captive, they had seen Orleg forced to take a potion which appeared to have killed the small gnome girl. She had been left on the table in the cave when all the gnomes escaped.

At this point, roused by all the commotion, Hugo's father came into the room. He took one look at the sad state of the small girl, and with a sideways glance at his shirtless son, grabbed some warm, dry towels that were near the Aga cooker in the kitchen and proceeded to strip away the wet shirt and all the wet clothes from her. Hugo's face turned red, and he looked away in embarrassment. Mrs Bennett pushed her husband aside and took up the idea, gently drying off the protesting naked gnome, finally wrapping her in the soft, warm towels. The heat from them started to settle the small gnome, and she snuggled down inside, not just for comfort but to hide her embarrassment as well.

Turning to Hugo, his mother ordered him to go upstairs immediately, take a shower and put on some warm, clean clothes. He was about to do so when his father said loudly to him.

"Before you go, get some of those old towels and give that dog a drying off." As he said this, the animal, who up to now had been quiet and watching all that had been going on, suddenly gave himself a massive shake, sending muddy rainwater everywhere.

"And while you're about it, you can clean up all that mess too," he added, pointing to all the splashes that now adorned everything within six feet of the table.

Hugo groaned and looked pleadingly at his dad as if to say, 'Do I really have to?' but a nod from his father confirmed the order. Without further comment, Hugo set to work. Finally, when all was clean and had satisfied his father, he trudged up the stairs to the bathroom and ran the shower.

Chapter 2

A New Home

The cleft in the cliff overlooking Hartland Quay was much smaller and more cramped than the two witches previous home in Westward Ho! It was also much draughtier than their old cave but at least they were sure that it would be secure from prying eyes, meddlesome little boys, gnomes and interfering 'Birds'.

Morgana and Putricia had now grown accustomed to the new bodies they had, 'acquired', from the journalist, Sue Redwell and the young Emma Jones. However, Putricia felt a little cheated that she had the smaller, weaker body of Emma. Since she was the elder sister, she thought that she should have been the stronger of the two. Although fully absorbed into their respective bodies, both kept getting flashbacks of their previous owners lives, Morgana more than Putricia. Morgana put it down to the fact that her body was that of a twenty-something-year-old, while that of her sister was of a mere child. Sometimes, the younger witch, not in body but age, would deliberately lie awake trying to remember the life and experiences that the young woman, whose body she now possessed, had lived.

Memories, of what she assumed must be of her family, kept coming back, together with an image of a young man who, even the witch thought attractive. Strange items also came to mind; a box on the wall with sound and pictures coming out of it, carts that pulled themselves along without horses. There were also funny little, what appeared to be, small books, that you held up to the ear and talked into. Their purpose was a mystery, except that she had discovered one in the pocket of the strange blue trousers which she had found herself wearing after regenerating. She had left it in the old cave, but one day, while she was examining it, the object had suddenly lit up and started to play music. Shocked by the sudden activity, she had dropped it, smashing the glass on its front.

A large tin can that had been a bright yellow in its prime, now a dirty soot-covered relic of its pristine past, bubbled away over the open fire. Wisps of steam shimmered over its top and the aroma of stewed rabbit permeated the area around it. Close by, curled up, was the large ball of black fur that was Snatch, the witch's panther-like pet. Its head, bearing the fangs of a sabre-toothed tiger, was buried deep in the centre of the coil to keep warm. Putricia stood up and poked the fire, which sent a bevvy of sparks high up into the roof. Using the same stick, she stirred the gurgling stew.

Snatch uncoiled his head from under its paw and looked expectantly at his mistress. She added a few more dried leaves and gave another stir, finally blowing and bringing the flattened stick to her lips. Carefully she blew again ensuring that it was cool enough to sample and licked the end of her makeshift spoon. With the slightest of a smile, she took an old tin can and used it to ladle two portions onto two wooden platters carved out of driftwood. She offered one to her sister, who looked at the meagre meal with a little less enthusiasm. The dejected pair sat down in silence and ate until both platters were empty. Snatch watched with anticipation, but no food came his way. He buried his head back down and covered it with his paw.

Morgana put down her plate and with a sigh, looked around the cave and then again at the plate.

"Sister, I know that you do not want to think about it, but we can do nothing here, it is so remote, and the winter will soon be upon us, do you think that we should move and find something more..." She was going to say, comfortable but then changed her mind and said, "convenient. After all, these new bodies we have are not as strong as our own were and we do not have any more of the potion left to go into another body if these fail."

"And where do you suggest we go?" her sister almost spat out.

"Well, I keep having dreams and thoughts that this body I am in had a home of her own, which was far more comfort...convenient to... this," and she waved her arm around the cave with disdain.

"And where is this, 'Home'? I fear that you are becoming soft." Putricia barked without looking up.

Morgana looked down in disappointment.

"I don't know." she sighed sadly to herself and picked up both platters. She took them to a small hollow in the side of the cave, where rain seeped down through the rocks.

She splashed them with water and put them to one side to dry. Glancing into the cooking pot and, seeing that there was still some of the stew that they had eaten leftover, she poured it onto the floor in a corner, at which point Snatch sprang up and devoured every morsel before the witch had even sat down.

The wind blew and the sea crashed below them but silence now reigned in the cave as both sisters sat quietly. Morgana was thinking about a new home and more comfort. At the same time Putricia planned on how she could kill that murderer, who was the father of that interfering boy who had destroyed all their careful plans to kill the gnomes. She inwardly fumed that this boy had somehow acquired, and had control of, the amulet of Excalibur. This treasure had originally been in their family for centuries and had given them the special powers that made them the great healers they had been when they were alive. It was her inheritance, and whatever happened, she was going to make sure that she got it back. Nothing and no one was going to stand in her way.

Chapter 3

Orleg's Homecoming

Much had been done at the Gnome Reserve over the previous few weeks to clean up and repair the damage done following the night of the attack by the two witches and the Cornish goblins. The owner and her staff had all worked non-stop to rebuild the village; restoring the houses of the gnomes that had been destroyed. There were also a few people that came and helped but had been given the excuse that a large dog had ransacked the village. However, they were not allowed to visit when the real gnomes were active.

A commemorative stone had been erected close to the centre of the small township. Engraved on it, were the names of those that had been killed in the attack, with that of Barguff at the top. He had played such a vital role in their enemy's defeat but had sadly been killed in his efforts.

By the side of the stone sat the young gnome, Chipper. He had picked some daisies from the lawn of the owner and was laying them beside the memorial when a Volvo estate car came up the drive and tooted its horn. All the gnomes scurried for cover, including Chipper, who hid under a log but was still able to see what was going on. The car skidded to a halt on the rough gravel and all four doors opened.

The reserve owner, alerted by the noise, looked up from painting the walls of one of the last houses to be repaired. She recognised the car and smiled as the whole Bennett family emerged. Mr Bennett grinned and waved at the owner as she came into view. Mrs Bennett appeared to be carrying a parcel in her arms and it wasn't until she was much closer than the owner realised it was a baby. Coming closer and preparing to admire the young child, she looked at its face. Her eyes suddenly lit up. She gasped.

"Orleg! You're alive. We all thought that you had died. Look, everybody! It's Orleg! She's alive!" The owner turned and shouted as loud as she could so that everyone, human or gnome, would hear. There was a scream from inside one of the small, gnome cottages and a plump female gnome rushed out, still with the suds of the washing she was doing covering her arms. She raced to where Mrs Bennett stood, holding her package and tore at the blanket to see who or what was inside. At the sight of her daughter, alive and well, she screamed again and burst into tears of joy.

Chipper sprang from his log and rushed over, eager to see his best friend. He jumped around Mrs Bennett's legs as he did not even come up to her knees and it was several moments before she noticed him. She bent down on one knee and gently laid her bundle on the floor in front of him. Wriggling between Orleg's mother, who was frantically trying to cuddle and caress her daughter, he brushed away the blanket and looked down at its contents.

21

There before him was the somewhat confused face of Orleg but as soon as she saw Chipper, she screamed with joy and pushed away the blankets and sat up. She looked around and noticed her mother and all her friends rushing towards her. She squeaked with glee, clapping her hands. While she kissed and hugged everyone around her, the Bennett family moved away, together with the owner and the two assistants, who had rushed out of the office to see what was the cause of all the fuss.

When back in the office, Mr Bennett explained how Hugo,

"And Jake," added Hugo.

"Yes and Jake." repeated his father. "As I was saying Hugo… and Jake, went back to the cave, against everything that had been said about never going there," he looked sternly at Hugo as he said this. "and found that Orleg was trapped inside. Fortunately, he was able to rescue her.

I must admit though, had he not done so, then I would not have fancied her chances of survival. She was in a pretty bad state when he brought her to our house. However, with some very careful attention by Julia and Stephanie here," his daughter blushed and turned her head away, "we were able to patch her up. So here she is."

Jake, firmly held on a lead and a new collar by Stephanie, wagged his tail furiously at the sound of his name. She bent down and rubbed his head.

Two of the elder gnomes started to come into the office to say 'Hello' to the Bennetts and to find out what had been going on, but when they saw Jake, they ran away screaming. They had previously seen him when he was working for Morgana, at which time he was certainly not friendly.

Hugo ran out after them and called to them to say that everything was alright and they need not be afraid. It was with much trepidation that they returned and poked their heads inside the office several minutes later. Seeing that Jake was firmly held on a strong lead by a young female Big Person and he was lying on the floor, they ventured in and joined in with the conversation and questions that everyone was firing at Hugo and Mr Bennett.

"Oh, I am sorry," the Reserve's owner broke in. "I'm forgetting my manners. Would anyone like a drink? A cup of tea perhaps or a Coca-Cola?" she said, looking at Hugo. He looked at his father, who never let him drink fizzy drinks as, he said, they were bad for the teeth. Then looking back at the owner he said, "A cup of tea would be nice."

His father smiled his approval and said, "Tea would be fine. All white with no sugar."

One of the assistants left to make the drinks and soon came back with a tray bursting with eight cups of tea and a plate of sticky cakes and biscuits.

"I brought a special one for you," she said, looking down at Jake. Kneeling, she patted its head and, from inside the pocket of her pinafore, she produced a large Doggy Treat. Jake rapidly jumped up, wagging his tail frantically. Gently taking the treat from her hand, he moved into the nearest corner where he quickly demolished it.

More gnomes joined the party, all eager to find out what had happened until the only people left outside were Oleg, her mother and Chipper. Orleg kept looking around until she said, "Where's Barguff?"

Chipper suddenly stopped laughing and jumping around, his whole attitude changing. With tears beginning to well up in his eyes, he hesitantly told the little gnome that her cousin had died in the battle. She burst into uncontrollable tears and took several minutes to settle down. Chipper took her hand, escorting her to show her the stone that had been set up as a memorial. By now both were in floods of tears. It wasn't until the Bennetts, with a great many gnomes, poured out of the office all cheering and shouting, that they managed to control themselves.

Hugo noticed the two gnome children and broke away from the crowd and went over to them. He knelt beside them and held their hands. Reading the inscription on the stone, it was as much as he could not to burst into tears himself. He wrapped his arms around them both and they cuddled up to his chest.

His mother looked over and saw the distress that the three of them were suffering. She dug into her handbag. After a little searching in the suitcase of a purse she always carried, she pulled out a large chocolate bar, unwrapped it and divided it amongst the three of them. The smell and taste of the chocolate seemed to do the work and they all started to cheer up and smile a little.

"Come on, Hugo. It's time to go," Mrs Bennett said softly, putting out her hand to help her son up from his knees.

Both Orleg and Chipper begged him to stay but a look from his mother made him say 'Cheerio'. After shaking hands and saying goodbye to what-seemed a never-ending stream of gnomes, the Bennett family, including Jake, climbed back into the car. With a final wave, it disappeared down the drive.

All the gnomes congregated around the now smiling

Orleg who, with great relish and quite a lot of embellishment and exaggeration, relayed what had happened to her after the witch gave her the potion.

It was very late when the party broke up and everyone went back to their various homes, with the small gnome girl still talking excitedly to Chipper as they went to her house.

Finally, the lights went out in the owner's house and one by one, in those of the gnomes. At last, all was silent except for the sound of the stream running through the village and the occasional hoot of an owl out hunting.

Chapter 4

The Interview

"Hey Sarg. Any news about those missing girls yet?" A young constable asked as Sergeant Cummings strode down the corridor of the police station. "What is it now; four weeks since they disappeared? I was sure that they'd have been spotted by now if they were still alive but there again, if they were dead, or drowned, their bodies should have surfaced, so to speak, by now.".

"Nothing yet," he replied as he looked up from the sheaf of papers he was carrying, "but we're not giving up yet. I am sure that they'll turn up, sooner or later."

Burying his nose back into the papers in his hands, he continued his march down the corridor and into the office of Detective Inspector Hyde. The office was empty and he threw the papers onto the desk with a loud bang.

"Don't damage my desk!" came a voice from behind him which made him jump.

"Sorry Sir!" he said snapping to attention. The unexpected arrival of his superior officer had surprised him and he blushed with embarrassment.

"Anything that I need to know about in all that?" D. I. Hyde asked him nodding to the papers.

"Not much. All the usual rubbish, nothing much of interest. At least not for you."

"Right then! Let's go and have another chat with the family who was supposed to be looking after the missing young girl. I had the funny feeling that last time we spoke to them, they weren't telling us everything they knew: especially their little boy. I'm sure he knows a lot more than he's letting on. Oh, and you'd better get someone from child services to come with us. I want to get him on his own and I need a witness."

The Sergeant picked up the phone and ten minutes later, both officers and an officer named Meg Black from child services were on their way to the Bennetts house.

Hugo had just arrived home from school and was burying his face in a jam sandwich when the front doorbell rang. His mother shouted from upstairs asking him to see who it was at the door. Putting the snack down on the kitchen table, he went to the front door, his mouth full of food, and opened it.

"Oh hello young man." the Detective Inspector said, in as friendly a voice as possible. "Are your parents at home? We want to ask a few more questions about the young girl, Miss Jones, who was staying with you."

At first, Hugo could not answer, as his mouth was still full and he tried his best to empty it as fast as he could before replying. He had just succeeded when his mother came up behind him to see who had called.

"Oh hello, Mrs Bennett," The senior officer said." I think that you know my sergeant and this is Ms Black from child services. We were wondering if we could come in and ask you and your son here a few more questions that may help us in our enquiries about the missing girl, Miss Jones?"

A little taken aback, Mrs Bennett looked at the three officials standing at the door and nervously invited them in. She showed them all into the lounge and asked them to be seated, followed by, "May I get any of you a cup of tea or coffee?"

The Sergeant was just about to say that he'd love a cup of tea when his superior declined the kind invitation. The D.I. then explained that they would like to talk to them, especially Hugo, just in case he had remembered anything else that might aid their enquiries.

"This is why we've brought Ms Black."

"Oh, please call me Meg," interrupted the young woman.

Hugo's mother grinned at her in acknowledgement while the inspector continued.

"As I was saying. Your son here, may have remembered some information which may be of benefit in our enquiries and with your permission." He paused a little for effect, "We would like to have a little chat with him."

Mrs Bennett looked and felt very nervous, unsure of what to do.

"I can assure you we will not ask any difficult questions and I am here to ensure that Hugo is not pressurised in any way," the child officer said, trying to reassure her.

Although not entirely comfortable with their request and wishing that her husband was there to back her up, she agreed and sat down in a chair away from the officers but well within earshot so that she could hear what was said. The detective inspector indicated to Hugo to sit down opposite them and then started to ask if he had remembered anything else about Emma's disappearance.

Hugo nervously feigned total ignorance and so, with a glance at each other, they decided to go down a different route, one they had discussed in the car on their way.

"What do you know about?" the sergeant hesitated and looked at the other officers, 'Gnomes'?"

Hugo suddenly felt himself blush but, trying to sound as ignorant as possible, replied that they are the little ornaments that people have in their gardens. The two police officers looked at each other, nodded and then proceeded.

"Do you believe that there are... genuine gnomes, not plastic ones, living in the garden?"

Again, Hugo tried to play it as if he was completely ignorant of what they were asking.

"What would you say if we told you that we have a video of real, live gnomes, which we think was filmed at the Gnome Reserve and where, according to our CCTV records, you and your family have been visiting? Most recently, just before the young girl went missing."

Hugo's mother watched her son and began to grow very uneasy. She could tell that the police knew more than they were saying and that if they did not tell them the truth, then they might not only get in trouble with the law but also hinder the police's ability to find Emma, and that was the most important thing. Looking very red in the face and with a hesitant voice, she said.

"I think that you had better tell these officers everything you know, son. I think that it would be best."

Hugo looked at her questioningly and then at the policemen. After a little pause, he coughed and then began,

"Well, you see. I was taking Jake. Oh! He's our dog. I was taking Jake for a walk when he started to chase after a rabbit and slipped his lead…"

Over the next twenty minutes, he told them the whole story of what had happened. Well, not quite the entire story. He deliberately left out any mention of the talisman, as he thought that they would take it away from him if they knew that he had it. He desperately wanted to hang on to it, in case it was needed, and besides, having it in his possession made him feel important, believing that it showed that he was a descendant of King Arthur. All the while, the Sergeant was taking copious notes and by the end, had almost filled his little pad.

Out of breath, Hugo sat back in his chair and looked at the three stunned people in front of him. It was several minutes before the Sergeant had finished writing and no one spoke until then.

Sitting as far back in his seat as possible, the Detective Inspector looked at his colleagues, then at Hugo and finally at Mrs Bennett, whose face was bright red with embarrassment.

After clearing his throat, he looked at Mrs Bennett.

"If you don't mind Ma'am I think that I would like that cup of tea now. With two sugars, he added as an afterthought."

The other officers nodded in agreement, still stunned at the story Hugo had recounted.

Mrs Bennett was pleased to have the opportunity to leave the room and while she waited for the kettle to boil, she went to the sink and splashed cold water over her face to try to reduce the flushing and the perspiration that was covering it.

Feeling calmer, she loaded a tray with four hot cups of tea, some sugar and a plate of chocolate digestive biscuits. Jake, who had been asleep in his basket all this time suddenly stirred as he heard the packet being opened and followed his mistress into the lounge as she took the refreshments into her guests. She set the tray down on the table and invited everyone to,

"Tuck in."

Hugo counted the cups and then realised that he had been left out, so he announced that he was going to get himself a glass of squash. While in the kitchen he took two of the remaining chocolate biscuits and was about to throw one to a begging Jake, when he remembered that dogs shouldn't have chocolate, so he quickly ate it himself.

Making sure that there were no tell-tail signs of chocolate left around his mouth, he went back into the lounge carrying a large glass of orange squash, followed by Jake. The animal went straight up to the plate of biscuits on the table but found it empty.

The child officer patted its head as she wiped the biscuit crumbs from her mouth.

"Well. That's quite a story you've told us, young man." D.I. Hyde coughed, as a biscuit crumb became lodged in his throat. "And where can we get in touch with this uh, uh, Bird thing?"

"It's not a thing." retorted Hugo, "and at the moment he's in Australia visiting his brother. Or at least I think he is. I haven't heard from him ever since we won the battle against the goblins."

"And you say that this, um, witch, Morg somebody, changed into the missing reporter Sue Redwell."

"Morgana," Hugo reminded him.

"Yes. Right. Morgana. And where d'you say she is now?"

"No idea," Hugo answered honestly. "A long way from here, I hope."

His mother grunted in agreement.

Just at that moment, the front door was heard to open and Mr Bennett came in after finishing a day at his practice. He threw his briefcase onto the chair in the hall and calmly strode into the lounge, shuffling a pile of letters that he had picked up. He was about to moan to his wife about there being more begging letters when he looked up and saw the visitors.

"Oh! Hello."

His wife jumped up and began. "Oh, hello, darling. This is Ms Black from Child Services. I think you know these other officers. They wanted to know if Hugo could remember anything that might be useful in their search for Emma and," she paused and looked at her husband as if to say, 'I hope that I've done the right thing.' "So I told Hugo to tell them everything."

Mr Bennett looked horrified and was about to say something when his wife blurted out that the police knew all about the gnomes at the Reserve and even had a film of them. After all, if it helps to get Emma back, safe and sound, then they needed to give them as much information as possible.

Her husband sat down in the last remaining chair, sighed and then looked at his wife with a resigned stare and nodded in agreement.

"Do you have anything that you would like to say?" asked the Detective Inspector.

Mr Bennett said that he didn't, and so the three officers got up to leave. Just then, he had an idea.

"Inspector. Sorry, Detective Inspector. I would like to offer a reward of…" He hesitated and looked questioningly at his wife, "A reward of ten thousand pounds for anyone who has information that will lead to the safe return of Emma, or has knowledge of her whereabouts," he added as an afterthought."

His wife's eyes lit up and she jumped up and hugged her husband.

The Inspector looked at them both and added, "Well if that's what you want, then we will let the press know, but of course, you do realise that most of the calls we will get will be from cranks and money grabbers. You always do when a large reward is involved, but it may help to turn up something or someone that can help." Mr Bennett nodded in agreement.

"Right, Sir. If you are sure, then we'll get it underway. "Turning to Hugo, he continued, "Thank you son, for telling us what you know. I can understand why you were a bit hesitant. The whole story is a bit bizarre. I must admit that we, down at the station, were a bit dubious about the film.

Right then, you two," he said, turning to his colleagues, "I think that we've taken up more than enough of these good people's time. Let's go."

After final pleasantries, the Bennett family watched the police car disappear and went back inside to mull over everything that they had been told and its consequences.

In the police car, all three were silent until the car had turned the end of the road.

"What a load of nonsense. That kid has got a fantastic imagination, I must say. He's been watching far too much television. Magical Birds, witches taking over the bodies of young girls. He'll be telling me next that he's related to … King Arthur. Huh" D.I. Hyde burst out laughing.

His fellow passengers just looked at each other, shrugged their shoulders and kept silent.

Chapter 5

Sue's Flat

The latter part of October was now beginning to become chilled. Morgana and Putricia wandered the streets of Bideford looking for the house that Morgana felt sure she would recognise as the house that held the flat where her body had once lived. At three in the morning, no-one stirred. Many of the streets were unlit, as a means of the council saving taxpayers money. Both sisters wished that they had not abandoned their old cloaks when they took on their new forms. The garments were ragged and torn but at least they were warm and helped keep out the wind. They hugged themselves to try to keep warm. Snatch lurked in the shadows, a little distance behind, occasionally disturbing the odd cat as it went about its nocturnal patrols. One throaty hiss from his relatively gigantic head invariably sent them scurrying away. Sometimes a dog would catch his scent and start to bark but none ever made any attempt to come close.

As with several nights previously, tonight looked as if it was going to be a fruitless exercise when Snatch raced over from the opposite side of the road and started to growl at them. He ran back and then returned to stand in front of them. They looked at each other and wondered what the animal was doing. Morgana looked over to where Snatch had run and suddenly she saw a house that stirred something in the depths of her memory.

She gasped to her sister that she thought that this house was the very one for which they had been searching. She unfolded her arms and dug her hand into the pocket of her jeans; the same ones that Sue Redwell had been wearing when she was transformed. Inside was a key. The two looked at the house, which was in pitch blackness except for some very small lights by the front door, illuminating the bell pushes and names of the occupiers. Checking to see that they were not observed, they crept slowly up the path to the house and looked at the writing under the illuminated signs. None of the names appeared to be familiar at first, but as Morgana passed her hand over the labels, she seemed to sense one that seemed to have meaning. Squinting at the label it read. "Sue Redwell. Flat 2. First floor." She repeated the name, over and over again in her head and with each repetition became more conscious of it.

"I think that this is it," she said enthusiastically to her sister and gently tried the handle of the door. It opened and a light suddenly engulfed them. They froze and Snatch raced to hide in the nearest corner. Keeping as still as possible, they looked around to see if they had been spotted. With equal suddenness, the light went out but the moment they started to move, it came back on again. It took several periods before they realised that their movement triggered the illumination.

Regaining a little of their confidence, they stealthily examined the front of each door that led from the corridor, now grateful for the illumination. No sign read 'Sue Redwell'. Disappointed, they turned and were about to leave when Putricia pointed to the stairs at the end of the corridor. Morgana nodded and with her sister in the lead, started up the darkened stairway. At the top, a light came on again, but this time, with only a short pause, they continued their search.

The first door they examined had a somewhat faded sign on the door encased in a small brass frame. "Sue Redwell". The two looked at each other and smiled in anticipation. Morgana withdrew the strange-looking key from her pocket and put it up to the lock. It took several attempts to insert it into the Yale keyhole, but with a faint click it turned and the door creaked open. Moving in quickly, they were about to close the door, when Snatch raced passed them and into the room, skidding to a rapid halt as he hit the darkness of the interior. Morgana silently closed the door. They each took a location to investigate aided by the dim glow that came through the windows from the half-moon. It was frequently hidden by clouds driven by the chilling wind that scudded across the sky. After only a few minutes they met back in the entrance hall and grinned at each other.

"I think that this will do very nicely," Morgana whispered to her sister who grimaced with less enthusiasm but had to admit that it would certainly be warmer than their present lodgings and even the cave at Westward Ho!

"But what if we're discovered?" she whispered to

her sister, who thought for a moment considering the possibility. Suddenly her eyes lit up.

"It doesn't matter if someone sees us, or at least me, because this is my house and I am supposed to live here."

"But what about me? And Snatch," Putricia added as an afterthought.

"Well," Morgana thought for a while. "Providing no one sees you, then you will be perfectly safe as well. I can go in and out to get all our supplies, while you and Snatch can stay inside, or else just get out at night."

Putricia was still not totally convinced but agreed, reluctantly. Even she had to admit the idea of spending the winter in their cave was growing less and less appealing. She was pleased that, as they could now both venture out in daylight, life had certainly improved. Besides, it will give them, or at least Morgana, chance to observe and spy on that murderer and his brat of a son and also that woman with him, who seemed strangely familiar.

During all this, Snatch had been sniffing around all the rooms and had found the bedroom. The animal buried its nose in and around the bed and when happy that it was safe jumped on and nestled down into the soft, warm duvet.

The two women spent the rest of the night exploring the flat and pulling out all of Sue's clothes and personal items, most of which they had never seen or knew what they were used for. Morgana was particularly ecstatic at the clothes in the wardrobe. She had never seen so many and, what added to her joy, was that they all fitted her. Even when first alive, she had never had more than two dresses, and they were both of very dull colours and coarse fabric. What she saw were bright and, so soft. She buried her face in them, feeling their texture and smelling the freshness of the delicate fabric. Putricia also was amazed at what she saw but was disappointed that the choice of what fitted her was much more restricted, as she was much smaller.

By the time that they had fully explored their new home, dawn was breaking. They were still wary about being seen, and so they sat down in chairs, the comfort of which they had never experienced and slept soundly for the first time since either of them had been resurrected.

Chapter 6

Hugo's Birthday

"Big day tomorrow," Mr Bennett announced to his son as they sat down for breakfast.

Hugo looked up from the scribble he had been doing on a piece of paper by his side.

"Uh! Yeh. Uh. What d'you mean?"

"Don't tell me you've forgotten what day it is?" queried his father. "By the way, what's that you're doing?"

"Oh, it's some homework we were supposed to do but I forgot." His father looked at him, disapprovingly.

"What day is it tomorrow, anyway, other than Saturday?"

"Saturday what?" his father grinned.

The boy sat for a moment and then a smile suddenly crossed his face.

"It's my birthday. Yippee! With everything that's been happening I quite forgot."

His father returned the smile and asked him if there was anything special that he would like to do, now that he had achieved double figures, to celebrate.

He thought for a minute and then answered.

"It may sound a bit silly but I would like to revisit the Gnome Reserve. I know that it's closed for the season but over the last few weeks, I feel that I've made a lot of friends there, far more than at school and it would be nice to see them all again. Perhaps mum can make some of her fairy cakes and take them with us. They've become quite famous since Bird told them how he used them to become invisible, and I know the gnomes would love to try them. Oh, and I would like to see Bird again, but I know that he's still in Australia so that won't happen."

"Ok then, I'll give the Reserve owner a call when I get to work and see if we can arrange a visit." His father looked at his watch and suddenly got up from the table.

"I'm late. Judy, my receptionist, will have kittens if I'm late again. You know, I'm supposed to be the boss, but my staff seem to have far more authority than I do."

He laughed, grabbed his car keys and jacket, shouted, "I'm off now. Have a good day," to his wife and rushed out of the door. Seconds later the noise of the Volvo disappeared up the road and all that was left was the sound of Stephanie's hair drier buzzing from the open door of her bedroom.

At school on Friday afternoons it was sports, and now that it was the winter term, that meant football, which Hugo hated. Not so much playing it but all the conversations that his fellow pupils had about it; who was the best team or player, or did you see that fantastic goal from somebody or other. All the boys in his class seemed obsessed by the sport, even a lot of the girls knew more than he did. He felt left out and, though he made a particular point of listening to the TV and reading the sports section of his dad's newspaper, he always seemed to be supporting the wrong team or something. When it came to playing, he still didn't know the difference between inside right and right back, with the result that few of the other players would pass the ball to him. This lack of confidence meant that he had never had the opportunity to score a goal during the whole time he had been at school.

Before school that day, he had been playing with the amulet he had found and had absentmindedly put it around his neck and forgotten about it. His mother had stressed that he should never take it to school as someone may try to touch it and get hurt.

That day, he was reluctantly getting changed for sports, when Timmy Wyatt, who happened to be the football captain and a bully to boot, saw the pendant dangling from Hugo's neck and shouted to everyone in the changing room that Bennett was a sissy for wearing a girl's necklace. Hugo's face went bright red and he turned away from everyone to avoid eye contact. At that point, the teacher's whistle blew and everyone ran out of the changing room onto the pitch, Hugo at the rear.

At the start of the match, the ball stayed at the far end and he was happy just to jump around to keep warm and look as if he was participating in the game. Suddenly a long ball from the other team's players sent it straight to Hugo's feet. He was not sure at first what to do, but suddenly, he felt a warm sensation on his chest, and without further hesitation, he took control of the ball and dribbled it passed at least five opponents before driving it into the net at the other end. Both sides just stood in amazement, even two girls on the touchline started to clap. All the players ran to him, slapping him on the back and congratulating him on such an exceptional performance; that was, all the players except the captain, Timmy Wyatt. Hugo went on to score another two goals in a similar fashion, the final one clinching the victory, making him the star of the match.

That night, while lying in bed, he replayed the match over and over in his head until the small hours of the morning. At last, sleep overcame him and he settled down, still with a big smile on his face.

He was awakened in the morning by a loud knock on his bedroom door from his mother, telling him that his breakfast was ready and getting cold on the table. He was still a little lethargic from his lack of sleep the night before and was slowly putting on his dressing-gown when he remembered that today was his birthday. Energy suddenly surged through his body, all feelings of tiredness evaporated. He rushed out to the bathroom but found it locked, with the noise of his sister singing, or that's what she called it, to herself in the shower. Giving up on getting inside for at least the next half-hour, he rushed downstairs, almost knocking over his mother as she carried a large pot plant from the kitchen, where she had been trimming its leaves, to the lounge.

"Careful! It's on the table," his mother scolded him as he skidded around the door into the kitchen. His father was sitting on one of the chairs by the table reading the newspaper. A large wad of letters of various sizes lay in front of him. Without putting down the paper, he wished his son a good morning and then pushed another pile of letters, which Hugo had not spotted, toward him.

"These are yours, I think?" He folded the newspaper

and grinned at his son, adding, "We are popular today, aren't we?"

Hugo looked at him with a big smile and grabbed the letter on the top. It did not have a stamp and had been hand-delivered. It was a pretty shade of pink and he was sure it smelt of perfume. His father smiled as he watched Hugo sniff the envelope. He caught his son's eye as he did so. Hugo blushed a little and set about slitting open the letter with a knife from the table. It was from a girl in his class who had seen him play football the day before and had become star-struck. As he read it, he could feel his face become redder and redder. Again, a point not missed by his father.

Hugo was unsure how to react, having never had an 'admirer' before and wasn't sure what to do. He reread the letter before putting it back in the envelope and carefully folding it before sliding it into the pocket in his dressing gown. He continued to open the remaining letters and cards, all from Aunts, Uncles and friends of the family. One from his grandmother enclosed a twenty-pound note, which he also slid into his pocket.

With all letters and cards opened, he pushed them to one side and without making any comment set about demolishing his bacon, eggs and fried bread which his mother had prepared, knowing that it was his favourite. Jake hovered under the table waiting for a titbit which frequently Hugo would slip him but today there was none and he slouched off to his basket.

"You've missed one," his father called just as Hugo was about to leave the table. He looked around and there, half covered by the brown-sauce bottle, was a very tiny gold-coloured envelope. He reached over and cautiously picked it up carefully examining the very neat but miniscule handwriting on the front, which read,

"Master Hugo Peter Bennett. The large house, with the tall tree, by the sea, Westward Ho!"

He was at a loss as to who the small card was from and how did they know that his middle name was Peter? He hated the name and never told or used it. He held the card between two fingers and twirled it around.

"Well don't just sit there looking at it. Open it!" His father said excitedly from his chair, as he was also intrigued to know who was the sender of such a small letter. With great care, so as not to damage the contents, Hugo slit open the envelope. Cautiously, he pulled out the sparkly card from inside and opened it.

"It's from Puchy! You know; the tooth fairy," he screamed in excitement.

"Well read it out then." said his father, who had now been joined by his wife, having heard the commotion from the lounge.

"It's very hard to read 'cos it's so small but I think it says. From Puchy and all the tooth fairies. Have a very happy birthday."

Everyone burst out laughing and Mrs Bennett clapped her hands.

"Who told Puchy that it was my birthday?" Hugo asked.

"Presumably the same person who tells the tooth fairies when your tooth has fallen out," his father chuckled

They all laughed again. At this point, Stephanie came in through the door, rubbing her wet hair in a pink towel.

"What's going on?" she insisted and everyone looked

at her and started to laugh again. Hugo handed her the card. Squinting her eyes to try to read the minute writing, she began to scream with laughter as well. They all took turns to read and reread the card and it was at least ten minutes before Hugo's father told him to take all the empty envelopes and papers out to the recycling bin, just outside the back door. Hugo's face dropped but did as he was told.

No sooner had he opened the back door when there was another scream of excitement, as he saw, leant against the recycling bin, a brand new racing cycle. He had mentioned that he would love this particular model several weeks before, as they passed the cycle shop on Bideford Quay, on their way to the solicitors dealing with his father's inheritance. At that time, his father seemed not to be paying attention, especially when he mentioned the price but now, here it was, in all its glory.

His parents and sister were now standing in the doorway and they said in unison,

"Happy Birthday Hugo."

He smiled, a little embarrassed but then mounted the saddle and unsteadily rode a few circuits of the garden. His father told him that he would need to make a few adjustments to the position of the handlebars and saddle but even as they were, Hugo's face beamed with pride and pleasure.

"Right then, now that's done, let's go," announced Mr Bennett. Everyone seemed to know what he was talking about; everyone, that is, except Hugo.

"Go where?" he questioned.

All his father would say was, "Wait and see."

After clearing away all the breakfast debris and putting

the dishes in the dishwasher, the whole family put on their coats and climbed into the car. Minutes later they were heading along the A39 out of Bideford. Hugo was at a loss as to where they were heading until he saw a sign advertising the Gnome Reserve. Excitedly, he confirmed with his father that this indeed was where they were going. With a nod and grunt from his father, he sat back, waiting impatiently for them to arrive when he could meet all the gnomes and the Reserve's owner again but this time in much happier circumstances. As they pulled up and alighted from the car, there to meet them was Bird, looking very suntanned, well, his feathers did seem to be a bit darker and more colourful, with a brown-paper parcel balanced under his wing.

Hugo ran up to him and gave him a great big hug. Releasing his friend, who looked a little overcome by the welcome, Bird handed him the parcel saying "Happy Birthday. It's a little something I picked up from Australia. Hugo tore off the wrappings and inside found a hat that had corks strung from around the brim and a boomerang. Hugo put on the hat, which was a little on the large size, and waved the boomerang at his family. A noise behind made him spin round. Before him were gathered all the gnomes, the owner and her assistants. They had all come out to meet him and wish him a happy birthday with little Orleg taking pride of place in the front.

The owner had prepared lots of sandwiches and cakes for everyone and Mrs Bennett added to the feast by bringing out, from the back of the car, two large tins of fairy cakes, which she had made the day before. Everyone settled down for a party. Even Jake was given a special cake that Stephanie had made out of meat and dog biscuits, though it was noticeable that the gnomes still gave him a wide birth, just in case.

Mr Bennett was just about to raise a cup of tea to toast Hugo and congratulate his son on reaching double figures when there was a buzzing around Hugo's head and Puchy landed on his shoulder. Hugo screamed with delight so loudly that the tiny tooth fairy fell off and landed on the table, almost falling into his cup of orange juice. Everyone laughed. He put out one finger and she climbed onto it.

"Happy Birthday," she squeaked, "I was very busy last night and I thought that I would miss your party."

Hugo handed her a small piece of one of his mother's fairy cakes and whispered as quietly as he could. "Thanks very much for the birthday card. I really did like it."

The little fairy blushed and buried her head into the piece of cake.

It was several hours later that, after a final sad visit to Barguff's headstone to pay their respects to their fallen friend, the Bennett family got back into their car and returned home, with Hugo still wearing his hat with the corks.

Chapter 7

The Site

"Ere George, what d'you think this is?" Charlie Plummer asked his fellow archaeologist, George Fellowship, holding up a D-shaped, heavily-rusted piece of metal.

"Looks like an old stirrup to me." replied his colleague. "Sling it with all the rest of the bits we found and let those, so-say experts, worry about it. I don't know about you, but I think it's time for a brew. How about it?"

The two men put down their trowels and buckets, and after much groaning, they stretched their aching limbs. After being on their knees for some time, it felt good to stand up. With a nod of his head, Charlie indicated to his fellow worker and they headed off to the makeshift tent at the far end of the site in which they were excavating. The location where, not long previously, its then-owner, Sir Richard Benson, was killed, when a lightning bolt hit the JCB he was driving. He was a distant relative of Sir Thomas Raymond who, in 1697, had murdered Stephen Lloyd and the young healer's relatives, who were subsequently hanged to cover up the crime, It was this property that had been inherited by Hugo's father in a weird twist of fate.

At the opposite end of the site, a small door, half-buried behind an accumulation of rubble and years of uncontrolled undergrowth, cracked open. After checking that no one was around, with a gentle creak, it eased open a little more. From behind this portal emerged a bent figure, completely covered by a tattered, well-worn black cloak. Only a small hole, where an eye should be, was left uncovered. The figure slid silently from the doorway to where the men had been working; moving stealthily to stay in the shadows wherever possible. On reaching the trays of finds, it checked that it was still unobserved and, when convinced, ruffled through the dirty and rust-covered artefacts gathered there. The emaciated and brown-spotted hands pushed and lifted the items, becoming more desperate as they searched. They seemingly did not find what the frustrated figure was looking for as there was a grunt of disgust and annoyance. The head of the apparition spun left and right, rechecking that it was still unobserved before returning to the door in the corner, which groaned again as it clicked behind the trailing threads of the cloak.

"Here! Did you mess up all these finds?" Charlie asked George accusingly.

"What d'you mean? I've been with you all the time. How could it be me?" George replied with a hurt tone to his voice.

"Well somebody or somethin's been at 'um because they was all neat and tidy when we left and look at 'um now, all messed up. You know, that Miss, what's 'er name who's in charge of this dig, will have kittens if she sees this mess.

Give me a hand to straighten everything up, then I don't know about you but I'm cold and it's nearly lunchtime. 'Ow about we do this then go to the pub for a pie and a pint?"

"Sounds good to me," responded his companion, and forty minutes later, they were seated in the White Hart, each tucking into a hot pie.

Chapter 8

Mrs Cartwright

"Sir! Sir! That missing reporter girl's been spotted by someone living opposite the flat she lived in." Sergeant Cummings shouted breathlessly, charging into the office of D. I. Hyde.

"Don't knock then," the senior officer said sarcastically, looking up from a sheaf of papers that he was studying. "What's this all about then?"

The sergeant, still fighting to catch his breath, explained to the inspector that they had received a phone call from an old woman who lived in the house opposite where the missing reporter, Sue Redwell, had lived. She said that she wasn't a very good sleeper and had got up in the middle of the night to get a drink of water. While in her kitchen, she noticed the security light in the reporter's flat go on and was sure that she saw the reporter open the front door and go into her flat. The inspector was about to say something when the sergeant forestalled him and continued that that wasn't all. She said that the reporter was accompanied by another person, a young girl, who looked very much like that other girl that's missing; that Emma Jones girl.

His interest sparked, the inspector pushed himself away from the table but, before getting up, he looked at the sergeant and asked him if he was sure. He didn't want to go out on another wild goose chase; after all, there had been several supposed sightings; especially after the announcement of the reward. The sergeant confirmed the details given by the neighbour and the girl had tallied with their descriptions. After all, it was the only lead that they had at the moment, so what did they have to lose.

Still not entirely convinced about the authenticity of the reports, but admitting that they needed some sort of break in the case, he rose, grabbed his hat and coat from the hook behind the door and the two officers left to interview the neighbour.

* * *

"Right now. Tell us exactly what you saw, Mrs Cartwright," asked D.I. Hyde, as the two officers sat down in the lounge of the neighbours flat, sipping the tea that she had made for them. The sergeant wiped a crumb of biscuit from the side of his mouth and flicked through his notebook to find a blank page.

"Well officer, it must have been about three o'clock in the morning, last night. I don't sleep well you know and I was feeling a little bit restless, so I got up to get a glass of water. When I was in the kitchen, I noticed a light come on in the house opposite. I knew that the young girl who lived there had been reported missing, I saw her picture on the telly several times and I thought it strange that there should be a light, so I decided to take a better look. The street lights had gone off and I couldn't see that clearly but as they..."

"You mean there was more than one person there?" interrupted the sergeant.

"Oh, yes. There were definitely two people; one much smaller than the other, more like a child. Anyway, as they passed through the door, the light from the security lamp illuminated their faces and I was convinced that the taller one was that reporter girl that you've been after. I did not see the face of the smaller girl but she followed the other girl into the flat. After the security light went out, I couldn't see anything, but a few minutes later, another light came on inside the house for a short while but I do not know from where."

"Well, thank you very much, Madam, you've been most helpful," the inspector said condescendingly, getting up and shaking Mrs Cartwright's hand. "What you've told us could be very useful. We will investigate what you've told us thoroughly." The two officers started to make their way out.

"It's not really important," the elderly lady whimpered, just before the policemen went through the door, "but wasn't there some mention about a reward?" She bowed her head looking somewhat embarrassed at mentioning it.

"Well, yes, there is." The inspector stopped and turned to look at her, "And if what you've told us leads to the finding of the unfortunate young women, then you will certainly be in line for it, but first we have to find her."

"Yes, of course," the old lady responded, still looking as if she had regretted asking the question in the first place.

As they walked down the path leading from the old lady's house, they noticed a twitch from the lace curtains covering her windows. They looked at each other and smiled, raising their eyebrows.

"What d'you think, Mike? Any truth in what she said?" The inspector looked questionably at his colleague as they sat back in the patrol car.

"Well, sir. There's only one way to find out."

Both officers eased themselves back out of the car and walked in unison across the road. After a search down the list of occupants on the front door, the sergeant rang the bell, signed, Sue Redwell. No one answered. They repeated the push three times but there was still no response. The sergeant was convinced that he had seen a movement of the curtain from one of the flats, but since he did not know if this was the flat that they wanted to visit, he could not be sure. After waiting several minutes, he said with a sigh.

"Well, that's it, sir. I suppose that we'll need to go back and get a warrant."

The inspector nodded his head in the direction of the car and a minute later, they disappeared down the road. The curtain twitched again as they left.

Chapter 9

The Dinner

Hugo slumped down on a chair in the lounge, exhausted after a long ride on his newest acquisition.

"Why do we have to live where there are so many hills?" he moaned to his mother who was sat opposite watching an antiques programme on the television.

"You'll soon get used to it," she said, but not fully paying attention.

At that point, the front door opened and his father came in unexpectedly. He threw his briefcase onto the seat next to Hugo. He explained to his wife that he had had an urgent phone call from the solicitors about his inheritance and they needed him to sign some more papers as soon as possible to avoid a potential legal delay. He rushed upstairs, washed and changed. With another slam of the door, he was out again. His wife looked up a little surprised but went back to her programme.

Hugo felt bored and decided to go to his room. It was already growing dark outside and he was tired of playing games on his computer, wishing that Emma could come round but knew that this was no longer an option. He sat and imagined what had become of her and wondered if Morgana's threat to kill everyone had, in fact, come true. Suddenly, he decided that he would give Bird a call. After all, although he had talked to him at his party at the Gnome Reserve, there had not been a chance to speak to him properly and find out what he did in Australia and if he found his brother.

Facing the wall, he called out, "Bird. Bird. Bird."

A few minutes went past and he thought that his friend was not coming but then, with a shimmering of the wall, he appeared, looking somewhat dishevelled. He explained that he had been helping put a new roof on one of the gnome's houses and had not had time to preen his feathers. After a preliminary chit chat, Hugo asked him about his brother. He gave a sort of embarrassed chuckle and said that his brother had grown so big that they were threatening to drive a tunnel through him. He wished that he had access to those witches' potion books because he was sure that they must contain a recipe for something that would reverse the original potion and make him shrink.

Hugo glumly explained to his friend about Emma going missing. He had mentioned it to him at the party but it was not the right time to go into details. He also confessed to Bird his fear that Emma had been captured and killed by Morgana but did not know where the witch was now living. The police had told him that they had had reports that she had been sighted near Hartland, about twenty-five miles away but it had not been confirmed. What was giving him the most concern however, was the report of her seen in the company with someone who looked very much like the reporter that had also gone missing a few weeks before. A person who, Hugo knew for sure, was now Morgana, but in another form.

At this, even Bird looked worried, as he knew that this was certainly a possibility, so he said that he would return to the Reserve and ask if any of them there knew any more about it. Hugo thanked his friend, shook his wing and without more ado, Bird shimmered back into the wall.

Hugo sat back on his bed. Although still feeling extremely worried, he thought that, now that Bird was on the trail as well, they might be in a position to learn more of the truth.

He must have dozed for a while, as nearly an hour had passed when he heard the front door slam and his sister's voice shout a 'Hello.' to her mother who was vacuuming the carpet in the lounge. Her shout was accompanied by the stamping of feet up the stairs and a loud bang from a bedroom door. Almost simultaneously the front door banged again and Mr Bennett came back home. The noise of the vacuum cleaner stopped and moments after, Hugo heard his mother scream with delight. Curious to find out what was going on, he ventured downstairs and into the lounge where he could hear the sound of his mother laughing.

Entering into the room, he saw both his parents in a strong hug. It made him feel a little embarrassed but when they saw him, they broke apart.

"How would you like to shake the hand of a millionaire?" his father grinned. "All the paperwork has been settled and the money's in the bank, so that's that."

"How much? How much?" Hugo demanded.

"That's my business," his father replied curtly, "but enough for everyone. Think, I can buy that new digital imaging system for my practice that I've always wanted and a load of other things."

"You mean you're not going to give up work?" Hugo asked in surprise, thinking that, if you had a lot of money, then you wouldn't need to work.

His father burst out laughing. "Money doesn't solve problems. In fact, it frequently causes them, especially if you don't have something to put all your mind and energy into. I like my job and I still have the responsibility to my staff and patients. If I gave up my job, then they would be out of work and besides, if I was here at home all day, then I am sure your mother would soon kick me out for getting in her way."

His mother grinned broadly and nodded her head in agreement.

"Right then! To celebrate, let's all go out for dinner tonight. Where's the most expensive place you can think of?" he said, looking at his wife.

"Well, there's that place near Exeter that's got a Michelin star but it is too far to go tonight and besides, I think you have to book up for weeks in advance if you want a table. Why don't we go to that smashing Chinese place in Fremington? I always enjoy going there and it's still not too late to book a table."

"Right! Chinese it is," confirmed her husband as his wife rushed off to the phone to book it.

"You look a mess, Hugs. If we're all going out, then I suggest you go and have a shower, providing that sister of yours hasn't drained all the hot water. I really don't know what women find to do in bathrooms that takes so long?" His father smiled and rubbed the top of Hugo's head and left to get changed himself.

True to form, Stephanie was still in the bathroom when he went upstairs. He banged on the door to tell her to hurry up. In response, there was a noise which sounded like a wet sponge hitting the door. He shouted to her that they were all going out to the Chinese restaurant and she'd better hurry up. Moments later, the door swung open, releasing a cloud of steam, laden with the smell of deodorant and talcum powder.

"Why didn't you tell me earlier? Nobody tells me anything that's going on. I am supposed to be seeing Marty tonight."

"You can bring him along if you want." her mother cried out from her bedroom, having overheard her daughter's rantings.

Hugo's heart sank. 'That's a good evening spoilt,' he thought, and resigned himself to hearing about how 'Marty did this, and Marty did that, and if it hadn't been for dear Marty, the world would have ended'. Braving the choking fumes of his sister's previous occupation, he went into the bathroom and showered.

On the way to the restaurant, they stopped to pick up Marty, who climbed into the back seat of the car next to Hugo. Hugo was about to look at his sister, and without his parents' or Marty seeing, put two fingers down his throat to annoy her, when as soon as the object of Hugo's action had strapped himself in, he slapped Hugo on the back and congratulated him on a fantastic game of football he had played a few days earlier. Hugo was at a loss for words, as he hadn't mentioned anything about it to his parents because he was a little shy of what they might say. Mr Bennett turned momentarily from driving and asked what all this was about. Marty recounted all that Hugo had done and had scored not only the winning goal but two others besides.

Hugo could feel his face getting redder and redder.

"Well, that explains the perfumed card," his father commented, followed by a very dirty look from his wife.

Stephanie's ears pricked up and she asked, "What card?"

Immediately her father dismissed it, realising that he had spoken out of turn. By the time they arrived at the restaurant, Hugo had wished that he had never played football. Throughout the meal, Marty kept asking Hugo about this defence move or that attack and how, if he had done this or that, he could have scored another goal. It wouldn't have been so bad if Hugo knew what he was talking about, so it was with great relief that the meal was finished and they all went home but not before dropping Marty off at his house.

As soon as they got back home, Stephanie insisted that he show her the card that had been mentioned but he said that he had thrown it away, whereas, in reality, it was under the pillow on his bed. As he lay down in his bed that night, he put his hand under his pillow to reassure himself that it was still there.

Chapter 10

Snatch's Capture

"Someone knows we're here," Putricia groaned at her sister.

"I'm sure they won't be back," she replied, but doubt was in her voice.

"We need to find somewhere else to live, and quickly. I'm sure that by now these bodies we've taken will have been missed and people will be out looking for them."

"We'll go out at first light and see what we can find. It will be very quiet then and there shouldn't be too many people around to see us."

"What about Snatch? If anyone sees him, they will surely know that he is not a normal cat."

"We will leave him here for now. He'll be quite safe. If anyone does try and come in, then he will frighten them off."

As soon as the first rays of daylight were visible in the clouded sky, the two cautiously ventured out to look for somewhere more suitable to live.

***

"Got that warrant you wanted, Sir." The sergeant waved a piece of paper over his head.

"Right then, get the team together and we'll see if that old woman was right. Oh, and don't forget to tell them to bring the ram. You never know, we may have to use it."

The sergeant nodded while the inspector finished his cup of tea.

***

"There's still no answer." The sergeant said to the inspector after ringing the doorbell of the flat of Sue Redwell.

"OK boys. You know what to do."

The three constables stood either side of the door while a fourth readied himself to swing the battering ram at the lock.

"Wait a minute." A voice called from below and a young man hurried up the stairs.

"Who are you?" the inspector barked.

"I'm Allan Carlisle; Sue Redwell's boyfriend, or at least, friend. You never know with her. I've got a key to save you using that… 'thing." beckoning to the battering ram in the constable's hand.

All the policemen looked quite disappointed. It wasn't very often that they had the chance to smash a door down.

"OK. Let him through," ordered the inspector and Allan approached the door. He went to open it but the inspector pulled him aside and told him to wait downstairs.

Cracking open the door, the inspector called out, "This is the police. We are coming in."

Nothing stirred and so, following Alan Carlisle's instruction, they moved up to the first floor and hammered on the door displaying the small sign 'S. Redwell'. There was a faint movement from inside but no other reply. Swiftly unlocking the door with the key from her boyfriend, the inspector threw the door wide open and all, except the constable holding the ram, rushed in. There was a ferocious growl and curdling hiss as Snatch flew at the inspector and one of the constables at the same time. Its claws ripped down the jacket of the constable and one of the legs of the inspector's trousers. All five policemen immediately backed away, kicking and screaming at the animal. After another slash at his legs, the inspector finally managed to reclose the door.

Everyone stood in stunned silence. Allan ran up the stairs hearing the commotion.

"What in the world is that?" one of the constables gasped as the shock wore off.

"I have no idea," replied one of the others, "but there's no way I'm going back in there. I've never seen anything like it. It looks like one of those monster creatures you see in books about dinosaurs."

"You!" Sergeant Cummings shouted at one of the constables. "Ring the RSPCA and get them around here as soon as possible. Oh! And you better tell them to bring a tranquilliser gun: a big one."

One of the constables moved a little way off and spoke into his lapel microphone, explaining to headquarters what had happened. He also instructed them that they should also send a medic as the D.I. and one of the constables had been injured.

A frantic scrabbling from the other side of the door made the assembly jump back again. One of the constables gingerly went up to the door to make sure that it was firmly shut. Meanwhile, the inspector sat down on the floor while one of the other constables, who said he was trained in first aid, ripped the leg of the blood-stained trouser off the inspector and started to try to stop the bleeding.

"Careful!" the D.I. exclaimed, but more from the fact that one of his best pairs of work trousers had been ruined, rather than the pain, though it was quite painful, he had to admit.

There was a cacophony of talking, with everyone debating on what the animal was, but slowly the noise died down as the overall shock took control. The murmuring was suddenly silenced by the sirens and screeching of several police cars arriving outside the flat.

Allan Carlisle, who had been ordered to stay downstairs, directed, what seemed a whole squad of police, many wearing flak jackets and carrying guns, up the stairs to where the D.I. was struggling to his feet, or rather his foot because he could only manage to hop. He rapidly explained the situation to the team's commander, who slowly approached the door and put his ear to it. He shot back as a fierce growl and the tearing of claws on wood was heard.

"I think we'll wait for the vet before we do anything else," he said with a noticeable tremor in his voice. He and all his team backed away as much as possible. Meanwhile, one of the officers announced himself to be a doctor and began to examine the wounds on the inspector and the injured constable. He dressed the wounds as best he could but then told them that they should leave and go to the hospital to get an anti-tetanus injection, just in case.

"I'm not leaving until I know what that... thing... is and it's either shot or at least tranquilised," the inspector insisted, hopping on his good leg.

About ten minutes later a man wearing a white jacket, but covered by a stab-proof vest, came up the stairs and announced that he was Tim Harrington, the vet.

A corridor opened up between all the policemen gathered in the narrow area and the vet looked at them wondering why they all seemed so happy to see him. They let him through to the front where D.I. Hyde rapidly appraised him of the situation. The confident look on his face suddenly turned to one of great concern. One of the constables closest to the door offered to open the door for him but he held his hand up and said that first, he would use the letterbox to get a look. The constable went up to the door and, with one finger, pushed open the flap of the letterbox as quietly as he could. The vet went on one knee to look inside and as he did so, several of the officers around him drew their weapons, which made him look even more worried.

He looked through the narrow opening but said that he could not see anything. He was about to get up when there was a massive bang, with the sound of tearing wood as Snatch bounded at the door. The vet fell backwards in a heap and all the officers rapidly stepped back almost colliding with each other.

"Nobody told me it was a monster we're dealing with!" Tim Harrington almost screamed in surprise as he wiped his brow. "I will need to adjust the dose in my tranquilliser gun. I was told it was a big dog but whatever it is, it is certainly like no dog I've seen before. Judging by that noise and the weight with which it hit the door, it sounds more like a big cat if you ask me."

There was a general hubbub from the policemen, which was silenced by another loud screech from behind the door, followed by more tearing of wood. The vet loaded his handheld tranquilliser pistol and then indicated for those there to stand back and give him some space. None of the policemen needed to be told a second time to stand well back.

The vet again lifted the flap of the letterbox, pointing the barrel of the gun through it. He then deliberately banged on the door. As predicted, Snatch jumped at the door and, as he did so, the vet pulled the trigger. The bolt found its mark, just below Snatch's neck, between its front legs. It roared even louder and pawed at the door with such ferocity that one of the door panels began to break up and the animal's paw reached out into the corridor causing all those standing there to jump backwards.

The paw scratched even further at the hole which was now getting bigger. Snatch's snout appeared and he growled again as he sensed the scent of the humans outside. For five minutes the pawing continued and one of the armed policemen closest to the door released the safety catch off his gun. Slowly, the noise and effort shown by Snatch slowly died down as the drug took effect. When all noise had ceased, the vet slowly cracked open the door. There was a little growl which made him close it again rapidly, but then a minute or so later he tried again. He opened it a couple of inches but then it stuck. Snatch had collapsed directly behind the door and it was only with the help of two of the policemen that they were able to open it sufficiently wide enough for the vet to put his head around and squeeze himself into the room.

He was amazed at what he saw. He had never seen anything like it in the whole of his career. He prodded the sleeping body with his foot, just to make sure, then, bending down, he grasped the hind legs and pulled the animal away from the door. All the policemen poured in, all anxious to see what they had been fighting. They stood in a semicircle around the beast, amazed at what they were seeing.

"You there!" the vet ordered, "give me a hand to tie its legs. I did bring a muzzle but I never expected something like this. The one I brought is far too small. Does anyone have a strap or something I can wrap around its jaws?" All the policemen looked at each other until there was a voice from the back and D.I. Hyde hopped into view, pulling a belt from around his waist.

"These trousers are finished, so you may as well have the belt." he moaned and threw it to the vet. However, the moment he did so he realised that it was a big mistake. As he hopped to keep his balance, his trousers, or what was left of them, started to fall and he had to rapidly let go of the wall that he was using to support himself to stop them falling completely. In the confusion and efforts to hop, hold onto the wall and support his falling trousers, he lost his balance and went sprawling in front of everybody. A couple of the police officers started to snigger, but one look from the inspector as he sat up from the floor stopped that immediately.

Eventually, they bundled Snatch into a tight package and the vet rolled him onto a small rug on the floor. After giving instructions to three of the officers to each grab a corner, they picked up their sleeping package and carefully carried it down into the vet's van waiting outside.

By now there was quite an audience outside from the neighbours and those passing. One young girl was scribbling in a note pad, while a man standing by her was taking photos. If only this young trainee reporter knew who this fearsome beast she was seeing belonged to and the circumstances that had led it to be there, she would not be looking so pleased with herself.

As the vet prepared to drive away, he asked one of the policemen to contact the North Devon Wildlife Park near Ilfracombe to get ready to receive a very strange new guest. The noise of the van starting made the crowd part and the vet drove off with his special cargo.

Back in the flat, the rapid response team was packing up ready to leave, their part now complete.

"Right then Tony, we'll leave you to it. I don't fancy your job of having to write a report on this lot. The superintendent will have you in his office for hours when you tell him what has happened," the team leader joked.

The Inspector was about to swear at his colleague but thought better of it with all the other policemen standing around, so he just grimaced and waved him goodbye, forgetting about his trousers which promptly started to fall so that he had to make a sudden grab for them. Looking around, he noticed a piece of cord in one corner.

"Hey, Sarge. Grab that for me," he ordered, pointing to the piece of rope. The sergeant obliged and the inspector wrapped it around his waist.

"Don't you think that you should go to the hospital with that?" the sergeant suggested, looking and pointing to the inspector's leg which had now started to bleed again.

"P'raps you're right," he replied, looking down at the trail of blood he was leaving behind him. "You there!" he ordered, pointing to a young constable whose face was noticeably white. "Lock this place down and make sure that nothing, I repeat nothing, is touched or disturbed. I want to make sure that whoever owned that ... thing gets the book thrown at him or her."

He took a long look all around, in case there was anything that needed his immediate attention. Painfully, helped by his sergeant, he hopped down the stairs and outside to a now increasing reception, who all gasped at seeing his injury.

"Move along now, ladies and gentlemen. There's nothing else to see here. Move along please." he announced to the waiting crowd who started to drift off as he climbed into the patrol car. With sirens blasting, it rushed to the A & E department at North Devon District Hospital in Barnstaple.

The remaining policemen relocked the front door of the flat and fastened blue and white tape emblazoned with 'Police Do Not Cross' across it. They met with Allan Carlisle, still waiting at the bottom of the stairs to see if there was any news of his girlfriend. The policeman said that as far as they knew there was no news but they would need to keep the key of the door when Allan asked for it back. He heard one of the officers say to his colleague as they left,

"If you ask me, if that young reporter girl was living there, then you can bet your life that that creature has eaten her." The other policeman nodded and grunted in agreement.

By the time that the boyfriend had driven off in his MGB GT, the road was quiet, except for the normal traffic.

Chapter 11

Reserve Rebuilt

Bird sat down on his haunches and fluffed out his feathers. It had been a long day but finally, the last house in the Gnome Reserve to be rebuilt was finished. Its grateful owner, Trickle, so-called because she was born where the spring that supplied the stream running through the Reserve came out of the ground in... well... a trickle, had moved back in.

It was beginning to grow dark and the weather was taking on that winter chill that occurs in November. He slowly strolled back up to the big house, alongside Hosper, who was dragging a spade behind him so that it made a clattering sound as it bounced over the stones in the path. As they entered the office of the house, one of the assistants handed them both a large steaming cup of tea, which she had freshly brewed when she saw them shuffling up the garden path.

"I think you two deserve this. You've both worked very hard, but it's all been worth it. I haven't seen the place looking so spick and span for a long time." As she said this, the owner walked in and gave the assistant a distant look, as if to say, "I do try to keep it all very tidy, honest."

The assistant blushed and went off to wash up. When she was gone, the owner confided to both Bird and Hosper that the assistant had been right; the whole gnome village sparkled.

"I have something here that I made for you, as a way of saying, thank you." From under the counter, she withdrew a massive cake, with the words 'Thank You Bird' written in pink icing on the top. Bird's eyes lit up with anticipation but Hosper looked a little disappointed, as he felt that he had worked as hard, if not harder, than Bird. The owner looked at him without emotion but then broke into a beaming smile and pulled from under the counter an even bigger cake, complete with a little gnome house made of marzipan, at its centre.

"This is for you and all the gnomes. I think there should be enough to go round."

Hosper clapped his hands and rushed outside, shouting to everyone within earshot to come to the house for a party. Within minutes, the office, kitchen and even the hallway was buzzing with gnomes, all holding great slices of cake, and some with traces of icing around their mouths, were going back for seconds, most prominently, Chipper, who was on thirds.

Having eaten a large proportion of his cake, Bird asked the owner if she would wrap the rest in a paper so that he could eat it later, which she did. Tucking the parcel under his arm, he wished everyone goodnight and left to have a well-deserved sleep in the Reserve's garage.

He was beginning to settle down when he felt something

move next to him. Stretching his neck, he looked around and saw Chipper snuggling up to him. Bird knew that his parents had been killed in the attack on the Reserve by the two witches and Snatch, not forgetting Jake as well. Despite many of the gnome families offering to take him in, he had refused, and now, it seemed, that he had adopted Bird as his new family. Fluffing his feathers, Bird moved his wing so that it covered the small gnome, and together they fell asleep.

Chapter 12

Another house

"How much would it cost to completely clear the site and redevelop it into, say, a block of flats?" Paul Bennett was asking the architect that he had hired to advise him on what to do with the piece of land he had inherited.

"You can forget that," James McKelvy sighed. "There's absolutely no way in which the planners would let you get away with that, although it is an ideal place to build a block of retirement homes. The local planners have already been inundated by archaeological groups and preservationist who want to see it used to build a museum or some form of social amenity. Some had even suggested rebuilding it as it was originally, as they still had the original plans for it from the sixteen hundreds when it was first built. I've got a meeting with the town council and planning department in a few days, so we'll leave any decisions until we've heard what they have to say. In the meantime, I think that it would be useful if we have a good look at the site together, to see if any other ideas spring to mind."

"Before we go, did you say that the plans for the original house were available because I would certainly like to see them before we make any decisions?"

The architect agreed with this proposal and said that he would contact the local museum, where they were kept in their archives, and get some copies made.

The meeting was adjourned and Mr Bennett arrived home to find Hugo looking very glum.

"What's the problem Hugs?"

His son cringed at the name, which he hated. "Oh it was football again today and after the last time everyone expected me to be like David Beckham again but everything went wrong and we lost five nil. It would have been six nil if our goalie hadn't managed to stop a ball, that I passed back to him, from going in the goal. If only I'd worn my talisman."

"What do you mean?" his father asked, sounding puzzled. Hugo admitted that, on the day he had scored all the goals, he had left the amulet on around his neck, by mistake he emphasised, because his father had told him expressly not to wear it to school. He said that all through the game, he could feel its warmth and power giving him strength.

His father looked at him very sternly. "There are no such things as 'lucky charms'. They are only objects that people put their faith in, and it is that faith that spurs them to do great things. In reality, they could do the same, with or without the charm. I know that your amulet does seem to have some inexplicable powers, and therefore may be an exception, but remember, it was you, not it that scored the goals, and if you can do it once then you can do it again."

He smiled at his son, who grimaced back, but Hugo did not feel convinced.

Two days later, Mr Bennett came home from work carrying a large cardboard tube. Hugo was sitting at the kitchen table, in the middle of finishing off some homework. Ever keen to find an excuse not to do it, he asked what was in the tube.

"Oh, you might find this quite interesting. It's the plans, or at least copies of them, for the mansion that originally stood on that plot of land that I got as part of that inheritance. They date back to the late sixteenth century and have been kept in the town's archives ever since. When that Sir Richard Benson was killed at that Time Team dig we went to, one of the reporters, I'm not sure, but I think that it was the same girl who went missing, started to plough through the archives to get some background research on the site and she managed to dig them up."

Eager to see them, Hugo pushed all his books and papers unceremoniously to one side, while his father removed the plastic top off the tube and pulled out the rolled sheaf of documents, which he proceeded to spread over the table.

At that point, Mrs Bennett came in with a large tray of crockery and cutlery.

"You can put that away for a start. I need that table to sort this lot out. It's all our mismatched crocks and cutlery. When I've sorted them out, I'm giving them all to the local charity shop, and they are coming round in ten minutes to pick them up so, scoot." As she said this, she lowered the tray onto the table, and using it, pushed both rolled up plans and Hugo's homework to one side, causing several school books to fall on the floor.

"Aw, mum!" Hugo complained as he bent down to retrieve his homework but all she said was,

"Shoo!"

Hugo and his father looked at each other, sighed and rapidly gathered all the papers together before any more were pushed onto the floor.

"You go and finish your homework in your bedroom and we'll have a look at these after dinner when we won't be in the way or be disturbed," Mr Bennett commented, but stressing the last sentence as he looked at his wife, who chose to ignore him.

When the table was finally cleared after their evening meal, Hugo's father pulled out the cardboard tube again and spread its contents over it. They had to use some knives out of the kitchen drawer to hold down the edges to stop the plans from curling back on themselves. Finally, after running his hands over the document to flatten it, he and Hugo looked for the first time, at what the old judge's house had looked like all those years ago. After filling the washing-up machine with the dirty dishes, Hugo's mother joined the pair as they ran their fingers over this bit and that, trying to imagine what it all looked like before it was left to decay into the pile of rubble that existed now. They had been studying the drawings for about an hour when Stephanie came in from her date with Marty. Out of curiosity, she also started to peer at the plans.

"What do those lines mean?" she asked, pointing at the plans.

"What lines do you mean?" her father asked. She

pointed to some very faint, almost invisible lines that seemed to lie below the much bolder lines of the main drawing.

Everyone's head dropped closer to the paper and slowly they all looked up, appearing mystified.

"I must say, you've got pretty good eyesight, young lady. Until you said, I hadn't even noticed them."

"Well, it's only when you look at the paper sideways so that the light reflects off it that you can see them."

Her mother moved to roughly where her daughter stood and confirmed that they were much more visible from that vantage point. Hugo and his father both got up and stood by the two women, nodding at each other as the lines became more evident. Mr Bennett rushed over to a drawer in a sideboard, and after a bit of rummaging, pulled out a large magnifying glass. Everyone fought to look through it to see where the lines extended. After a few minutes, Mr Bennett put it down and said that it was impossible to see the lines well enough to make out exactly where they went, after all this is only a photocopy, so he proposed that the next day he would go to the museum in his lunch break and have a look at the originals.

By the time they had rolled up the plans and replaced them in the tube, it was quite late, and so it was decided to go to bed. It took Hugo over an hour to finally get to sleep as he pondered over and over in his mind what the old judge's house used to look like, and what was the meaning of the strange faint lines shown under the main plan.

Next evening, everyone was excited to know the results of Mr Bennett's investigation, and as soon as he opened the door, they all pestered him to understand what he had found out. He playfully delayed giving an answer saying that he needed a cup of tea and have a shower; however, he rapidly gave in, because he also was eager to share his findings.

"Well," he began. "You were right Steph; those were lines under the main ones. The originals show them up much better. What it seems is, that before the old judge's house was built, there was another house on the same site. The Judge's house was constructed on top of it. The lines we can see is the plan for the original house. The museum curator could not be sure, but he thinks that, to save completely redrawing the plans for the new house, they were overdrawn on the plans for the original building, presumably to save money, as skilled architects were few and far between in those days. So it looks like we have got two sets of plans in one. While I was there, I sketched in the faint lines on my copy from the original, and here it is."

With a flourish, he pulled out the updated plans from the cardboard tube and laid it on the table, which had been left deliberately clear for such an occasion. He had enhanced the faint lines by marking them in red pen, and yes, it did show another house under the second.

"The museum curator asked me to hold fire on any further site development until he had researched the findings and consulted with the local archaeological groups. I agreed, providing that it did not take too long."

With ideas buzzing about what they might find and speculation, if any of the original building was left, it took up most of the evening but finished with them all deciding to visit the site at the weekend, complete with the plans and start their investigation.

Chapter 13

The Witch's Return

Morgana was in tears as the two sisters looked at their flat and the damage and devastation inside, especially to the door. The intrusion and damage to, what she had hoped would be her home, was bad enough, but what upset her most was the disappearance of Snatch. He wasn't the most amiable of pets but he had been her only companion for almost as long as she could remember. She was aware that he was cowardly but she also knew that he could be vicious as well. If he was out there by himself, there's no telling what he might get up to.

Putricia was far less concerned about, 'that stupid animal'.

"Good riddance if you ask me," she cruelly jibed at her sister. "That settles it; we have to move. Now! Pack up everything; we're going back to our cave at Hartland. It may not be as cosy as here but it is safe from prying eyes."

"But what about Snatch?" her sister pleaded.

"He can find his own way back," was her only reply.

Slowly and laboriously the two women repacked all their belongings, Morgana adding many of Sue's clothes to her burden, having fallen in love with them. Besides, she told herself, strictly speaking, they were hers anyway. With a backward glance as she walked away, Morgana joined her sister and headed back to Hartland.

It was a miserable journey, with Morgana fretting about losing her pet and her sister planning further revenge and atrocities on all those that had dared to invade her privacy. She kept repeating over to herself and muttering,

"They'll pay for this. You wait and see."

The slash in the rocks was uninviting when they finally arrived. Morgana looked around at the very place that she had been so desperate to leave. She silently swore that she would not stay there a moment longer than she had to, even if it meant leaving her sister behind. That evening, and for several days and evenings later, she left the cave while her sister was resting, determined to find a new home. A safe, new home.

Chapter 14

The Beast of Exmoor

Hugo woke, still feeling elated about the thought of investigating a hidden house. At least he hoped it would turn out to be a mysterious house and not just a pile of rubble. He was sauntering down to the kitchen for breakfast when he noticed his parents looking very glum-faced at something they were reading in the local newspaper. When they saw Hugo, they looked at each other and then at their son. His father handed him the paper. Emblazoned across the front page was a picture of Snatch with the headline, *'Beast of Exmoor Caught! Alive!'*

Hugo gasped when he read it and gave his parents a concerned look. Reading on, the article describing how the police had gone to a flat in Bideford, looking for the missing reporter, after a tip-off, but instead of finding her, they were confronted by a ferocious beast. Two police officers had been severely injured in its capture. It went on to say that the animal; described as a huge black cat with large fangs, was bravely sedated by local vet, Mr Timothy

Harrington, whose selfless action saved more officers from certain injury, or worse. The animal is, at present, under tight security at the North Devon Wildlife Park, where experts from across Britain are studying it. Following the publication of details and pictures on the internet, the Wildlife Park has been inundated with requests from Zoos all over the world to exhibit this unusual animal, which definitely lives up to the description of that creature, known locally as, '*The Beast of Exmoor*'.

Hugo lowered the paper, not knowing what to feel. His parents looked at him but said nothing.

He turned and ran up to his bedroom, taking the paper with him. He shouted out that he had to tell Bird because it meant that Morgana and Putricia were closing in again and that was something none of them wanted.

Bird emerged from the wall looking very irritated.

"There's no need to shout that loud to call me," he roughly chided Hugo.

Saying nothing, Hugo opened up the newspaper and held it in front of Bird's face. At first, the animal was surprised, but then it saw the picture covering most of the front page, and asked Hugo to read out what the article said. When he had finished reading it, Bird sat back on his haunches deep in thought.

"And it says Snatch was found in a flat in Bideford?"

"Yes," shouted Hugo, now almost panicking. "The same flat that Morgana, or at least the girl she was before she became Morgana, lived in, in the centre of Bideford. If Snatch was there, then she must be there, as well as Putricia. I am sure that they are still after us. I'm very worried. I think mum and dad are too."

He sat on the edge of his bed and looked at Bird, waiting for a reply. His friend thought for several minutes during which Hugo's parents came in. He looked at them and then they all looked at Bird.

Eventually, he looked up and said that; in his opinion, if the police had found and captured Snatch in the flat of the missing reporter, then it is highly possible that both witches would have left. What was likely, however, was that they would probably try and rescue him. If the police had any sense, then they should keep a very close watch on the animal.

Standing up and stretching, he announced that he would return to the Gnome Reserve and ask if anyone there would be prepared to mount a watch on the wildlife park, where they were keeping Snatch. If they did this and either of the witches tried to free him, then at least they may be able to locate their whereabouts and take what action that seemed appropriate at that time. Everyone nodded, and after a final glance at the newspaper that Hugo was still holding up, he shimmered through the wall, leaving the three of them there.

"Well, we can't stay here all day," Mr Bennett said, breaking the silence. "I have work to go to and you have school, so I suggest that we leave this matter in the hands of Bird and get on with our lives as normal, or at least as normal as possible." This idea spurred everyone into action and they all left, to continue their days as best as they could.

Chapter 15

Burglary?

"You there!" the inspector called to a young constable who was passing his office. "Give that missing reporter's boyfriend fellow a call and ask him to meet us outside her flat at 11 o'clock. He may be able to tell us if anything is missing when we go and have a look at the place, providing there aren't any more dangerous animals in there."

He rubbed his injured leg and eased it off the chair on which he had been resting it. Two hours later, he was standing next to a crimson MGB GT, leaning on its roof, talking to Allan Carlisle.

"Sorry to disturb you, sir," a forensic officer broke into their conversation, "but I think that you'd better come and see this. It looks like someone has already been in the flat before us. The tape is broken and the inside has definitely been disturbed."

"What!" the inspector yelled. "I ordered the strictest of security on the place. Can't anyone around here follow simple orders anymore." Turning to Sue's boyfriend, he apologised and said, "I'm sorry, sir but it certainly looks like that we'll need you now to identify, wherever you can, what is missing or out of place. We have to wait a while to allow the forensics team to do their bits and then we can go in. I apologise for taking up so much of your time. I hope you understand."

The young man nodded and the inspector limped off towards the flat, determined to find out who had been in charge of keeping the flat secure, and venting his rage on them.

It was almost three hours later that all the work was completed and fresh blue tape secured around the doorway but this time a constable, who looked very bored, stood on guard outside, as the last patrol car disappeared down the road.

Back in his office, D.I. Hyde sat rubbing his injured leg, which was now throbbing badly after all the standing at the crime scene. He tried to concentrate on the pages of paper crying out for attention on his desk, but the throbbing just seemed to be getting worse. He called his sergeant and told him to sort out all the papers as he was taking the rest of the day off as sick leave. The officer inwardly groaned as he looked at the pile and then at the inspector. He watched him as he limped out of the office and down the corridor, then, when sure he was out of earshot, swore loudly and banged the desk

Unobserved by the constable patrolling outside the crime scene, Bird looked around inside. He was searching for clues as to where the two witches might have gone. Not that he wanted to meet them again but he felt that if he knew where they were, he would be in a better position to keep the gnomes and Hugo's family safe. Finally, not finding anything that might help, he disappeared through the wall and returned to the Reserve to see if his friends there had found out any information which might be useful.

Chapter 16

Bideford

Morgana looked at herself in the fragment of a mirror propped up against a small outcrop in the wall of the cave. She felt impressed with the way she had transformed her appearance using the clothes that she had taken from Sue Redwell's flat. She had tied her hair into plaits and pinned them to the top of her head, which she covered with a small blue peaked cap pulled low over her eyes to hide her face. She wore a pair of denim jeans, a thick red woollen sweater covered by a heavy coat with the collar pulled up. She was pleased with this, as it not only helped to disguise her but was warm. The cave was now becoming very cold as they had not dared venture out very far to collect driftwood for a fire.

"Yes," she said to herself and twisted and twirled in front of the mirror, happy that, for the first time in as long as she could remember, she felt like a woman again and not some wretched old hag. Her sister had argued that it was still too soon to leave the safety of the cave but Morgana insisted that if she did not go out, then they would have nothing to eat. Putricia scolded her sister, but inwardly was jealous, and what made it worse was that she was cold. She was wearing two of the jumpers that had been brought from the flat, to try to keep warm but they did not fit well and made her look like a child who was wearing her mother's clothes to try to make her look grown-up. If only she had her sister's body instead of this… child's.

It took over an hour of walking before Morgana reached the village of Hartland. On several occasions, she had had to take a detour to avoid meeting people who might see and possibly recognise her, despite her disguise. She was almost at the outskirts of the village when a car drew up and stopped. The driver wound down the window and asked if she would like a lift. She had never been in a vehicle of any sort in her life, other than a cart, the last one of which took her to her execution.

The driver was a young woman about her apparent age. Morgana hesitated at first, as up to now she had had very little involvement with any other human, except her sister and the young woman, in whose body she now existed. She did not count those stupid gnomes and goblins, or even that interfering little boy and his weird friend, whom he called 'Bird'. However, she was wet and cold. The driver looked pleasant and so she accepted. Before the woman drove off, she asked her passenger to put on her seat belt and it took Morgana sometime before, with a little help from the driver, she managed to put it on.

The car pulled away, at what seemed breakneck speed and Morgana found herself holding onto the seat with all her strength. The driver, who introduced herself as Victoria, smiled as they hurtled around the narrow twisting roads, typical of North Devon. Morgana did not want to give her the name she used now, not that anyone would know it. Also, she did not want to use the name of Sue Redwell, so said that her name was Anne, which it had been before her execution, and that she was visiting friends. Victoria said that she was going to Bideford and was that where Anne wanted to go? Morgana answered that that would be fine, so she sped up and headed for the town.

The novelty of the journey was now beginning to thrill Morgana, and by the time they reached Bideford, she was trembling with sheer excitement. Victoria parked the car and invited her passenger to go for a coffee. She was not sure what going for a coffee was, but enthusiastically accepted the invitation.

To avoid awkward questions, Morgana said that she was a stranger to this area and had lived in a remote area and was not used to big cities.

"I would not call Bideford, a big city," laughed Victoria and they both went into a small café in Mill Street, just off the High Street. Morgana looked around at the variety of cakes and sandwiches available; it was certainly something she had never seen before, even when she was alive and, as for the coffee, she had never tasted anything as delicious as this before either. She was alarmed when Victoria started laughing at her and looked around to see if there was another reason for her new friend's amusement but there was nothing. Still smiling, Victoria opened her handbag and pulled out a small mirror which she handed to Morgana. The witch took the object with some trepidation, in case she saw that her transformation was beginning to wear off and she was unaware of it, but as she looked, she also burst out laughing. All around her upper lip was a ring of coffee foam which made her look as if she had a moustache. Taking a tissue that Victoria handed her, she wiped the foam away but it took several minutes for her laughing to stop. It was the first time that Morgana could remember laughing for a very, very long time

The two women sat making small talk, or rather Victoria did, as she did most of the talking, but after about half an hour she said that she had to go, and gave Morgana her address in case she wanted to keep in touch. Morgana thanked her and was interested to see the coins she used as payment for the bill. There had been some of these coins when she was living, albeit for a very short time, at Sue's flat and realised that she would need to get some if she... she corrected herself, they, were going to survive in this new era.

Now warm and dry, she left the café and started to wander around the town, trying to keep as low a profile as possible. Everything was so different from the time that she had lived there. The river was wider in her time, and tatty, semi-derelict houses and warehouses littered the banks. The High Street still stretched up the hill, but all the shops and houses were different. The only landmark she recognised was the bridge with its many arches, now in stone, though it was wooden when she knew it, however, its design and position were unmistakable.

She was standing at one end of the structure when she looked up. On the wall of a large stone building, was a blue sign which was in commemoration of the three women that were hanged for witchcraft in 1682, Temperance Lloyd, Susanna Edwards and a name that suddenly brought tears to her eyes, Mary Trembles; her mother. Morgana felt faint and unsteady. A passing woman asked if she was alright but all Morgana could do was to start to run from that place. She did not know where she was going and did not stop until she came to a chain-linked fence, against which she put her hand to rest.

The moment she touched the rusted wire, a strange feeling coursed through her body and she felt as if she had been there before. She looked through the netting and began shaking with fear and anger as she recognised the ruined site. Although now just a flattened ruin, she knew that this was the house that she, her sister and her friend, Mary Edwards, had been taken to, and where her cousin Stephen Lloyd had been horrifically murdered by that butcher of a judge, Sir Thomas Raymond.

The euphoria of the car journey and the joy of talking with her new friend over the past hour suddenly drained and all the hate and anger that she had had before she had taken over this young woman's body returned. She pulled at the fence and rattled its links. A passing little girl looked at her, giggled and ran on. Several hours later, sitting exhausted, back in the cave, she related to her sister all that had happened that day. They vowed to return to honour their friends and parents; each reconfirming their goal; the death of all those associated with their execution.

Chapter 17

The Ruins

Mr Bennett turned the key in the padlock securing the gate of the chain-linked fencing. The lock and its attached chain fell away with a clang as it hit the support post. All the Bennetts stood at the entrance of the old judge's house and looked for signs of anything that might give a clue to the faint lines on the plans. Hugo's father found a convenient flat surface and, taking the enhanced drawings out of their cardboard tube, laid them out as flat as he could, trying to orientate them to the directions shown.

"Right! You go over there," he ordered Stephanie and indicated to the Eastside. "You cover that side," he said to Hugo, pointing to the South, "and your mother and I will have a look over here."

All four went in their various directions, every now and then coming back to the plan to see if it showed anything that might help. Mr Bennett picked up an old stick and started to use it to slash away at the tangle of weeds and brambles that had invaded every nook and cranny.

After about twenty minutes, Stephanie cried out. Everyone looked up and started to move towards her, but she had only scratched herself on a thorn and pulled a hole in her tights, which, she complained, were brand new on that morning. Ten minutes later, she sat down nursing yet another big scratch on her arm and moaning that it was a waste of time and there was nothing left but a pile of old bricks and stones.

The others ploughed on investigating for about another fifteen minutes but had nothing to report. All feeling very dejected at the anti-climax, they headed for the gate. Mrs Bennett was just passing a particularly dense section of bramble when she thought she heard a noise. Backtracking, she pushed aside the thicket from where it had seemed to come as best she could to see. Her husband told her to hurry up but replied that she would not be a minute. Bit by bit, she inched her way inside the tangle. She had reached almost as far as was possible that the vegetation would allow when she saw a small wooden door, half of which was above ground but the other half was concealed. She shouted to her husband to come and have a look at what she had found. All three quickly came and, using sticks and their feet, they battered down some of the overgrowth so that they could see more clearly. All looked pleased that they had discovered something that might explain the mystery lines on the plans.

It certainly did look like a door that might lead to some structure below ground level. With some effort and a great many scratches, Mr Bennett forced his way through further, until he could touch it. He gave it a push but it did not move, so he pushed harder and it cracked open; just a fraction but no more. Putting his face up to the crack to look inside, all that met him was blackness. He moved away and looked at his family, who all burst into laughter. When he asked them what the joke was, his wife pulled from her handbag, her make-up compact, opened it and, using the mirror, showed him his face which had black, brown and green streaks from where he had pushed his face against the old door.

From over their heads, a loud clap of thunder sounded and it started to rain. Everyone looked up and started to back away from the door as the shower became more intense.

"I think that's about it for today," Mr Bennett said, pulling up the collar of his coat.

Stephanie had already started for the gate and everyone followed after her. Everyone raced back to the shelter of the car with Mr Bennett bringing up the rear as he had to relock the chain back on the gate, or thought that he had.

The rest of that day it never stopped raining and Hugo was becoming bored with playing on his computer. There weren't any programmes on the television that interested him, so he decided to call Bird, more for the company than anything else. His friend appeared looking very wet and bedraggled, as he explained that he too had been caught in the storm. Hugo talked to him about the judge's house plans and how they had discovered the possibility of another building under the ruins. He also described the door that they had found. Suddenly Hugo had an idea.

"You can move through walls, can't you? Well, why don't you go to the site and see if you can move through the door and tell us what is on the other side?"

Bird looked a little doubtful about this and then looked outside at the rain which was still hammering it down.

"I'm sorry but I can't do it now because I still have loose ends to tie up at the Gnome Reserve but I will try in the next few days and let you know. By the way. None of the gnomes were prepared to go within a hundred miles of Snatch to watch him if they could help it, so I am afraid that we will have to rely on the people at the wildlife park to monitor him."

Hugo groaned in dismay.

There was a sudden knock on his bedroom door and Hugo jumped off his bed in surprise. His mother entered carrying a cup of juice and a sandwich. She was surprised to see Bird but asked him if he would like some as well. The creature jumped at the offer, and before long she reappeared carrying a whole plateful, plus two fairy cakes. Hugo looked at Bird's plate and then at his meagre sandwich, but Bird's plate was empty before Hugo had finished his. Fluffing out his feathers, which sprayed water droplets everywhere, he thanked Hugo and his mother, said goodbye and shimmered through the wall.

At dinner, Hugo asked his father when they could go back to the ruins to see if they could open the door. He did not tell him that he had asked Bird to do some investigating of his own.

"We'll have to wait till next weekend," he replied, "because by the time I get in from work, it's dark and it is difficult enough getting through those brambles in the daylight let alone trying at night. Besides, there is supposed to be a security patrol at night and we don't want to upset their arrangements. Also, I have been in contact with the archaeological team about the plans and they have asked that we do not disturb anything until they had had a chance to examine the site themselves."

Hugo felt a little disappointed but realised that his father was right and let the matter drop.

***

Behind the door at the ruins, the cloaked figure barricaded more wood against it; to keep out any, unwanted guests.

Chapter 18

Another New Home

The rain had not stopped for two days and the cave roof was dripping continuously, making it even more uncomfortable for its two occupants. After seeing the houses and buildings in Bideford and the easy accessibility of food and facilities, Morgana had finally persuaded Putricia to move again. Redressing in her previous disguise, she helped her sister to also find something that fitted and that would allow them to blend in, without being noticed. Finally, by tying up one of Sue's skirts and tucking in a large, yellow, cotton blouse, she completed her ensemble by putting on a navy anorak. It covered her hands as the sleeves were too long, so she turned the cuffs back on themselves. Finally, they set off on the long journey to Bideford.

This time they were not as fortunate as before and were not offered any lifts, so it was early afternoon before they arrived, each feeling very weary. Morgana found some coins in the pocket of the anorak, and endeavouring to impress her sister, took her to the same café as she had been to before. She implored her sister to try not to look so nervous as she noticed a person looking at them while they both had a cup of coffee and a cake. When it was time to go, she gave the waitress the coins she had, and was pleased to get some of them back, including some copper ones she had not seen before. By the time that they left, it was already beginning to grow dark and Morgana was keen to show her sister the plaque on the wall of, what she had found out to be, the town hall. Putricia looked at the memorial and started to cry, which made some women passing, look at her. To avoid further attention, Morgana ushered her to the site of the ruins, at which point her sister's tears abruptly stopped as she gazed in horror at the scene of their ordeal centuries before.

Running her hands along the chain-linked fence, Morgana moved along its length until she came to the gate. She rattled the chain, and to her surprise, the padlock fell away. Looking around, she motioned to her sister and they quickly moved inside the site's perimeter, closing the gate after them. Despite the deepening gloom, they inched around the site, replaying in their minds the events that had happened there so many years before. Putricia noticed an area where the overgrowth had been flattened and inched her way along it. On several occasions, she had to disentangle her anorak from the clinging thorns of the brambles. Ahead of her, she saw the small wooden door, still half covered in bracken. Quietly, she called for her sister to join her and they realised that this was the very door through which they had entered the building on that fateful day. They pushed it but it did not move. They pushed harder. From behind the door, they could hear the cracking and splintering of wood and the door started to move. Using all the force they could muster, the door finally moved sufficiently enough for them to squeeze through.

The stench of centuries of rot and decay greeted them but a warm draught of air swept through the corridor in front of them. The light from outside was now very dim and very little penetrated the area in which they stood, in silence. The warmth of the air around, seemingly coming from ahead, surprised them, nevertheless, they welcomed it. It was a great respite from the chilled weather outside and the rain, which had now become more intense. Unwilling to face the journey back to the cave at Hartland and unable to see ahead of them in the corridor, the sisters agreed to stay there that night and explore the next day. Morgana commented to her sister before settling down, how ironic it was that the site of their demise should now be the site of their protection. A rat scurried deep into the blackness of the corridor as the two settled, as best they could, for the night.

Chapter 19

Snatch's Plan

The Wildlife Park was swarming with scientists, representatives from museums and zoos, as well as the nosey and curious. Normally closed at this time of year, the arrival of Snatch had created such international interest that they had decided to reopen, resulting in trade being busier than at the height of the summer season. The animal had become an international celebrity, with its picture broadcast over several television channels and nearly every newspaper in the country. Even the nation's most eminent naturalist had asked to come to do a 'Wildlife Special', and the park's staff were making great efforts to spruce everything up ready for the broadcast.

Snatch paced up and down his enclosure, desperate to find a means of escape. It snarled and roared at the mass of faces that were pressed up to the security fencing. It had been reinforced; not to keep Snatch from escaping, but to resist the pressure of the people pressing up to it. The noises made by the animal did not frighten away the unwanted viewers; instead, it only increased their enthusiasm, especially the children, many of whom had taken days off school to visit the attraction. The only aspect of his capture that Snatch had enjoyed was the regular feeding with fresh meat, not the dead rats and left-overs that he had existed on while in the ownership of Kadavera and Morgana. Nevertheless, he was desperate to get back to them and away from all these unwanted potential victims.

As he patrolled his territory, he had noticed a small space below part of the perimeter fence. Conscious of the myriad eyes watching him in daylight, he kept clear of the area to avoid it being noticed by one of his keen-eyed observers. He decided to wait until darkness had fallen when he knew he could enlarge it, and if all went well, make his bid for freedom.

Chapter 20

The Archaeologist

Mr Bennett sat at the breakfast table reading the report on the incredible creature that had been captured and was now resident at the Wild-Life Park, thinking, 'If only they knew the truth about that animal, it would fill up the front covers of every newspaper in the world.'

Folding the newspaper, he drained his cup of coffee and started to open his mail, which had just been delivered. The pile was still so large from those pleading for a donation or telling a hard-luck story, that the postman had to knock on the door each day to deliver them, as they would not all fit through the letterbox. He had opened about five, which were all now resting in the waste bin, when he saw one that looked very official, with the franking mark of a firm of local solicitors. Opening it, he found it was in connection with the house owned by Emma's parents, the late Mr and Mrs Peter Jones. As legal guardians of their only surviving family member, Emma, they were inquiring as to their proposals on the future of the property, as there were still outstanding payments on the mortgage. If these were not forthcoming by the first of January, the following year then the bank holding the mortgage would foreclose the arrangement and repossess the property, in lieu of debt. As solicitors acting for the deceased couple, they would be grateful to know of the Bennetts' plans.

With everything that had been happening and the general confusion, together with Emma's disappearance, he had not even considered the house, now effectively owned by Emma, if she was still alive. He folded the letter and pushed it into his briefcase for his attention later if he had a free moment at work. Shouting goodbye to his children and receiving mumbled groans from upstairs, he gave his wife a peck on the cheek and rushed off to his practice.

Hugo slouched into the kitchen and poured himself a bowl of cornflakes, which he dowsed with milk from the fridge. Taking them over to the table, he pushed his father's newspaper to one side to make space for the bowl. Glancing at the paper, he saw the face of Snatch on the front cover. Forgetting his cereal and grabbing the paper, he flattened it onto the table. Quickly, he read through the article and studied the picture staring out at him. Although he was pleased that the beast had been captured; after all, it was one less problem to deal with, he somehow felt sorry for it as its picture gazed back at him.

Stephanie ambled past him, deliberately knocking his chair but as she looked at what he was reading, she snatched the paper from him and rushed over to the window to read it herself. Hugo was about to swear at her and chase her when his mother came in. He moaned to her about what Stephanie had done. She strode across to her daughter and tore the paper from her grasp and was about to give it back to Hugo when she saw the article and picture herself. Taking a seat at the table, she started to read, making both Hugo and Stephanie shout in complaint.

Hugo asked his mother if they could visit the Wild-Life Park and see Snatch again but this time with the protection of a thick wire fence between them. Even Stephanie joined in with the request but their mother told them that they already had had enough time off school, what with chickenpox, Emma's parents' accident and her subsequent disappearance. The only time available would be the weekend and they had already planned to go back to the judge's house at that time, which meant there would not be any opportunity.

"Besides," she went on. "if you had read the article, then you will have seen that due to demand they have had to instigate a booking system for tickets and they have already sold out for the next five weeks."

The two children moaned but consoled themselves that they had both seen Snatch first hand, long before anyone else.

That evening, Mr Bennett sat discussing the meeting he had had with the solicitor acting on behalf of the estate of the late Jones's. Since there was still a possibility of Emma being found alive she would still be entitled to the house; therefore, they had decided that he would use some of his inheritance to clear the mortgage on the home on her behalf. This choice would make it hers in her own right, if and when she returned.

"After all," he smiled, "what's the point of having money if you can't do someone a favour with it."

His wife smiled as well but in the back of her mind, she was still not sure if they would ever see their ward again.

Her husband explained that the legalities might take some time, especially as the beneficiary to the estate was herself missing; however, they would get matters started and take things as they developed. The solicitor had recommended that they arrange for a good security system to be installed to prevent thieves and possible squatters, entering the property. Mr Bennett asked his wife if she would arrange that with the same firm that handled the security at the site of the judge's house, as he was very busy at work and did not have the time to sort it out himself.

Disappointed that he could not visit Snatch, Hugo went to his room to collect his books and bag for school. He remembered that it was football again that afternoon and suddenly thought of his talisman. He also recalled that his father had told him that it was not the lucky charm that brought him success but having confidence in his own abilities. He was not convinced, however, and decided that he would take it with him anyway, to see if wearing it previously and the success it gave him on the pitch, was a fluke, or if it really made him invincible, as told in the legend.

With a shout from his mother, telling him that she'd be waiting in the car, he ran downstairs and was on the point of slamming the front door behind him when he remembered that he had not picked up his games kit. Returning to the kitchen, he grabbed his bag from the cupboard and was about to leave again when Jake jumped up at him, trying to get some attention. Without realising it, the dog's paw caught in the cord holding the pendant around Hugo's neck. The knot in the thread separated and the amulet fell off, landing on the rug by the front door. Oblivious to its loss, Hugo joined his mother and sister in the car and they left for school.

That morning, on her return, Mrs Bennett spent her time arranging with the security firm to fit alarms to the house where Emma's parents had lived and attend to some business matters concerning the money and property that had been inherited by her husband. As part of her travels, she happened to be passing the site of the judge's house and stood by the fence looking in. She had been there with her family, but had never had a chance to look at it by herself. She approached the gate and noticed that the padlock was not locked properly. Taking advantage of this, she pushed the gate open and went in.

It felt very strange being there, almost as if she had been there in the distant past but she knew that that was impossible. After all, she had come from Reading, which was several hundreds of miles away, yet the feeling was so strong it seemed uncanny. She carefully made her way over to where they had seen the small wooden door. She was sure that it was fully closed when they left but now there was a definite crack in its opening. Trying to avoid the brambles catching her tights, she pushed her way to the door and gave it a slight push. It moved, only slightly but more than when they were there before. She pushed again but this time with a little more force. A warm vent of air covered her face together with the smell of decay. Another push and the door gave, just enough to allow her to squeeze through. Before her, was total blackness, which did not improve even after several minutes as she allowed her eyes to become accustomed to the darkness. Placing her hands against the walls, she shuffled forwards, but after even a few yards, she realised that, without a torch, any progress would be futile. Retracing her steps, she eased her way back through the opening. As she turned, the daylight blinded her for a few moments. On opening her eyes, a middle-aged man was standing in front of her. The shock of seeing him made her jump, and it was only after he had apologised to her for giving her a shock, that he introduced himself as Tom Broadbent, the senior archaeologist in charge of this dig.

He had just arrived himself, and had seen her go in through the doorway. Thinking that she might have been a trespasser, he had followed her to investigate. It took several minutes before she could compose herself enough to explain who she was and what she was doing there. She mentioned to him about finding the fine lines on the old plans and about their theory that there might be something left of the original building below the ruins. He said that he had also seen the plans as part of his initial investigations into the history of the site and the structures that had stood there. He went on that, from his research, he, or rather his team, had found out that the site had been occupied since at least six hundred AD when Bideford was just a small community that had become established there. The settlement had stood in that spot as it was the first location from the estuary where the River Torridge could be forded. All the original wooden structures had long since disappeared and besides, at that time, the river was much wider, which is why the present site was a good way from its present banks. The first stone building recorded there was in the thirteenth century but it was washed away by a massive flood in about fourteen thirty-five. Since then there have been four buildings on that area, the last being that of the late Sir Thomas Raymond.

Mrs Bennett was fascinated by all that he had to say and asked him if he would like to come to dinner so that he could meet her husband and family and tell them all that he knew. They arranged a date for that evening and she left feeling very pleased with herself at finding out so much.

Chapter 21

Breakfast

The disturbance by Mrs Bennett in the corridor had woken Putricia from her sleep. Suddenly alert, she squinted in the direction of the noise but saw only blackness. She rubbed her eyes, and as she did so became aware that she was covered by several newspapers, as was her sister. Brushing them aside, she poked her still-sleeping partner, who woke with a start. Putricia immediately put her fingers over her sister's mouth to prevent her from making any noise. They could hear the sound of two people talking close to the doorway. Not daring to move, they maintained their silence until the voices stopped and the sounds of the two intruders had moved away. Morgana looked at her sister when she felt it was safe and it was only at that moment did she also noticed the layer of newspapers that had covered her. She asked Putricia if she had put them there, but each had thought that the other had done it while they slept. They were confused when they realised that neither of them had blanketed themselves with the papers. A small chink of light, shining through a small crack from above them now allowed them to see where they had been sleeping. It was a small room. One end had rotting wooden shelves nailed precariously to the wall, some with old pots still standing on them. They both agreed that it must have probably been a storeroom. As they passed directly under the light source, it illuminated a part of one of the newspapers now covering the floor. Putricia glanced down and suddenly stopped, gasped and pointed at the paper. Her sister followed her gaze and also let out a small cry.

Partially highlighted by the beam, was a picture of Snatch. Both sisters made a grab for the page but Putricia was successful and pulled the page closer to the light and read the article printed below the picture of their pet's face. Morgana strained to read it over her sister's shoulder, so Putricia laid the paper on the floor directly below the light beam and both read, each occasionally groaning as the article described the animal as dangerous, vicious and the 'Beast of Exmoor'.

When they had finished reading and rereading the newspaper, they agreed that they must rescue their pet, to save it from those stupid people who had captured it. They were sure that some of them would want it to be put down and stuffed so that it could show it off in the local museum. The two agreed that trying a rescue in the daylight would be impossible and foolish, so carefully collecting and folding the remaining papers, they put them to one side and continued the exploration of their new residence.

From the dimly lit area from where they stood, they could see nothing but blackness but following the line of the wall, they inched further into, what?

The corridor suddenly came to an abrupt stop, but turning to their right, a very dim light could be made out. With nowhere else to go, they felt their way forward until they came to a small flight of stone steps which seemed to descend into another room from which the light source came. Holding onto each other, more for mutual support rather than finding their direction, they made their way forward until, after a slight dog-leg bend, they entered a room with a smouldering lamp on a table in the centre of it. At each end of the table was a cracked china plate on which lay a small loaf of bread which was in two pieces. An equally cracked pitcher of water with two small cups stood beside it. Cautiously the two approached the table and felt the bread, which they were astonished to find, was fresh.

Each looked around for the owner of the food but could see no-one. Furtively, Putricia picked up one portion of the loaf and started to eat. It tasted so good, just like that which she remembered her mother making when she was a young girl. Seeing her sister eating prompted Morgana also to start but she was aware that this might be someone else's breakfast and so she tore her portion in half and only ate one part. Each had not realised how hungry they were. They smiled at each other as they poured two cups of the water and rapidly drank them down, followed by a second cup.

They looked at each other and then around the sparsely-furnished small room. In the centre, there was a rickety table, on which stood the glowing lantern. A single chair was leaning against one wall and a small cooking pot was hanging from a trivet in one corner. It was immaculately clean, unlike the caves in which they had previously lived, which seemed to have always been littered with debris. However, what surprised the sisters more than anything else, was the scribbling on the walls. Each of them glanced at the neat but shaky handwriting, in what seemed to be charcoal. As they read, recognition dawned and they poured over the writings more closely.

They were not familiar with everything, but all of the writings they did recognise were the recipes and formulas for many of the potions they had made in the cave at Westward Ho! They were totally confused. Who had written these: moreover, who knew what the recipes were in the first place? As far as they knew, only they were aware of these formulas and no one else had the books in which they were written. Who had invaded their space, stolen their property and deigned to copy them onto the walls in this strange place?

Each looked at each other in bewilderment, tracing and reading the small script with their fingers. One section of the writing particularly interested Morgana, who went to the table and picked up the lamp which she took back to the section of the wall she had been studying. Putricia complained that she could no longer read her part and went over to where her sister stood, stunned by what she was reading. As she approached her sister, she drew in a breath as she read the title; '*Life Eternal*'.

The women were transfixed as they read down the list of ingredients and brewing instructions. Morgana returned to the table and sat on the small chair. Minutes later she was joined by her sister who, shaking slightly, asked,

"Is that what I think it is?"

Morgana nodded and replied, "What is this place and

who has been living here? That formula describes how to resurrect a body near to death and keep it alive for centuries. It is that potion which is the reason we are still here now. Whoever lives here has been responsible for keeping us alive." The pair gazed at each other and then around the room as if someone would suddenly appear but all remained silent.

Putricia suddenly stood up and took hold of the lamp, turned up its wick to give better illumination and announced to her sister,

"I am determined to find out who and what is going on," and started to leave the room into the corridor that led from it. Morgana joined her and they set off on their exploration, not knowing who, or what to expect, or find.

Chapter 22

Puchy's Disappearance

Hugo was almost in tears when he arrived home from school that evening. His mother was busy cooking and preparing the dining room for the arrival of their guest. She did not notice her son's distress at first as she was preoccupied with her work but thought it strange when she saw him crawling on all fours around the kitchen floor. When she asked him what he was doing, he looked up and broke down. Tearfully, he told her that he had lost his talisman. He explained that he wanted to take it to school to wear it during football to see if it gave him good luck. He was positive that he had put it around his neck before leaving for school, but when changing before games, he noticed that it was missing. His mother tried to reassure her son that it would turn up at some time but deep down was equally concerned, as she knew that this was no toy and its power to burn almost everyone may cause some significant damage to its finder.

To settle Hugo's obvious distress, but more for her peace of mind, she joined him, looking everywhere where he might have lost it and a few other places besides, but they could not find it. When his father came in from his practice, he also joined in the hunt when they told him what was missing but he also reprimanded his son for disobeying him and said to him that it was a good lesson for him to remember.

Tea time was a sullen experience that evening and Hugo decided to go to his room to do his homework, which amazed his parents, as this was most out of character for him but they did not argue about it. Mrs Bennett busied herself continuing the preparation for the dinner for their guest that evening. At the same time, her husband searched out all the information he had about the Judge's house, including the plans which he laid out to flatten before Tom Broadbent arrived.

Feeling very dejected and bored, Hugo emptied his school bag on the floor to see if the amulet had fallen inside, but it hadn't. To pass the time, he picked up his homework and began to work on it.

The sound of the doorbell ringing, shortly followed by the noise of the front door slamming shut, suddenly roused Hugo. He realised that instead of doing his homework, he had fallen asleep. Only a fraction of the essay he was supposed to write had been completed. He had already had a reprimand for not handing it on time the day before and he knew that, if it was not completed that night, he would be in further trouble when he returned to school next day. Sitting up on the edge of his bed, he started to complete the essay.

His parents were surprised to see his light still on when they went to bed and looked into his room to check on him. Surprised at actually seeing him working, they wished him goodnight and told him not to be long but it was after midnight when he finally threw his book on the floor and climbed into bed. He didn't even bother to clean his teeth, which made him feel just a little bit guilty.

The next morning was frosty, which for the middle of November was unusual. His father had to scrape the ice off the windows of his car before he could go to work and he asked Hugo to do the same for his mother. Reluctantly and with a prompt from his mother, he put on his jacket. Jake thought that this was a sign for a walk and jumped up and pawed the door but Hugo pushed him to one side and eased himself through the door, using his foot to prevent the dog from escaping.

The cold hit him as soon as he closed the door and small clouds of breath surrounded his head. Fortunately, the ice was already beginning to soften in the early-morning sunshine and it did not take long to clear it from the car's windows. He was about to return indoors when there was a loud 'splat' and there, streaked across the windscreen was the dropping of some large bird. Hugo swore silently under his breath and looked around. A very irritated white seagull was perched on the wall next to the house. He bent down and picked up a pebble and was about to throw it at the offending creature when a high-pitched voice rang out,

"Hello, Mr Hugo."

He looked around and then saw the reason for the seagull's obvious irritation. Seated on its back, with a leg either side of its neck, was Chipper. The young boy gave a broad smile as he recognised his friend who, in dismounting from the twitching bird, slipped and fell on the ground, which, for a human, was not a long way but for a small gnome, it was a considerable height. The seagull, free from its unwelcome burden, gave a loud squawk and took off, circling twice before disappearing over the hill behind Westward Ho!

Hugo rushed over to his small friend, who was getting up from his fall. Despite the accident, he gave a broad smile as Hugo bent down to help him to his feet. Chipper brushed down his bright blue coat and pink trousers, finally straightening his floppy red hat and held his hand out to shake Hugo's.

"That was Hosper's taxi and I'm not used to such a large bird," apologised the little gnome, still smiling.

Hugo smiled back and asked what he was doing there, especially on such a cold morning, as he knew gnomes hated the cold.

Chipper's face changed and he began to look worried. He explained that he had invited Puchy, the tooth fairy, to come over to the Gnome Reserve the previous night, to play. On arriving, she apologised but had just received a message that a young girl in Bideford was about to lose her tooth and had to rush over to be ready to exchange it for a coin when she went to sleep. She said that when she had finished her work, she would return to the reserve to spend the evening with her friend, but never returned.

"I've called and called her many times since then," Chipper went on, now with tears beginning to mist his eyes, "but there's no reply, which is most unusual for Puchy. She is always very prompt when you call her."

Hugo went over to the small gnome and put his fingers around him to try to comfort him. Chipper forced a smile.

"I'll tell you what," the boy said, in such a way as to sound confident that everything was all right. "I'll give her a call and see if that does any good."

Chipper nodded enthusiastically, while Hugo stood up and, in a firm voice shouted, "Puchy, Puchy, Puchy." He and Chipper looked around expectantly, but the small tooth fairy failed to appear. Hugo cleared his throat and shouted even louder, but still no Puchy. He gave his little friend a concerned look, then, with as much force as he could muster, he called out the tooth fairy's name three times again. As he finished calling, the front door of the house opened and his mother put her head around it and asked what in the world he was doing. Then she noticed Chipper and gave him a broad smile. The little creature grimaced back, and Hugo, now very worried himself, explained the problem to her. She reassured them that there was probably a very straightforward explanation of why Puchy could not come but if Hugo did not hurry up, he would be late for school. Her son looked downhearted and tried to argue with his mother that he should forget school and look for his friend.

"After all, she helped us when we were in trouble," he protested.

"I'll tell you what," she replied, "after I've dropped you off at school and taken young Chipper back to the Reserve, then I will see what I can do."

As she finished saying this, Stephanie came to the door looking very irate, carrying a large duffle bag, seemingly crammed with books, but when she saw the small gnome her demeanour changed and she smiled and went up to him and put her finger out to shake his hand.

"Right! Go and get your bag Hugo and all of you get into the car." She was about to get into the Volvo herself when she saw the large splash across the windscreen left by the seagull. She swore under her breath and went back into the house; returning with a yellow sponge and a large bucket of water, which she threw at the windscreen and used the sponge to wipe it all down. Finally, with a slam of the front door to the house, they all left.

Almost an hour later, Mrs Bennett pulled up outside the Gnome Reserve. She and Chipper went to the office, where a somewhat distraught owner was talking to Hosper, the new head of the gnome community. When they saw the pair coming through the door, they both gave a deep sigh of relief. The owner went up to caress Chipper but Hosper pushed her aside and began telling off the now, somewhat-cowering, gnome.

Mrs Bennett quickly explained the situation as regards Puchy, and Hosper eased away but still admonished the youngster for taking his seagull without permission. When everyone had calmed down, Hugo's mother suggested that they all call the tooth fairy and see if that helped. Forming a rough circle, they all stood to attention and in unison, loudly called; 'Puchy, Puchy, Puchy!' and waited. They called again but no small fairy appeared. Everyone looked glumly at each other, wondering what had become of their diminutive friend.

Chapter 23

Snatch's Escape

Night had almost fallen. Wisps of pink hung over the darkening sky as Snatch uncurled himself from the corner of the compound where he was imprisoned. The effects of the tranquilisers the staff vet at the wildlife centre had used on him earlier in the day, had almost worn off. Scientists from around the globe had prodded and probed him, taking samples of his blood, fur, and skin, they even removed one of his teeth and gave all the rest a thorough clean and polish. His head was still feeling a little disorientated but as he began to walk around it rapidly cleared. He could hear the clank of buckets and wire doors slamming shut as the staff finished feeding and cleaning out their various charges. As darkness finally consumed the attraction, all that could be heard was the hooting of an owl and the occasional whooping of the howler monkeys from the other end of the site.

Snatch licked the small trace of blood from the corner of his mouth, a reminder of the dental treatment he had been subjected to as part of a health check. It was certainly a strange feeling, being able to feel the silky smoothness of his teeth instead of the almost constant niggling from the debris left from several meals previously. The sharp edges from that broken tooth that had plagued him were now gone, as was the tooth. He had damaged it when he had bitten too hard on a bone that his mistress had thrown him several months before. Instead, was the still oozing socket left from its extraction.

The security lights cast strange shadows as he prowled around his compound, sniffing the air for any trace of man. Slowly, his meanderings became a pattern which, with each circuit, became more confined, till ultimately they centred on a small area of the fence at the far end of the enclosure. He leaned against the chain-linked wire and watched as the bottom pulled away from the ground leaving a small space. With each contact, the fence was eased out of the ground a little more until he judged it to be sufficient to allow his escape. His red eyes glistened in the glow of the security lights as, with only a slight squeaking from the rusting wire of the fencing, he squeezed and wriggled himself under the mesh.

Staying in the shadows, he eased himself around and between the various enclosures, trying, wherever possible, to stay off the paths which were illuminated, albeit dimly. Finally, with an easy leap of the entrance gate, he was free.

He took a deep breath and sniffed the air. He could not sense his mistress but he could smell the scent of the sea and human habitation. He recognised some familiar odours that he had encountered from his excursions when hunting for fresh meat for his mistress. It was during these killing sprees that he became known as the 'Beast of Exmoor'. The scents told him which way to go, and with a final satisfying look back at the wild-life centre, he headed back; towards Westward Ho!

Chapter 24

Ancestry Revelations

"What in the world are you doing?" Mrs Bennett asked her husband as he cleared the kitchen table of everything and began to pull a large roll of paper from a cardboard tube he balanced under his arm.

"Oh! When I was at the surgery this morning, a courier delivered this." He wiggled the cardboard container under his arm. "It's from Jasper and Harding. You know, the heir hunter people who discovered my inheritance. It came with a note, which said that it is the family tree they used to track me down. They had now completed all their investigations and thought that I would like a copy of their paperwork."

Mrs Bennett's eyes lit up and she rushed to help her husband uncurl the very large sheet of paper as it was pulled from the tube. They both laughed as they rolled out the sheet, for as they pushed on one end, the opposite end rolled back. It reminded them of the slapstick comedians they remembered from their childhood, who had a similar problem when they tried to put wallpaper on a wall.

However, this time, the two adults did not end up covered in wall-paper paste as those performers did.

Eventually, using a variety of kitchen tools, they had the sheet as flat as they could, and started to follow the lineage of Mr Bennett's ancestors back through the ages. They were both stunned and impressed at the work that Jasper and Harding had gone to, researching all the various lines of the many families that made up the tree. Unfortunately, their investigations had only taken the tree back to the mid-1800s. This lack of information disappointed Mr Bennett, as he was hoping that it might go back as far as Sir Richard Benson in 1682, so that it would corroborate the story that Hugo had told them as to the reason for the witches' vendetta.

"Why don't you try that website that is advertised on the television; Ancestry something? In fact, after seeing your tree, I think that I would enjoy doing a bit of investigation into my own." announced his wife. "Since the children are away doing their own thing, there's no time like the present. Where's that laptop of yours?"

Mr Bennett, without taking his eyes off the paper, spread out on the table, grunted and nodded to the worktop, next to the fridge, where he had dropped his briefcase and laptop. He had left it there as he struggled in with the large tube on returning home from his surgery. His wife marched over to where it lay and with a flourish, picked it up and made her way into the lounge.

Minutes passed, then a shout came from the lounge.

"Darling! What's your password?"

Mr Bennett looked up from his studies and walked, glum-faced into the lounge.

"What's wrong with you?" his wife asked on seeing his face. "I only asked you for the password to this stupid machine."

"It's not that." Her husband replied. "but I've been studying that family tree in the kitchen. From what I can make out, it seems that everyone, at least on the male side, has died at a very early age. There are only a few 'causes of death' stated, but each one was premature and not particularly pleasant. One, a Thomas Bennett, was a farmer and 'fell' into his threshing machine in 1904. Another, Gordon Bennett..."

Mrs Bennett gave a muted giggle at the name, which was returned by an angry stare from her husband which made her blush with embarrassment.

"As I was saying," he continued, "Gordon Bennett was mysteriously drowned in the river, despite being a strong swimmer, in 1863. There are also three more cases of death by unusual causes, documented in the information that the heir hunters sent."

"That's very interesting," smiled his wife, "but why the sad face?"

"Remember what Hugo said about the witches. They're staying alive with the sole purpose of destroying the descendants of that judge, Sir Richard Benson or whatever his name was. If that is true, then it includes me... and Hugo, he added as an afterthought. I haven't checked yet as regards the female line of the tree, but if that is also included in the witch's plan, then it also includes you and Stephie."

Mrs Bennett's face suddenly dropped and she looked pale and slightly shocked.

"Whatever you do, don't tell the children what you have discovered. They have enough to worry about at the moment, what with Emma's disappearance and all that has happened at the Gnome Reserve. We need to do a lot more research before we come to any conclusions. After all, there may be a very logical reason for your family's history and we don't want to make them any more afraid than they are now.

I think that we had both register for this ancestry site and find out as much as we can... and as quickly as we can., Julia Bennett added as an afterthought.

"Now. What's that password?"

Two hours passed in silence as they both busied themselves in investigating and tracking down their respective family origins.

The silence was broken by a car pulling up outside the house. Moments later, Stephanie burst in through the front door in tears.

"What's wrong with you, Steph?" asked her mother as her daughter passed the lounge doorway.

"Marty's ditched me!" she screamed, and ran up the stairs and into her bedroom, slamming the door behind her.

The intense concentration of the previous two hours was broken and Mrs Bennett chased after her daughter to determine the problem. Mr Bennett looked up from his studies and sighed.

Carefully pushing away all the kitchen implements holding down the scroll, he re-rolled the paper and fed it back into the cardboard tube. Seconds later, Hugo and Jake came in through the back door, both covered in mud.

"Get that animal out of the kitchen and clean him up before your mother sees it! The same goes for you. You look as if you've been rolling down a hill," shouted his father.

This fact wasn't far from the truth either, for Hugo had been trying to get back into the cave from the Abbotsham cliff entrance, but there was no way that he would ever admit this. Hugo and the dog reluctantly retreated to the utility room, where the animal was given a bath, or rather a shower, from the hosepipe.

Finally, re-entering the kitchen, his father looked at the dog and then at Hugo. Without saying a word, he pointed to the stairs and his son trudged slowly up to the bathroom where he splashed water over all the visible spots of mud, wiping the excess off in the towel, and then went into his bedroom to change his clothes.

For the moment, all concerns about the ancestry and the premature deaths of the Bennett's family members was forgotten. Stephanie's sobbing echoed around the house and Mr Bennett decided that it was a good time to go to the chip shop and get something for them all to eat. With all the time spent on chasing up their long-lost relatives, no thought or effort had been given to making anything for dinner.

An hour later, it was a very subdued Bennett family that scrunched up the chip papers before throwing them in the recycle bin. The only cheerful person, or should I say animal, was Jake, who had eaten most of Stephanie's meal, as she said she was not hungry.

With all the effort of digging, trying unsuccessfully to get back into the cave, Hugo was tired, and so it was not long after the meal that he, and everyone else, went to bed.

The sound of his sister's crying slowly subsided as he drifted off to sleep. By ten o'clock, the whole house was silent.

No-one was aware of Jake sniffing the air and pawing at the door to get out, no-one except a dark shadow with yellow fangs, many miles away.

Chapter 25

Puchy's Misadventure

Evie McLachlan was feeling very pleased with herself; she had caught a fairy.

She was six years and five months old. Ten minutes before, she had been lying in her bed playing her tongue against the loose tooth in the front of her mouth. The tooth had been wobbly for about a week and now was only held into her jaw by the finest of a thread of gum. Her mother had told her that when it fell out, she had to put it under the pillow of her bed, so that, when she woke the following morning, she would find that the tooth fairy would have visited and replaced the tiny piece of enamel with some money. Her mother even suggested that she pull it out for her daughter to speed up the process. The real reason, however, was that she was fed up with her daughter flicking the tooth from between her lips, especially when in company.

Her mother had told her as she went to bed that night that, if the tooth had not fallen out by morning then she would get a tissue and pull it out for her. Evie was determined not to let this happen and frantically pushed it back and forth with her tongue to separate the thread holding it in.

Puchy had been preparing for over a week for her visit to Evie's house and she knew that tonight was to be the night. Clutching a pound coin, she waited outside the young girl's bedroom window, waiting for the thread of gum holding the tooth to finally break and then for the donor to fall asleep so that the transfer could be completed. Evie, on the other hand, had different ideas and she was determined to, not only see but to catch her very own fairy.

As soon as her mother had kissed her goodnight and left the room, the small child rose from beneath her duvet and picked up, a small plastic box with a picture of Barbie painted on the top, from her toy cupboard. She returned to bed, covering her head with the duvet. With a little trepidation, she forced the loose tooth between her lips and then compressed them together. It had the desired effect and the tiny tooth, along with a spot of blood, fell onto her pillow.

Unable to see the object clearly, as it was almost dark, she rubbed it between her fingertips. Part of it felt smooth and shiny but the other side felt a little rough and sharp. Carefully, she positioned the tooth in front of the half-open box which she had pushed under her pillow, keeping it close to the edge so that it would be easier for her to close it when the time came.

Puchy sensed the vibration of the tooth coming out and passed through the window into the child's bedroom, ready to do the changeover. She waited and watched the slow rise and fall of the duvet as the little girl slept and then flew down onto the bed next to the pillow. Silently she pushed her small arm under the pillow, feeling for the tooth. Suddenly, without any warning, there was a movement from under the duvet followed by a loud 'snap' as the Barbie box passed over her and the lid closed.

The little tooth fairy was stunned as the box was withdrawn from beneath the pillow and waved in the air by the triumphant child. The shock of the shaking had made the small fairy drop the pound coin she was carrying and was struck several times by it as it rattled around inside the pink box.

Finally, the box became still and Puchy was able to calm herself down. She did not feel worried by her capture, more annoyed that she, for the first time in her life, had misjudged a child and allowed it to get the better of her. All she needed to do was to pass through the box just like she usually did with the windows of the children she visited. However, because of this child's effort to capture her, she was determined that she would not leave the money she had brought. Feeling around, she found the coin. Holding it tightly against her chest, she walked up to the wall of the box and pushed to go through, but nothing happened, except that she banged her nose on the box wall. She tried again, but the wall held firm. She started to panic and ran at the wall, this time hurting her nose so much that it began to bleed.

The box started to move again but rapidly came to a stop. A faint light came on, shining through the translucent plastic of the box and then the lid began to open, followed by a blue eye peeping through the crack. Puchy heard a triumphant giggle and then felt that someone was calling her name. She knew that it was Chipper calling but try as she might, she could not escape from the box.

"Hello," the eye said. "Are you the tooth fairy?"

"Yes!" Puchy said indignantly but then changed her tone and pleaded to let her go.

"All my friends said that you do not exist, and that it was our parents that put money under the pillow when our teeth fall out. I'm going to take you to school tomorrow and show them that they were wrong and you really do exist after all."

"Oh please let me go," pleaded Puchy and at the same time felt the call from both Chipper and Hugo as well. Since each of them was calling, she thought that it must be something very important and so she desperately asked again to be let out.

Suddenly, there was a noise like the sound of a door opening very carefully. The lid of the box slammed shut. The small fairy was swished around inside as it was moved. After a moment it became still and everything went dark again. A minute or so passed and then Puchy felt the box carefully sliding from under the pillow.

"Oh. Isn't that sweet? Look, darling. Little Evie has put a box under her pillow for the tooth fairy to put the money in," muffled voices were heard to say. Puchy felt as if her prison was being carried. Lights flashed through the box as it was transported from room to room, finally coming to rest after a sliding feeling, followed by total darkness and silence.

It took several minutes for the small creature to compose herself. She approached the side the box and tentatively tried to pass through but the wall held firm.

'I don't understand why I can't pass through this box?' she thought to herself and gave it one last try but to no avail. She sat down on the pound coin and started to cry. She suddenly stopped as she sensed that everyone was calling her name at the gnome reserve, but then started to cry again even louder as she began to appreciate her predicament.

As soon as Evie woke up the following morning, she pushed her hand under her pillow to retrieve her box but all she found was the two-pound coin, left there by her parents. The disappointment of not finding her box was quickly forgotten as she rushed to show her parents her 'prize'.

The box stayed covered by an old headscarf in the bottom of a draw of Evie's parents' bedroom.

Chapter 26

Julia Bennetts Ancestry

"Thank goodness they've gone." sighed Mrs Bennett, as the car door slammed behind Hugo and his sister as she dropped them off at school. Her husband had left for his dental practice half an hour before and after a ten-minute drive back home, she would have the whole day to herself.

It was a Monday morning and the whole family, being at home over the rainy weekend, had left the house in a terrible mess. The atmosphere had been made worse by her daughter being in a foul mood all the time following her breakup with her boyfriend, Marty.

In many ways, she was glad that her daughter had packed her boyfriend up, though technically, it was he who had given her up. She had always found him to be a bit pompous, but for a sixteen-year-old boy, she supposed that it was normal. She hoped that Hugo would not end up such a pain in the neck.

With no-one else in the house, Jake jumped up and generally got in the way as he vied for some attention until, in desperation, Julia Bennett shut him in the utility room while she got on with her cleaning. It wasn't until after noon that she finally decided to stop and make herself a cup of coffee. Opening the utility room door, she let the dog back into the kitchen and put into his bowl, half a tin of dog food. It disappeared before she had time to put the kettle on for her coffee. With reluctance, but more to stop the dog from whining and worming between her legs, she dished out the other half of the tin.

Feeling that she deserved a rest after all her hard work cleaning, she sat at the kitchen table and opened the latest copy of 'She' magazine. She was just about to start to read, when the kettle clicked to indicate that it had boiled. She pushed herself out of the comfort of the chair and made a cup of coffee. She was putting the top back on the coffee jar when the lid slipped from her grasp and fell onto the floor. It bounced and rolled into the far corner of the kitchen where it spun a few times, then came to a halt. Mrs Bennett shuffled over and bent down to pick it up. As she did so, there, underneath the lid, she saw a glint of something. Looking closer, she noticed that it was Hugo's medallion. Smiling, as she thought of her son's relief at retrieving his lost treasure, she picked it up, stalling to appreciate its warmth, and put it in her handbag, assuring herself that it would be safe in there. Returning to her seat, she fingered through the pages of her magazine while sipping her coffee.

With the housework more or less done and Jake sleeping contentedly in his basket, the house seemed unusually silent. The only noise, coming from that of the waves rolling the pebbles on the beach close by. The storm, out at sea the night before, had created large breakers, which were now crashing onto the rocks a short distance from their house. Despite their violence, it seemed to give an atmosphere of calm within the protection of the house and Julia Bennett felt at peace for the first time since the disappearance of Emma.

Dismissing her thoughts on where the young girl was, or who or what she had become, she decided to log onto the internet and do some more investigation into her ancestry.

She had gone back four generations when she noticed a familiar surname regularly coming up. The name of 'Edwards'. The name seemed to ring a bell but she could not think where or why it should be significant. The further she went back in time, the more frequently it seemed to occur, especially in the female line. The other point she noticed was that she, or at least Stephanie, would be the last of the line. When they died, unless Hugo had children, the family name would effectively die out.

After several hours of work, she had traced her relations back to the first census in 1841, but here her efforts came to a halt. Enthused by her progress, she was determined to try to go back even further. This search would involve some leg work and visits to local churches to check on their parish records. She hoped that they might be able to tell her, who married who and if and when, their children had been baptised. She was thinking about continuing to do more research when the front door banged shut and Hugo and Stephanie came in. A glance at her watch startled and amazed her to see how late it was. She had been engrossed so much in what she was finding, that she had not noticed the time passing. She had not even started to prepare dinner for her family. She told her children to grab a sandwich for now and they would all go out for dinner as soon as their father came in.

Stephanie moaned and disappeared up into her room. Hugo was delighted at the thought of a Big Mac and a large Coke if only he could persuade his father to go to McDonald's.

"Before you get any ideas, we won't be going to McDonald's," his mother announced almost as fast as the idea popped into his head. Hugo moaned but then asked what his mother was doing on the computer.

Eagerly she showed him what she had been doing and the progress she had made in tracing her ancestors. She waited for her son to praise her for her efforts but he just stood there, gazing at the screen, grim-faced.

"What's wrong with you?" she inquired of her son and looked at the screen and then back to her son.

"You're descended from the 'Edwards'!" he almost screamed, and pointed to the screen at the recurrence of the name throughout the tree.

"Yes. I noticed that. It seemed a bit strange to me as well but I couldn't think why the name sounded familiar," his mother responded still looking back and forth at the screen and then her son. "What! Does it matter?"

"It matters because the name of one of the witches from Bideford that was hanged at Exeter in 1682 was 'Susanna Edwards'. If it is true, then you are related to Kadavera and possibly Morgana and Putricia."

His mother put her hand to her mouth and sat down in the chair next to the laptop. She was quiet for some time before suddenly switching the computer off.

"Don't you dare say anything of this to your sister

or your father until I have done some more research to confirm it, one way or the other. They've both got enough to worry about without this adding to their problems."

Hugo nodded but he felt knotted inside as he thought about the possibility that, each side of the family had a hereditary vendetta against each other. He had promised not to say anything to his father and sister but he had not agreed to keep quiet to Bird. He was determined to call him as soon as he could do so, in private. His mother stood up and walked into the kitchen to make herself a cup of coffee to calm her nerves. Hugo started to go to his room but then had a sudden thought and ran back to his mother.

"Mum. Do you remember when we went to the reserve, when we were fighting Morgana and Putricia and they saw you, they seemed to be confused by your being there? If you are related to them, they may have recognised you and that is why they had the reaction that we saw."

His mother did not answer but slowly nodded and continued to make her coffee.

Half an hour later his father arrived home and after a short discussion with his wife, he shouted up to Hugo and Stephanie for them to come downstairs quickly as they were going out to dinner.

The meal was a little strained, with Stephanie still upset about her breakup and Hugo and his mother wanting to say what they suspected but scared to do so. The only cheerful person was Mr Bennett who had been to the BMW dealer with the possibility of buying a brand new, top of the range estate car to replace their ageing Volvo. He bored them all, spreading the brochures of the various models over the table, asking them what they thought about the special features, most of which were of no interest to anyone else except when it came to colour. This decision broke the tension, as each wanted their own choice. Mr Bennett had chosen black or silver, Mrs Bennett demanded a bright red, Hugo wanted British Racing Green while Stephanie insisted on pink, at which everyone else groaned.

It was quite late by the time that they all arrived home and as they entered the house, Jake ran around them wanting to be let out. Mr Bennett opened the back door and the dog ran out into the garden. After running around and doing his toilet, he stopped and pricked up his ears. He pushed his nose high in the air and sniffed. His tail beat from side to side and he sniffed again. The garden fence was no obstacle as he cleanly vaulted over it and ran along the road, stopping periodically to listen and smell the air in the stillness of the night.

The Bennett family were all heading for bed when Hugo remembered that he had some maths homework to do. He asked his father if he would give him a call next morning so that he could do it then. His father frowned but said that he would and all disappeared into their various bedrooms.

Hugo just beat his sister into the bathroom to wash and clean his teeth. Had he not, then he would have had to wait for what seemed ages for her to do, whatever teenage girls have to do in a bathroom that takes so much time.

Finally, the house became silent as the family settled down. Waiting for a few minutes longer to be sure, Hugo faced his wall and whispered, "Bird. Bird. Bird."

A short time passed and Hugo was about to call again when his friend appeared through the wall. Bird was surprised by the lateness of Hugo's call but as he listened to the story that his friend related about his mother's ancestry, he became serious and forgave the time of the summons.

By the time the tale had been discussed, it was the early hours of the morning and both started to yawn. Bird reassured Hugo that he would do his best to find out whatever he could, and with a fluff of his feathers, he melted through the wall.

Hugo pulled his duvet over himself and within minutes was asleep.

Chapter 27

Friends Reunited

Snatch hunched down behind a hedge, belly almost flat on the floor. He slowly inched his way closer and closer to the young deer as it grazed just twenty metres away, making sure that he was well downwind of the unsuspecting animal. Fifteen metres, ten metres, five. Snatch's strong back legs tensed, ready to pounce.

The cat flew through the air as if it was a feather caught in a breeze and in one movement felled its prey and broke its neck with a single bite from its strong jaws. The attack had been so swift and silent that the peace of the night was undisturbed and the background noise of screeching owls and humming insects never stopped.

The victor stood over the vanquished and looked around to ensure that no other predators, that might try to capitalise on the kill, were around. Snatch's sharp teeth and fangs made short work of the carcass, leaving very little, other than skin and bone.

With a final lick of its lips, the large animal started to move away but suddenly became aware of a noise behind him. Crouching, it turned and made itself as flat as it could against the moist grass of the moor. The sound came closer and Snatch prepared to pounce at whatever was tracking it. Over the top of the undergrowth, it could see flashes of what appeared to be yellow fur. It approached silently; the only noise was the swish of the vegetation as the intruder bounded up and the crunch of it as it landed. Snatch's tail flicked noiselessly back and forth as he tensed for another kill that night. He launched himself at the oncoming foe only to realise, at the peak of its jump, that his quarry was none other than Jake. With a mid-air twist, that would have delighted any Olympic diver, the large cat changed direction and landed in front of and to one side of the panting dog.

With tails wagging they licked and smelled each other. Snatch retreated to where it had killed the deer, and without any further instruction, Jake buried its nose in the carcass to recover any juicy morsels that his friend had missed.

Both satisfied, they gave each other a final lick and headed across the hills and valleys of Exmoor towards Bideford and Westward Ho!

Chapter 28

The Police's Quandary

"Well. This is certainly the most unusual case that I have ever come across." voiced the chief constable, as he eased himself up from his desk and started to pace around his office.

D. I. Hyde had just finished explaining to him the dilemma he faced with the investigation into the vandalism at the Gnome Reserve and the disappearance of the woman and young girl several weeks before. The inspector had insisted that the forensic team leader, Bill Sutton, be present at the meeting, which originally had been planned as a dressing down for the inspector for lack of progress in the case. However, after talking to the two officers and seeing the casts of the footprints but more convincingly, the pictures and video recovered from the mobile phone of the missing reporter, the chief constable was now as confused as the men standing before him.

"And what about that incredible story from that young boy you interviewed? Do you think there was any truth in it? It seems too far-fetched to be credible but all the facts did seem to corroborate what he said was true."

He was staring out the window of his office, his expression, that of a very confused man.

"The press is still clamouring for answers as to the fate and whereabouts of that reporter and young girl but if I tell them this... load of rubbish," he put his hands to his head and pushed back what little hair remained, "then I, I mean, *we*," he emphasised, looking at his two colleagues standing before him. "will be made to look like total idiots and we can all say goodbye to our jobs and pensions."

He turned and slumped back down in his chair.

"Go out and get me some real evidence. Something that won't make us all look like total fools. And find those two women." He almost shouted. "If we can get them back, then at least we can satisfy the press. The trouble at the Gnome Reserve we can bury, or at least try to, without getting us into more trouble and making the force look like complete idiots."

The two officers stood, and with an arm and finger pointing to the door from their superior, they turned and left the room. As the door closed, they heard the chief constable swearing and thumping his desk.

"That went well." Bill Sutton said to the detective as he breathed out heavily. D.I.Hyde looked at him and raised his eyebrows.

"Come on. I know it's early but I don't know about you but I could do with a drink," gasped the inspector. Without further ado, the men headed for the exit of the station and the pub a little way down the road.

In his office, the chief constable pulled open the bottom drawer of his desk and withdrew a half-empty bottle of scotch whiskey. Taking a small glass, he poured himself a generous shot and drank it down in one gulp. Tearing a tissue from the box on his desk, he carefully wiped the glass, and together with the bottle, replaced them in the drawer. With a loud sigh, he pulled a thick file of papers towards him and started to plough through its contents.

In the pub, the two police officers, each with a half-full pint of beer in front of them, sat in a corner desperately trying to find a solution to their dilemma, but slowly realising that the only explanation of the problem was that given by that little Bennett kid, however far-fetched it sounded.

Chapter 29

The Judge's Site Resident

The shadows danced across the walls of the corridor as the lantern dangled from Morgana's outstretched arm. Putricia held onto the belt of her sister's jeans as they carefully made their way through the many passages of the ruined house they now sought to call home.

The two moved forward slowly but with each step, felt that they were going deeper and deeper underground. Turning a corner, they were confronted by a staircase going down, but what was surprising and made them somewhat apprehensive, was that at the bottom of the flight was an illuminated lamp. Morgana hesitated, unsure what this meant and who, or what they might encounter but Putricia pushed her from behind so that she had no option but to go forward, and down.

Although not a long-distance, it took several minutes and several pushes from Putricia, before they reached the bottom. Looking around and waving their lantern in every direction to get a better look, they saw before them, a large, arched room that had been, at some time in the past, a wine cellar, for around the sides of three walls were old wine racks; some even had the odd bottle left in them.

At the opposite end of the cellar, another lamp burned, emitting a fine plume of black smoke from its top. It illuminated a tidy area, equipped with a Windsor-style chair, a large solid-looking wooden table and several very old cupboards, most of which were covered by peeling paint. The very end wall, which was not covered by wine racks, was instead, covered by shelf after shelf of ancient books, many bound in leather and in the corner was a fireplace, with a scorched, black cauldron hanging from a hook above its centre.

On seeing the pot, Morgana felt a deep sense of sadness, remembering the similar cauldron that she had been forced to leave behind in the cave at Westward Ho!

But wait. This was her pot. She was sure. The closer she looked at it, the more she recognised it. There was that little chip out of the rim, the dark yellow streak down one side where she had spilt one of her experimental potions, which, try as she may, she could not remove the stain and finally the broken leg underneath its base. How was it that it was here, but what was of more concern was, who had moved it?

The women moved around the room in silence, each with one eye on what they saw but the other looking out for whoever, or whatever lived here, because, without a doubt, someone did.

They each made a circuit of the room, after which, they met by the table and looked at each other. Morgana pointed to the black cauldron and in an excited whisper said, "Look! Look! Over there. In the corner. The cauldron.

It's mine. It's my old one from the cave at Westward Ho! We abandoned it there when we moved."

"Well, what's it doing here, then?" shot back her sister.

"I don't understand what's going on. Who lives here and how did my cauldron come to be here?" Morgana continued. "Look at those books over there. They're potion books and some of them I recognise."

"Shush!" Putricia suddenly called out, gripping the jumper that her sister was wearing. The two stood as if petrified.

"What's wrong?" whispered Morgana, pulling her sister's hand away from her jumper but not letting go of it.

"I think I heard something." Her sister replied as quietly as she could and started to move away from the centre of the room and towards the flight of stairs that brought them there.

In the distance, from inside the corridors through which they had previously come, came the sound of a very soft shuffling. The two backed away and returned to the corner in which the fireplace stood. Bending, they eased their way into the spaces on either side of the large pot and waited.

Time seemed to stand still as they cowered in the alcove.

"Put the lantern out," Morgana ordered Putricia. With a swift blow, the light was extinguished and they were left in the shadows.

The shuffling slowly came closer and could be heard coming down the stairs at the far end of the room. It stopped and the two women held their breath in anticipation. Morgana put out her arm so that she could hold her sister's hand but as she did so, her sleeve caught the chain holding the cauldron above where a fire would be.

The chain suddenly fell back against the pot and let out, what seemed to be, an ear-splitting, *clang*.

A black shadow dived from out of the doorway by the stairs and Snatch bounded into the room.

The two witches jumped, making the cooking pot emit another loud clang but then sprang from their place of refuge. They ran towards their pet but instead of it running up to them, it turned to the wall and started to growl and spit. Morgana slid to halt but Putricia backed up into the space she had previously occupied beside the cauldron.

Morgana started to approach the cat again but it growled and slashed its tail angrily: Never taking its eyes off the wall.

"What's wrong with you? You stupid animal," Putricia shouted from her refuge.

The animal, crouching and looking ready to spring, but not taking its eyes from the wall, gave a loud growl.

Suddenly the wall began to shimmer and Morgana and the cat took a step backwards. Putricia crouched behind the cauldron, causing it to emit yet another loud clang.

As they looked at the wall, a small, hunched figure started to materialise, until, after what seemed an age, it finally stood in front of the trio.

"Who are you?" Morgana shouted, more in fear than in wanting to know the answer.

The figure shuffled forward, making Morgana and Snatch back away, though the cat continued to hiss and spit.

With its head bent low, it was impossible to see who or

what the visitor was, but without raising its head, it made for the table and chair. When there, it slowly sat down.

Putricia eased herself from inside the fireplace, and together with her sister, closely followed by her pet, formed an arc around this strange being. Several minutes passed as each studied each other until, finally, with only a slight rise of its head, the figure spoke.

"Welcome to my home, Morgana, Putricia; or should I say; Anne Trembles and Jane Trembles. I am glad to finally meet you, in the flesh, as it were."

The two witches stood up straight and stepped back. Snatch whimpered and retreated behind them.

Chapter 30

The Box

The air inside the small box was now becoming stale and Puchy was feeling very hot and a little panicky. Her stomach gave a loud gurgle. She realised that she was also feeling very hungry and had not had her meal of flower-nectar before she left her home for that evening's work.

She had tried pushing and kicking at the inside of the box but all she succeeded in doing was hurting her toe and bending her frail wings. She sat in the corner of her prison and started to cry but then scolded herself for being so weak. Her voice was beginning to fail from all the shouting she had done, pleading for someone to let her out, but to no avail.

She thought of all the things she had done in her life; from being a child and dancing between the petals of the giant sunflowers surrounding her home in the summer, to the time when an enormous beetle attacked her as she slept under a mushroom. She thought back to more recent times when the witch, Kadavera, had caught her and how she had escaped, with the help of Barguff, Hugo and Bird.

"That's it!" she shouted, to no one in particular. "Bird. I'll call Bird. I'm sure that he will come and save me and she tried to shout his name but only a squeaky wheeze came out from her throat. All her calls for help had made her throat dry, and try as she may, she could not sound out his name.

She slumped back down in the corner and started to cry. Tears flooded down her cheeks and her nose began to run. One huge tear ran down to the side of her mouth and instinctively put out her tongue and licked it off. It tasted very salty but even that morsel of liquid felt refreshing to her parched throat. Suddenly she had an idea.

Using her finger, she stroked her cheeks, mopping up the tears that were rolling down and then she pushed her finger into her mouth and licked off the moisture. However, as soon as she started to do this, she began to feel much happier and stopped crying. With as much courage as she could muster, she banged her knees against the box wall, hoping that the pain would make her cry again but all it did was to make her angry.

She fell back into the corner and rubbed her knees, which felt very painful.

"Think of something sad," she said to herself and thought back to a time in her life when she was distressed and unhappy. There was that time when her pet caterpillar had died and all that was left was a brown shell. A single tear fell but then she remembered how the husk had suddenly become alive and turned into a beautiful butterfly, which made her happy. She remembered how she had fallen from a tree and broken her wing but this did not even make one tear run. There were those times when her brother and sister fairies would make fun of her because she was so small but then she remembered the hugs and cuddles that her mother had given her when she had run home in tears. Her whole life passed through her memory but nothing seemed bad enough or sad enough to make her cry. She started to think of Bird and that nice little boy called Hugo, who had helped her escape from that horrible witch. Her mind drifted, until she remembered her friend, Barguff, and how he had helped in her rescue but also how he had died trying to help save the gnomes from the witches and the goblins. She recalled how he was always so cheerful and positive about life and never let anything, or anyone get him down.

Tears began to flood down her face and she was so engrossed in her thoughts that she forgot the purpose of why she was thinking them until one very large tear fell onto her grazed knee which made it sting. The pain brought her back into consciousness and she rapidly licked around her mouth and used her finger on her cheeks to mop up the liquid. She had to stop now and then, to push herself into making herself sad again to keep the flow of tears going but after several minutes she composed herself and tried to call out Bird, Bird, Bird.

At the first attempt, all she succeeded in saying was Bir... Bir... Bir... Swallowing as hard as she could and licking her lips she sat up straight and cleared her throat as much as she could and then, as loud as she could, called out, "Bird! Bird! Bird!"

Although not as loud as she would have liked, she felt pleased that she had been able to say it. The effort had left her throat feeling very sore, and although she tried again to call her friend, she found it impossible to make any noise at all.

She slumped back in the corner, breathing heavily after all the effort and the effect of the thinning air. Slowly her eyes closed and she slid down the side of the box and lay motionless on its floor.

Chapter 31

The Tunnel

It was the weekend and Hugo was lying in bed watching a cartoon on his television. His mother was against him having a TV in his bedroom but after a great deal of arguing and little or no back up from her husband, she had capitulated and allowed her son to have one. However, it was on the condition that it was only used at weekends when he did not have to go to school.

The phone rang downstairs and his father answered it. Several minutes later he heard the receiver being replaced and him telling his wife that it was Tom Broadbent, the archaeologist, on the line. He had asked if they would meet him at the site of the judge's house at mid-day that day so that he could discuss with them the plans to excavate the old ruins.

Hugo's ears pricked up at the prospect of going back to the site. He was sure that there was more there than just a load of old bricks and stones and was eager to find what lay behind that rickety wooden door that his mother had found.

Jumping out of bed, he quickly washed, and sort of cleaned his teeth. Then rushing downstairs, called out to his father, "Can I come with you, Dad?"

"My my, what big ears you have." smiled his father and glanced at his wife, raising his eyebrows. "Yes. OK. But no messing about. These archaeologists can sometimes be pretty strict on what and who is allowed onto their dig, or whatever they call it. Even though I own the site, they have far more say over what happens there than I do."

Hugo turned and walked into the kitchen where his mother was engrossed, studying the large sheet of paper spread in front of her that was her, ever-growing family tree. Looking up, she announced that she had now gone back to 1786 after a friend of hers, who worked in the Bideford library, had been able to trace some old parish records where her family name had appeared.

"What's for breakfast?" Hugo asked.

Her face suddenly became stern. "Anything you care to make," she replied sarcastically and returned to her studies.

"Are you coming with us to have a look at the judge's site?" he asked. He poured a large portion of Cheerios into a bowl, followed by some milk, which he managed to splash over the work surface where he stood, unable to sit at the table because of his mother's family tree.

His mother looked up. Seeing the puddle of milk, she ordered him to mop it up and then said that she had promised Steph that she would go with her to the hairdressers. She had agreed to take her so that she could have a makeover and change her hairstyle to try to make her feel better after her boyfriend trouble.

Hugo was secretly pleased that his sister wasn't coming.

She always seemed to spoil everything for him, especially for the last few days, when she did nothing but mope about and complain about everyone and everything. He could tell that even his parents were becoming a little fed up with her attitude.

While Hugo waited for his father to tell him when he was ready to leave, he thought that he would tell Bird about it. He remembered that his friend had said that he might try himself to get through the wooden door on the site. Hugo did not want Bird to be there while that archaeologist man was visiting.

Back in his bedroom, Hugo called out Bird, Bird, Bird and waited. After a few minutes, the wall shimmered and his friend appeared looking a little dishevelled. He explained that he had been playing hide and seek with Chipper and had fallen down a bank into a mass of thistles while he was searching for the young gnome. He said that he was pleased Hugo had called him at that moment because it meant that he could stop having to entertain the small creature, who seemed to have adopted Bird as a surrogate father.

Hugo quickly explained about his and his father's trip to the judge's site and how there would be this expert with them who may be able to discover and tell them what was under the ruins. Hugo was about to continue when Bird held his wing up and motioned for his friend to be quiet.

Bird's expression changed and began to look serious.

"I've just had a call thought from... I think it was Puchy but it wasn't very clear and she hasn't called me again. I tried to call her back but there was no reply.

Since you no longer need me to go to the site, I will

find Puchy and see what she wants. It is very unusual for her to call me this early in the day as she is usually fast asleep after visiting all the children who have lost a tooth. Let me know what you find out about the tunnels. I will see you soon."

With a wave of his wing, the wall shimmered once more and the animal was gone.

Hugo did not give any more thought to Bird; instead, he ran downstairs and asked his father if he could have another look at the enhanced plan of the judge's house site before they went. His father looked at the kitchen table. His wife was still leaning over her family tree, which now covered the whole of it. He beckoned his son to go into the lounge with him, where he unrolled the large sheet and spread it out over the small coffee table, using the placemats from it to resist the paper rolling back up again.

Hugo traced his finger over the lines that indicated the rooms and passageways of the original house, trying to envisage in his mind the directions they would need to go, if they managed to get in at all that is.

Mr Bennett looked at his watch and rerolled the plans. He slid them back into the cardboard tube and told Hugo to get his coat.

A voice rang out from the kitchen, "And change your trousers and shirt. Those are too good to go scrambling around in tunnels. There are plenty of old clothes in your draw." Hugo looked at his father, who just hunched his shoulders and grinned.

Although the remarks had been primarily aimed at Hugo, his father suddenly felt a pang of guilt and went to his room to change to something more suitable for the project ahead. Twenty minutes later, the two, parked the car and approached the wire fence.

Tom Broadbent came up to them and cheerily shook their hands.

"I am very sorry son but I am afraid that I can't let you come with us into the tunnels as they are considered very dangerous and potentially could collapse. Health and safety regulations say that I can't let you accompany us."

Hugo looked at his father with a very glum face. He had so been looking forward to exploring the tunnels and now all his hopes had been quashed. His father rubbed his head, ruffling his hair.

"Never mind Hugs, I am sure that when we have been down and certified that it is safe, then Mr Broadbent here will let you have a look.

"Don't look so disappointed, Hugs, did you call him?" Tom Broadbent looked enquiringly at Mr Bennett.

"Oh, his name is Hugo really, Hugs is my nickname for him."

Hugo blushed and felt a little belittled by his father, calling him Hugs in front of someone else.

"As I was saying, Hugo. Don't feel too upset about not being able to accompany us because I have a very important job for you to do, while you're up here waiting for us. I don't know if you noticed on the plans but somewhere over at the far end," he pointed to where he meant, "is an old well. We, archaeologists, love looking in old wells as they are often the source of artefacts that people have discarded. Sometimes they also contain treasure that someone has hidden."

Hugo immediately cheered up at the prospect of finding a treasure and could not wait for his father to unlock the gate so that he might start his quest. He was about to make his way over to the far side of the site when his father picked up a large stick and handed it to him.

"You may need this," he said. "There are a lot of brambles at that end of the site and you can use it to knock them down."

Hugo took the rod and waved it around his head a few times, then, with a smile, he ran across the site to the far end.

Mr Bennett watched his son starting to beat down the undergrowth and then turned. With Tom Broadbent following, he made his way to where the small doorway stood, firmly closed.

"Here, put this on." His companion stated and handed him a yellow hard hat. "Health and Safety, you know."

Mr Bennett smiled and complied with the order. As he approached the door in the corner, he prepared himself for the force that he expected to have to use to push it open. To his surprise, it gave with only the slightest of pressure. He stood back and waved Tom in front of him, as per health and safety instructions from Mr Broadbent. Both men switched on the torches they had provided themselves with and ducked as they entered through the half-buried door.

Hugo slashed away at the mass of tangled vegetation before him. He trampled whatever he could so that bit by bit the area became flattened. Now and then his stick would strike something and his heart rate would race but on each occasion, it turned out to be a large stone or rock. After half an hour, he began to feel weary and stopped to look at where the two men had disappeared. He looked at his watch. 12.45. He decided to carry on until one o'clock then have a break and wait for his father. Picking up the stick, he attacked an exceptionally large patch of bramble. The blow landed and the branch hit something so hard that it broke in two with the longer section buried in the dense bush.

He looked at the broken stump of the stick and then used his foot to push away the vegetation to try and locate the broken piece. His foot found the remains of the stick and he started to pull it out but suddenly realised that its end was jammed in a crack in what appeared to be a small wall. His heart jumped. Was this the well, or just another block of piled-up stones? Using the remains of the stick " and his boot, he slowly cleared some of the growth from around the wall. It began to form a circle. Almost panicking with excitement, he jumped and pushed on the remaining vegetation.

Suddenly, as he rested for a few seconds before continuing his attack, he felt a small rumble under his feet. Standing still, he looked around to see what had caused it. Another louder vibration made the ground below his feet shake a little more. He jerked his head around, looking for what might have caused the tremor. It was then that he noticed a small plume of dust coming from the doorway through which his father and Tom Broadbent had passed.

He ran to the spot as fast as he could, falling twice as his feet became entangled in the undergrowth. Ignoring his bloodied hands, he finally reached the doorway and looked inside — total blackness but with dust rising out of it.

"Dad! Dad! Are you in there? Speak to me!"

He prayed for an answer, but none came. Oh, how he

wished that his mother had let him have a mobile phone. Most of his friends at school had one and they used to tease him that his parents didn't trust him enough for him to have one. Pulling his shirt from his trousers, he held the tail over his mouth to keep out the dust and started through the doorway.

He had only progressed about ten metres when, through the fading light, he came face to face with a large rockfall which had completely sealed the corridor. He made a futile attempt to move the debris but soon realised that it was pointless. He sat down to catch his breath and it was then that he was sure he heard a faint laugh.

Chapter 32

Evie's Disappointment

"Look, Grandad. I've lothsed my tooth." Evie lisped and pushed her tongue through the gap in the teeth of her upper jaw.

"Did the tooth fairy leave you anything?" her grandfather asked, smiling and rubbing her head.

"Yeth. She left me two pounds but I got her."

"What do you mean, you 'got her'?"

"I caught the tooth fairy!" she screamed with obvious delight.

"You caught the tooth fairy? Well, where is it?" questioned her grandfather.

"I put her in my box," the six-year-old said excitedly and jumped up and down.

"Come on then. Let me see."

The young girl ran off into her bedroom and could be heard rattling through her toy cupboard.

"Mummee." A cry rang out from her bedroom. "Where's my pink box? I can't find it and Grandad wants to see the tooth fairy I caught."

"The what?" questioned her mother, who appeared at the child's bedroom door, wiping her hands in a tea towel after just finishing the washing up.

"My pink jewel box. You know, the one with Barbie on the front that Santa got me last year."

"Oh, that one. Well when did you have it last?" she enquired, but then suddenly remembered tidying it away in the drawer the night before.

"Have a look in the bottom drawer of my bedroom sideboard, darling. I may have put it in there. You should learn to be tidier and put things back where you found them," she chided her daughter and walked back into the kitchen.

Evie jumped across her room and eagerly pulled open the drawer. There, on top of some pillowcases, lay the pink Barbie box. Grabbing it, she held it in the crook of her left arm and carefully lifted the lid with her right hand making sure that the fairy could not escape.

The lid was only halfway open when she looked inside. Curled up in the corner was the lifeless body of Puchy, together with a pound coin and the small remains of the child's tooth.

Evie flung back the lid and poked the corpse with her finger, flicking it around the box to see if it was alive but the small fairy did not respond. After a few more flicks around the container, the small child picked the body up by the tip of its wing, looked at it as if it was a dead insect and was just about to drop it into her waste bin when the wall in her room began to shimmer.

The little girl jumped backwards, too frightened to scream as Bird appeared, seemingly out of nowhere.

At first, he also was surprised to see the small child and was on the point of melting back into the wall when he noticed what the girl was holding between her thumb and forefinger. He raised himself and grabbed the body in his beak without any hesitation. Giving the child an angry look, he was about to disappear back through the wall when Evie suddenly regained her voice.

"Mummee...Mummee...there's a monster in my room."

The noise of a breaking teacup sounded from the kitchen and her mother raced into her room only to see the final shimmers of the wall as Bird and his precious cargo left the scene.

Evie's mother gazed at the wall and then at her daughter who was now clinging to her leg.

"What is it my sweet? Where's the monster?" She said, sympathetically, as she bent down to pick up her trembling child.

"There was a monster, honestly Mummy. It took my tooth fairy and disappeared through that wall there." The little girl pointed to the part of the wall that her mother was sure that she had seen shimmering as she entered the room.

Her mother looked all around the room but saw nothing, and unsure of what she had thought that she had seen, she stroked her daughter's head and consoled her, suggesting that it must have been a trick of the light or something.

Eventually, the child settled and her mother sat her back down on her bed.

The pink box was open beside her.

"Oh look darling, the tooth fairy has left you another present." Her mother pulled out the one-pound coin plus the tooth fragment out of the box. "Go and show this to Grandpa and tell him the tooth fairy escaped."

Evie grabbed the objects and ran from her room back into the lounge where she could be heard giggling, telling her grandfather all about what had occurred. He smiled and gave her another pound to match the one she was holding.

Her mother meanwhile ran her hand over the wall in Evie's room, still unsure of what she had seen.

Chapter 33

The Past Revealed

"My name is Susanna Edwards."

"No! That's impossible. You're dead. You were hanged with our mother. You're lying!" screamed Putricia, stepping forward.

The figure raised her skeletal arm and the young witch backed off, however, as the hand emerged from the shroud of black cloth, a flash of light reflected from the ring on its finger. A ring identical to those worn by the intruders with the exception that this one held a large clear stone.

The flash stunned the two witches into silence as they each recognised it as being the master ring of the guild of healers to which their parents had belonged.

"My name is Susanna Edwards, and yes, I was hanged with your mother Mary and Temperance Lloyd, but I did not die like them.

From time immemorial, my family have been healers. Our power of healing was well known and respected. Over the centuries, we had accumulated much knowledge from a study of herbs and minerals and their medicinal properties. However, the main source of our power came from an amulet reputed to have come from the sword of King Arthur himself; Excalibur. It was the power of this talisman that made our work seem magical and many other healers became jealous and branded us as witches."

Morgana started to speak to tell Susanna that they knew of the amulet and what was more, who had it but the woman held up her hand for silence.

"As well as the power to heal," the voice beneath the cloak continued, "it also had the power to protect the bearer from harm."

"Then why was it then that our mother and Temperance died and only you survived?" burst out Putricia.

Again the hand was raised for calm and she continued. "As I was saying, the amulet gave the person who was wearing it, its protective power. However, the only people that could touch it were the direct descendants of King Arthur himself. Anyone else who it came into contact with it was burned and unable to hold it. For this reason, your mother and our friend, Temperance, could not possess it.

As we were being wheeled on the cart on the way to our execution, my mother, Ruth, was able to get close enough to pass me the amulet.

When the trapdoor of the gallows was sprung, I was knocked unconscious, which made me look as if I was dead but the talisman saved me from dying."

The cloaked figure paused, seemingly lost in the horror of that moment as the memories flooded back.

Morgana was about to speak when Susanna continued. "Although I was alive, my hands and feet were tied and I could not move or escape from my bonds. All three of us were left hanging for three days, during which the crows and rats took their toll on our bodies. I was able to wriggle a little to fend off the worst of the attacks but even so,"

She broke down and started to sob inconsolably. It was several minutes before she was able to continue.

"I… I am afraid to even look at myself."

She broke down again, laying her head on her arms that she folded on the table.

The sisters were paralysed by the story and stood in front of the crying figure, unsure what to do.

Slowly the noise of the crying eased and finally stopped as the figure made to compose herself.

"So how did you escape?" Putricia asked when she thought that the woman had recovered enough.

"At the time I did not know because I was drifting in and out of consciousness but I later found out that my mother, Ruth, had come in the middle of the night, while the whole town slept, and cut me down. She used an old hand cart to take me away but because she was very old and frail at that time, could not take me very far. Therefore, she hid me in a coffin which had been made for herself and paid a travelling tinker to take her, and it, away from Exeter, to a cave in the north of the county, where she had played as a child. It was there that she tended me and tried to heal my wounds using the amulet.

Unfortunately, the effort of seeing me hanged and the stress of travelling the width of the county was too much for my mother and she died before she could fully heal me so that I was left hopelessly disfigured."

Again the woman broke down into floods of tears. Morgana approached her and went to put her arm around her by way of comfort but the figure angrily pushed her away. Taken aback by this reaction, Morgana stepped back to where her sister stood.

It was over fifteen minutes later that Susanna was able to carry on with her story, of how she had existed in the cave for many years, only venturing out at night, in case anyone saw her. She had often visited the homes of the two sisters, her daughter, Mary, and their cousin Stephen, as they grew up in the village of Appledore, not far from where she lived in her cave.

All the while she had used her knowledge of herbs and minerals and the power of the amulet to experiment on, not only keeping herself alive but also making herself invisible to enable her to move around more freely without being seen. It had taken many years but finally, she discovered the secret.

It was while she was watching them one evening, that she was discovered by Stephen and forced to say who she was and why she was spying on the family. After hearing the story, the young man had agreed to help her in her work and equip and furnish the cave which she called home. On several occasions, Stephen had borrowed the amulet to help him perfect some of the potions he had devised.

She happened to be watching the family's house on the day when the judge summoned them to his mansion. Under her new-found power of invisibility, she had followed them and witnessed the fate of her cousin, Stephen. She was horrified at the brutality of the attack and the viciousness and arrogance of the perpetrator and vowed that she would kill him, whatever it took. She had followed the servants, who had been tasked with the disposal of his body in the river. When they had finished their gruesome task and left, she had followed the body as it floated up the river, until it became snagged on a branch, near the bank. She waded into the icy water and pulled it from the river.

At first, she thought that Stephen was dead but then she discovered that he was wearing the amulet and was still alive, though very severely injured. She had found a small boat tied up, close to where she was, and under cover of darkness, used it. With the turning of the tide, she navigated it down the river, around the estuary where the Torridge met the river Taw and across the infamous sand bar, which has been the demise of many a ship. They finally landed outside the entrance to her cave, in what is now called Westward Ho! but which, at that time, was uninhabited.

In the cave, she had feverishly worked to heal Stephen, but like herself, he was not able to fully recover from the vicious damage to his body and ended up as deformed as her.

They had both witnessed the execution of her daughter Mary and the two sisters, Anne and Jane Trembles and it was they who had rescued the bodies from the gallows and brought them to the cave.

The physical disabilities of her and Stephen and the lack of the necessary herbs meant that they were not able to bring all the women back to life at that time but were able to treat and maintain them so that they were in a state of suspended animation.

At the women's execution, they had heard Mary swear the curse on the judge, his offspring and all those responsible for the death of the three. Over the centuries, she and Stephen had methodically ensured that the curse was fulfilled.

Unfortunately, one night, while out gathering drift wood for a fire, Stephen had lost the amulet, which was the essential ingredient in what was keeping them alive over the centuries. Try as they might they were unable to trace its whereabouts. Without it, they both became weaker until eventually Stephen succumbed to his deformity and died.

Although growing progressively weaker, she had continued her experiments and was able to make a potion that not only kept her alive but was able to resurrect her daughter, Mary.

By that time the bodies of the three women were in a very poor condition and she could not bear to look at them or call them by their names. Just the memory of how they had been and how they had now become, filled her with sorrow and so she renamed them Kadavera, Morgana and Putricia.

So it was, that Mary, or Kadavera, came back into existence, while the other two 'slept on'.

She was ashamed of her appearance and did not wish her daughter to see her so distorted. Therefore, she left Kadavera and all her potion books in the cave while she went to find a new home but all the time she would watch over the three women.

Morgana and Putricia stood in front of Susanne in stunned silence for several minutes, unable to take in the story that they had just heard.

Suddenly Putricia looked up and almost shouted,

"We know where the amulet is!" But at that very moment, there was a noise from the corridor leading to the chamber in which they stood, which drowned out her words.

A light flashed on the wall, illuminating the stairs ascending to the corridor, where they heard the voices of two men.

Morgana grabbed the fur of Snatch's neck and without another word, all three women and the cat disappeared into the shadows

Paul Bennett and Tom Broadbent entered the room, flashing their torches around and into every corner, amazed at what they were seeing. Their beams focused on the chair and table, then the cauldron and the shelves of books and bottles.

"Someone's been living here, I'm sure," said Tom, looking at his colleague.

"Yes they do!" screamed a high pitched voice and Susanna Edwards materialised in front of them, shortly followed by Putricia and Morgana, who was still holding Snatch. She let him go and he hissed and spat at the two men and began to circle them.

The suddenness of the encounter left the two men paralysed and unable to respond until, at last, Paul Bennett shone his torch at Morgana.

"You!" he shouted, remembering the face from his time during the battle at the Gnome Reserve.

"You!" screamed a voice from behind him. "Murderer!"

He swung his torch around to where the sound came from, to reveal Putricia and another figure in a black hooded cloak. Both were slowly closing in on the two men.

Tom Broadbent had not moved or blinked, his hands and his torch slumped by his sides.

"Who are you?" Mr Bennett shouted. "And what do you want with us?"

My name is Susanna Edwards and you are the last in the line of the descendants of those that were responsible for the execution of myself, my two friends, my daughter and these here."

She waved her hand at Morgana and Putricia. "But that was centuries ago. You can't blame me for that. We are as innocent of that crime, as you were of being witches. If you kill us, then you are no better than the judge, because you are killing innocent people."

"Ah. That is where you are wrong." The voice rang out from under the cloak. "You see I *was* a witch and a very good one too. I helped many people to get better from their suffering but what did I get."

She suddenly threw back the cowl from her cloak and everyone, even Morgana and Putricia gasped in horror. Snatch ran behind the cauldron, whimpering.

Before them stood the most hideous sight that any of them could imagine, half of her face was missing and the other half was covered by what appeared to be boils, so that there was no resemblance to it being human at all.

Several seconds went by as each, including the sisters, in turn, turned their heads away, unable to look at the sight before them.

Momentarily stunned by the revelation before him but recovering somewhat, Paul Bennett grabbed the jacket of the still immobile Tom Broadbent and ran to the staircase, dragging the zombie-like man behind him. Almost pulling the archaeologist up the stairs, the two raced back along the corridor and towards the small wooden door that meant safety.

Susanne replaced the cowl over her head and took a small glass jar from one of the shelves. She threw the container in the direction of the stairs and as it passed through the air, it left a glittering trail behind it. However, its flight did not stop as it approached the stairwell. Instead, it flew, like a guided missile up the stairs and along the corridor following the fleeing men.

They could see the daylight of the doorway as they ran along the corridor then suddenly, there was a sudden flash of light and the wall of the tunnel fell in on them.

A little laugh could be heard coming from the chamber deep in the bowels of the earth.

Chapter 34

Bad News

Bird laid the still body of Puchy on Hugo's bed and called for his friend, Hugo, to come. He called again but the house was empty. He was unsure what to do, especially with his lack of hands. He saw a glass of water on Hugo's bedside cabinet, and with no other ideas of if or how he could revive the small creature, he picked it up and dribbled it over his little friend.

There was a slight twitch as the water splashed over her, so he continued to pour even more. With a wretching cough, the tooth fairy suddenly revived and threw her arms around to fight off the torrent.

Over the next few minutes, the tiny fairy began to recover and asked Bird for a drink of water instead of being drenched with it. When satisfied, she sat up and brushed herself down and then tried to fly up onto the bedside cabinet to be at more eye level with her rescuer, but found that she couldn't. The trauma of trying to get out of the box had bent one of her wings so she could only buzz around in circles. She started to cry but Bird reassured her that he was sure that Hugo, or more likely his father, should be able to make it better.

"Where are Hugo and everyone else for that matter?" she asked, but Bird just ruffled his feathers, unable to answer the question.

Over the next few minutes, Puchy explained what had happened and how she had been caught.

"It's my own fault," she sighed. I am usually very good at spotting children that are pretending to be asleep when I visit, but this little girl was an exceptionally good actress and caught me out. I will certainly remember her when her next tooth falls out. I may even avoid calling on her but I will see how she behaves in the meantime.

The tooth fairy sat back on the bed and began to nurse her injured wing.

"Do you have anything to eat, Bird?" she asked. "I'm really hungry. I haven't eaten for a long time and I'm feeling a little faint."

Bird looked around to see if there was anything that Hugo had in his room that he could feed to his little friend but saw nothing.

"Jump onto my back," he suggested to the small fairy, "and we can go downstairs into the kitchen. I am sure that there will be something down there and I do not think Mrs Bennett will mind."

A few minutes later, they were both tucking into a large spoonful of honey from a jar Bird had discovered in one of the cupboards, when Julia Bennett walked in through the back door. After overcoming the surprise at seeing the pair in her kitchen she listened to the story of what had been happening to Puchy, carefully tended her wing and did her best to straighten it. She used a matchstick as a splint to help it to heal and told her to leave it on for a few days.

The tooth fairy looked sad, and at first, explained that she had to return to her home because she still had many more children to visit, but Hugo's mother comforted her and told her that she could stay at her home while her wing healed. As for the children with missing teeth, then she was sure that the other tooth fairies would be able to stand in for her until she was back to full fitness.

Puchy smiled at this idea and imagined all the honey and sugar she would be able to have while she stayed at the house.

Mrs Bennett went over to the kettle and filled it to make a cup of coffee for herself. She had just finished making it and was holding the mug when the phone rang. She smiled at the pair and went to the wall and picked up the receiver. Seconds later, the cup of coffee smashed on the floor and she went very pale.

Without any explanation to the two friends, she grabbed her car keys from the table and rushed out of the house, slamming the back door. The two looked at each other as the sound of a car accelerating away echoed from outside.

Chapter 35

The Cave In

"Help! Help! Somebody help me!" Hugo screamed as he tore into the pile of rubble where the small door in the corner of the site had once stood. Dust still hung around the air, and now and then Hugo could feel, rather than hear, the sound of more falling masonry.

With bloodied hands, he ran to the fence surrounding the site and yelled for someone to come to his aid. A small car approached and Hugo ran down the road in front of it, waving his arms. The driver squealed to a stop and angrily opened the door to admonish the stupid child.

Hugo grabbed his arm and pulled the middle-aged, well-dressed man to the pile of rubble.

"Please help me! My dad's in there somewhere and he may be hurt."

The man took one look at the dusty ruin and then at Hugo.

"Are you sure your father is in there?" he said, looking sternly at the shaking boy in front of him.

"Yes! Yes!" Hugo screamed, "and another man."

The driver looked at Hugo and then at the rubble in front of him. Plunging his hand into the pocket of his jacket, he pulled out his mobile phone and dialled 'Nine. Nine. Nine.'

By the time he had explained to the operator the situation and finally finished the call, two other people; an elderly lady and a young man with a shaven head and tattoos over each arm, had ventured into the compound to see what was the cause of all the fuss. Quickly taking in the seriousness of the situation, the young man raced over to the rubble and started to tear at the rocks and stones filling the entrance to the tunnel. Meanwhile, the lady, who introduced herself as Mrs Miller, took Hugo's hand and led him over to a large raised area and sat him down and asked what had happened.

Hugo tried to resist her pull, not wanting to leave the scene of the accident, but she spoke to him calmly, to reassure him that everything would be alright and not to worry. Slowly his panic started to calm. Meanwhile, the young man, now aided by the car driver, was frantically pulling away at the stones filling the tunnel entrance and tossing them behind them. More people started to arrive and joined in the excavation.

After what seemed like hours, the sirens of the emergency services could be heard wailing in the distance. A young police constable ran breathlessly onto the site, quickly pausing to look at the rubble, and the men frantically tossing stones and debris hither and thither, and then came up to Hugo and Mrs Miller.

As soon as Hugo saw him, he jumped up and ran to him, pleading for him to help his dad, who was trapped in the tunnel. The constable took hold of the young boy's hand and led him back to where he had been sitting. At the same time, there was a flash of blue lights as the fire service arrived. The fire crew calmly walked to where the men were attacking the rubble and started to talk to the tattooed youth. An older officer approached the trio sat on the mound and asked, to no one in particular, what had happened.

Hugo, with tears streaming down his face, started to explain what had happened but in his panic, he did not make himself clear.

"It's alright son. Calm down and tell me slowly what has happened and who is trapped," the fire officer calmly but firmly, said to him.

Fighting back his tears, Hugo explained about his father and another man, who he thought was called Tom something or other, had gone into the tunnel to find some archaeology that might explain it being there in the first place. He told them how he had heard and felt a tremor and saw the dust rising from the tunnel entrance, followed by the sound of a rockfall.

While Hugo was talking, the policeman was making notes in a small pad he had taken out of his pocket.

"Thank you. What did you say your name was?"

"Hugo Bennett," Hugo replied. "And my dad's name is Paul Bennett. He's a dentist."

"Well, then. Thank you, Hugo. Now you stay here with this lady and I will go and find out what is happening. When I know, I will come back and tell you. By the way, is anyone else of your family here?"

"No. I came here with my dad and that Tom man. My mum went out shopping."

The fire officer turned to the policeman and asked him if he could try and track down the young boy's mother and get her down to the scene of the accident. He then left and went over to where three firemen were now using shovels and crowbars to loosen and remove the rubble. The tattooed man and the car driver, plus another man who had joined in the rescue, were sitting, sweating and covered in thick dust on a large stone near the entrance. They were all drinking from water bottles given to them by the fire crew. A large crowd was now beginning to form at the gate but was being held back by two more police officers who had joined the rescue effort.

The young officer next to Hugo asked him if his mother had a mobile phone. Hugo said that she did but did not know the number; however, he did know his home's landline number.

The policeman dialled the number. It rang four times and was then picked up by a happy sounding woman.

"Hello. Julia Bennett. How may I help you?"

Chapter 36

Morgana's Dilemma

*S*usanne and Putricia smiled broadly at each other as they heard the loud bang and the sound of falling masonry, however, Morgana did not. There was something that Paul Bennett had said that was playing on her mind.

'If you kill us, then you are no better than the judge who killed you because you are killing innocent people.'

The words kept rolling around her mind and she could not shake them off. She thought of all the gnomes and goblins that had died and the animals and creatures she had destroyed in her experiments. Even the body she now stood up in, although technically alive, she had robbed its rightful owner of its use.

"That's it! That's it!" screamed Susanna. "We've killed them. We've killed them all. Our job is done. Your vow is complete."

"You've forgotten that young brat of a son of his," corrected Putricia. "He is still alive. He has yet to be killed and most painfully too, as he has thwarted all our plans but we will have to be careful because he has our inheritance."

"What!" screamed the black figure. "You mean *he* has the amulet?"

Putricia nodded sheepishly and even Morgana looked up from her thoughts, feeling embarrassed that they had not brought the fact to Susanna's attention more forcibly.

"Why didn't you tell me before? Are you sure; absolutely sure?"

"We tried to tell you earlier but your story seemed more important," Morgana said apologetically, "but we have both seen it." He definitely had it when we were at that stupid gnome place but that silly Bird animal also had it when he tried to rescue one of the gnomes."

"Then it can't be the real talisman because it can only be held by a member of my family, as rightful descendants of King Arthur," shouted Susanna, with an air of glee in her voice. Morgana insisted that it was, saying that the animal held it by the feathers of its wingtips.

"Nevertheless, we will take no chances. We have all come this far and I am determined not to be denied the fulfilment of our vow at the last minute by a scrawny little boy and a stupid bird." the cloaked woman said menacingly and beckoned the two sisters to follow her down a small corridor hidden behind the cauldron. As the three emerged from an entrance hidden behind a wall of ivy, they looked at the chaos they had caused and smiled, except Morgana, who stood back in the tunnel, feeling troubled.

Chapter 37

The Rescue

The emergency services were working flat out to try to rescue the trapped men. The whole area was now almost illuminated by blue flashing lights. A large JCB drove through the gate, which made Hugo almost panic, remembering what happened the last time one was brought to the site and its fatal consequences.

A woman was fighting her way through the hordes of onlookers that surrounded the wire fence. She was arguing with the policeman standing guard at the gate. A minute later, Mrs Bennett was escorted, by the same officer, to where Hugo sat, still holding the hand of Mrs Miller.

He jumped up at seeing her approach and ran to her, tears streaming down his face. Mrs Miller also rose and walked over to where the two Bennetts' stood, each in floods of tears. She went up to the pair and introduced herself.

"Hello. My name is Otterly Anne Miller. Please come over here and sit down and I will fetch the fire chief who will explain what is happening."

She led them back to where she and Hugo had been previously sitting and then left to find the fire chief, who seemed to be in charge. Meanwhile, through sniffs and coughs, Hugo explained to his mother what had happened and they hugged each other in comfort.

It was only minutes later when Mrs Miller returned with the fire chief in tow. He introduced himself as George Flattley and quickly explained what they were doing to expedite the rescue of her husband and Mr Broadbent. He had almost finished his explanation when there was a cry from the workers at the tunnel.

"Sir! We've found them!"

The fire chief apologised for having to leave and rushed to where the workers were carefully removing bricks and rubble from around what was thought to be, a person. Hugo, his mother and Mrs Miller also rushed over to the scene. As they watched, Mrs Bennett, with her fist in her mouth to try to control her emotions, clung tightly to Hugo with her other hand.

As soon as there was space, a young man in a blue overall and yellow hard hat jumped down to the body lying there. He was carrying a small bag from which he withdrew a stethoscope.

Pulling back the shirt from the patient, he indicated for silence and felt and listened for a pulse. Getting up from his knees, he shook his head. One of the workers standing next to him took a small packet from his pocket and unfolded a silver emergency blanket which he spread over the body.

Mrs Bennett screamed and rushed forward but she was held back by a policeman standing some way back from the excavation. Hugo, however, being smaller, was able to wriggle past. He dashed to where the men were working and managed a glimpse of the victim before the shroud covered it. He gazed at the figure, lying bloodied and twisted, covered in dust and mud but almost shouted in relief as he realised that it was not his father.

"It's not dad!" he shouted and ran back to his mother screaming, "It's not dad!" as he went.

He ran into his mother's outstretched arms and screamed again,

"It's not dad! It's that other man, Mr Broadbent."

There was another scream from about five metres away and a woman ran forward shouting out,

"Tom! Tom! Let me see him. Please let me see him. I'm his wife."

A female police officer quickly walked over, put her arm around her and escorted her to a waiting police car.

"There's another!" A shout rang from the tunnel and several workers in yellow hi-vis jackets ran forwards and started to throw more bricks and stones from the pile of debris.

The same, blue-suited man ran back and jumped back down into what was now a deep pit.

Reluctant to see, what might be the body of her husband being dragged out from the debris, Mrs Bennett gripped the hands of Mrs Miller and together they walked slowly forward. Hugo however, ran forwards again to see whatever he could.

As before, he saw the worker put his hand into his pocket and pull out an emergency blanket. He stepped back and put his hand to his mouth, standing, fixated to the spot. His mother joined him and put her arm around his shoulders.

Time seemed to stand still as they watched the body being slowly cleared of debris and the doctor check it for signs of life.

He stood and gave a thumbs-up sign to two paramedics who were standing on the banks of the pit. They grabbed a stretcher and an emergency pack, and aided by the workers, made their way into the tunnel. The doctor placed a face mask over the body's nose and mouth and started to administer oxygen. He then inserted a drip into its arm and then covered the casualty in the silver blanket but this time the face was left uncovered.

Mrs Bennett and Hugo rushed over to the stretcher as they lifted it out of the hollow and accompanied it to the waiting ambulance.

Minutes later, with a scream of sirens, the ambulance, with all the Bennetts', made its way at speed towards Barnstaple and the North Devon District Hospital.

At the far perimeter of the site, there was a scream and a curse from Morgana.

"You've failed! You've killed the wrong person!"

She looked angrily at Susanne and Putricia and strode back into the small opening in the underground complex from where they had emerged.

Chapter 38

Stephanie's Breakup

Bird and Puchy gazed at each other for several minutes as the noise of Mrs Bennett's car accelerating away slowly died away. It was only when the back door slammed open and a very angry-looking Stephanie stormed in that their attention returned to that moment.

She looked around and was surprised to see the two in front of her. Their presence seemed to calm her down a little and she forced a smile.

"Where is everybody?" she asked, going over to the fridge and opening the door to see if there was anything in it which she could snack on. Bird craned his neck to see if there was anything in it which he could eat himself. The young teenager grabbed a large wedge of cheese, and closing the fridge door with her foot, tore off a large chunk, which, after slumping down on one of the chairs next to the kitchen table, she proceeded to eat.

"Well! Where is everybody?" she demanded.

The angry tone of her voice stirred the two into breaking their silence and they tried to explain what had happened at the same time. With her mouth full of cheese, she raised her hand and pointed to Bird. Spraying crumbs of her snack over the table as she spoke, she asked him to explain what was going on.

Bird approached and leant against the table, explaining how a little girl had captured Puchy and that he had taken her back to the Bennett's house after her rescue. As for where everyone else was, he did not know, except for the fact that Mrs Bennett had received a phone call and had anxiously rushed out in response.

During the explanation, Bird had been eyeing the remaining piece of cheese which Stephanie had left in the centre of the table. She saw him looking at it but deliberately chose not to offer it to him.

"What's wrong with you?" Puchy asked the young girl. "You don't look very happy."

Stephanie suddenly looked up, her face contorted with anger. With a barrage of cheese fragments, she screamed, "I hate him! Hate him! Hate him! How could he? How could he? She's not even pretty."

Tentatively, Bird asked, "Who do you hate?"

"Who do you think?" came back the shouted response. "That disloyal, evil, self-opinionated imitation of a human being who thinks himself to be God's gift to women! That's who."

"Oh, you mean, your friend Marty."

"Don't you ever mention his name again in this house. He is certainly no friend of mine!"

With a thump of her fist on the table, she pushed herself away and ran from the kitchen and up into her bedroom. Puchy and Bird could hear her crying but were afraid even to attempt to try to go to comfort her in her present state.

Bird looked helplessly at his friend, then hunched his shoulders and in one movement of his wing, swept up the remaining wedge of cheese, plus the crumbs scattered over the table, opened his beak, and they were gone.

Over an hour passed as the two friends settled into the comfy chairs in the lounge while they waited for Hugo, or one of his parents to return. They were drifting in and out of sleepy consciousness when the phone started to ring. The noise woke Bird out of his daydream and Puchy jumped up and tried to fly but found that the matchstick splint in her wing only allowed her to spin round on her back, like a dying Bluebottle fly.

The phone rang for, what seemed several minutes until mercifully it stopped. Bird and Puchy were about to settle down when the ringing started again. It went on for some time until Bird heard a thump from upstairs and Stephanie's heavy footsteps go into her parents' bedroom where there was an extension. The ringing stopped, followed after a few seconds, by a scream and the sound of the young girl crying.

'That boyfriend of hers must be trying to apologise,' thought Bird but only for a second as Stephanie suddenly burst into the kitchen, with tears flooding down her face and screaming,

"Dad's been injured! He's in hospital. Mum and Hugo are with him. I need to get there. A man with him has been killed."

Bird and Puchy jumped up as the distraught girl ran around looking for the telephone number of anyone that she thought might be able to help. Without thinking, she scrolled through the numbers on her mobile phone and pressed the connect button. Impatiently stamping her feet and gazing at the dial, as if it might speed the connection, she waited for the phone to connect. After what seemed like hours, a voice answered.

"Hello, John Edmunds,"

"Please help me," Stephanie pleaded and, through a flood of tears and loud sniffs, she quickly explained the situation.

"I'll be there in five minutes." The voice on the phone reassured her and she put down the phone and slumped into one of the chairs, sobbing loudly.

"What's happened?" Bird almost shouted.

It took several minutes for Stephanie to regain enough composure to be able to reply but when she had finally told them of what she knew, they too were looking tearful.

As she finished her explanation, the front doorbell sounded. Stephanie grabbed her phone and a large piece of kitchen roll on which to blow her nose and wipe away her tears and rushed out to find Mr Edmunds at the door, with Marty and his mother waiting in their car. Without any pleasantries, the man and the girl jumped into the car and within seconds could be seen disappearing up the hill towards the link road and the hospital in Barnstaple.

"Come, my friend!" Bird exclaimed. "Jump on my back and we'll see what's been happening for ourselves."

A minute later, the house was empty and silent.

Chapter 39

The Hospital

The journey to the hospital seemed interminably long. Marty wrapped his arm around Stephanie, who went over and over again what little she knew of what had happened. Mr Edmunds dropped his three passengers off at the entrance to Accident & Emergency and went off to find a parking space, which, given the amount of activity and the number of people inside the department, was going to be difficult.

Mrs Edmunds strode purposefully up to the reception. She explained who they were and why they were there, and then, following the instructions, the polite but obviously harassed receptionist had given her, led her followers to the lifts. Impatiently they waited for the doors to open. A man lying on a trolley and an old lady in a wheelchair were pushed out of the lift before the three could enter. Mrs Edmunds pressed the button for the floor she wanted and they all stood in paralysed silence as they ascended.

The doors to the lift parted and they were all about to exit when Hugo and Mrs Bennett stepped in. As soon as the two women saw each other, they broke down and hugged each other. They would have stayed like that had it not been for a somewhat irate man, moaning about the cost of parking his car, getting in with them.

Through the tears and snuffles, Hugo's mother explained roughly what had happened to Mrs Edmunds and that they had been asked to wait in the cafeteria for now, as Mr Bennett was undergoing surgery.

Both women had almost finished their coffees and Hugo was finishing off his second Coke when a very frustrated Mr Edmunds stormed up to them.

"D'you know, I've been around that carpark so many times looking for a space that I feel dizzy."

His anger vented, he put his hand on Julia Bennett's shoulder and asked how things were and if there was anything he could do. He seated himself opposite Mrs Bennett and she went through again as much as she knew.

They were suddenly distracted by a very distraught, middle-aged lady, surrounded by three other people. She was being pushed in a wheelchair through the centre of the corridor leading to the exit.

"I think that is Mr Broadbent's wife," Hugo mumbled softly. "I think it was her that I saw at the ruins. She was screaming something about her husband."

Mrs Bennett turned and looked at her. Rising, she went across and, with as much sympathy as she could, introduced herself. The woman in the wheelchair renewed her crying, calling out that it was her fault. After only a few minutes, while her friends exchanged addresses and telephone numbers with Mrs Bennett, she returned to the table, obviously upset at the woman's accusations.

For over an hour and a half, they all sat at the table, only occasionally leaving to visit the toilets to relieve themselves of the copious amounts of tea and coffee they were consuming, more as a distraction than because they were thirsty. Finally, a young man in a blue scrub suit came up to where they were seated and pulled up the remaining empty chair.

He explained that Mr Bennett was now out of surgery and was stable. He pointed out that he had severe head injuries and, had the patient not been wearing a hard-hat he, most certainly, would not be alive today. However, his injuries were extremely extensive and there was a strong possibility that he might not survive, or if he did, he could be severely disabled.

His wife broke down in floods of tears, followed by Hugo and Stephanie. The doctor suggested that they all go home for now as Mr Bennett had been induced into a coma and there was nothing they could do by being there.

Mrs Bennett forced a smile and thanked the doctor, who rose, turned and left.

Mrs Edmunds suggested that she drive Julia's car and take them home while Mr Edmunds would follow and pick up his wife after she had dropped them off. Mrs Bennett wasn't about to argue. Still in floods of tears, they left, not knowing if they would ever see Mr Bennett alive again.

Bird, in his invisible state, with Puchy hiding under the feathers on his back, had been standing in an alcove, listening to all that was said. They both had been fighting to hold back their tears as they heard what the doctor had said but were unable to offer their sympathy, for fear of being seen.

"If Hugo's father dies, then I am going to kill all those witches, whatever the cost." Bird whispered. Puchy nodded in agreement and together they also made their way back to the Bennett's house.

Chapter 40

Putricia's Plan

Out of the corner of her eye, Putricia watched Morgana disappear back into the entrance of the underground ruins. She smiled as she surveyed the devastation and chaos that lay before her. Slowly, she moved closer to Susanna, who was relishing in her handiwork.

"I think that we have a problem," she whispered.

Susanna looked at her and from her expression, Putricia could tell that she had noticed it too.

"My sister is becoming weak. If we do not do something, she will destroy all that we have set out to do."

The elder witch nodded and her face looked stern.

"I'm sure that it is due to that body she's occupying. She told me that she keeps getting flash-backs to situations and happenings that never happened to her in her old body. She is beginning to take pity on these murderers. If we are to finish and fulfil our vow, then she must be stopped, or at least controlled." Putricia gave a wry smile as she said this.

"I agree but what do you propose?"

Putricia moved even closer to her fellow witch and quietly whispered, "Swap bodies."

Susanna looked up in amazement at the suggestion but then the younger witch explained that, in her present form, that of a useless ten-year-old girl, she was not able to use her full potential but, if she had the young, firm, athletic body which now resided with Morgana, then she would be more powerful and be able to fulfil her vow more rapidly. Also, with Morgana transferred to a child's body, she would become far more…controllable.

Susanna looked doubtful for a few moments and then chuckled. "You've been planning this for some time, I can see."

Putricia looked away in feigned embarrassment.

Susanna continued, "We will have to be very careful because, in the potions you took to take over your present bodies, the 'victim's' body dies."

"I have already thought of that," chortled Putricia. "While we were living in that cave by the sea and while my sister was out getting food, I worked out how the recipe could be modified to keep both of us alive. I even tried it out on a badger and a fox that I managed to capture. The result was almost perfect but I know where I went wrong and have fixed the problem."

Susanna chuckled again, amazed at the cunning and deviousness of the younger witch.

With a final admiring look at their handiwork and the resultant rescue teams, police, fire crews and the now hundreds of spectators, most of who were holding, what looked like, multi-coloured torches high above their heads, the two witches turned and followed Morgana back into the depths of the tunnels.

"We need food," Putricia shouted irritably to Morgana as all three re-entered the main chamber of the ruin. "And not your usual scavenging's. I want proper food. Go out and get us some." Although Morgana, in her present form, was much bigger and taller than the ten-year-old body hosting Putricia, she was the more dominant of the pair and deep down Morgana feared and distrusted her sister. With a glance at Susanna, whose look confirmed Putricia's order, the young witch went over to the wall where the hooded jacket that she had taken from the flat of Sue Redwell during their brief stay there, hung and put it on, throwing the hood over her head. With a last look at her companions and Snatch, who licked his lips, as if to say, 'Don't forget me.' she left.

There was still a mass of activity around the area of the cave-in but she skirted past, keeping her head low. After a short walk, she reached the bottom of the High Street. She stood staring at all the bright lights in the shops and the myriad of items for sale. It made her jealous of all the people milling around who seemed able to buy those luxuries. As she stared, she slowly became aware of some very unusual items for sale in the shops. There were pumpkins and wooden brooms displayed in windows of clothes, sweet and even butcher shops. The further she walked, the more she became amazed at the weird clothes and pointed hats on show. She was even more surprised when she saw some children, out with their parents, actually wearing these items and made hideous by the paint that covered their faces.

She was about to turn and head back to the ruins when there was a tap on her shoulder. Panicking, she spun around, to be confronted, not by one of these hideous creatures that were walking the streets but by the smiling face of the young woman who had given her a lift in her car some weeks before.

"Hello," she said cheerfully. "Remember me? I'm Victoria. I gave you a lift a few weeks ago. I saw you from across the street and thought that it would be nice to have another chat. Would you like to come for a coffee?"

At first, Morgana felt that she should run but then remembered the last time she had had coffee with Victoria and the joy it gave her. Rapidly composing herself, she smiled at her acquaintance and pulled the hood of her jacket back from her head. "Oh hello Victoria," she mumbled nervously but then, regaining some of her confidence, she smiled and said that she would love to have a coffee.

"Great!" beamed Victoria, "But first I need to get some money from the hole in the wall."

Morgana was at a loss of how you could get money from 'A hole in a wall' but was intrigued and followed her friend to a large building with the name 'Lloyds' emblazoned above it. Victoria approached a box-like structure set into the wall of the building and pushed a small card into it. Morgana remembered seeing a similar card in the wallet that was in the pocket of the coat she was wearing. She watched in amazement as, after pushing a few buttons on the machine, a little door opened and a thick wad of money emerged, which Victoria rapidly tucked into her wallet, together with the small card, finally returning it into her handbag.

Suddenly Morgana had an idea. "Wait, please. I need some money too," and she dug into the pockets of her coat to find the small card that she had. Finally, she found it, and following Victoria's example, she put the card into the machine. At first, it would not go in until her friend explained that the card was upside down. Finally, the card slid into the box and a message requesting a 'PIN' came onto the screen. She hesitated and Victoria, sensing her confusion explained what it meant. Morgana had no idea what the PIN was and was about to panic when something seemed to click in her memory and she keyed the numbers 1682. It wasn't until she had pressed them that she realised the significance of that combination. It was the year that her mother was hanged. She was mesmerised at the thought until a little nudge from Victoria brought her back to reality.

"How much do you want to withdraw?" her friend prompted.

Morgana gazed at the amounts displayed in front of her. In all her life she had never owned more than a pound at any one time yet here she was being offered ten, twenty, fifty, even a hundred pounds. Her heart was pounding at the thought of so much money; she pressed the twenty-pound button. Seconds later there was a bleep from the box and her card reappeared from the small slot into which she had placed it. Taking it, there was another click from the little door and a crisp twenty-pound note fell out.

Full of excitement, she held the note up to show Victoria, who did not seem interested.

"Right! Let's go and get that coffee," her friend announced and strode off in the direction of Mill Street, the other main shopping area in Bideford.

It was over two hours later that the two women emerged

from the café and said their goodbye's. Morgana, or Anne as Victoria knew her, had been eager to find out why the shops were full of strange clothes and items that seemed out of place. She did not want to appear unintelligent in front of Victoria and had only slowly brought their conversation round to the subject. Victoria had explained about Halloween. Gradually all became clear to Morgana as she remembered the celebration of *All Hallows Eve* that had occurred in the years before her execution. It was the story that all the mothers told their children about how the dead came alive on that night, though, in her day, all the families stayed indoors to protect themselves from the ghoulish activity that might occur, unlike what she saw now.

Her excitement about getting the money, learning about this strange witches' festival and the pleasure at being able to talk to, what she now regarded as a friend, had made her forget about her primary mission, to get food. By the time she had left the café, many of the shops had closed but as she made her way back through Mill Street, she saw a shop called CO-OP still open. She watched as people entered and picked up small metal baskets, so she followed suit and entered. She was astounded at the choice of food and drinks displayed there and it was not long before her basket was full. Again she studied the other shoppers and watched as they went to a series of small desks where they unloaded their purchases and filled white bags with their contents, finally handing over one of those strange cards to the woman seated at the counter.

Joining the queue at one of the desks, she slowly approached the seated woman.

"Do need some bags, Luv?" the woman asked with a cheerful smile.

"Oh! Ah! Yes," Morgana replied hesitatingly and then transferred all the items in her wire basket, into two of the flimsy white bags.

"That'll be seventeen pounds and twenty P," the woman chanted.

Carefully, Morgana pushed her card into the small black box that sat on the counter, as she had seen the people in front of her do, followed by the same number that she had used at 'The hole in the wall' as Victoria had called it. A few seconds elapsed and a small roll of paper spewed out of the box. The woman tore it off and handed it to her. She picked up the bags and was about to leave when the woman at the desk shouted to her.

"Don't forget your card Luv!" and waved it at her. Morgana smiled and took the card. She turned, feeling very proud and pleased with herself and eager to return to the ruins to tell the other two of her adventure.

Chapter 41

Julia's Revenge

That night, the lights never went out in the Bennett household. None of them could sleep. Mr and Mrs Edmunds and their son Marty had stayed until the early hours but had finally left. Dr Peter Goodfellow, Paul Bennetts friend, had heard about the accident and had called round. He had given them all a strong sedative before seeing them all to bed and then leaving.

Julia Bennett lay in her bed, drifting in and out of sleepy consciousness. Her worry and concern at the start was slowly changing into anger, which grew as the hours ticked by. By morning, she had made a clear plan to confront those evil women and bring them down, by whichever way she could. She had made up her mind that they would pay, and pay dearly for the damage they had done to her family, Emma and everyone else they had destroyed… whatever it took.

In the early hours of the morning, she decided that sleep was impossible and went down into the kitchen to make herself a drink. On entering, she found her daughter sitting at the kitchen table with her head resting on her arms but fast asleep. A cold cup of coffee balanced precariously between her hand and the edge of the table. She had obviously had the same idea.

Her mother was about to wake her but then thought better of it. Taking the cup, she poured its contents down the sink. She then placed a large bath towel, that she kept by the door in case Jake, who was curled up in his basket, snoring, oblivious to anything that had happened, ever came in wet, over her daughter's shoulders. Fortunately, she had washed it the day before and it was clean. Stephanie stirred and gave a small moan but did not wake.

Mrs Bennett looked around her kitchen, wondering if she would ever see her husband slumped in the chair in the corner, reading the newspaper, again. She started to well up but told herself to have positive thoughts and controlled her tears. She filled a glass with water from the tap on the sink and returned to her room.

Her peace was shattered at 8:30 by a ringing of the doorbell. Shaking her head to clear it from the sleep that had finally fallen on her, what seemed only minutes ago, she twisted to get out of bed but then heard the footsteps on the landing of one of her children who, she hoped, was going to answer the door. Falling back on her pillow, she pricked her ears to hear who the visitor might be and she recognised the voice of Peter Goodfellow. She was preparing to get up when there was a knock on her bedroom door and, after a short pause, he eased his head around.

"OK if I come in?" he asked. "I was just passing and thought that I'd pop in to see how you all were."

Julia pulled the duvet up to her chest and pushed her hair to one side, thinking about what mess she must look. She grimaced and replied that, 'she'd had better nights'.

"I've checked on Paul this morning and he's holding his own at the moment but he's still in intensive care and so I would not recommend you going to the hospital until he has been revived from the coma that he has been put in."

Julia looked concerned, yet relieved at the same time. In her present state, she doubted that she would be able to drive safely to the hospital anyway. She thanked her visitor for all that he had done to help. He smiled and fumbled in the bottom of the briefcase he was carrying and pulled out a small, plastic bottle of tablets, which he held up and shook.

"Take one of these, every six hours," he announced, shaking the bottle again. "There's enough in here for you and the children but only give them one every twelve hours; otherwise you'll have zombies walking around you. Be careful because they will make you feel drowsy, so under no circumstances are you to drive, but they may help you to get through the next few days a little better." They smiled at each other.

At that point, there was a nervous tap on the door and Hugo poked his head around.

"Is it OK if I come in?" he asked, and as he entered, they saw he was carrying two large mugs of tea. His mother started to well up with tears again as Hugo had never, ever, even offered to make her tea, let alone do it.

"That's very thoughtful of you, my boy." the doctor said pleasantly. "And how are you today?"

Hugo forced a grimace but then broke down in tears and fell onto his mother's bed. "It's all my fault!" he screamed.

"If I hadn't found that stupid cave and those evil witches, then none of this would have happened. It's all my fault! It's all my fault!"

His mother sat up and put her arm around him, stroking his hair. "Don't talk rubbish," she admonished him, "it's more to do with that wretched inheritance than you've ever done. If your father hadn't been given that site, then he would never have been in that tunnel in the first place."

Now it was her turn to break down in tears.

Dr Goodfellow broke open the seal on the bottle of tablets and emptied two light yellow tablets into his palm. Picking up the cup of tea which Hugo had brought for his mother, he passed it to her plus one pill and the other to Hugo. Julia Bennett looked at him as if to say, 'Do I have to?' but his look told her she did, and with a sniff, swallowed the tablet. Hugo followed suit, taking a slurp of tea from his mother's cup.

"Right. I'll leave you for now. I'll call by later this afternoon to see how everything's going. Oh, give one of these..." he shook the bottle of tablets, "...to Stephie when she wakes up. It may help. I'll let myself out."

With a final smile, he turned and a minute later could be heard driving away.

The noise of him leaving must have woken Stephanie and she slouched into the room, looking very much the worse for wear. She lay down beside her mother and gave her a hug which was returned. All three lay on the bed for several minutes until a bark from downstairs broke the silence as Jake demanded his breakfast. Hugo got up and wearily said, "I'll go." Pulling his dressing gown around him, he left and after a short while, the sound of Jake's metal bowl scraping over the kitchen floor as he chased the food in it, was heard.

It was almost 9:30 by the time his mother and sister appeared in the kitchen. Hugo was sat at the kitchen table scribbling in a notebook. His mother asked what he was doing and got the reply, 'homework'. The shock of Hugo doing his homework voluntarily was unheard of but she let it pass, knowing that her son was doing whatever he could to distract himself from worrying about his father.

At just after 10:00 the doorbell rang and, on opening the door, Mrs Bennett was pleased to find, Mr and Mrs Edmunds and Marty. They immediately asked how everyone was and if they could be of any help in any way. Hugo's mother invited them all to come in and as soon as Marty entered the kitchen, Stephanie ran up to him and broke down in his arms.

"Why don't you two go and sit in the dining room?" Julia Bennett whispered to the two teenagers and ushered them into the next room. "I'll bring you a cup of tea in a moment," she called as she turned and went back to her guests.

They all sat huddled around the kitchen table speaking in hushed tones, going over and over what had happened but both Bennett's being very careful not to mention or implicate anything about witches or magic.

To settle everyone's curiosity and concern, Hugo's mother decided to phone the hospital for a progress report but, after she finally got through to the right department, was politely informed that there was no change.

It was 3:30 by the time that her guests finally left, accompanied by Stephanie, who had packed a small bag and arranged to stay over that night, her 'difficulties' with Marty seemingly resolved. As the front door closed and the sound of the Edmund family's car drifted away, Julia Bennett gave a loud sigh.

The repeated talk of what had happened over the last five and a half hours had helped to calm her down, at least from the sorrow point of view but the anger she had felt earlier that day had grown and she knew that if she did not do something about it, she would explode. The only way that she thought that these feelings could be released was to confront those responsible, namely the witches.

"I'm just popping down to the supermarket," she called to Hugo who had retreated to his room.

He acknowledged her comment and she made for the kitchen back door. It had just started to open when she had a thought. 'What if they try to attack me?' She looked around and her eyes fell on a small knife that she used for preparing vegetables, resting on the draining board next to the sink. Without thinking, she grabbed it and threw it into her handbag. Again she started to leave but then she had another thought, 'how would she find her adversary?' She hovered at the door, not knowing what to do, then a slight movement, as Jake found a more comfortable position in his basket in the corner of the kitchen gave her an idea.

She picked up his lead and said, "Walkies!"

Jake was immediately awake and jumping up to be let out.

"I may not be able to find those evil things but I am sure that Jake will know exactly where they are." She called up to Hugo explaining that she was taking Jake with her and she received a grunt in reply.

Twenty minutes later, she and the dog were standing at the gate of the fence that surrounded the scene of the accident. A policeman was on guard, protecting the property from the still several journalists and those just curious, that were milling around. She explained to the officer who she was, showing him her driving licence as proof. She told him that, in all the confusion of the previous night, her husband's wallet, containing all his credit cards and personal documents, had gone missing and she wanted to see if she could have a quick look to see if she could find it.

The officer was very reluctant at first to let her pass but after several pleas and some genuine tears, he let her through but warning her to stay well clear of the area marked out by blue and white tape. With a slight smile, she and Jake ducked under the tape that crisscrossed the gate where they stood. She moved around the entrance area slowly, appearing to look for the wallet but slowly letting her course pull farther from the entrance and all those who may be watching her, all the time encouraging Jake to "Find 'em."

A tug on the lead finally told her that the dog had picked up the scent and, as quickly as she dared, she moved to the far side of the site. Jake pawed at a stone that, to all intents and purposes, looked like an old gravestone but from the scratches on the surrounding ground she could see that it had been moved, and recently. Kneeling, she brushed the earth from the stone, revealing an old iron ring. Bracing herself, she gave it a hefty pull. To her surprise, the stone moved without almost any effort to show a staircase leading down into a tunnel.

Hitching her clothes around her and with a final glance to make sure that she was not observed, she and Jake began to tread carefully down the stone stairway.

Chapter 42

Sue's Sighting

"Excuse me, Sir, but I think that you would like to see this." A smartly uniformed WPC stood at attention as she handed D.I. Hyde an A4 sheet of paper.

He snatched it from her unceremoniously and started to read.

"Go and get sergeant Cummings. And tell him to be smartish," he ordered her.

The young woman raised her eyebrows and turned to carry out her order. She poked her tongue out as soon as she was out of view of the officer, something which was observed by an older secretary who was seated in a glass-fronted office facing the corridor. She gave the WPC the thumbs up as she passed, which made the policewoman blush.

It was a good ten minutes before she located the sergeant and passed on the message. As they both strode back to the D.I.'s office, she told him about the contents of the paper, which she had read as she took it to the detective's office.

"She's been spotted!" the detective shouted to his

sergeant as he stepped into his superior's office. "By the way, you took your time, didn't you?"

"Who's been spotted? Where?" the sergeant replied, not wishing for the detective to know that the WPC had already briefed him on the way up to the office.

"That stupid reporter woman who went missing ages ago but this time we've got proof." He handed his sergeant a piece of paper and printed on it was a rather fuzzy picture of a young woman. Despite the lack of clarity, it was evident that this indeed was the young reporter Sue Redwell."

"Where was this taken?" the younger officer asked.

"Outside Lloyds Bank on the High Street in Bideford. She took out twenty pounds from her account." D.I. Hyde almost shouted back with glee. "At least that proves she's alive." he went on and then suddenly turned, looking angry. "I thought that you were supposed to have suspended that account?"

"Well, it's a good job I didn't." snapped back the sergeant, "otherwise, we wouldn't have this lead."

D.I. Hyde was taken aback by the anger in the reply from his sergeant and was about to admonish him but then thought better of it and ignored the response.

"I want heightened 24-hour CCTV surveillance of that bank, in case she comes back again. Leave the account open because if she can't access it, we may lose her again. If we can get her, then I'm sure that we can get that other kid who ran away. I'm positive that the two are connected."

The detective smiled and looked at the piles of paper on his desk. *'If we can find those two women, then I can bin nearly all of this. And the chief constable will stop nagging me about our lack of progress,'* he thought to himself.

Turning back to his sergeant, the inspector waved his hand, gesturing for him to leave.

"Well! What are you waiting for?" he shouted.

Without replying, the sergeant gathered the papers and photo and went back to his own office where he sat down and started the paperwork necessary to start the surveillance, muttering oaths and curses on his superior under his breath.

Chapter 43

Confrontation

J ulia had only gone a few yards when the light reflected from the entrance was on the point of disappearing. Opening her handbag, she took out her mobile phone and switched on its torch mode. The tunnel sprang to life and its slimy, algae-covered walls made her shiver. Gripping Jake's lead even more firmly, she made her way forward, stopping at every other step to listen for any sounds and to try to penetrate the gloom ahead. Jake was busy sniffing at every stop, seemingly enjoying the adventure. Suddenly he stopped and sniffed the air, then, with a sharp tug, started to run forwards, pulling his handler with him. It took all her effort for Julia to get him back under control but finally, the leash became limp and the whimpering animal moved at her pace.

About a minute, which seemed like an hour, after entering the tunnel, Julia halted and switched off her phone. In the distance, she could make out the glow of a flickering light. It was very faint but definitely there. A tremor of excitement ran through her, or was it fear, as she pulled her coat more tightly around her and continued to move forward again. Jake must have sensed her nervousness and hung back. As she slowly shuffled forward, the light ahead became brighter, giving the corridor in which she stood an even more eerie and overbearing atmosphere. She could feel her heart pounding inside her chest and hoped that its noise wouldn't give her away. Ten feet away, a doorway was outlined in the gloom and again she stopped, fighting the urge to turn and run. Gathering Jake's lead close to her, so that the animal was almost wrapped around her feet, she took the final steps and stepped into the doorway.

Peering around the stone pillars that made it, she looked around and into the room. At the far end stood Emma, for that is how she still thought of her, stirring a steaming liquid in the cauldron over the fire. The girl giggled as she lifted a ladle full of the contents and a stream of, what appeared to be, liquid gold flowed from it back into the pot. Susanna was seated in a chair made from driftwood. She seemed to be sewing her cloak, for all she wore was a rough-looking shift-type dress and a black hood. The thick, heavily-worn folds of cloth lay before her, balanced on her knees. Her face was uncovered and the sight of her damaged and distorted features made Julia almost wretch.

Suddenly, Jake barked and jumped forwards, pulling the leash from Julia's hand and ran to where Snatch was curled up as close to the fire as it could without catching fire himself. The two witches jumped up and screamed. Susanna tried, in vain, to cover her head with the cloak but only succeeded getting it tangled around her neck. Putricia, flew back against the wall, dropping the ladle into the cauldron. Jake, on the other hand, was nuzzling Snatch as if he was a long-lost friend.

There was absolute silence for what seemed minutes, though in reality, was only seconds.

"You!" Susanna screamed so loudly that the sound reverberated around the chamber. "Traitor!" she spat, now beginning to regain control. "How dare you invade our home. You traitor! You're one of us yet you live with that murderer."

"Or did," broke in Putricia, who also had now regained some of her composure, and gave a gloating smile.

Seeing this, Julia could feel the anger inside her start to build and she marched forwards, toward the pair, who instinctively fell back.

The shouts and accusations from the two women before her dispelled any feelings of fear and apprehension that had been with Julia only a second before, and was replaced by sheer anger.

"You tried to kill my husband and my son, not to mention all those gnomes. You've even taken over the bodies of two innocent people. It's not me who's the murderer and traitor; it's you. You sought justice and I commend you for it but now, you have become guiltier of the same crimes inflicted on you, than those who killed you in the first place."

"Don't listen to her!" Susanna screamed out and began to move forward but Julia stood her ground, gripping her handbag, ready to pull out the knife concealed in it should it become necessary. "Do you think that after centuries of looking like this," she threw back her cloak and let it fall to the floor, revealing a body of skeletal proportions, topped by her grossly disfigured head, "that I am going to fail in my vow for the sake of a stupid woman, her pathetic, murderous husband and her interfering brat of a son."

Mrs Bennett turned her head as the sight of the hideous creature in front of her revealed herself. Putricia, who, although still shocked at the appearance of her friend Susanna, saw her opportunity to overpower the interloper and made a lunge for Julia. A bark from Jake made Hugo's mother look up and she saw the attack coming, just in time. Without thinking, she gripped the strap of her handbag and swung it as hard as she could at the charging witch. As the bag turned in front of Putricia's face, she screamed and dropped to the floor, blood pouring from a gash in her cheek.

Julia Bennett was as surprised as the two witches at what had happened and was sure that her bag had not even touched the witch, still in the form of the young girl, Emma. Automatically she started to move forward to see if she could help but then realised who and what she was about to help and thought better of it. Gathering her bag to her chest, she felt underneath it, thinking that the knife inside must have somehow worked its way out and that the blade must have caused the wound, but the bag was intact. Still puzzled, she started to open her handbag to see if the knife was still there when suddenly Susanna screamed.

"She's got it! She's got our inheritance! I can feel it!" and she too made a movement as if to attack Julia, but Hugo's mother was ready for the witch and made to swing her bag again at the pathetic figure in front of her. The witch stopped her attack and stepped backwards. "Give me our inheritance and I promise that I will let you live."

Julia was at a loss for words, as she did not know what the witch was talking about and as far as she knew, she did not have anything that belonged to these characters. "I don't have your silly inheritance or anything else of yours for that matter. As for you letting me live, well I believe that it's me that is going to let you live but I promise you, that if you try to hurt any of my family, then I will find that inheritance of yours and destroy it… and you as well."

Julia Bennett could feel her face flushing and beads of nervous sweat running down her cheeks but the shock of the injury she had inflicted on the young girl, who was now lying on the floor, had made her anger diminish. She started to back up and retrace her steps out of the chamber into the corridor, closely followed by Jake who jumped around, wagging his tail as if it was all a game.

The corridor was in total darkness and Julia was aware that she was at a disadvantage, being unfamiliar with the layout and direction. Before the light from the room finally disappeared, she reopened and rummaged in her handbag until her hand fell on her phone. Gripping it, her hand shaking uncontrollably, she switched on its torch mode again and was pleased to see the space ahead of her was empty as the beam of light from the phone illuminated the way forward. Keeping her back to the wall, she inched her way along the corridor, all senses on high alert, until finally, she saw a glimmer of subdued daylight ahead of her. As the window of light became larger, she noticed a familiar silhouette framed by it. Jake had run on ahead and was now sitting at the entrance, his tail swishing from side to side. He barked as he saw the flash of light from the phone and stood up, obviously still enjoying the adventure.

Julia Bennett had hardly made it outside when the phone in her hand started to vibrate and ring. Swiping the screen, she answered the call.

"Oh. Hi Julia. This is Peter Goodfellow."

"Oh. Hello Peter. How are you?"

"I'm fine thanks. I'm glad I've found you. I've been trying to call you for the last ten minutes but your phone kept going to voicemail."

Julia looked at her screen and sure enough, there were three missed-call messages.

"I think that you'd better get over to the hospital as fast as you can," the doctor said solemnly. "There's been a change in Paul's condition and I'm afraid it is not looking good."

Julia didn't finish listening to the conversation. She threw her phone into her bag and ran as fast as possible to where her car was parked. With tears streaming down her face, she manoeuvred her car out of the car park, ignoring the blasts from the horns of the other vehicles and barged her way out and across the junction where the entrance to the car park met the main highway. Without glancing left or right she drove across the old Torridge bridge at breakneck speed, heading for Barnstaple and the North Devon District Hospital.

Chapter 44

Coffee

Morgana was about to step off the pavement to cross the road next to the old Torridge bridge when a small, silver-grey car screeched past her and sped over the bridge. The surprise made her drop one of her bags and she stooped onto one knee to pick up the few items that had tumbled out. As she stood up, a young man approached her and asked if she was alright. Even when she was alive, she had never had much dealings with young men, other than her cousin and she could feel herself blushing. What was even stranger, was that deep down in her memory she felt that she recognised the person, yet she could not recall from where or when. Without replying to the stranger, she gripped the handles of the bags and ran, almost crashing into another car as she went. As she ran, she could hear someone call out the name 'Sue, Sue', but she paid it no heed.

Finally, she reached the fence of the ruin and skirted around it to where the concealed hole was, a few yards from the tunnel entrance. She could feel her heart pounding in her chest but she was not sure if it was due to the running or the embarrassment and excitement of meeting the young man, who, now she thought on reflection, was quite handsome.

With a backward glance, to ensure that no one had seen her, she headed into the darkness of the tunnel clutching her parcels and thinking how pleased Putricia and Susanna would be when she showed them the delicacies she had bought.

On returning to the main room, she was surprised to see it in chaos and her sister lying on her bed with blood covering her face. Susanna was desperately trying to staunch the flow using some dirty rags that had been one of the sheets that had covered the bed. As she applied pressure on the wound with the cloths, Putricia flinched and cried out in pain.

Morgana dropped her bags, being careful not to smash any of the contents, and rushed over to her sister. Pushing Susanna to one side, she ordered her to get a bowl of clean water and add a spoonful of salt to it to clean the wound. Selecting the unused parts of the sheet, she tore off several more pieces and dipped them in the water that Susanna had brought. At last, with frequent moans and yelps from her sister, the bleeding was finally staunched and she was able to clean around the wound to make her sister look less battered.

Putricia's skin was ashen from the shock of the injury and Morgana told her to lie still while she fetched her something to make her feel better. While Susanna sat by the patient, Morgana went to where she had left her parcels and rummaged inside the bags. With a triumphant smile, she pulled out a jar of instant coffee; the same brand that she had drunk in the café which she had visited with Victoria. She had never made the drink before and was not quite sure if she was doing it right but she had carefully watched the waitress in the café make it and was convinced that she was doing it correctly. At last, in front of her, was a mug of the steaming brown liquid and she could not resist taking a sip to see that it was correct. Perfect. Just as she remembered from the café.

Carefully, gripping it with both hands, she went over to Putricia and, with Susanna's assistance, helped her sister into a sitting position. She handed her the mug of brown liquid and urged her to drink it. Putricia and Susanna eyed each other suspiciously but, with encouragement from Morgana, Putricia began to sip the coffee, slowly at first but then with more enthusiasm as the warmth and taste of the liquid filtered down into her stomach. Susanna, intrigued by the aroma that came from the mug, pulled it away from Putricia before she drained it and drank the dregs herself.

"What is this stuff?" she questioned Morgana.

"It's called coffee," Morgana replied and then went on to explain about her visit into the town, meeting her friend, Victoria, getting money from 'the hole in the wall' and buying all the goodies still lying in her bags on the floor.

Susanna could not contain herself and ran over to the bags and started to pull out the contents, feeling and sniffing each item. She had to continually push Snatch away, who also was curious about the unusual aromas that emanated from the bags. Drool trickled from the corners of his mouth as he sensed food. The coffee had revived Putricia somewhat and she crawled from her bed, eager to see and taste what other delicacies her sister had brought back.

It was a full ten minutes of sniffing, tasting and eating food that they never knew existed before when Putricia yelped as she was trying to cram a large piece of French loaf into her mouth. The effort had stretched the wound in her cheek and a bead of blood reappeared. Morgana looked at her sister and gently wiped the droplet away with a serviette which she retrieved from her pocket, having placed it there before leaving the café.

Raising herself from her patient, Morgana walked over to the fire below the cauldron and threw the soiled tissue into it, where it momentarily flared and then died back to its previous orange glow. As she turned, she noticed the content of the cauldron, its golden-coloured liquid still swirling as if alive. She immediately recognised it as the elixir she and her sister had used to take over and inhabit the body of another person. It puzzled her for whom this batch could be for. She was about to question this, when there was a crash from the other side of the room. Susanna had dropped a small plate containing the remnants of their meal which had been balancing on her knee.

While her friend grovelled on the floor picking up the pieces, Morgana went back to Putricia and checked her wound to make sure that the bleeding had stopped.

"What happened to you?" she asked her sister, studying the wound, and, over the next ten minutes, the story of Julia Bennett's visit came out.

Chapter 45

The Miracle

Tears streamed down Julia Bennett's face as she careered down the roads on her way to the hospital. On several occasions, she had to swerve or brake hard to avoid other vehicles as her watery eyes distorted her vision. She was oblivious to the sounds of the horns from other drivers as she swerved to overtake. With a squeal of tortured rubber from her car tyres, she turned into the car park at the hospital, pounding the steering wheel while she waited for a ticket to be issued and the barrier raised. Every space was occupied and she had to drive around twice, becoming more anxious and frustrated with every circuit before she saw a car reversing and preparing to leave. Another car was waiting for the space but Julia accelerated and squeezed into the bay before the other driver was aware of her presence. The lady driver blew her horn in anger but Julia lifted two fingers at her and ran to the entrance, almost falling down the stairway that led from the car park.

Without stopping, she ran through the entrance, past the café and shop, to where the lifts were located at the far end of the corridor. She just missed one of them as she skidded to a halt and hammered on the up button. Impatiently she waited, trying to control her tears and hoping for all that she was worth that she would not find what she feared the most.

Finally, after what seemed an eternity, the lift doors slid open. It was occupied by two orderlies who were pushing a trolley with a very large old man balanced on the top, who was groaning loudly and seemed in imminent danger of falling off. Behind them were two women, the younger of them in obvious distress and was being comforted by the other who, by the similarity of the faces, Julia took to be the mother.

Mrs Bennett was ready to push round them to get the lift operational but on seeing the tears of the young woman and the worried look of the other, she stood back to let them pass without hindrance. The sight of other people with obvious serious concerns made her realise that she was not the only person who was troubled and it made her calm down a little. When the lift compartment was empty, she walked in and pressed the button for the third floor.

The doors had almost shut when a young man in a blue scrubs-suit, wearing a stethoscope around his neck and virtually running, shouted from down the corridor and waved his hand to get Julia to hold the lift. She was about to ignore his request but then, with the two women fresh in her mind, she put her foot in the doorway. The doors shuddered a little and then slid back open. The young man, Dr Mike Grayling according to the badge he wore, gasped a grateful *thank you* to Julia as he joined her and also pressed the button for the third floor.

In silence, the two stood as the doors closed and the lift made its way, at a tediously slow pace thought Mrs Bennett, to the third floor, at which point the doors slid open with a grinding sound. Both occupants almost ran out together, each matching each other's stride as they marched down the corridor, passing busy wards on either side. Finally, they turned into the same small side ward, ending up at the end of the bed in which lay Mr Bennett.

Beside the bed, Hugo and Stephanie already stood, holding hands. As their mother entered, they ran toward her and all three hugged. Stephanie burst into tears and Hugo was not far from it. Also by the bed was Mr Bennett's doctor friend, Peter Goodfellow. He was also dressed in a blue scrub-suit and was adjusting the pulse oximeter attached to the patient's finger and looking at the machine that was bleeping regularly and showed a red display that flickered between 94 and 96.

Dr Goodfellow smiled weakly at Mrs Bennett as she came into the room and then entered into quiet whispering with his colleague who had joined him. After several minutes the two separated and Dr Goodfellow came over to where the Bennett family stood in a huddle.

He indicated them all to move into a corner where there were two chairs. Stephanie and her mother each sat down while Hugo stood behind his mother.

"I am afraid that Paul is in a very bad way." the doctor started. "He has received major trauma to his head and neck as well as injuries to other parts of his body. We have tried to make him as comfortable and pain-free as possible but, I hate to tell you this… his chances of survival are very poor. You must all prepare yourself for whatever happens.

All three of the Bennett's burst into tears and sobs. Even the doctor took off his glasses to wipe his eyes. Julia looked through her tears at the face of the doctor to almost plead with him to say that he was wrong but all she got was a slow shake of his head.

"I have to go to attend to my other patients now, but Dr Grayling here will be just down the corridor should you need me. Let him know and I will come."

With a final look at his friend, lying motionless on the bed and the myriad of monitors bleeping and flashing around it, both doctors left the room, leaving the Bennett family alone.

Mrs Bennett got up and went over to her husband's bedside, where she sat down on the single chair already there. Hugo and his sister lifted the chairs from the corner in which they had been sitting and moved them over to the bedside as noiselessly as they could. Stephanie sat by her mother while Hugo squeezed his chair between two bulky machines that beeped regularly, on the other side of the bed. Stephanie gripped her mother's right hand as her left hand reached out to tenderly grasp that of her unconscious father. As she touched him, the sound of the machines around suddenly changed for a moment but then returned to the rhythmical monotone as before. Mrs Bennett looked up, encouraged at the change of tone but as it returned to its previous beat, she looked down again, lost in her thoughts.

For several hours the Bennett family sat by the bedside, hardly wishing to talk, as each did not know what to say. Periodically Dr Grayling came in and checked the monitors and asked if the family would like some food or a drink. None of them felt hungry but they each requested and received a bottle of water.

It was now quite dark, and apart from the occasional visit to the toilet, none of the Bennetts had left the room. Suddenly the tones on the monitors began to change, becoming erratic. All three woke from their daydreams and thoughts and were immediately alert. Julia Bennett was about to go out to find doctor Grayling when he and a nurse burst through the door pushing a trolley, loaded with more equipment, before them. Politely but firmly they asked all the family to wait outside, which they reluctantly did. From outside they could hear a great deal of activity from inside the room. Doctor Goodfellow suddenly appeared as he raced down the corridor and entered the side ward, with only the fleetest of acknowledgement of the family standing outside.

For over twenty minutes they all stood, motionless, arm in arm, listening to the beeps and pauses of the monitors in the room and the muffled conversations of the workers within, until, with a final bleep, the commotion stopped and all went silent. A minute later, the door of the ward opened and Peter Goodfellow emerged. His face, flushed but drawn, said everything. As he looked at Julia Bennett and her two children standing in front of him, all he could do was to shake his head before he started to cry, moving forward to embrace them all in a hug.

The quartet stood there without speaking, lost in their thoughts, the silence only broken by the sniffs and coughs as they tried to hold back their emotions. At last, the sobbing group split apart and all moved slowly into the now silent ward.

"I'll leave you alone for a while., choked Peter Goodfellow and, after removing his glasses to wipe his eyes, he left, closing the door quietly after him.

The three Bennett's stood, almost petrified, looking at the bed and the motionless body resting on it. Its face was partially obscured by the pipes and tubes still attached and it took several minutes before any of the trio dared to approach the bed. The two women returned to their seats which they drew up beside the bed while Hugo sat on the other side. Mrs Bennett reached under the sheet covering her husband and withdrew his hand, which she gripped and gently stroked. Hugo pulled his chair closer, making a loud, scraping noise. His already flushed face became even redder and he sniffed as quietly as he could, fighting to be brave and show that from now on he was the man of the family.

For several minutes they all sat in silence, each with their thoughts. Hugo tried to dismiss the idea that this was all his fault. If only he hadn't discovered Kadavera's cave and poked his nose in, none of this would have happened and his father would still be alive. He was sure that his mother and sister were thinking the same and that they would blame him for the rest of his life. These thoughts suddenly overwhelmed the young boy and he burst into a flood of tears. He dug into his pockets to find a handkerchief or tissue to blow his nose, which was now streaming down his upper lip.

His mother, seeing his plight reached for her handbag and rummaged around inside it. At last, she drew out a small cellophane bag of tissues which she passed over to Hugo. As Hugo stretched over the body of his father to take them, a small object, that had become attached to the packet, fell off and landed on the chest of Mr Bennett's body. As it touched the sheet, it started to glow with a golden hue. The glow increased until the three seated around it had to shield their eyes. None of them knew what was happening and Stephanie began to scream hysterically.

Without warning, the machines still attached to the corpse, sprang into life and lights flashed and beeps sounded. The glow slowly subsided until finally, Hugo was able to uncover his eyes and look at the object that was its source.

"My amulet! Look! It's my amulet!" he screamed, but his mother and sister did not look at it; instead, they were gazing, wide-eyed and open-mouthed at the body lying in the bed. Its eyes were open and it was smiling, somewhat asymmetrically, due to the thick tube protruding from its mouth.

The door of the ward slammed open. Peter Goodfellow and a portly nurse charged into the room. Without ceremony, they pushed passed Mrs Bennett and her daughter and stretched over the bed. The nurse switched back on some more of the machines while the doctor pulled back the sheet covering the body and started to listen for a heartbeat with his stethoscope.

As the sheet flew back, the small golden object that had been resting on top slid off and into Hugo's lap. Quickly he grabbed it to stop it falling on the floor and held it firmly in his fist. He could feel the unusual warmth from it that was always there when he touched it.

Two more nurses and Dr Grayling burst into the small ward, amazed to see the monitors flashing with signs of life. The room was now becoming crowded as another nurse, pushing a large wheeled cart, entered, banging the door loudly with the machine. Julia Bennett stood, hand in mouth, trying to see what was happening around the bodies of the medical personnel fussing around the bed. Hugo and Stephanie also rose, eager to see what was happening to their father.

At last, Dr Goodfellow broke away from the group and faced the three Bennett's.

"Well!" he sighed loudly. "In all my years as a doctor, I have never seen anything like this before. I do not know if any of you have been praying for a miracle but we surely have seen one today. Paul is alive! Not only that, all his injuries seem to be healing at a phenomenal rate. If this keeps up, then he will be out of here in no time."

A broad grin spread over his face, which was echoed by the smiles of relief and utter joy on the faces of all the Bennett's.

"I'm sorry to have to ask you," continued the doctor, "but we need to do a lot of checks on Paul, so could you all go outside and wait in the nurses' station so that we can proceed."

Julia nodded but before leaving, she pushed through the swathe of blue scrubs and gripped the hand of her husband, giving it a hard squeeze. Her husband's eyes flickered open and he gave a small smile. Smiling back, she gave another squeeze of his now warm hand and pushed her way through the sea of blue around her. She beckoned to her children and they followed her out, making their way, down the corridor to the nurses' station, where they met a large coloured nurse arguing with a fresh-faced young man. He was holding an iPad and insisting on seeing "the miracle man" as he called him. Julia heard the words "North Devon Journal" and guessed that he was a journalist. The nurse, however, stood her ground and minutes later, he reluctantly left.

After making sure that he had not secreted himself around the corner of the corridor, the nurse, who introduced herself as Cheryl, turned to the three Bennetts and invited them to sit down, at the same time asking if they would like a drink. Mrs Bennett looked up and said in jest, "A bottle of champagne would be nice but I'll settle for a coffee; white with no sugar."

The nurse turned to the children and they each said that a coffee would be nice but then Hugo decided that since his mother was not in a position to object, he changed his mind and asked for a Coke.

"Oo," Stephanie joined in. "May I have one too?" and she smiled at her brother.

Julia Bennett looked at them disapprovingly but then smiled, after all, they had something to celebrate and one Coke would not stop the world.

When the nurse had left to get the drinks, Hugo held out his hand in front of his mother and opened his fist. The gold medallion sparkled and still emitted a faint glow.

"Where did you find it, mum? And what was it doing in your handbag?" he asked, smiling broadly at being reunited with his favourite possession."

His mother was taken aback at the sight of the medallion but then remembered finding it under the carpet in the kitchen. She remembered tossing it into her handbag as she rushed out but then had forgotten all about it. Suddenly a thought crossed her mind as she cast it back to the confrontation she had had with the two witches. '*If that amulet was in my bag when I swung it at that young witch, then it must have been that which made the slash on her face, not the bag itself. It was trying to protect me.*'

"Mum! Mum!" Hugo was prodding her as she had become lost in her thoughts. She quickly roused herself and came out of her daydream.

"The medallion saved Dad. Didn't you see it? As soon as it touched Dad's chest, it brought him back to life. Don't you remember when I was talking to you about it ages ago, I said that one of its properties was that of healing and protecting its owner? I know Dad doesn't own it but since he is my dad, then my ownership must, sort of, count."

His mother's thoughts jumped back again to the bag incident but the return of Cheryl, the nurse, with their drinks stopped any further discussion. Hugo pulled from his pocket one of the tissues his mother had given him and, under the pretext of blowing his nose, wrapped the golden disk in it and carefully placed it in his trouser pocket, pushing it well down to ensure that he did not lose it a second time.

Peter Goodfellow's footsteps were heard striding down the corridor and into the nurses' station. The ear to ear smile on his face said it all and each of the Bennett family returned it.

"I don't know what happened there." he said, nodding his head towards the ward from where he had just come, "and I can only apologise for any distress it might have caused you all but we all thought that Paul had not survived. Even the monitors showed him to be dead. What went wrong and what happened to cause it all, I am really at a loss to explain. I can only apologise again."

Hugo was fighting to contain himself and tell the doctor about the medallion and it was that which had caused the miracle but a side look from his mother made him keep quiet.

"We have several more tests and treatments that we need to do for Paul and, as a precaution, we have sedated him to allow a faster recovery, so what I suggest to you all is, that you go home, for now, have something to eat and have a good nights' rest. The way everything is going, Paul should be able to leave in a few days."

Suddenly, Julia Bennett broke down into tears; the emotional rollercoaster of the last day catching up with her. Peter Goodfellow reached over and gave her a hug which was joined in by Hugo and Stephanie. The nurse handed the distraught woman a handful of tissues which she used to mop up her tears.

At last, Mrs Bennett returned to her usual calm self and, after thanking the doctor and the nurse profusely, she wrapped her arms around her children and escorted them out of the hospital and into the car park.

It took several minutes to remember where her car was parked, resulting from the state that she was in when she arrived, and it was a big shock when she came to pay the parking charges. She consoled herself that at least her husband was safe and well and that made it all worthwhile.

Surprisingly, everyone was quiet on the drive home, all still stunned and shocked by the events of the last twenty-four hours, as well as being physically and mentally exhausted.

Chapter 46

Further Investigations

"Excuse me." Allan Carlisle leaned over the reception counter at the central police station in Bideford, trying to attract the attention of a young officer who was seated at a desk, typing painfully slowly, on a computer keyboard.

"Yes, Sir. And what can I do for you?" the young policeman said, stretching in his chair and making a scraping noise as he pushed himself away from his desk. As he walked to the counter, he stretched again, rotating his head to ease the pressure on his neck.

"I'd like to see whoever is in charge of the Sue Redwell case. You know, the journalist who went missing a few months ago."

The officer nodded and returned to his computer, tapping the keyboard with one finger. After a few minutes and repeated sighs of frustration, he finally grinned and looked at his inquisitor.

"That would be Detective Inspector Hyde," he said, as his grin became broader. "I'll see if he is available if you would like?"

Allan nodded and the young officer picked up a phone sitting precariously close to the edge of his desk. After a few minutes, most of which he seemed to be talking to a woman he was trying to impress, he looked up and told him that sergeant Cummings, D.I. Hyde's deputy would be down shortly. He invited Allan to sit down in one of the chairs opposite the reception, which he did.

He did not have to wait long before sergeant Cummings entered and warmly shook his hand.

"It's Mr. um, Carlisle, Miss Redwell's boyfriend, isn't it? We met soon after your girlfriend went missing."

Allan nodded and followed the sergeant to his office, which he indicated with a nod of his head as he held the door to a corridor open. When comfortably seated, the police officer asked what he could do for him. The young man explained about his meeting with Sue in the street when she had dropped her shopping and the fact that she seemed not to recognise him. He was concerned that she might be suffering amnesia or something similar and was wondering if there had been any progress in finding her.

The sergeant admitted that, despite a few unconfirmed sightings, they had no firm idea of where she was, though, he did admit that she had been reported being seen, again unconfirmed, in the company of a young girl, who had also been notified as missing. He thanked the young man for coming in with the information and reassured him that they were following up on every lead and his sighting helps to confirm that she was still in the area.

After final pleasantries, the two shook hands and Allan turned and left but made a personal vow that, if the police could not find her then he would.

Returning to his car, he put another hour onto the parking ticket and then backtracked to the place where he had last seen his missing girlfriend. Looking around to take note of anywhere she might have gone, he turned and headed in the direction to where she had run, hoping that by chance, or some miracle, he would bump into her again. He assured himself that, if he was that lucky, then he was determined that she would not escape this time, even if it meant kidnapping her.

With the old Bideford bridge on his left, he walked past the library and stood beside a derelict hotel. Looking around him to see if he was being observed; he did not want to appear to be or accused of being a vandal, he checked out the rotting, graffiti-covered plywood doors securing the building, thinking that she may have sought refuge inside but although the doors were rotting, the locks appeared to be brand new and firmly shut. He then remembered that the police had mentioned that they had already gone over that particular building with a fine-toothed comb, as it had become a favourite haunt of *'the lower end of the social scale'* as the constable had told him. Shrugging and pulling his jacket around himself to ward off the fine drizzle that had started to fall, he continued out, toward the limits of the town. He eyed every building and alleyway for signs of where Sue might have run to, but there was no trace of her; or anyone for that matter. He realised that, beyond where he stood, there wasn't anywhere of any significance that she could use as a refuge. There were some old converted warehouses but businesses used these and people would notice if she lived there. The only place between where he was and the nearest residential estate, was the site of the ruins of the old judge's mansion. '*She can't be there.*' He thought to himself, '*it's just a pile of old bricks.*'

For the sake of having nothing better to do, he walked on until he came to the fence surrounding the ruins. He checked the lock on the gate, but this was well secured.

"Oy! You there! What d'you think you're doin'?"

A tall, well-built man, in his late fifties, or so Allan guessed, dressed in a security company uniform was approaching him. The young man's initial instinct was to turn and run but then he thought that if anyone were likely to have seen his girlfriend, then he would be that person.

Allan waited for the guard to come near and then explained who he was and what he was doing. The security officer shook his head, saying that, ever since the tunnel cave-in, the monitoring of the site had been a major priority. There was no way anyone could get past their company security monitoring system, which was on twenty-four hours a day.

"I'm sorry, Sir, but not even a mouse can get in here without us knowing about it," the guard, whose badge gave his name as Bert Adams, said confidently, "but I wish you the best of luck in finding your friend."

He gave Allan a polite salute and then headed back to the warmth of his little cabin, which the young man had not noticed before.

The drizzle was now turning into rain and the sky was rapidly becoming darker and more overcast as dusk approached. Allan pulled the collar of his jacket up to try to keep dry and was about to turn to go back, when he noticed, what appeared to be smoke, filtering through the ruins at the other end of the site. He looked around to see if he could see any signs of a fire which might be a source of the smoke but could see none. Suddenly the heavens opened and a strong wind sprang up and all traces of the smoke disappeared. Allan felt a trickle of rainwater run down the back of his collar and neck and decided that he would have to check this out, but not now. Pulling his jacket as tightly as he could around himself, he ran back to his car as fast as he could.

Sinking into its leather seat, he sat and panted, trying to catch his breath. '*I must do a bit more exercise,*' he thought to himself. Easing his sodden trousers from around his legs, he turned the ignition. With a roar from the car's wide-bore exhaust, he flicked the gear stick into first and the MG sped off, back to his flat.

Chapter 47

Putricia's plot

Morgana lay in her rough bed of old sacking on the far side of the room away from the fire, which had been blocked from view by Snatch's large body, lying prostrate in front of it. She could hear the gentle breathing of her sister and the courser rasping of Susanna some yards away. They had all retired, satiated, after the first proper meal that any of them had had for what seemed, ever.

Despite her tiredness, she could not stop wondering why her sister or Susanna had brewed the body-transmorphing potion and who had they planned on using it on. She and her sister now had perfect bodies and ran her hands over herself, enjoying the smoothness and suppleness of her skin. She shuddered at the thought of what it had been, up until her fortunate meeting with that inquisitive reporter woman. The only solution was that it must be for Susanna so that she could get rid of the disfigured shell she was at present inhabiting and exchange it for a new, younger and more active host. Finally, the excitement of the day caught up with her and sleep overcame her concerns.

The slow, rhythmical sound of her breathing was just what Putricia had been waiting for. Despite having to overcome her temptation to fall asleep, she had lain awake, waiting for this moment. Softly calling out Morgana's name, she watched and waited for a response. Her sister did not move.

Slowly throwing back her sacking blanket, she raised herself and went over to her dormant sibling. Lightly prodding her, she again waited for a response but when none came, she tip-toed over to the cauldron and picked up two small cups she had deliberately placed by its side.

Her movements alerted Snatch who was still lying at full length in front of the now dimming embers. He growled quietly at being disturbed but on seeing his mistress, turned his head and returned to whatever thoughts large cats dream about.

With the slightest sound of a bubbling gurgle, she filled the cups with the swirling golden solution from within the large pot and held them close to her chest as she carried them over to where Morgana was curled up.

She again called her sister's name to check that she was still asleep. Seeing no movement, she took a deep breath and put one of the cups to her lips. Looking around the room to check that she was not seen, she took one more deep breath and drank half its contents. Its bitter taste made her screw her face up in a grimace which surprised her. Then she realised that the last time she had tasted it, she had the distorted and insensitive body of her resurrected self, which lacked many of the finer senses that her new body had given her.

She shrugged off the cold shiver the liquid gave her as she swallowed the remaining potion and leant over her sister. Drop by drop she tilted the second cup, emptying its contents into the mouth of the sleeping figure in front of her.

Almost as a reflex action, her sister swallowed the liquid, periodically licking her lips. The cup was almost empty when she suddenly opened her eyes and was instantly awake and made to get up. Putricia pushed her down onto the bed and before she had time to react, forced the remaining liquid into her mouth.

Morgana began to panic and fight off her attacker, screaming and demanding to know what was happening.

"I want your body," came the gloating response from the grinning head that leaned over her.

"You want my bod...Why? I don't understand?"

"Why should you have all the fun with the beautiful adult body you've got, while I'm stuck with this silly child's form, so we're just going to do a swap."

"No! No! You can't! You mustn't! Please stop!"

Morgana looked up into the cruel, smiling face peering down at her. Its form already becoming blurred when another joined it. The distorted features of Susanna blinked in and out of focus as the potion started to take its effect.

"It wasn't finished. The potion wasn't finished," choked Morgana, coughing as she spoke.

"What do you mean, it wasn't finished?" Putricia's smile had gone and was replaced by a worried look. She shook her sister and repeated. "What do you mean, it wasn't finished?"

Morgana had been thinking about this as she tried to go to sleep earlier. When she had seen the golden potion in the cauldron, she had immediately recognised it and what it could do, but she had also noticed that the gold colour was the wrong shade and realised that one vital ingredient had been omitted. Since at that time she was not aware that it was to be used, she gave it no heed but now that she found herself as the recipient, the thoughts of what might result flashed through her mind.

"What do you mean, the potion isn't finished?" shouted both Putricia and Susanna in unison.

"You forgot to add the…"

"The what?" screamed the sister, who also was now becoming delirious.

Suddenly she slumped to the floor, stretching out her hand to contact that of her sister, for without physical contact the transfer would not work, but try as she may in her semi-conscious state, she could not reach her hand.

Without warning, Susanna gave Putricia a firm kick which projected the flailing witch the few inches she needed to make contact. As unconsciousness took over the two witches, Putricia stretched out and caught the limp fingers of her sister. A strange golden glow enveloped the two bodies, growing brighter and brighter. Susanna stepped back and shielded her eyes as the light became more intense. The two bodies writhed on the floor as if being tortured and Susanna had to look away as she began to fear what she and Putricia had been planning with each other while Morgana had been out shopping.

Slowly the two shapes on the floor began to change, the smaller becoming larger and vice-versa. The golden light suddenly changed, turning to a vivid red and then through the colours of the rainbow, fading, finally, to a deep shade of blue.

Susanna uncovered her eyes and looked at her two confederates lying prostrate on the floor in front of her; motionless, except for an occasional twitch. She felt a movement around her legs and, looking down, found Snatch nestling up to her, half in fear and half in curiosity.

The bodies lay for several minutes with no signs of movement, not even any breathing. Susanna was tempted to bend down and check to see if they, or just one was still alive but she refrained, as she had been instructed by Putricia that at no point was she to touch the bodies, as it would confuse the magic, leading to serious consequences. Ten minutes had now gone by and there were still no signs of life from either form lying on the floor.

Susanna could not contain her concern any longer and bent down to touch, what had been Putricia but now had been transformed into the size and form of Morgana. Immediately she contacted the body, a bolt of electricity shot up her arm and threw her backwards, causing her to trip and fall over Snatch who was cowering behind her. Immediately she knew that she had made a mistake, for the body began to writhe and twitch, finally becoming still again.

The old witch sat where she had fallen, not daring to move, hoping beyond hope that she had not caused a problem by disobeying her instructions not to touch the bodies before they recovered. Her worry was further exaggerated as the final words of Morgana bounced around in her head. '*The potion isn't finished!*'

The smaller of the two forms in front of her began to move; slight twitches at first, followed by longer stretching movements until, with a long yawn, the eyes flickered open. They gazed haphazardly around at first but finally came into focus on to Susanna, still sitting, open-legged, on the floor, with Snatch firmly trapped beneath them.

The person gave a faint smile and reached up and rubbed her eyes; however, the smile gave way to a look of horror as she moved her hands away and saw their size. A child's size.

She rubbed her eyes again, looking at the backs of her hands, the palms and fingers, her arms and finally her body. Shakily she turned and stood up. She felt her face, her body and looked down and saw the shortness of her legs.

"What have you done to me?" she screamed hysterically. She lurched around the room looking for a mirror or some reflective surface whereby she might see herself as a whole but none could be found as anything that might show Susanna her true distorted self, had been removed many years previously.

The screams and terror of this new smaller person were joined by a loud coughing from the other body still lying on the floor. Both witches fell silent as it began to writhe on the floor. Without warning, a shrill, ear-piercing scream came from its mouth and the eyes flicked open wide.

Its chest rose and fell rapidly as gulps of air flowed in and out of the mouth. Slowly the breathing became lighter and more regular as the form appeared to become more relaxed. The person, for Susanna was unsure of who was who, lay still for another few minutes, the breathing now settled to a normal depth and frequency. The eyes opened and closed several times until the hands moved and were used to give them a rub.

With a loud yawn, the body raised itself from the floor

and began to feel itself, but something was wrong. The person now standing before an open-mouthed Susanna and the small person next to her was unable to move her left arm. It tried and tried but it was evident that the limb was paralysed. There was an almighty scream as the transformation had been incomplete.

Susanna's heart began to pound as she realised that the limb that was paralysed was the one she had touched during the recovery.

"What have you done to me?" it screamed.

"What you mean is, what have you done to me?" screamed the smaller person. "This is your fault. You deserve everything you have because you deceived me. You're my younger sister, yet now, through your stupidity, we are both at a disadvantage."

Despite only having the use of one arm, the larger woman, who Susanna now confirmed was Putricia from the reference to the younger sister, launched herself at her smaller sibling, knocking her to the ground. A tangle of arms and legs ensued as the two fought on the floor. Snatch jumped and growled as the two tore at each other. It was only by Susanna forcing herself between the two that brought the bout to a standstill. Although the physical part of the fight had stopped, the shouting and bickering continued for several minutes until both were exhausted.

Moving to opposite ends of the room, each slumped onto the floor, rubbing their wounds and familiarising themselves with the sensations of their new bodies. Susanna tried to act as intermediary but, in the now smaller body of Emma Jones, Morgana pushed her away, knowing that she had been party to the plot from the beginning.

'Why, why, why, did she do such an underhand thing?' thought Morgana, rubbing her head, releasing handfuls of hair that had been pulled out during the struggle. She knew that her sister was dissatisfied having to live in a child's body, but didn't she realise that she would rapidly grow up into someone probably taller and stronger than she had been. How could she even contemplate such a deception, let alone carry it out?

Suddenly she remembered the potion that she had seen brewing was not complete and began to panic. She had always been better at potion-making than her sister, which was why she had noticed the mistake but she was not aware of what the lack of its final ingredient of thistledown extract would have on the overall effect of the mixture.

Ignoring the other two women, who were wrapped in each other's arms in the corner by the fire, she walked, somewhat falteringly, to the table on which the potion books lay open. Rapidly turning the thick curled pages, she desperately scanned the scripts to find any reference to *Extract of Thistledown*. At last, she found a page that briefly inferred that its power involved that of longevity and something to do with memory, the rest of the page was indecipherable. In the past, something had been spilt on the page, making the ink run into a dense grey sea of blurred symbols.

Closing the volume with a loud bang making the other two and Snatch look up, she decided that she could no longer trust her roommates and realised that it was time to leave and go out on her own. Her sojourns into the town when in the body of Sue Redwell had given her a taste for freedom and although she now appeared as a young girl, she was sure that she would be able to survive alone. Her experiences had also made her realise that, perhaps that wretched little boy's mother had been right and in their fight for revenge, she and the other two had become as guilty, if not worse, as the perpetrators of the crimes against her, her friends and family.

Morgana was about to start to gather together her few precious possessions when she became aware that she was still in the clothes she had been wearing before the transformation. Since these were of adult size, they almost fell off her as she moved. Ignoring the others, who were now considered enemies, she marched over to where Putricia had kept her clothes and started to grab whatever she could find. Putricia began to get up to stop her but Susanna pulled her back down as she realised what was happening.

Choosing the warmest of the garments available, Morgana changed into them and pushed the rest into the plastic bag that she had brought the shopping in from town. Without a word, she marched out of the room, down the tunnel, and out into a very uncertain future.

Chapter 48

Bird's Message

Bird had just started to eat the last slice of bread left in the bread bin when the front door to the Bennett's house flew open. He had been expecting them to return at some time and had prepared sympathetic speeches and expressions of how sorry he was about the fate of Mr Bennett. He had also considered what he was planning to do by way of revenge against the witches, so he was quite taken aback when they all came in with beaming smiles on their faces.

Before he had a chance to say anything, Hugo rushed up to him and gave him a hug which, despite his size, nearly threw him off his feet.

"He's alive! He's alive!" screamed Hugo. "The talisman saved him. It saved my Dad!"

Bird sprayed a mouthful of crumbs over Hugo, slightly winded by the onslaught. After regaining his balance and composure, he wrapped his wings either side of his small friend and asked him what he was talking about.

Mrs Bennett, seeing the presence of Bird, asked him if

he would like some tea and cake. Bird blushed, or at least changed colour, which was his equivalent. He declined the cake, for he knew that he had eaten the last one several hours ago, but accepted the offer of some tea. As she turned there was a faint buzzing from behind and Puchy flew up from where she had been sitting beside a bowl of roses.

"Oh, hello, Puchy." Julia Bennett smiled, "I'm sorry I didn't see you there. I suppose you would prefer a sugar lump wouldn't you."

Puchy nodded and fluttered her wings as best as she could; the matchstick still restricting her movements. Hugo's Mother turned and went into the kitchen while Stephanie ran up the stairs to her bedroom, muttering something about looking an absolute mess. Meanwhile, Hugo sat on the sofa with Bird and Puchy at his feet. He began to tell them the whole story of what had happened to his dad, and the miracle the talisman had brought about.

He had just reached the part where the talisman fell onto the chest of his father when the crest on Bird's head sprang up and changed colour from a deep purple to a bright red. Bird stood up and appeared to be listening to something.

"I am sorry, Hugo, but I have just had a call from Chipper to say that he is in trouble and needs my help."

Puchy gave a little squeak and fluttered onto Bird's shoulder as if trying to listen to the thoughts that he was receiving.

"I'm sorry but I must go. It sounds important," apologised Bird and, with a slight, pop, he and Puchy disappeared.

At that moment, Mrs Bennett had reappeared, carrying three cups of tea and a sugar lump on a saucer. She heard the pop and saw her guests disappear.

"Well I'm not surprised he disappeared," she said, looking a little annoyed. "Those two, or should I say, that large friend of yours, Hugo, has eaten everything in the house. I'll have to go out and do some shopping if we are to have anything to eat today. You and Stephanie behave yourselves while I'm away." She put the tray of cups of tea down onto the table, went into the kitchen to get a shopping bag and then, with a slam of the front door, she got into her car and drove off to the shops.

Hugo quickly drained one of the cups and sat back, digging into his pocket to find the amulet.

Carefully he unwrapped it from the tissues he had used to hide it in at the hospital and rolled and twisted it around in his fingers.

"Let me have a look at that thing," Stephanie demanded as she came into the room and saw what her brother was holding. At first, Hugo was reluctant to surrender his prized possession but after some moaning from his sister, handed it over. She too rolled it around in her hand. It was the first time she had held it and was surprised how warm and smooth it was; it even seemed to glow brighter as she held it.

"Do you think that it was this that saved Dad, or do you think that the machines at the hospital were just on the blink?" she asked Hugo.

"You saw what happened. What do you think?" he replied.

She looked at it one more time and then announced that she was going out to see Marty and tell him and his family the good news. Hugo reminded her that their mother had told them to stay in, but she ignored him and a minute later she had left, leaving Hugo alone.

Chapter 49

Bragnar's Good Luck

Chipper licked the tips of his bleeding fingers. He had been desperately clawing at the walls of the hollow log in which Bragnar, the goblin, had imprisoned him.

Earlier that day, Chipper's curiosity had got the better of him. He had commandeered an unsuspecting seagull and forced it to fly to Penzance in Cornwall, in the South West of England. He knew the remaining goblins that survived the fight with the gnomes at the Gnome Reserve and their subsequent infection with chickenpox, lived there. This disease, which they had contracted from Hugo's sister, Stephanie, had decimated those that had escaped the battle and the small gnome was both curious and concerned as to what had happened to them.

Chipper had mentioned to Oleg that he would have liked to know what had become of them but avoided telling her that he planned on visiting. The journey from the gnome reserve to the remote area above the cliffs near Penzance had been very bumpy and the seagull, which the small gnome had requisitioned, had taken objection to being hijacked. It squawked continually all the way there, especially when Chipper pushed his tiny pointy toes into the soft flesh under the bird's wings as he steered it into a landing.

The remaining goblins of his clan had ostracised Bragnar for leading such a wild and stupid attack on the Devon gnomes, though many of the leaders at that time, secretly admired him for having the audacity to try. However, the resulting decimation of the clan from the fighting and the disease that nearly destroyed them all had demanded a scapegoat, and he was it.

He had made his home in a badger set, about one hundred metres from the cliff edge and was sitting at the entrance, sharpening a small dagger. He used it for almost everything, from slicing his food to attacking his enemies, number one of which at this time was that stupid Bird and his human companion. If it weren't for their interference, then the battle would have been won in the goblins favour and he would now be considered a hero, as well as the undisputed leader. Instead, he was confined to living in this damp, boggy, insect-ridden badger's hole; rejected and despised by what remained of his clan.

He had heard the seagull screeching overhead long before he could see it. At first, he ignored the noise as it was the norm around that part of the cliffs where he had taken up residence but its persistence and unusual tone made him look up at it as it circled overhead. He was about to ignore it, as it rose and fell in the updraft from the cliff when he became aware that something was not right. The outline of the bird was wrong. He rubbed his eyes and looked more closely. It was then that he saw a small figure clinging to its back. He knew that the only creatures that travelled that way were gnomes. He put down his sharpening stone and gripped the blade. Without taking his eyes off his prey, he stood and stealthily tracked the incomers.

Chipper did not want to land too close to where he thought the goblin camp was and was unsure of what reception he would receive if he were observed. He forced his transport to drop him some distance from their village, where he felt it would be safe, unaware of the proximity of where their ex-leader was eyeing him.

The landing had been rough and the small gnome had grazed his knee in the fall from, what was a great height for someone so little; the back of the large gull. He was bending down, giving it a rub when there was a bang on his head and he fell to the ground, unconscious.

How long he had been out, he was unaware but regaining consciousness realised that he was no longer on the top of the cliff on which he had landed. Instead, he was surrounded by the rough feel and stench of rotting wood. As his head became clearer, he looked around only to realise that he was trapped inside an old tree trunk. All entrances and exits were blocked so that there was no way of escaping. The only light coming in was from an old knothole and above it, was what appeared to the small gnome, as a large green eye.

There was a loud bang on the side of the tree as Bragnar hit it with a large stone he had picked up.

"Wake up my nosey friend. So good of you to call. I suppose you would like some cake and some nectar, wouldn't you?"

Chipper was about to say that that would be nice when he realised that the eye above him was being sarcastic.

"Who are you and why have you imprisoned me?" screamed the little gnome, trying to sound as brave as possible but inwardly feeling very scared.

"Why? Don't you recognise me, you stupid creature? After all, you and your friends tried to kill me enough times." The eye peering through the hole blinked and then curled up as if the owner was grinning.

Bragnar. Chipper slumped down onto the soft, damp, rotting wood pulp that lined the floor of the log. A large woodlouse suddenly appeared and flexed its grey, tank-like body as it meandered up the inside of the trunk, its seven paired legs working in a wave-like rhythm as it passed close to where the gnome was seated. Of all the goblins he could have met, this one was his worst nightmare.

"What do you want with me?" he said a little shakily.

As soon as the goblin realised who he had captured, he could not believe his luck. He knew that this was a golden opportunity to get his revenge on those who had created the solitude and ignominy in which he now found himself.

At first, he just wanted to kill his prisoner, but then he thought that this would not get him his real prize; that infernal boy and his bird friend. For several hours he paced up and down next to the log. His captive had screamed at first but now lay silent realising that there was no escape. He went through all the permutations of what he could do. Finally, he kicked the log, and trying to sound as sympathetic as he could, put his mouth to the knothole and whispered, "Little gnome. Little gnome. You have landed in some very dangerous territory for one so small and I only put you in this log to keep you safe. You banged your head when you fell off that silly seagull and hurt yourself. If you could contact your bird friend, then he could come and take you home safely. How would you like that?"

Chipper looked at the large pair of lips moving above the knothole and thought about punching them but realised that this would probably make the goblin more hostile. The small gnome sat for a few moments and pondered his predicament. At present, he decided that he had no real options but if Bird was here, then he was much bigger and stronger than the goblin. He reassured himself that, between the two of them, they could defeat his captor, even if it meant a very stern telling off, not only from Bird but everyone else back in the reserve.

"Thank you for helping to save me Mr Goblin, if you wait a few minutes then I will send him a message." Sitting well away from the opening in the trunk, he looked around and then whispered, "Bird. Bird. Bird." He waited a few more minutes and then repeated his call.

Far away, back in the Bennett's house, Bird's comb on the top of his head tingled and changed colour.

Chapter 50

Allan's Mistake

Allan Carlisle waited until the security guard went back into his small hut after doing his rounds of the ruins site and then quickly eased his way between the security fence and the remaining intact wall of the ruin. Stealthily, he headed to where he was convinced he had seen smoke rising the day before. He swore as the sleeve of his camouflage-design anorak caught on a rusty piece of wire sticking out from the fence. The coat was brand new and he had purchased it especially, only a half-hour earlier so that he would not be noticed in his planned task. Fortunately, he saw the snag before any real damage was done. Keeping low and in the shadows, he inched his way between the wall and fence until he reached a point where it ended and he was able to move more freely into the site. Keeping a check on the guard's hut, he negotiated his way to where he thought he had seen the source of the smoke.

The area was littered with small holes and depressions, any of which could have been the vent for the smoke. He was on the point of giving up when he noticed an area where the nettles and brambles appeared to have been trampled, creating an indistinct path. Pulling his jacket tightly around his body, to stop it getting snagged again, he followed the trail and was delighted to see that it led to a small opening between two low walls.

He'd only eased himself into the opening by a few metres when he saw, what was a set of stairs going downwards. They were thick with moss and creeping ivy but a bare patch in the centre of each tread was clear and was showing signs of having been recently used. The way ahead was dark and so Allan dug into a pocket of his jacket and pulled out his car keys. Attached to the fob was a small torch that his firm gave out as freebies to potential customers. The light carried the logo of his company and its name and phone number. He pressed the small button on the side and a beam shot from the trinket; despite its small size, it was surprisingly powerful.

Keeping to the worn parts of the steps, partly to prevent any noise from the crunching of the vegetation and also to lessen the risk of slipping on the slimy surface, he cautiously made his way down the steps, holding onto the green, algae-covered wall for support. The end of the flight came sooner than he expected. Ahead lay the gaping blackness, of what appeared once to have been a corridor. The walls still had bits of plaster attached to them, some parts with signs of paint reflecting as he flashed the light in his hand around them and into the darkness ahead.

Again, the floor ahead showed a track where something, or somebody, had walked. Slowly, with all senses on high alert, he moved forward, scanning the floor and walls with the small torch. Progress was slow as he checked every nook and cranny for anything that might give him a clue if he was on the right track of finding his girlfriend.

Suddenly, he became aware of a faint, sweetish smell, as if someone had been cooking, and sensed that he must be getting near to where, he hoped she might be, or at least where she had been. Ahead there was a glimmer of light and his heart began to thump inside his chest. Moving forward a little faster, encouraged by the illumination, he came to the entrance of a large room. He doused the torch and looked around the grim space. Its size and layout suggested that at one time it had been a decorated wine cellar but now most of the paint had peeled from the walls, yet it was still remarkably tidy and had recently been cleaned. There was a glow of a fire in the far corner, and as his eyes became accustomed to the dim light, he could see the outline of a figure.

The person was stirring something in the large pot hanging over the fire and it was from this that the sweet smell he had noticed was drifting. The figure turned sideways to study a large book by its side and at once Allan saw that it was his girlfriend, Sue.

He called out her name and she spun round in shock. He rushed across the room towards her. She jumped up with a small scream and started to back away. He called her name again as he approached until he was within a metre of her. He could tell by the look on her face that she was shocked to see him but the blankness of her expression made him realise that she did not recognise him.

"It's me, Allan," he said as sympathetically as possible, approaching her and putting his hands on her shoulders. She tried to retreat further but her back was against the wall.

There was a slight movement behind him and he started to turn to see who or what it was when something very heavy fell onto his head and the last thing he could remember was a sort of high-pitched scream followed by blackness.

Chapter 51

Emma's Return

Hugo was at a loss of what to do, now that everyone had left. He went into the kitchen, only to find that his mother had been right and every cupboard was devoid of anything edible. Bird had made sure of that. The only thing he found was a half-full bottle of orange squash, so he put some into a tumbler and walked back into the lounge. He was about to sit down when there was a ring of the front doorbell. Still holding his glass, he went to see who it was. Through the rippled glass of the door, he could see that it was a person about his height and thought it might be one of his friends from school come to see how everything was. As the door swung open, the glass dropped from his hand and he stood paralysed to the spot.

Before him stood the figure of Emma, who he knew, in reality, to be Putricia, the witch. It took him several moments to recover any form of movement, during which time the girl stood there, also seemingly paralysed.

"May I come in?" the person eventually said, which broke the rigour that had affected Hugo.

His first reaction was to slam the door in her face and run but as he was about to do so, she said pleadingly,

"Please let me come in. I am not who you think I am and I promise, I am not here to hurt you."

Hugo partially closed the door, ready to give it final slam in case he needed to, and gazed fixedly at the figure standing before it.

"Please, Hugo, I think that's what you are called, but, I am… Morgana. I have come to offer you my help."

You're not Morgana. You're Putricia and I don't believe you. Go away, or I will call my mum."

"She's not here. I saw her leave. That's why I need to speak to you alone before she gets back," the girl said insistently. "Please! You have to let me in to talk to you. You are my only hope and the only hope of your friend whose body I possess."

Hugo was torn between fear and curiosity. He peeped again at the figure before him and then felt that, if there was a struggle, then she was only just a little bigger than him and he would probably be able to hold his own if it came to a fight. Suddenly he felt a warm sensation in his trouser pocket and put his hand into it. His fingers made contact with the source. His courage suddenly increased as he fingered the talisman. His fingertips danced over the metal and it seemed to make him feel invincible.

Stretching himself to his full height, he pulled open the door and indicated for his guest to enter.

She came in very suspiciously, trying to avoid the broken glass on the floor and looking around into every corner. Hugo showed her into the lounge and told her to sit down. Remembering his manners and, forgetting who he was talking to, asked if she wanted a drink. The girl nodded and Hugo backed out of the room, into the kitchen, where he prepared two tumblers of squash. As he filled the glasses from the tap, he realised how stupid he had been, leaving Putricia, or whoever she called herself these days, alone in his house and rushed back into the lounge, spilling much of the drinks onto the floor. He needn't have worried for his visitor was lying face down on the settee crying. As he re-entered the room, she sat up and tried to appear as if she was not distressed but her tear-streaked cheeks made no doubt of her state of mind.

Nervously, Hugo handed her one of the glasses but did not sit down, just in case he needed to make a fast getaway. She tentatively took a sip of her drink and then, realising that it was tasty, she almost drained the rest. Putting down the glass, she looked sheepishly at Hugo and explaining how his father's words at the battle with the gnomes, describing the actions of she and her sister were worse than the crimes committed on them, had been playing on her mind and she had realised that he was right.

Tearfully, she went on to explain about his father's *accident* and how she had tried to dissuade her sister and Susanna not to go any further with their vendetta.

There was a noise from the front door of the lock being turned and Mrs Bennett came in from her shopping trip. She screamed Hugo's name with annoyance as she almost slipped on the broken glass of the tumbler and the wet splodges from the spilt drink. Hugo's visitor sprang up and raced behind the settee on which she had been sitting. Hugo also jumped up and ran out to meet his parent.

She was starting to admonish him, pointing at the glass on the floor, explaining that someone could have been seriously injured on it when Hugo managed to tell her they had a guest. His mother stopped her ranting and looked questioningly at her son.

"P... please don't be angry mum but I think that you had better prepare yourself for a shock," Hugo whispered, trying not to let the person in the lounge hear what he was saying.

His mother put down the shopping bags she was still holding, subconsciously smoothed her hair and looked quizzically at her son. Hugo beckoned her into the lounge and stood back as she entered the room.

The scream she emitted would have woken the dead. She automatically backed out of the room and the centre of her attention cowered behind the settee.

"It's not what, I mean who, you think," shouted Hugo, trying to calm his mother down.

She suddenly ran into the kitchen, almost slipping on the drink that Hugo had spilt in there, and grabbed the first make-do weapon she could find, a sweeping brush. Holding it like a staff, she rushed back into the lounge and stood by the door, like a lioness protecting her cubs and pushing Hugo behind her.

"Get out of my house!" she bellowed. Her adversary fell on all fours, with her arms over her head, behind the refuge of the sofa. Mrs Bennett started to move forwards, now brandishing her weapon like a sword.

Hugo pushed past her and stood between the two combatants.

"Mum! Stop! You don't understand! Putricia, or

Morgana, I'm not sure which, has come to help us. Honest. Just listen to what she has to say."

Hugo tried to sound as calming as he knew how but all the time he was gripping the talisman in his pocket... just in case.

His mother stopped shouting and appeared to calm down a little but still held the broom outstretched in front of her. The intruder slowly uncurled from behind the furniture and timidly looked over the top at her attacker. Hugo straightened himself up and suggested that they all sit down and explain what was going on. His mother held her ground but after much coaxing managed to persuade the girl to come and sit on the sofa instead of hiding behind it. Slowly and hesitantly, she began to tell the whole story of her original life as a healer and execution; her years as a living corpse and subsequent resurrection. She explained her commitment to the curse which she and her fellow victims vowed, right through to where she had stood in front of the Bennett's at the gnome reserve. It was then that Mr Bennett had spoken of how they were now guiltier criminals than those on which the curse had originally been laid. His words had made her rethink her life, and she had realised that what they were trying to do was wrong. She went on to explain that she had tried to convince her sister and Susanna.

"Wait a minute. You mentioned her before, but who is this *Susanna* person?" asked Hugo.

"Susanna... Susanna Edwards; she was one of the original three witches hanged at Exeter. She was the mother of Mary... Mary Edwards. I think that you knew her as Kadavera."

Hugo stepped back. He had very wretched memories of

her and became concerned that the person sitting in front of him was out to get revenge, for him causing her death.

"You mean that she is still alive, even after all this time?"

"Yes." came back the reply. "Of the three originally hanged for witchcraft, she was the only one who was genuinely a witch. It was because of her and our cousin Stephen, who is now dead, that Mary, Jane... Jane Trembles, my sister and myself Anne Trembles, that we survived and subsequently brought back to life. It was her that caused the roof to fall onto those men in the tunnel."

Hugo felt like a bolt had hit him and his mother stood up straight and gripped her broom even more tightly. She was about to say something when the girl continued.

"Much of Susanna's power came from the amulet of Excalibur and this is why she is desperate to get it back, as without it she will not be able to exist for much longer unless she can find another body to inhabit."

"What do you mean...*inhabit*?" questioned Hugo's mother, who had lowered the broom as she became more and more engrossed in the story being told.

The girl looked nervously at herself and then, with a hint of embarrassment, explained how, by using a special potion, they were able to take over the body of another person. Then, tearfully, she went on to tell about her taking over the body of the woman who they knew as Sue.

"Sue Redwell," interjected Hugo. "The news reporter."

"Yes, that's right," came the reply. "I never knew her last name because the potion wipes the memory of the person taken over and I only knew my new body's name when I was recognised by a young man when I was out shopping."

She then continued to explain how her sister, Jane; or

as they knew her, Putricia, had been jealous of the young, adult body she, Anne, had and the child's body that she had acquired. Spurred on by Susanna, Jane gave her some of the transformation potion which she had made and had swapped bodies. This change had resulted in Anne now appearing as Emma and Jane becoming Sue Redwell.

Other than Hugo's small outburst, the two Bennett's had stood spellbound. Mrs Bennett had lowered the broom entirely and was now perched on the side of one of the armchairs.

There was a long silence as she finished before Hugo asked, "So, to be sure. Who exactly are you and what do we call you? Morgana? Emma? What!"

"I am Anne…Anne Trembles, who you knew as Morgana. I do not know the name of the young girl whose body I inhabit, though I did find it familiar when you mentioned it. I would prefer it if you call me Anne. The name Morgana was given to me by Susanna, to avoid anyone suspecting who I actually was. I have never liked it."

"But what has happened to the real Sue Redwell and our friend Emma? Are they dead?"

"No, they aren't dead…exactly. They are still in their bodies but our will keeps them from surfacing, though occasionally some of their being escapes and we remember facts and occasions that happened in their life."

"But what happens to them if you die?" questioned Hugo further.

"I am not quite sure," admitted the girl, "but if our spirit is lost, then the subdued body should come back."

"So let me make this clear," Julia Bennett said softly. "If

we want to get our Emma back..." she paused, "...we have to kill you."

The witch suddenly lost all colour in her face and looked shocked. After several minutes of looking at Hugo and his mother, in turn, she covered her face and began to cry, nodding her head and whispering, "Yes."

Chapter 52

Chipper's Mistake

Bird was not *too* concerned when he received the call from Chipper. That young gnome was always getting himself into scrapes and Bird thought this was just another one, though he did wonder why his young friend was calling from Cornwall. As he circled the spot where the call came from, he noticed that no one was around. As he landed, he dropped his invisibility. He had eaten so much at the Bennett's house that he felt somewhat lethargic and staying invisible took so much energy. Softly calling Chipper's name, he was pleased to get a response from what appeared to be an old, rotting log. Walking over to it, he banged on the flaking bark. A small voice came from a small knothole halfway along. He put his eye to the hole and, in the gloom of the inside, saw his little friend. Chipper saw Bird's eye and part of his beak through the hole and started to scream a warning but it was too late. A strong, thick net appeared from nowhere and completely engulfed the would-be rescuer. Bird fought and struggled, but the more he did so, the more he became entangled in the mesh, until realising that escape was useless and he collapsed onto the floor, his head resting on the log.

"Bird! Bird! Are you alright? I'm sorry. I tried to warn you." Chipper fell back onto the spongy, rotting fibres that encased him and gazed forlornly at the hole in the trunk, praying that the happy face of his friend would appear.

"Oh! How stupid could I have been to even think about trusting that devious goblin? Now, look at what I've done. I've got Bird and me into trouble." Chipper started to cry.

Immediately there was a loud bang on the side of the log and Bragnar shouted for him to keep quiet. The goblin walked around his prey, gloating and kicking Bird in his belly as he lay entangled in the net.

"Well! Well! Well!" he taunted. I knew you were stupid but I didn't think that you were that much of an idiot. I am very disappointed. I was expecting a much more formidable foe. You made it so easy. Now I have you two, all I need is that obnoxious little boy but at least I have the bait."

Carefully lifting the edges of the net, the goblin took a rope, and despite his captive's renewed protestations, he started to tie his legs, followed by wrapping the cord around his wings and finally his neck. When he felt sure that his prize was secure, he untangled the net and lifted it off the trust-up body in front of him with a flourish.

Bird gave a wriggle but rapidly realised that this goblin was well trained and escape was not an option...at least, not yet.

"Call that boy and tell him to come here...alone," Bragnar shouted. Bird stayed silent.

"Did you hear what I said!" screamed the goblin pushing and kicking his captive.

Again there was no reply.

"If you don't call him then I'll… I'll kill your little friend."

Bird still said nothing, so Bragnar kicked away the stone that he had used to block off the entrance to the log and reached inside, grabbing the small gnome by the leg. He pulled him out and stood in front of Bird with Chipper dangling upside down from his outstretched arm.

From the belt around his waist, he drew the long curved knife he had previously been sharpening and pointed at the wriggling creature before him. Bird winked at his minute friend and, taking a deep breath, he disappeared.

The goblin became suddenly confused and shocked. All of the work he had undertaken to capture his foe and yet he had disappeared before his eyes. He twisted around, trying to see where he had gone, and without realising, eased his grip on the small bundle he was holding. Chipper did not need a second chance. Bending upwards, he gripped his own feet and plunged his sharp little teeth into the hand, holding him. The sudden bolt of pain made Bragnar instinctively open his hand and release its contents.

Chipper fell to earth with a bump, but in a split second, he jumped up and ran to what he thought was a safe distance from his captor. Turning, he shouted at the goblin, trying to taunt him so that he would move away from where Bird had disappeared. Sure enough, the goblin started to give chase. Although Chipper was much smaller than his adversary, he was very much fitter and was easily able to maintain the distance between himself and his chaser.

This distraction was what Bird had hoped would happen and had counted on the stupidity of the goblin in his plan. When he saw that Bragnar was almost out of sight, he repeatedly went in and out of invisibility. Slowly he began to get smaller and the threads holding his legs and wings began to loosen. Finally, with a wiggle and a stretch, the ropes fell away.

Bird looked around to see where his friend had gone. In the distance, he could hear the screams and curses of the goblin as he continued to pursue his foe. In no time, Bird's long strides allowed him to join the fray. The sight of his captive, free and now attacking him, made the goblin jump around in furious anger.

Bragnar seemed confused as to who to attack. He held his knife out in front of him and slashed at whoever he thought nearest. First, it was Bird, and then Chipper would run in front to divert the goblin. Without realising, the battleground edged closer and closer to the cliff edge.

Bird was backing away from Bragnar when he tripped over a small gorse bush and fell. The goblin seized his chance. With an almighty bound he flew into the air and landed on the outstretched wing of Bird. In one flowing movement, the attacker rolled and plunged the dagger into the nearest piece of soft flesh he encountered. Unfortunately, he was unable to contain the momentum of his jump and as he rolled away, the edge of the cliff became perilously close. With a scream of success of landing a blow, he threw his arms in the air. The dry, sandy earth beneath him started to give way and he began a slow slide to the precipice of the cliff edge. He grabbed at any vegetation he could touch to slow his descent but inch by inch the cliff drop-off became closer. With a pitiful scream and a scrambling of limbs, the goblin disappeared from view.

Chipper ran over to where he had seen Bragnar fall, and being careful not to go the same way, peered over the edge. There was no sign of the goblin but the undercut of the cliff did not allow him to see the base of the cliff. He stretched out as far as he dare, to look where the goblin had landed but eventually he decided that it was obvious that no one could survive a fall from that height and moved away from the edge.

The small gnome gave a cheer and looked back at Bird to share the feeling of victory but when he turned, His fellow adversary was lying, immobile, stretched out on his back, some metres away.

Chipper ran over to his friend, still exhilarated with the victory but as he approached, he could see a large stain developing under, his still outstretched, wing.

"Bird! Bird!" screamed the gnome. "What happened? Are you alright? Speak to me!"

Painfully Bird turned and looked at the young gnome.

"I'm sorry Chipper but Bragnar caught me with his knife and I think that he has seriously injured me."

Chipper began to cry but Bird asked him to stop and to help him close his wings as the injured one would not move. With this, Bird told the gnome to hang onto his neck and he would try to get them back to where they might get help.

"Where can we go?" pleaded Chipper, now realising that it was his fault that they were in the predicament in which they found themselves.

"We must get back to Hugo's house as fast as we can, while I still have some strength left. He has a doctor friend who may be able to help me."

Chipper nodded and threw his arms around his friend's neck.

With great effort, Bird stood up, and summoning what reserves of strength he could muster, made himself invisible and started the journey back to Westward Ho!

Chapter 53

Susanna's New Body

The pain and pounding in his head brought Allan Carlisle back into consciousness. He tried to lift his hand to rub his head but another pain, in his wrists, brought him further out of his foggy haze. He attempted to move his legs but found even this was impossible. As his head cleared, he was able to open his eyes. In the dim light of a fire in the distance and a single candle, flickering and sputtering on a table in the middle of the room in which he found himself, he could see very little. Unconsciously he gave a muted groan and saw a pair of dirt-encrusted legs walk slowly towards him. He tried to turn his head to see the feet's owner but the pain in his head as he attempted any movement, stopped him.

"Where am I, and who are you?" he managed to mutter, somewhat incoherently.

Another pair of feet joined the first but these were wearing trainers, albeit dirty as well.

This set of feet pushed him so that he rolled over onto his back. As he looked up, he had to close his eyes as the rolling sent shivers of pain throughout his head and body. At last, as it subsided, he opened his eyes.

Susanna looked down at him, her face and head uncovered, so that her distorted features, surmounted by a hideous, almost toothless grin filled his vision.

He closed his eyes and gave an involuntary scream as the sight came into focus. The face let out a hoarse laugh, which was repeated by another standing just behind. Opening his eyes again, he searched the dim light for the source of this second laugh.

"Sue! Sue! Is that you? What's going on? Help me. Please."

The second face grinned and gave a familiar laugh.

"What's going on?" he repeated.

"Welcome my friend," the face replied. "We are delighted to see you, despite not being invited, but since you're here, we would like you to help us with... a little experiment."

Both faces gave a hideous cackle.

Allan twisted and struggled to free himself and get away but the pain of each exertion wracked his head and he rapidly realised that his bonds had no sign of giving; in fact, the more he moved, the tighter they seemed to become.

"Sue! Sue! What are you doing? It's me, Allan... your boyfriend. Let me go."

The name of Allan seemed to ring a bell in Putricia's mind, making her hesitate but she shrugged the memory off and knelt on the floor next to their prisoner.

Roughly she took his head, twisted it upright and wedged a piece of firewood between his teeth. The man fought to spit it out but she held it firmly and wrenched it back even further making the corners of his mouth split and bleed.

Susanna hobbled slowly over to the cauldron hanging above the glowing fire and dipped into it a small earthenware cup which she had picked up from the table. An iridescent, golden liquid dribbled from its brim and spilt onto the floor.

Returning to the hapless victim on the floor, she dripped the liquid, slowly, from the cup into his gaping mouth. He wretched and coughed as it stung and burned his mouth. Fighting not to swallow, drop by drop it seeped into his throat so that he found it impossible to breathe. With a gulp, he had no choice and began to swallow the mixture, gasping between each mouthful.

Slowly the bitter taste and burning sensation began to subside and he began to feel light-headed and started to relax.

The two women smiled at each other as the potion began to take effect but then became serious. Susanna looked at the cup still in her hand and with a final look at Putricia, lifted it to her lips and drained its remaining contents. She dropped it on the floor, shattering it. Wiping her mouth with one hand, she knelt down and then lay down beside the trussed-up body. Putricia pulled a large knife from the table and severed the ropes holding the body and freed its hands and arms. Susanna reached out and gripped one of Allan's hands, her small bony palms, almost dwarfed by the fleshy, muscular digits of the adjacent body.

Her eyes closed and her body began to twitch and writhe. As the minutes ticked by, Putricia watched in awe as the body of her friend slowly diminished in size. The rough shift dress she wore slowly becoming no more than a limp rag.

Hours passed and Putricia became worried that the transformation process had not worked and Susanna had died. She remembered from her own experience how fatal it would be to touch the subject before the transformation was complete and she subconsciously looked at her own, still paralysed arm resulting from her body swap.

The candle on the table finally ran out of wax and the flame guttered and died. The sudden loss of light brought Putricia to her senses and realised that she had fallen asleep but for how long she did not know. Going across to a small cupboard, she took out another candle and lit it from the fire. Snatch was curled up in front of it, totally unconcerned as to what had been happening. He growled as she pushed him to one side to get at the only part of the fire that was still alight. As the candle slowly increased its intensity, she went over to a stack of wood and withdrew some thin twigs and two thick logs. She threw the twigs and wood onto the embers, sending a plume of sparks into the air. As she watched them rise and then disappear, a groan came from the other side of the room. Snatch, again raised his head but then resumed his sleeping posture.

Putricia raced over to the form lying on the floor, unsure of what to do or what to expect. Slowly the body became reanimated and finally sat up. Putricia was about to speak to it but was not sure who it was. To be safe, she walked back to the wood store and picked up a large branch which could be used as a club if needed.

The body before her looked around and finally at her.

She raised the stick but then the body spoke in a deep, manly voice.

"That won't be necessary, my friend. Give me a mirror."

Putricia smiled and dropped the stick. She strode over to the cupboard and from deep within it, pulled out a fragment of a broken mirror. She brushed its surface with her hand and passed the smeary shard to the person at her feet.

The figure twisted and turned her face and body to see itself in the reflection. For several minutes it just looked, admiring what it saw. Then with a deep male laugh, which Putricia had not expected, the man said.

"Well, my dear friend, how do I look? Am I not handsome? Now that I am a man, think of all the things I can do instead of being trapped in that hideous female form."

Putricia grinned but felt a little afraid, as she was still trapped as a female, albeit an adult female, instead of that weak girl's body she had before.

The man raised himself from the floor, pulling away the remaining ropes that had tied his alter ego, and strutted around the room still holding the mirror and gazing at himself as he moved.

"I'm hungry," he announced. Get me something to eat."

Putricia felt offended at the tone of the command but went over to the cupboard and pulled out everything that was left in there. Snatch lifted his head and sniffed as he sensed the smell of food and waited impatiently for any scraps to fall his way, which they never did.

With a wipe of his hand across his mouth, the man sat back, looked at his companion and said, "Well, my friend, I think that all went much better than we had hoped. Now

I think that it's time to fulfil our vow and finish what we started to do."

Putricia smiled.

Chapter 54

Mr Bennett's Return

"Daddy's home."

A loud cry rang out from Stephanie's room, from where she had been looking out of the window and had seen a large, white Jaguar car, which she recognised as belonging to their doctor friend, Peter Goodfellow.

She hurtled down the stairs, skidding to a halt just before Hugo had made it and they fought to open the door. Throwing it open, they both ran outside and saw the doctor helping their father out of the back seat. As soon as he saw them, he threw his arms open and bent down, giving them each a massive hug as they rushed into his arms. His wife appeared at the door, brushing down her dress and smoothing her hair. Both smiled and he stood up. She ran up to him, hugging and kissing him. Hugo and Stephanie looked at each other in embarrassment.

The car door slammed shut and Mrs Bennett broke away from her husband's embrace and went over to the doctor, hugging and kissing him as well, which made

Hugo feel even more nervous than he had been previously. Eventually, they all moved back into the house and returned to the lounge. Mr Bennett suddenly stood still, fixated at the door. Standing before him, holding tightly onto the edge of the settee, was Putricia.

Mrs Bennett pushed passed him and ordered the men to sit down. Doctor Goodfellow did so without further ado but Mr Bennett stood still at the doorway.

"What is *she* doing here?" he demanded, glaring at his wife.

The doctor made to get up, thinking that he had suddenly interrupted a family argument.

"Please sit down, Darling," Julia Bennett said in a consolatory tone to her husband, putting herself between him and the terrified young girl still gripping the settee. "And you as well Peter. I will explain and I think that you need to know the truth."

"Steph, be an angel, will you go and make us some tea and bring those cakes that I made from in the kitchen. You help her as well, Hugo." She gave a nod of her head to them both, which they interpreted as, get out. The message was received and both of them left the room.

"Close the door on your way out, please."

Hugo looked at his sister, each wishing that they could hear what was said.

The two children had both eaten a cake and had a mug of orange squash before they considered that it would be acceptable to return to the lounge with the tea and remaining cakes.

The tension, evident in the room when they left, had subsided but it was still strangely quiet.

Anne, as they now called Morgana, was sitting curled up in the corner of the settee looking much less terrified but still uncomfortable.

Mrs Bennett was in mid-pour of the tea when there was a gentle tapping at the French- windows.

Getting up and pulling the curtain back, she initially could not see anything and was about to turn back when there was another frantic tapping at the bottom of the door. Looking down, she saw Chipper, hammering for all he was worth on the glass.

Pulling the doors open, she was about to ask the gnome what was the matter when the little creature ran inside and shouted as loud as it could.

"Quick! Please come! Bird's been hurt!"

Julia Bennett looked in the direction of where Chipper was pointing and saw a large, greenish mound in the middle of the back lawn. At first, it was unrecognisable, but as she stared at the fluttering feathers, she suddenly yelled.

"It's Bird! Look!"

Everyone turned and gazed out of the window.

"Quick!" screamed Chipper. He's been hurt!"

Hugo could not understand why the bundle outside appeared to be green. It certainly wasn't Bird's normal multicolour appearance but as he led the rush outside, he rapidly realised that the colour was because his friend was covered in blood, which, in Bird's case, happened to be green.

Everyone stood around the injured animal and Hugo knelt and cupped his friend's head in his arms.

"Do something!" he pleaded, looking at everyone standing around.

Dr Goodfellow was in awe at the creature lying before him. He had only just learned of the existence of the animal and, in truth, he was a little sceptical of what he had been told but here it was, before his eyes.

Everyone focused on him, silently suggesting that he take charge. Taking the unspoken request, he moved forward and, clearing his throat, asked everyone to move back to give him space. Going down on one knee, he carefully lifted the wing that was the source of the injury. Bird gave a faint groan and a jet of green blood shot out.

"Quickly! Fetch me some towels and, Julia, go into my car and get my bag. I think one of its arteries has been severed and it's lost a lot of blood." 'If that's what you call it.' He said under his breath.

He dug into his pocket and pulled out his car keys which he threw to Mrs Bennett. She and Stephanie ran back into the house, with Stephanie returning moments later carrying all the tea towels from the kitchen. Peter Goodfellow grabbed them and pushed them over the wound, trying to staunch the bleeding. Julia Bennett returned moments later, thrusting his bag at the doctor. Hugo continued to hold Bird's head and stroke the crest on its top, which was now a dull grey instead of its usual bright purple.

The doctor opened his bag and drew out a multitude of dressings and bandages, which he applied as best as he thought. Bird's groaning was becoming weaker with each application.

Finally, with a groan from the doctor this time, he stood up and said quietly,

"Well, that's the best I can do. I'm not a vet but I don't

think even the best vet in the world could do much better with such an unusual creature.

"Is he going to be alright?" screamed Chipper, who was dancing between the legs of all the humans, trying to get a better view of his friend.

"I don't know," replied the doctor, slowly shaking his head. "I think that he has lost a great deal of blood and his chances are marginal. We need another of those miracles that we had with you Paul if he is to survive."

The mention of *miracles* made Hugo jump up and shout. "I've got it!"

Everyone turned and looked at him. He fumbled around in his pocket and pulled out the medallion.

Morgana saw the object and suddenly felt a surge of desire for the treasure, which she and the other witches had been searching for, for centuries. She fought to stop herself rushing forwards and snatching the relic as it glistened in Hugo's outstretched palm but before she could move, the boy was back on his knees forcing the object under his friend's wing so that it made contact with bare flesh. Everyone waited...

Seconds passed, which seemed like hours but there was no glow or blinding flash as it did when he had done the same to his father. Hugo moved the amulet to see if it needed to be in better contact but, other than making Bird groan painfully; there was no effect.

"What's happening?" he cried. "Come on. It worked on dad, why won't it work on Bird?"

His father stepped forward and kneeling beside his son, cradled him and suggested that Bird was not human. The talisman was designed to protect men, not animals.

Hugo looked forlornly at his father, almost pleading for him to do something but all he could do was to shake his head slowly.

Hugo started to cry, which, in turn, made Stephanie begin as well.

Other than the sniffing of the two children, everyone stood, looking at the dying animal in front of them.

"Please don't die," sobbed Chipper. "I'm sorry. It's all my fault. I didn't mean to get you into trouble." He fell on the floor, face to the ground, hands over his head; his body heaving from crying.

Chapter 55

Walk in Daylight

Dusk had just fallen when, hand in hand, Susanna and Putricia emerged from the tunnel of the ruins. Susanna moved tentatively, still unsure if she could exist in daylight. Gingerly she manoeuvered her new body outside the blackness of the tunnel, expecting severe pain and ultimate death but there was none. Slowly realising that the curse of being confined to darkness had been lifted, she stretched and looked up into the still light sky, albeit becoming darker. The two witches looked at each other and grinned. Hesitatingly, they went forward and started to walk along the faint path leading from their home.

"Hey you two!" a voice rang out and they saw a man in a uniform striding towards them. "What you doin' in there? Don't you know this is private property?" He walked quickly towards them, speaking into a walkie-talkie as he approached. He was about five metres away when he recognised the man he had stopped the day before.

"Oh! It's you again. Look, I told you yesterday that this whole site is out of bounds to the public. If I catch you messing around anywhere near here in the future, then I'll call the police and have you arrested for trespassing. Do you understand?"

The two looked at each other, confused but angry at the encounter. Without answering the guard, they walked in the direction he was pointing his arm. They eased themselves around the security fence gate which the guard had left ajar and out into the town. The dwindling crowd of shoppers and office workers swerved around them as they all headed home after a day at work.

They melted into the crowd and the guard returned to his office looking puzzled. He rummaged through the pile of papers on a shelf and after a minute, pulled out a creased up sheet. He looked at the picture of the face printed on the page and then picked up his mobile phone.

"Hello. This is Bert Adams. I am the security guard working at the old judge's house ruins. I think that I have just seen that young woman who was reported missing some time ago, you know, that reporter girl. She was with a young man and they were messing about in the ruins. I thought that you might like to know."

"That's very thoughtful to let us know," came the reply. "We'll send someone over to you as soon as possible and you can tell them what you saw." After repeating his name and giving his exact location, he hung up the phone and sat down, feeling very smug with himself and waited for the police to visit him.

In the town, Susanna and Putricia looked like any average couple and were unnoticed by anyone, which surprised Susanna as she still thought herself as the deformed creature, whose memory she had left in the ruins. As they passed the shop windows, their reflections beamed back at them. Each lifted their heads proudly as they gazed at their images, that of a young couple, satisfied with what they saw.

Susanna gawped in awe at the multitude of goods on sale in the windows as they walked by, envious of all she surveyed and longing to have many of the items displayed. For centuries she had been confined in that abysmal room, only daring to venture out on the darkest nights well away from anywhere or anyone that would challenge her. The scraps she had survived on were no more than discarded rubbish in this affluent society.

"We need to get some food," she whispered to Putricia, still shocked at the deep tones of her, new male, voice. "What did Morgana use to buy the food she brought back?"

"Her companion looked at her and remembered her sister showing her a small card and mentioning something about a 'Hole in the wall' but look as they may, neither person could see a hole in any wall that gave out money.

"See if that man had anything with him," said Putricia, pointing to the pockets in the clothes that Susanna now wore. The witch plunged her hands into all the pockets. In one was a small bunch of keys, that had a trinket hanging from it with the letters 'MG' emblazoned on it. In another, was a strange, flat object with a glass front and a peculiar design of a bitten apple on the back. In one of the pockets, inside the green and mottled brown jacket, she pulled out a folding wallet which, when she opened it, was found to contain several notes which she recognised as money; the same as those Morgana had shown her after returning from her shopping trip. Also, in a small compartment in the wallet were several coins of various shapes, sizes and metals, all bearing the head of a woman. Susanna picked up the shiniest one in the pile and twisted it around in her fingers. It was a weird, round object made up of a gold-looking outer part and a silver inner section. She put it to her mouth and bit down on the disk to see if the metal was truly gold but it was such a long time ago that she had last touched a gold coin, and even then it was a fleeting encounter, that she did not know if it was real or not. Her action brought a smile to her face as, for the first time, she realised that her new body had teeth, something her old self had not had for as long as she could remember.

A small cake shop, towards the end of the street, was clearing its shelves as they passed and they peered into its window. The shop assistant looked up at them and smiled. Susanna initially tried to avoid making eye contact but then a groan from her stomach forced her into the decision. Clutching her coins, she entered the shop.

"Yes, Sir. Can I help you?" the matronly assistant asked. Susanna was taken aback at being called Sir but then remembered who she now was, and looked at the display of breads and cakes displayed before her. Pointing to several of the cakes and a single, long, thin loaf of, what she thought looked like bread, she indicated her choice but said nothing.

"That will be three seventy-five." came the response from the assistant. Susanna was not sure what three seventy-five was, or looked like. She held out the coins to the woman who looked at him somewhat sympathetically. She took some coins from the outstretched palm but then looked worried.

"I'm sorry, Sir, but you don't have enough here for what you have bought. Susanna became a little flustered but then, remembering the paper money in the wallet, pulled it out and gave it to the assistant. She was a little taken aback but opened the wallet and withdrew a single note. Going over to the till and pressing some buttons; the number 3 75 lit up in a small window on the top of the machine. After putting the money in the drawer at the bottom, she withdrew some other coins and passed them, together with the purchases and the wallet to the man standing in front of her. Without looking at what she had given him, her customer turned and quickly left.

'Must be foreigners,' the assistant thought to herself and continued to clean and tidy the shelves in preparation for closing.

Outside, the young couple hurried away, gazing into the bags of food as they went.

Chapter 56

Morgana to the Rescue

"I think that I may able to help," came a soft voice from behind the circle of people standing around the, now failing, Bird.

Everyone turned and looked at the small figure of Emma standing there.

"I think that I may be able to help to make him better," she repeated and started to make her way forward to where the animal lay.

Bird opened his eyes and they could see the look of fear that sprang into them as the girl knelt beside him but he was helpless to do anything.

Morgana examined Bird and then stood and asked if she could use the kitchen. Mrs Bennett nodded and escorted her in. Everyone else stood transfixed, not knowing whether to stay with Bird or go into the kitchen to see what was happening.

The witch rushed around the kitchen, pulling open drawers and searching for the ingredients she needed but was unable to find several vital components. She asked

Julia if she had any of them but Hugo's mother shook her head in disappointment.

She glanced at her watch and excitedly said that the shops in the village might still be open if she rushed. Grabbing a bag from out of a cupboard, she seized her car keys from the table and rushed off.

The front door banged and the sound of a car screeching away filled the air. Paul Bennett broke away from those gathered around Bird and went into the kitchen where he found the young girl stirring a large saucepan of a bubbling liquid. She pushed him aside as she moved quickly around the kitchen sniffing and tasting every box and spice she could find on the shelves. The floor was rapidly becoming covered in spilt food ingredients and discarded packaging.

Less than fifteen minutes later a car was heard to draw up and Julia Bennett rushed back into the house carrying a large bag of vegetables and, what appeared to be, leaves of various plants, some of which still had the earth attached to them from being torn from the ground. She passed them to Morgana who sniffed each one, selecting some and rejecting others, which she tossed onto the floor.

Hugo's mother looked disdainfully at the mess and groaned. She grabbed a sweeping brush and threw it to her husband, who was standing awe-struck by the outer door. He caught the broom and with a firm command, Julia shouted.

"Sweep it!"

Stunned by the ferocity of the order, he gripped the brush and started to sweep the debris from the floor without argument.

Hugo ran through the door shouting, "Hurry, please

hurry. I think he's dying." He looked pleadingly at his father and then the two women feverishly chopping plants and an assortment of powders and spices. Tears were welling up in his eyes and he wiped his nose with the back of his hand.

"Won't be long now, son," his father reassured him but none too convincingly. "Go and comfort your friend and we'll be out as fast as we can."

Hugo turned and left. His father was about to ask how it was going but a frustrated look from his wife made him keep quiet and he too went out.

Chipper was explaining to Hugo about their encounter with Bragnar and how Bird came to be injured.

"I didn't mean to get into trouble. I just wanted to know what had happened to all the goblins after the battle," he sobbed. "If I hadn't been so silly then none of this would have happened. It's all my fault."

Hugo put his hand around the small fellow and did his best to comfort him but saying in his mind that it definitely was his fault and how stupid could he have been. He thought back at the acts that he had done in the last few months and felt sorry for his tiny friend. His actions had also been the cause, not only of the injury to Bird but to his father and all the gnomes that had perished in the battle at the gnome reserve.

All the colour had now drained from the comb on Bird's head and his breathing became shallower by the second. The back door slammed and Morgana and Hugo's mother came out carrying the saucepan.

They knelt beside the injured animal and while Julia Bennett gently lifted Bird's head, Morgana spooned the dirty-blue liquid from the pan into the patient's beak. Bird's head was limp and lifeless. Much of the potion drained out onto the lawn where it sizzled.

Peter Goodfellow rushed over and lifted his head and neck, indicating Morgana, or as he had been introduced to her, Anne, to spoon more of the liquid into the beak. As she did so, he gently massaged Bird's neck, encouraging the medicine into its stomach. Eventually, Morgana stopped the feeding and sat back on her heels. With difficulty, she pulled the ring off her finger and then gasped in horror.

"What's wrong?" screamed Stephanie, who hadn't taken her eyes off the young girl, fascinated by what she was doing.

"It's the wrong ring! This is my sister's ring. She forgot to change it when she took over my body. Mine is blue; this one is red."

"Does it make a difference?" shouted Hugo, fearing it had gone wrong.

"I don't know," replied the girl. "I have never tried this without my own ring."

Nervously she held the ring between her fingers and gently stroked it over Bird's head, down his neck and onto where Hugo assumed his heart must be. She held the ring there for several seconds when it began to glow. The intensity increased, changing the colour of everyone and everything around them to a brilliant red. Everyone had to look away as the light became intense.

Suddenly it went out and they all rubbed their eyes to regain their vision. They all looked at the creature lying motionless on the ground before them. Morgana indicated for them to move back and once more she passed the ring over the body. This time there was no light, just a slight crackling and the smell of singed feathers.

The witch stood up and looked at everyone. Their eyes all seemed to ask the same question.

"Did it work?"

The answer came almost immediately as Bird gave a deep breath and then a rasping cough.

Hugo knelt and touched his head.

"Bird, Bird, Are you all right? Can you hear me? Are you all right?"

With a flicker, the animal's eyes opened and the first signs of purple bled into his comb. Everyone cheered and rushed forwards.

"Keep back! Give him some air!" Shouted the doctor and everyone took a step back. He knelt beside his patient and gathered his stethoscope from the lawn where it had been thrown. He indicated for everyone to be quiet while he listened to where he guessed Bird's heart might be. A minute later, he stood up and grinned.

"I think the patient will make a full recovery."

Everyone gave another cheer and Chipper ran to Bird and gave him as big a hug as he could, making him wince.

While everyone was celebrating, the doctor went over to Morgana and took her by the hand. "I must congratulate you on what you did there. Paul has told me who you are and what you are. I realise that with your history, saving, what was your arch-enemy, took a great deal of courage and humanity." She looked at him, smiled, but said nothing. He was turning away when he looked back at her. "You must let me have the recipe for that potion sometime. You never know when I might need it, especially with some of my... clients." He looked at Bird and Chipper.

She smiled and subconsciously replaced the ring on her finger, where it sparkled for a second and then returned to normal.

Everyone gathered around Bird, who was rapidly gaining strength. Mrs Bennett ran back into the kitchen and returned with a large bag of cakes she had bought when she had been out shopping. Chipper took one and broke it into small pieces and took great delight in feeding it, crumb by crumb, to his recovering friend.

Morgana went back into the lounge and sat in the corner by the window, watching everyone outside. She felt emotionally torn and was unsure if she had done the right thing. It would be easy to keep silent and let her enemy die, which would have put her back into the good books with Susanna and Putricia. On the other hand, they hadn't played fair with her, so why should she help them. She gazed at the ring on her finger, wondering what they were doing now but, what was worse, what they were planning to do. She knew that they would not give up their vendetta and she started to feel nervous about her personal safety if they ever found out what she had just done.

Chapter 57

The Witches' Interrogation

The river Torridge had never looked so beautiful in the shimmering pink sunset. It had been over three centuries since Susanna had seen it in daylight, or rather twilight. The two sat on a bench on the quay facing the river, enjoying a feeling of freedom. They had finished the bread and cakes and felt satisfied with their day's work.

The wind was springing up and Susanna pulled her jacket close up to her but she could see Putricia beginning to shiver.

"Do you want to go back home?" she suggested. Putricia nodded and they headed back to the tunnel.

They were about to slide between the fence and the wall at the ruins when there was a shout.

The guard had spotted them and as he waved his arm, they could see that he was holding something close to his ear with the other and speaking into it. They tried to hurry but Susanna caught her coat on the same piece of rusty fence that Allan had done earlier but this time the wire held her fast, giving the guard chance to catch up with them.

"Stay right where you are!" he shouted as he breathlessly approached, pointing his torch at them. "I've told you two twice before that this is private property and you are trespassing. I've called the police and they will be here shortly so don't you dare move. I've had enough of vandals like you."

Susanna struggled to free herself but the muddy ground underfoot and the wire caught in the anorak she was wearing made it impossible. Putricia fought to help her but she also slipped in the mud and, as they lay there, the guard towered over them, preventing their flight.

Very little time had passed when there was the sound of a siren and blue flashing lights illuminated the scene. Two officers approached and looked at the two, mud-caked individuals sitting on the floor.

One of the officers talked to the guard while the other unhitched Susanna's anorak from the wire in the fence.

"Right, you two. You're coming with us," he announced authoritatively and guided them towards the police car. He opened the rear door and indicted for them to get in but Susanna hesitated. She had seen the vehicles around the streets on the times that she had been out at night, but she had never been in one and was not sure what to expect.

The officer held her arm and with his other hand on her head, pushed her into the back seat, followed seconds later by Putricia.

"Put your belts on." the policeman ordered but neither of them knew what he meant and looked questioningly at each other. The other officer joined him, and without checking the belts, the two slid into the front and drove off. Both passengers gripped their seats and each other as they sped, at what seemed to them at breakneck speed, to the police station.

As they drove off, two bright green eyes watched them go. Snatch, had heard the commotion from within the tunnel. Venturing out to investigate he gave a deep throaty growl and began to follow in the direction where he had seen his mistress go.

...

"Well now m' lad. I see you found your girlfriend. Where was she hiding?"

Sergeant Cummings was leaning over a table in a small interview room, staring at the young couple seated before him. A female officer stood by the door.

Neither of his interviewees answered. The detective looked at them and then at the woman officer.

"Right then if you want to play it that way, we'll start from the beginning."

"Name?" He looked at Susanna. He repeated his request but receiving no answer, looked at the file on his desk. "From this file, it says that you are Allan Carlisle and live at 25 Shore Road. Is that correct?"

Neither person answered.

Showing signs of frustration, he turned to Putricia. "Name?"

There was a loud bang as the door to the interview room flew open and in marched D.I. Hyde.

"What's the story?" he asked the sergeant.

"They aren't answering," he replied, somewhat embarrassed in front of his superior.

"Oh, yes. We'll see about that," indicating for his sergeant to get out of his chair and let him sit down.

Taking the chair, the inspector took a quick look at the files on the desk and then pushed them to one side.

"Right then you two, I haven't got time for messing around. Either you tell me what's been going on or I'll have you arrested for wasting police time for starters."

He turned to Susanna and asked for her full name.

The shock of being arrested was wearing off and her livid hatred of authority following her previous experiences was coming to the fore.

"Susanna Edwards," she spat back, haughtily.

"Oh! One of them," the inspector replied, looking around at his sergeant and grinning.

"And who are you?" he said sarcastically to Putricia.

Buoyed by Susanna's attitude, she replied firmly.

"I am Jane Trembles."

"Look you two," replied the inspector, sitting back in the chair. "I don't know what you two are playing at because we know, perfectly well, that you are Allan Carlisle and Susan Redwell. I could now have you arrested for wasting police time and obstruction but that would involve a great deal of paperwork and even more wasted time, so since it now appears that you are safe and well." He turned to Putricia, "And you seem to have helped us in our work finding her." He looked at Susanna. "On this occasion, I am going to let both of you go, but if I hear that you have caused any more trouble, even if it's littering, I will throw the book at you. Do you understand me?"

The pair in front of him showed no emotion but glared at him, making him feel uneasy.

"Get out!" he ordered them, pointing at the door.

They looked at each other with satisfied smiles and left.

"Do you think that that was right, sir?" questioned the sergeant who looked at the policewoman standing next to him.

"Look," replied the inspector. "That woman is a reporter and they always say that they will not reveal their sources. I don't know what she and her boyfriend were playing at but whatever it was, I can think of far better things to do instead of chasing after them and their silly games." He pushed himself away from the desk and with a sigh, said, "As far as I'm concerned, it's case closed. Right, let's go and catch some real criminals."

Sergeant Cummings looked at the policewoman, hunched his shoulders and, mimicking the inspector, said to her.

"Right, let's go and catch some real criminals."

Both officers grinned, gathered up the files on the table and left, still smiling.

Chapter 58

24 Shore Road

Eager to get away from the police station, the two witches hurriedly walked in the opposite direction to their underground home. It was now quite dark and more familiar to Susanna who, up to now, had only known the town at night.

"Where are we going?" Putricia asked.

Susanna smiled and replied. "To this body's house."

Her companion looked confused, so she explained. "Didn't you hear that idiot back there. He said that I lived at 25 Shore Road. If we can find it, then we can stay there."

Putricia smiled broadly, remembering the comparatively luxurious conditions she had found when she and Morgana had had their brief stay at the house of Sue Redwell. She had realised it was the name of this body she now owned, as the policeman had called it so.

For the next two hours, they wandered the streets of Bideford searching for Shore Road, not daring to speak to anyone in case they were rearrested. Eventually, they returned to their starting point, feeling very exasperated at the time they had wasted. They were also now beginning to feel very cold and tired. They sat down on a bench overlooking the river, wondering if this place existed. An elderly man carrying a stick, accompanied by a stiff, old terrier dog, shuffled up to them. He looked at them as they shivered.

"You shouldn't be out in this cold," he mumbled to them as he limped passed.

"We're looking for Shore Road?" Putricia answered, out of impending desperation.

"Oh. If you go up there," he pointed ahead, "and take the second turning on the left, you should find it there."

Without any acknowledgement, they jumped up and walked briskly in the direction which the man had said.

"They could have said, 'thank you', Jasper," he complained to his dog, who had lain down while he had been speaking. With a tug on its lead, the animal slowly got to its feet and together, they shuffled along, into the gloom of the street lights.

The two witches arrived at the road which the old man had indicated but saw no road sign. They each recognised it from their previous search but as it was not sign-posted, they had not stopped. Still unsure, they walked along searching for anything that might tell them that this was indeed, Shore Road. Putricia noticed an illuminated name-plate on one of the houses and quietly went up to the door to investigate. *J Evans 49 Shore Road, Bideford,* it read.

She rushed back to her companion, looking pleased. Together they followed the numbers backwards until number 25 stood before them. Glancing left and right,

Susanna groped in the pockets of the coat she was wearing and finally found the set of keys she was looking for. One by one, she tried each key in the lock and on the third attempt it turned. Slowly, opening the door, they inched inside, feeling their way in the darkness. Splitting up, each looked into the different rooms, checking to see if there was anyone else there but, meeting back at the door they smiled, realising that they were alone... and safe.

Putricia was a little disappointed, as this house was much untidier than the one she had been in earlier but knew that it was far better than their hole under the ruins. They each tried to search for some candles or an oil lamp to give them some light but finding none, made their way around the house studying each room and opening every cupboard to see what they could use.

Susanna entered one room and opened one apparent cupboard. There was a sudden flash of light from the inside. Quickly she slammed the door shut but then slowly reopened it. The light came on again and she quickly closed it again. A third time she pulled the handle on the white cupboard but this time she just cracked it open. The light blazed out from the opening, illuminating the rest of the room, showing that it had a sink and several pots and pans stacked to one side of it. There were also several rags and papers lying around on a small table surrounded by three wooden stools.

Putricia had been alerted by the light coming from the room and joined Susanna. They knelt together in front of the cupboard and felt chilled by the air coming from it. Slowly Susanna eased the door further and further open. The witches grinned as they saw that it contained food;

cheese, milk, butter, eggs and several other items in packets and boxes which they did not recognise. Each grabbed what they could and gorged themselves on the cupboard's contents.

Leaving the door wide open, to give as much light to the rest of the house, they moved to a room next door and sat on a long soft chair in front of what appeared to be a large black mirror with *Sony* emblazoned on its base.

Curling up, they started to discuss their adventure and also on what they needed to do to complete their quest but excitement and tiredness had taken their toll and both were asleep in minutes.

They had been asleep for quite some time when a scratching noise at the front door awakened Putricia. After several nudges, she managed to arouse Susanna and together they listened intently as the sound grew in intensity.

Looking around in the dim light of the early dawn, Putricia saw a large, long bag of, what appeared to be, sticks with large wooden or metal L-shaped heads. Pulling out two of the heaviest, she handed one to Susanna. Brandishing them above their heads, they crept silently towards the source of the noise.

As they approached the door, the noise stopped, as did the pair, and they stood, statuesque, listening. After several minutes of silence, Susanna whispered that she thought that whatever had caused the noise had gone. Slowly, and as noiselessly as possible, with Putricia standing behind her with her stick raised high above her head, she eased the catch on the door. The door had only just cracked open when a heavy weight from the other side hit it and it flew open, knocking Susanna to the floor and Putricia almost off-balance.

With one giant leap Snatch bounded in, skidding on the polished wooden floor, coming to rest against the wall. The two witches gasped; initially with shock but then with relief as they discovered the source of the scratching. Snatch, leapt to his feet and approached the pair, growling softly and nuzzling Susanna.

Putricia put her hand out to stroke the animal but he raised his head and sniffed the air. Seconds later he was in the other room with his head in the white cupboard, demolishing anything and everything he could find that was left and might be considered edible.

Putricia followed him into the kitchen and was surprised to see that the pet was standing in a large puddle of water. At first, she thought that the animal had urinated but then she realised that the water was coming from the white cupboard, resulting from the melting ice which she had noticed in it when she had opened it the previous evening.

Snatch appeared unconcerned as he bit through containers and packaging, devouring their contents. A carton of milk fell onto the floor into the puddle, turning it white. Without hesitation, Snatch started to lap up the liquid until the surface was almost dry. With the floor covered in wrappers and debris, the animal looked at his owners as if nothing had happened. They looked at each other and, for the first time in a long time, they laughed.

Snatch looked at each of them, unfamiliar with this strange noise but then, sensing no danger, left, sniffing and exploring each place in turn, finally settling on a large cushion in the room where the two witches had been sleeping. Turning slowly several times, he looked at the witches as if to say '*What have I done now?*' Burrowing his head beneath his paws, he went to sleep.

As if this was a hint, the two witches looked at each other, smiled, and returned to their beds.

Chapter 59

The Faulty Potion

"And that's the whole story," concluded Mr Bennett. He had just finished telling the social worker about the return of Emma, or at least a story that the previous day, the whole family had concocted to explain the young girl's disappearance, for what had now been two months.

When he had first alerted the authorities that she had returned, they had tried to take her into care; *"For her protection"*, they said, but with help from Dr Goodfellow, the child protection agency had agreed to allow her to stay again with the Bennetts'.

Mrs Bennett had counselled Morgana into as much of the life of Emma Jones as she knew so that she would be able to fit back into society. The Bennett's had used the excuse that Emma was suffering the after-effects of the loss of her parents and was suffering from amnesia. This, they thought would fill in any spaces in her memory, especially when she returned to school where they knew that she would be bombarded with questions.

In the meantime, Bird had made a full recovery but had moved back to the Gnome Reserve, where no one would notice him, as the attraction had closed for the winter. Chipper was his constant companion and fussed over him like an old mother hen. He still felt guilty that it was he that had caused his friend's injury in the first place. All the other gnomes treated Bird like a king and showered him with an array of gifts, mostly food, which Bird gave himself the excuse of eating, for if he did not, he told himself, then it might offend the little people.

It was running up to Christmas and Mrs Bennett was thinking of buying Emma some new clothes, as up to the present she had been wearing the same things that she had originally brought with her, plus a few items of Stephanie's which she had outgrown. Julia asked Emma to come into her bedroom so that she could get the right size, but when she measured her, was amazed at the rate at which she had grown. Julia recognised that girls were developing earlier than in her day but also realised that Emma was now physically, more of a woman than a young girl. She even joked about it to her husband that evening.

It was only a few weeks after Christmas; the first Emma had had since before her execution. Even then, it had been a very modest affair with no presents or fancy food. Quickly Julia Bennett realised that Emma was beginning to grow out of the new clothes she had been given. She was now wearing the same size as Stephanie. The two spent a great deal of their time together, shopping for clothes, which they often swapped. Hugo began to feel left out as the two girls seemed to distance themselves from him.

Julia Bennett began to worry at the seemingly abnormal

speed at which Emma was growing and, when he was on a social visit, asked the advice of Peter Goodfellow. Without her being aware, he observed Emma, confirming that the speed at which she was developing far exceeded that of a normal ten-year-old girl. Also, when visiting the school to pick her and Hugo up, a teacher approached Julia and expressed her concern that Emma was being talked about behind her back by the other children about her size and physical maturity. She was worried that it might be affecting her, mentally.

Eventually, when the house was empty of everyone else, Julia cornered Emma and voiced her concerns, asking if she had realised what was happening.

As soon as she mentioned her observations, Emma broke down and started to cry. Julia put her arm around her and, after she had calmed a little, admitted that she had also noticed the speed at which she was ageing. Emma then told Julia about how Putricia had made the potion that had caused the transformation from her being in Emma's body into taking over Sue Redwell's. Morgana had always been the better at potion-making and when she had seen and smelt the fusion potion Putricia had made, realised that her sister had omitted the extract of thistledown. At that time, she was not sure what effect that this omission would cause but had now realised that it's lack resulted in accelerated ageing.

Julia Bennett sat back, stunned.

"If you are ageing abnormally fast, how long do you have to live?"

Emma burst into tears again, admitting between the sobs that she didn't know.

"But you were able to live a long time before you

transformed?" queried Julia. "So it shouldn't be a problem, should it?"

Emma explained that the potion that she and the others had used to extend their lives would only work on their original bodies and she did not know what would happen when she became too old for the body she now occupied.

"But, if you...die...Then what will happen to the real Emma?" Julia said with some trepidation, dreading the answer that might be given.

"I don't know," Emma cried.

Julia sat back, not knowing whether to hug Emma or hit her for taking another's body without their consent.

At that point, the front door opened and Hugo and his father came into the house. Emma jumped up and ran up to her room, almost knocking into Hugo and his father.

He watched her dash up the stairs, wondering what the problem was. Walking into the lounge, Mr Bennett saw his wife sitting with a very red face and on the verge of tears. She looked at him, motioning for him to follow her up to their bedroom, where she explained the conversation and revelations she had had with Emma. It was Mr Bennett's turn to have a red face now and both hugged and cried.

Chapter 60

Susanna's Final Solution

For over three hours, Putricia and Susanna sat at the kitchen table talking about how they could wreak their vengeance on, not only the Bennett family but their renegade compatriot and regain their ultimate objective; the talisman; their inheritance.

Susanna left to get a drink of water. Passing a mirror on the wall, she glanced at it and was shocked to see that a bushy beard covered her face. She looked again, getting closer to the mirror to get a better look. Tentatively she stroked her face and burst into laughter. She had forgotten that her body change was also a sex change.

Her laughter brought Putricia to her side and together they stroked the hairy mass and laughed.

Putricia then took a closer look at herself in the mirror and suddenly realised that in her previously dark brown hair, there was a streak of grey. Not just that, lines were developing in her forehead, where before it had been smooth. She rubbed them to see if they would disappear but they remained.

Susanna left her looking at herself and went into the kitchen and took a pair of scissors from a drawer which she had noticed during her initial exploration. Returning to the mirror, she pushed Putricia to one side and began to trim her beard with the scissors. Putting them down, she looked at the face gazing back at her. It smiled and, turning left and right, admired what it saw. The slight hint of grey in the beard made her look quite distinguished, she thought. Even Putricia expressed her admiration at his appearance and had to remind her that he was a she.

"Fire. That's what we can do!" exclaimed Susanna.

Putricia looked at her in amazement. "What are you talking about?" she questioned.

"Fire. We can burn those murderers out." Susanna smiled at Putricia who, suddenly realising what her friend meant, grinned back enthusiastically. They went into the room in which they had been sleeping to formulate a plan of how to finally end their adversaries' lives.

"We will kill five birds," Susanna emphasised the word *Bird's*, "with one stone…or match", she corrected herself.

Putricia looked bemused but then realised that her friend meant the whole of the Bennett family; including that silly bird creature that Kadavera had created, which had interfered with their plans on too many occasions.

"But what about Morgana?" she asked. "What shall we do with her?"

"When she realises that we have won and fulfilled our vow, she will come running back. We can deal with her then. After all, it would be a shame to waste such a youthful body… in case we should ever need one." Susanna smiled knowingly at Putricia, who grinned back. Leaning over the table, they discussed their plan in hushed whispers, even though there was no one else in the room except Snatch. He was lying curled up on the carpet in front of the window; the evening sun, bathing him in a blanket of orange light.

Chapter 61

The Reversal Potion

Bird was making one of his regular visits to the Bennett's house and the conversation turned to the time when Kadavera had first captured him.

"Please call her Mary... Mary Edwards," pleaded Morgana. "She was Susanna's daughter and my best friend. Kadavera is such a disgusting name and was devised by Susanna to frighten all those who heard it. Before all the troubles, she was a very clever, happy person and a very loyal friend. Hearing her called by that foul name does not give her justice."

Hugo thought to himself that he did not believe that she was a very 'happy person'; in fact, as far as he was concerned, she was just short of being a devil.

"I'm very sorry," Mr Bennett continued his conversation, "but we have only known her by that name. I apologise and will try to remember in future."

Bird reminisced about his days after hatching and his first memories of being brought up in a zoo with many other birds and animals. It had not been a happy time, as the owner of the zoo was very unkind and many of his friends died of hunger and ill-treatment. It was only by being able to run fast that he and his brother had been able to survive when the lion in the collection had escaped. The owner had returned one evening, very drunk and forgot to lock its cage. It had rampaged through the zoo, killing and eating as many of the other inmates as it could catch, which sadly included Bird's parents. He recalled how pleased he and his brother were when an old lady found them and took them back to her home, which was in a cave, next to a pebble-strewn beach. She had promised to feed and shelter them but as soon as they entered the cave, she had trapped them in a cage. She had forced them to eat and drink an assortment of strange potions. Over time, he and his brother started to transform, from their original size and shapes, to what they saw before them at that time, except that his brother had never stopped growing. It was because of this that she threw him out of the cave, as he began to take up too much space.

"I did not know what became of him until many years later when the witch..." Bird stopped his story and looked at Morgana and quickly apologised, "I'm sorry. I meant to say, Mary Edwards."

He continued: "Mary Edwards had brought into the cave a small bear-like creature which she had stolen from a sailor while he was sleeping. While I was talking to this animal, it emerged that my brother had stowed away on the sailor's ship when it had been docked in Bideford harbour and had ended up in Australia. He had escaped into the outback but because he was continually growing, he became well known to all the local animals living there, including this bear.

When I visited him some time ago, he asked me if I could find a way of reversing the effects of the potion, as he was now so big that he was unable to move and was finding life very dull, being in the same place all the time."

Bird stopped talking and looked at Morgana pleadingly. "Well, is there?"

She looked back at him, having been listening very uncomfortably to his story as she recognised many of the things he had described, which she had also done to the animals...and the gnomes, in the cave.

Everyone now turned to face her, which made her even more irritable.

"I don't know," she whispered, after a long pause. "If there is a reversal mixture, then it will be written in my potion books, but they are still in Susanna's home, in the tunnel under the ruins of the judge's house. If I go back there, then they will surely kill me, especially if they have found out that I have helped you."

"In that case!" exclaimed Mr Bennett, "I will go. After all, it's my property and I can do what I want with it."

"Oh, no, you won't!" screamed his wife. "You almost died; no, you definitely did die the last time you went there. I'm not going to risk that happening again." She looked at him, red-faced and with eyes that were beginning to well up with tears.

"We'll organise a proper excavation party," Peter Goodfellow butted in. "We can arrange for special emergency equipment to be available and heavy lifting gear, just in case. If enough of us go in at the same time, then, if those witches..." he blushed and looked at Morgana, then went on, "if those *women* are there, then we should be able to overpower them."

Julia Bennett still looked angry but everyone else, except Morgana, smiled and nodded at the plan.

It took several days to organise the expedition. The local archaeologist club tried to stop it as they said that it was an important site of local, and probably, national interest. They insisted that it should be treated as such but Mr Bennett finally persuaded them to change their mind when he offered to finance a proper excavation after he had made his own investigations. He deliberately did not mention precisely what his aim was, for fear of them asking questions, the answers of which would require him to tell them the whole story.

Chapter 62

The Vanishing Potion Books

Susanna gazed at himself in the mirror in the bathroom. The two witches had now become aware of their rapid ageing, though neither wanted to admit it. His hair and beard were now so grey that it was impossible to hide it. Putricia finally decided that something was drastically wrong and confided in her friend her fears.

"I think that there's something wrong with us. We are getting older much faster than we should. If we can't find a way to slow it down, then we may die before we can complete our vow."

"I agree," Susanna replied, still gazing at her reflection and stroking her beard. "We need to get our potion books to see if there is something that we can make to stop us from ageing so quickly."

Returning to the lounge area in the house, they sat down, pushing aside the remnants of their last meal, the plates having been licked clean by Snatch. He had been released to *hunt*, as their supplies of food from the cupboards in the kitchen were almost exhausted, as was the money that had been in the wallet of the young man Susanna had fused with. Morgana had told them of the card she had used to get more from, what she called, 'a hole in the wall of a shop' but she had taken it with her when she had left.

"We will go tomorrow night," Susanna suggested. "It will be easier to get in as there won't be many people around. We only have to deal with that guard on the gate and that should be quite easy, especially if we can get him to take some of this." She waved a small vial of green liquid in front of her and rotated it in her fingers.

Putricia smiled in agreement as she recognised the liquid as a strong sleeping draught, which she had used herself on many occasions, to subdue the victims that she had used as part of her experiments.

...

The air was chilled as they arrived at the site of the ruins. The pair stood in horror at the view in front of them. The wire fence had been removed along one side, replaced by a fluttering blue ribbon with 'Private Property. No Admittance' emblazoned along its length.

A large, yellow JCB digger was parked along one wall together with several other machines. What displeased the pair the most was that the whole area was now brightly illuminated with floodlights. Two security guards were sitting in a small hut with an open brazier burning in front of them. They were warming their hands on the steaming cups of whatever they were drinking.

Putricia turned to her friend with a look of astonishment, frustration and anger.

"What's happening?" she said, almost choking. "We can't go in now. Somebody will see us. Let's go back before we're spotted."

"Wait here," Susanna ordered. Pulling up the collar of his coat, the apparently middle-aged man went forward and up to the guards. He asked if he could warm his hands for a few minutes. While they were distracted, he slipped into their drinks some of the green liquid…and waited.

Slowly, the conversation of the two guards became incoherent until they slumped in their chairs. Susanna poked each one to make sure that they would not present a problem and, when assured, sat them up, to give the impression that they were awake, just in case anyone checked on them. Satisfied with her work, she returned to her partner and together they boldly went forward and entered the tunnel which had now been fitted with a string of small lights.

On entering the underground room, they found large boxes of tools and equipment. Susanna groaned as she saw that her beloved cauldron was missing. She moved over to the empty space and scuffed the ashes that had warmed it with her foot.

"They're gone!" A scream from the other side of the room echoed around the chamber. Susanna spun round to see Putricia scrabbling around in the cupboards that had held the precious documents.

"They're not here!" she sobbed. "They've taken them! Everything's gone!"

Chapter 63

The Potion

Morgana poured over the ancient papers laid out on the table in the lounge of the Bennett's house. All the family, including Bird, craned their necks to see over her shoulders, trying to decipher the faded script written on them. To them, the writing seemed to be just a mass of squiggles and blotches, but Morgana was flicking through them as if they were pages of a paperback. As she turned the sheets, she made notes on a pad by her side. Hugo tried to read what she was writing but, to him, it seemed like a jigsaw of symbols and letters that made no sense. As time passed, one by one, the Bennett's left; either to eat, or, in Mr Bennett's case, to go to bed. He had been up since the crack of dawn to supervise the excavation of the ruin's site and had been working hard physically on the project and the retrieval of the potion books. Eventually, only Bird was left by the witch's side, helping her, as much as he was able, to lift and move the heavy volumes. She worked unceasingly to find the ingredients she needed to make the potion to halt the ageing that she was experiencing, as well as the remedy to reverse the growth of Bird's brother.

With a loud sigh, she slammed the book she had been intently working on, shut, which made Bird jump. He had been on the verge of nodding off. He looked at the clock on the wall. It read 3:18. Morgana slumped into a chair by the table and smiled an exhausted smile at him.

"I think that I have found a solution to solve your brother's problem but..." she hesitated and tears began to form in her eyes.

"But what?" asked Bird.

"The only way I can find to stop my ageing so rapidly would be for me to give up this body and return it to its previous owner."

"But what will happen to you?" questioned Bird, fearing that he already knew the answer.

"I will die," whispered the woman.

Without any further conversation, she rose and went to her room, leaving Bird alone. The silence of the night was only broken by the clock ticking on the mantelpiece and the crashing of the waves beating against the shingle and rocks on the beach outside.

He moved to where Morgana had left the books and began to leaf through the curled, mottled-brown pages. The musty smell of the ancient parchment reminded him of his time, trapped in a wooden box in the cave, while Kadavera poured over the fading text in her efforts to find the recipe for a potion that would allow her to exist in daylight.

As the clock ticked and the waves crashed, the pages were turned, with Bird's wing-tip scouring each line.

"Wake up! Have you been down here all night?" Julia Bennett patted Bird's wing as she brushed past him on her way to feed Jake. He had also been curled up, fast asleep until the slop of his mistress's slippers on the carpet had roused him. Within a second, he had jumped up, shaken himself vigorously and was waiting at his bowl, ready for his breakfast.

Bird groaned and twisted his head to see who or what had disturbed him. He let out another groan and stretched his neck, slowly turning it left and right.

"Are you OK?" Mrs Bennett asked as she scooped the dog-food from the tin into Jake's bowl, fighting to prevent the dog from knocking the spoon from her hand as it jostled to get at the morsels.

"My neck is stiff," croaked the animal. "I must have fallen asleep and slept awkwardly."

Julia Bennett put down the empty tin of dog food and went over and gave Bird's neck a gentle massage. He felt very embarrassed and moved away, but at her insistence, he let her proceed and within seconds felt a deep feeling of relaxation spreading over him.

His euphoria suddenly came to an end as Stephanie shuffled into the room, trying to tease out the tangles in her hair with her fingers.

"You're up early," her mother commented, as her daughter turned and went into the kitchen. Mrs Bennett heard some muffled comment about meeting a friend but didn't pursue the mumble.

"I found it!" Bird exclaimed, now that he had finally woken up. "Quick, I must tell Morg... I mean, Anne." He jumped up, knocking his chair over, but left it as it was. He raced out of the room and up the stairs to where Morgana slept.

Mrs Bennett was about to ask what he had found but he left so quickly that there was no time for a reply. With a frustrated sigh, she picked up the fallen chair and was about to close the open potion book, when there was a scream from the doorway;

"Don't! Don't touch it!" Bird re-entered the lounge, closely followed by a very untidy Morgana who looked as if she had just been pulled from her bed.

The two raced over to the table, and ignoring Mrs Bennett, began to pour over the open pages of the book. The witch seized her notebook and a ballpoint pen that she had been using the previous night and started to make copious notes in some, seemingly indecipherable, writing.

They were still turning pages and whispering to each other when Mr Bennett came into the room, carrying a newspaper that had just been delivered. He glanced at the pair and then at his wife, who just shrugged her shoulders as if to say, 'Don't ask me. I have no idea what is going on.'

As usual, Hugo was the last to appear, looking as if he had been dragged through a hedge backwards. He barely gave anyone else an acknowledgement as he looked around, then went into the kitchen to see what he could find for breakfast.

"Well! What's all the secrecy?" Mrs Bennett demanded as she carefully placed two cups of steaming tea on the table in front of the whispering duo. They each looked at the tea and then at Julia Bennett who stood over them with a look of frustration.

"Bird may have found the recipe for a potion that will help me to stop ageing and extend my life. It may also let... Emma, is that what you called her?" Julia nodded. "Let her have her body back."

"That's great," Paul Bennett, who had been listening to the conversation, broke in.

"It's not that great," responded Morgana, "because I will need another body to move into."

The two Bennett's looked at each other as they realised that if she went ahead then they may get Emma back but it will mean someone else ending up in the same situation as her.

"I am very much against it but Bird here has insisted that, until a better solution turns up, I can share his body.

"What do you mean 'Share'?" queried Mr Bennett.

"Bird found a page in the potion book which gives a recipe which will reverse the mistake made in the potion that Putricia gave me but to make it work I need to change bodies... again.

However, the body that I take over must be a willing subject because if it isn't, then our two minds would be in conflict and we may both end up becoming insane.

I am sure that none of you would like to be a volunteer but Bird and I have become friends over the past weeks and since he is no longer the animal he once was, he suggested that we join together... permanently."

"But he's my friend too," came a voice from the doorway and Hugo stood there looking flushed as if about to cry.

"Don't worry," Bird consoled him, "You see, the good part about this, is that you are the owner of the talisman from Excalibur's scabbard. The secret of the potion is, that to make it work, it needs the five jewels that also encrusted the sheath."

"What are you talking about?" protested Hugo.

"This!" Morgana shouted and thrust her arm at Hugo. At first, he stood back, thinking that she was about to hit him but then he looked at her hand and saw the large red stone in the ring on her third finger.

Hugo went up to her hand and nervously took hold of it so that he could study the ring and its stone which sparkled as he twisted it back and forth in his fingers.

"Kad... I'm sorry, Mary Edwards had one of those, but hers was green," he said, almost to himself. I found it when she... died." He looked nervously into Morgana's eyes expecting her to be angry since he was instrumental in her death. He thought he saw a flash of hostility, but on reflection, he might have been mistaken.

"You mean this one." She felt around her neck and pulled out a delicate gold chain which held a small locket and another identical gold ring, except that, the stone in this one was green.

"That's the one. That's the one," repeated Hugo, rushing up to take a closer look. "Where did you get it? I hid it under some stones after Mary had died. I thought someone had stolen it." He made to take hold of it but Morgana pulled back and grasped the jewellery in her hand.

"It wasn't stolen. It was... reclaimed," she said in a tone which made Hugo feel as if he had been the thief.

"But what do the rings have to do with my amulet?" Hugo demanded.

"As you know, Excalibur, or rather its scabbard, was decorated with jewels. There was the amulet, plus five large precious stones; one green, one blue, one red, one clear and one black.

These jewels were bequeathed to Susanna Edwards' ancestors and were passed down, together with the amulet, as their inheritance. The stones were made into rings and were used to give the wearers the power to heal. As part of the regeneration process, the rings are the source of the power which allows it to work. Each of us was given a ring by Mary when she resurrected us after our execution." She subconsciously rubbed her neck. "This ring was Mary's." She opened her hand to reveal the green stone. "Mine was the blue one, Jane, the red and Susanna kept the clear one."

"But what about the black one?" queried Hugo. "Who had that?"

"The black one, which incidentally was the most powerful of all of them, was owned by Stephen, my cousin and Susanna's nephew."

"What happened to him? Has he been resurrected as well?"

Morgana lowered her head and whispered, "He's dead. He saved us all but in the end, he couldn't save himself."

Hugo backed away, feeling embarrassed at asking the question. He wanted to know what had become of the black stone but he could tell that Morgana was upset, so he decided to change the subject a little. "What has the amulet got to do with the jewels?" he asked, almost apologetically.

The witch looked at the rings in her hand and rubbed them tenderly. "The amulet controls them all. Individually they have some power and together, their effect is multiplied but if the charm is added to them, then they make the bearer invincible, which is why they were part of Excalibur.

"You mean, that if someone had all the rings and the amulet then they could do what they wanted and no one would be able to stop them?" interrupted Mr Bennett who had been listening to the conversation in stunned silence.

Morgana nodded. "That is why Susanna, and all of us," now it was her turn to look embarrassed, "are… were… so desperate to get the amulet. It would give us infinite power and allow us to fulfil the vow we all made before we died."

Everyone was silent for several minutes as the implication of what she had just said soaked in.

"Whatever happens then, we must make sure that the rings are kept apart, or at least that the amulet is never allowed to come in contact with them," Paul Bennett announced authoritatively.

The image of the amulet lying in an old sock in his bedside cupboard drawer flashed into Hugo's mind.

"Right, we've got no time to waste," interrupted Julia Bennett. "What do we need for this potion of yours? The quicker we start, then the less damage will be done. Make a list of what you need… Anne." She did not want to call her Morgana any more as it kept reminding her of what, and who she really was.

Morgana turned and smiled at her and then busied herself, writing down a long list of ingredients. She passed it to Julia, who looked at it and grimaced.

"I'm not sure where we are going to find all this but… here." She thrust the paper into her husband's hand. "Make yourself useful and get as much of this as you can. Hugo and Stephanie can help you."

Stephanie looked at her watch and moaned. "But mum I said I meet Marty in an hour."

"Right then. He can help as well," she answered back and pointed to the door, indicating that they get moving.

Hugo looked at his father, questioning his mother's authority, but he just hunched his shoulders and ordered him and his sister to get their coats.

Ten minutes later, they were on their way to Barnstaple to see if they could fulfil the list.

It was quite late when they returned and as they opened the front door, an overpowering, sweet-sickly smell hit them. Following its trail into the kitchen, they found the two women sitting at the table drinking tea, while a large saucepan, from which the smell emanated, bubbled on the stove.

Morgana rushed over to the bags that Mr Bennett had dropped beside one wall and started to rummage through them, examining and smelling each item. Each one was arranged in piles around her. Taking the contents from one stack, she brushed the table clear of debris onto the floor and began to unwrap, cut and chop up the various ingredients, which she then added to the saucepan. Multicolour vapours streamed from beneath its rattling lid and on several occasions, there was a loud hiss as some of the contents spilt over onto the hot stove.

Hugo's father looked at his wife and then the waste, strewn over the floor. She hunched her shoulders and returned his look with one of apparent helplessness. He walked over to the fridge and took out a bottle of beer for himself and passed Hugo a carton of cold orange juice.

The smell in the kitchen suddenly took a turn for the worse and Mr Bennett decided that it was a good time to leave. With Hugo following closely, they left, shutting the kitchen door behind them to try to contain the smell.

For several more hours, they could hear and smell the activity in the kitchen, despite the sound of the television being turned up to drown it. Hugo had taken himself to bed and his father was nodding off on the settee in the lounge when the door opened and his wife came in and flopped, exhaustedly down next to him. She looked at him with tired eyes and sighed.

"Anne is just finishing off but she thinks that it is complete. She had to modify the recipe a little because some of the ingredients weren't quite right but at least she seems satisfied, but time will tell. It needs to stew overnight, so she and I are going to bed. You can clear up!"

Her husband could see that she was exhausted and didn't argue but when he entered the kitchen; it was like a tornado had hit it. Rubbish covered the floor, with plates, dishes and kitchen paraphernalia piled on every work surface. Muttering under his breath, he pulled a broom from the cupboard and started to sweep the floor, with emphasised frustration at every stroke.

Chapter 64

The Fire

The Bennett house was silent. The only noise was coming from the crashing of the waves on the pebble beach and the faint moaning of the breeze as it eddied around the nearby trees.

A sudden crack of a rotting twig made Jake twitch in his sleep as he lay curled up next to the radiator, extracting as much from its residual heat before the timer on the central heating brought it back to life at six o'clock.

Another crackle, followed by a strange smell, roused him and he lifted his head and sniffed. He lay his head back down between his stretched-out paws and was just about to close his eyes again when a sudden breeze from outside caused the strange odour to increase. Reluctantly, but driven by curiosity, he stretched and stood up, meandering slowly to where he sensed the smell had originated. He pushed open the door from the kitchen into the hallway with his nose and stood as he watched two shadows through the glass of the front door. They were pouring a vile-smelling liquid through the letter-box and before he had time to react, it burst into flames.

The startled animal barked furiously at the shadows who immediately melted into the night. Unable to give chase through the flames, Jake ran up the stairs and began to bark and paw at the door to Mr and Mrs Bennett's bedroom. It seemed like several minutes before Mr Bennett, dressed in his dressing-gown, opened the door. Jake jumped up at him, still barking loudly. Mr Bennett was about to admonish him and push him away when the smell of the smoke hit him. Almost simultaneously, the smoke alarm in the ceiling at the top of the stairs started a piercing scream. Mr Bennett ran back into his room and ordered his wife to get up immediately and get out of the house. He then ran into all the other bedrooms screaming *"Fire"* and ordering everyone to snatch some clothes and get out.

Grabbing his mobile phone, he dialled *Nine, Nine, Nine,* and ran downstairs to see what and where the problem lay. At first, he thought that the women had left the gas stove on and was planning in his mind what he was going to say to them but as he reached the bottom of the stairs, he saw that the fire was not from the kitchen but coming from the front hall-way and door which was now a blazing inferno, making escape that way impossible. Rushing into the kitchen, he seized the small fire extinguisher kept next to the cooker and fired it at the flames but it was no match for their increasing intensity.

He realised that now, the only exit from upstairs was through the area he was occupying currently. Screaming as loudly as he could for everyone to hurry up, he could see that there were only seconds before the flames would engulf the area, trapping them.

Hugo sped down the stairs, half in and half out of his dressing gown. Stephanie and Morgana closely followed him, with Mrs Bennett and Jake bring up the rear. With only seconds to spare and fighting to breathe, in the thick, black, acrid smoke, they all rushed through the kitchen and out to safety through the back door. No-one spoke. Each looked dumbfounded as the fire licked through the windows sending plumes of dense black smoke, interspersed with flames, into the first signs of dawn.

Hugo forced his gaze from the inferno and looked around.

"Where's Bird?" he asked, to no-one in particular.

All those around him looked at him and then at everyone else but there was no Bird.

Panic suddenly overcame them all as they realised that, in their urgent need to escape, no-one had thought of waking Bird who, when last seen, was asleep in Mr Bennett's study. Hugo made to rush back into the house to try and find his friend but his father caught him and passed him over to his mother.

"You all stay here and I will go round the house and see if I can find him. Whatever you do, under no circumstances are any of you to move from here. Do you understand?"

He did not wait for an answer but pulled his dressing gown tightly around him and ran to the back of the house.

Hugo started to cry and hugged his mother. The two girls just held each-others hands quietly weeping, tears running down their faces. Mrs Bennett was fighting to control her tears and fears, not only for Bird but also now, for her husband who, she was afraid, might try to do something silly; heroic, but foolish nevertheless.

A little way down the road, two figures, dressed in hooded anoraks, marched purposely away from the scene. They frequently turned and looked backwards. Their faces, dimly lit by the street lamps, were smiling.

In the distance, the scream of the sounds from the emergency services overcame the crackle of burning wood and the occasional pop and bang as something exploded. Flashing blue lights pierced the glowing light of dawn as, one by one, the various fire engines and police cars screeched to a halt. The dancing yellow flames reflecting off the bright red of the vehicles made it look like a scene from hell, and as far as Mrs Bennett was concerned, it was.

Rapidly she discussed the situation to the chief fire officer who quickly came up to her. He asked if there was anyone left inside. She was about to explain about Bird when she saw her husband appear from around the back of the house. She looked at him as if to say '*Is everything alright*' and he understood, nodding his head but still looking grim.

To save answering the officer's questions, she pointed to her husband and instructed the fireman to talk to him.

Mr Bennett confirmed that everyone was out and no, he had no idea of how the fire had started, only that it seemed to have originated in the hall by the front door. The officer looked concerned but was then called away by one of the other firemen as some other details needed attention.

A female police constable came up to them and invited them to sit in their patrol cars as the early morning was chilly and they were only dressed in their night attire. Up to that point, no one had noticed the temperature due to the heat from the fire but as soon as it was mentioned to them, they all started to shiver and welcomed the protection and warmth of the vehicles.

The children sat in the constable's car while the adults were directed to one which had just arrived and was driven by a plain-clothes policeman.

As they got in, he turned and they recognise him as Sergeant Cummings.

"Well, you are keeping us busy these days," he said jokingly.

The Bennett's grimaced.

"Right now. Tell me what's been going on?"

Mr Bennett explained what had happened and where he thought the fire had originated, which made the sergeant's eyebrows lift. He was about to continue with the questioning when there was a tap on the window and the door of the car was opened by, what appeared to be, a paramedic.

"I'm sorry sir, but we have to get these people to the hospital to get them checked out." The sergeant was about to protest when the paramedic opened the rear doors to the car and ushered the two out and into a waiting ambulance. Inside, the two girls and Hugo were already seated. Jake bounced around with excitement.

As soon as the ambulance moved off and they were alone in the back Mrs Bennett whispered to her husband, "Is Bird alright?"

He looked around to check that the driver and his companion were out of earshot, then explained that Bird had become trapped by the smoke and had been unable to smash through the double glazing of the window. Fortunately, Mr Bennett had arrived and managed to break through it using a concrete garden gnome that had been bought by Hugo to remind him of his adventures and which he had stood on a pedestal on the rear lawn.

Hugo chuckled to himself that the gnomes had saved him this time, instead of the other way round.

His father went on to explain that he had managed to rescue their friend but he had suffered several burns to his feathers and had inhaled a lot of smoke.

"I tried to get him to come out and get treatment but he said it would create too many problems and so I rang Pete Goodfellow, again. He's going to wish he'd never met me. Anyway, he said that he would come as soon as he could and look at Bird. In the meantime, Bird would hide in the tool shed until everyone had gone."

The sirens stopped and the ambulance pulled up outside A&E at Barnstaple Hospital. They were offered trollies as they went in but the adults said that they would prefer to walk, but Hugo jumped on one and grinned as the orderly pushed him and the two girls into the waiting area.

It was broad daylight by the time they left. Mr Bennett started to order a Taxi to take them home but just as he was about to phone, Stephanie's boyfriend's parents turned up. In all the confusion, Stephanie had still had the instinct, or addiction as Hugo thought as she explained its presence later, to grab her mobile phone and while everyone was being checked, she had phoned Marty to tell him what had happened.

Mr Edmunds insisted that they all return to his house, after all, there was no point going back to their home, as everything, if it wasn't burnt, then it would be soaked in water from the fire engine. They all gratefully accepted the offer, especially Stephanie, and minutes later they drove off.

It was three days later that the fire services gave them permission to return to the house, or what remained of it. Mrs Bennett wept as she looked at the scene of devastation that confronted them. Mr Bennett, notebook in hand, walked around the perimeter, looking at the structure and going through his mind the choices of repairing it, or pulling the whole building down and starting again. He would have to wait until the insurers had been to assess the damage before he made that decision. '*At least I can afford to rebuild it.*' He thought to himself and thanked his ancestors for his inheritance.

He conveyed this idea to his family to cheer them up, and despite the scene in front of her, Stephanie smiled as she imagined all the new dresses and clothes she could buy, to replace those which had been destroyed.

Hugo meanwhile was subdued. Although many of his possessions had little monetary value, they played a very sentimental part of his life. He kicked at the gravel on the drive as he looked at where his bedroom had been. But wait, it was still there. The windows were intact and there was no sign of any damage to it, at least not from the outside. He made to go in but he was held back by his father who had been warned that it may not yet be structurally safe and only his father and the contractor, who was wearing a bright red hard-hat, were allowed to enter.

Hugo turned away noticing Morgana sitting on a stone in the far corner of the garden. She had her head in her hands and was crying. He walked over to her and sat down beside her. He was tempted to put his arm around her by way of comfort but thought better of it, after all, physically, she was a grown woman and not the apparent small girl several months his junior.

"Why are you crying? After all, you haven't lost anything," he said, as conciliatory as possible.

"I've lost everything," she sobbed.

"What do you mean, you've lost everything? You only had a few clothes and they can be easily replaced."

"You don't understand," she said with a note of hysterics in her voice. "All my potion books have been destroyed as well as the potion I made to keep me alive. Without them, I will die and I can't make any more without the books."

At this point, she broke down and Hugo instinctively put his arm around her.

His mother had noticed the pair and went over to them. Hugo, now himself in tears, explained to his mother the problem. She suddenly looked glum and also sat down beside the girl and wrapped her in her arms. All three were crying.

Mr Bennett, also in a red helmet, could be seen occasionally as he carefully picked his way around, what remained of his house. He kicked at piles of ash to see if anything could be salvaged but was rewarded by clouds of dust and soggy debris sticking to the toe of his shoe.

"Have you seen enough?" James Arkwright, the insurance assessor, called to him from, what had been the kitchen.

Paul Bennett made his way down to join him and they walked back to Mr Arkwright's car.

"Well, Mr Bennett, from what I can see, there is very little point in trying to restore the property. The intensity of the fire has severely weakened its structure and it would cost more to repair than rebuild. It's funny though; the flames damaged everything except the small bedroom upstairs and the area around the cooker in the kitchen. It even left your stew intact, though, I must admit, when I lifted the lid, it didn't smell edible."

The insurance representative smiled and grimaced.

"I need to wait for the forensic report on the source of the fire before my company can give a final figure for the rebuild but in the meantime keep all your receipts and bills for your living expenses etcetera and submit them when you are ready. Nice to meet you. Good luck and goodbye."

The man got into his blue Ford Mondeo and, with a final wave, drove off.

Mr Bennett turned to find what had happened to his family. All three were now gathered round Morgana in tears. He walked over to them and asked what the problem was. His wife, sniffing back the tears, explained about the loss of the books and the potion and that Morgana, sorry Anne, would die.

He made to look as if he was upset but then broke into a beaming smile.

Everyone looked at him, almost with disgust.

"I've just had a chat with the insurance assessor and he says that the house is beyond repair but what did surprise him were the two areas that weren't damaged. The first was your bedroom Hugo." Hugo's eyes lit up. "And the other area was around the cooker in the kitchen. He even commented on the foul stew that was left."

Morgana pushed the arms of those around her away

and ran over to the house but Mr Bennett caught her arm to prevent her from going in.

"The house is still pretty dangerous. You all wait here and I will see what remains and bring it out."

Nervously they all stood, pacing and stretching to see what he was doing. After a short while, he emerged through the blackened doorway holding a large saucepan in front of him. He set it down in front of Morgana's feet and said,

"You know. This stew does smell a bit off," and he lifted the lid and pretended to take a big sniff.

Morgana wrapped her arms around him and kissed him, which surprised not only him but his wife as well and she felt a pang of jealousy.

"Wait here." He motioned to everyone and returned into the house. A minute later he appeared, staggering under the weight of the several volumes of potion books, clearly unmarked by the inferno. "These really must be magic," he joked. "Everything else around was a cinder but these are unscathed."

Just then, Hugo remembered his amulet.

"Dad! Dad! Did you say my room was unscathed too?"

"Yes. Mr Arkwright said that he couldn't explain why so much damage had occurred to the rest of the house but your room was completely untouched."

"The amulet! Don't you see? The amulet is in my room and it protected itself. That's why my room was not damaged. I'll go and get it."

"Oh no you won't," his father said, holding him by the arm to stop him running off. "I'll get it. You wait here!"

"But it's hidden," Hugo insisted.

"Well, OK. But you stay right next to me and you wear

this." His father took off the hard-hat and put it onto his son's head where it immediately slipped over his eyes. Removing it, Mr Bennett adjusted the inside strap and replaced it. This time it stayed in place.

Together they entered the house and five minutes later emerged with Hugo holding high in his one hand the pendant while in the other he clutched as many of his toys as he could carry. Even his father had his arms full of the rescued trophies.

The following days were spent finding replacement accommodation and all that was necessary to make life comfortable again.

Mrs Bennett wanted to rent a large farmhouse on the outskirts of Bideford but Mr Bennett insisted that it would be unsuitable for work and school for the children, so they settled for a large, Victorian, gentleman's residence adjacent to the River Torridge. It was secluded, yet not far from the shops and amenities and school. It even had its own slipway into the river which made Hugo keep on insisting that they buy a boat.

During this time, they had a visit from Peter Goodfellow. He looked a little worried as he stepped inside their new home. He looked around and gave a nod of approval as he saw the potential of the property but then he pulled Mr Bennett away from the others.

"I've had a good look at Bird and generally he is not injured too badly but much of his plumage was singed. It will take at least six months for him to moult and get new feathers.

Until this happens, then he will not be able to fly or make himself invisible. I have brought him here; he's in the car covered by a sheet, but I thought that you should know before I bring him in."

Still covered by the sheet, Dr Goodfellow marched his strange patient into the house and with a flourish, pulled it off.

Everyone was standing around him and gasped when they realised that their friend was nearly bald, all his bright plumage, what was left of it, looked decidedly grey and moth-eaten.

Mr Bennett immediately wrapped his arm around the creature and led him into the kitchen. On the table in front of them was a large plate of fairy cakes which his wife had baked especially.

"Welcome back and help yourself," he said as cheerfully as he could.

Bird looked around at all his friends who were watching him intently but then, without any further hesitation, he leaned his long, but now scraggy neck, forward and ploughed into the goodies. Everyone laughed and it broke the air of pity that had prevailed moments before.

While everyone was involved with Bird, Peter Goodfellow pulled Mr Bennett to one side.

"Paul. You know you were telling me about Emma, sorry Anne, or is it Morgana? Well anyway, you said that she was planning to do some sort of, body merging, with Bird so that the real Emma can get her own body back. I have to warn you that in Bird's present condition, I feel that if she goes ahead, then the end result will not be predictable."

"Do you mean that the potion will not work?" Paul Bennett asked nervously.

"In my opinion, and I may be wrong as I have no

experience whatsoever in this sort of thing, but I think that Bird will not survive in his present condition and even if he does, then he will, almost certainly, never be the same Bird that we all know."

Hugo's father's shoulders sagged as he realised the implication of what his friend had just told him. If they did nothing, then Morgana and the body and soul of Emma will die of accelerated old age and if they went ahead with the transfer, then Bird and the essence of Morgana may never be the same... If they survived in the first place.

That evening, when the rest of the family had retired to bed, he sat in the lounge and told his wife about the conversation he had had with Dr Goodfellow. It was a tearful couple that ascended the stairs and closed the door to their bedroom.

Chapter 65

The North Devon Journal

Putricia sat on the small settee in the lounge of 25 Shore Road and picked up a copy of the North Devon Journal that had been delivered through the letterbox, to see if there was any mention of the fire. As she opened the paper, the front page showed a picture of the house fully ablaze with flames licking from every window. She called out to Susanna and gloatingly pointed to the picture. The pair smiled at each other but as they read down the article, their faces turned to a sneer as they realised that everyone had survived. The sneering turned to hysterical anger as they read that, among the survivors was a woman, named as Emma Jones. They were even more shocked when they looked at a picture of the family and saw that the small girl that had left them was now a fully mature woman. They looked at each other and their own rapidly ageing bodies and then back at the picture.

Susanna turned towards Putricia and screamed at her; "It's your fault. You said that you could make the fusion potion but now look what's happened. If we can't get an antidote very soon then we will die and all the sacrifices I have made over the centuries will be wasted, all because of you and your... incompetence!"

She lashed out at Putricia, sending the paper and the small table in front of them, flying. Putricia, in turn, returned the blows but rapidly realised that her adversary had a man's physic and would easily win any physical fight. In desperation, she ran out of the room and locked herself in the bathroom as it was the only room she could think of where she could remember that had a lock on the door.

Susanna kicked, battered and screamed at the door but Putricia refused to open it. Finally, after at least half an hour of hysterics and shouting everything calmed down until she nervously whispered from behind the door that she was sorry and pleaded with her friend to forgive her.

With her energy spent, Susanna relented as she realised that fighting would not achieve anything.

Suddenly Putricia threw open the door of the bathroom and raced down the stairs, shouting out, "Where's that paper! Quick, find that paper!"

Susanna ran down the stairs after her, confused as to what was happening. She found Putricia kneeling on the floor with the front page of the paper spread out before her. Not finding what she was looking for, Putricia seized the page and ran over to the window where there was more light. With a beaming smile, she turned to her friend and poked her finger repeatedly at one point on the sheet.

"Look! Look!" she said excitedly, still stabbing her finger on the page. Susanna could not clearly see what was there and pushed the hand aside so that she could take a closer look. At first, all she saw was the Bennett family and that accursed woman who was previously their friend. She looked quizzically at Putricia who, triumphantly, told her to see what was pictured behind and to the left of the group. Susanna looked down again and slowly her grimace turned to a smile and then to a shout of joy and she threw her arms around her friend, all thoughts of animosity, gone.

The two almost bumped heads as they peered down at the image. Just behind the group was a series of steps and, although slightly obscured by a lavender bush, was, what at first glance, appeared to be a box but on closer examination was… a pile of books. Old books. Old potion books.

When they finally stopped hugging each other, Putricia explained that while she was sitting in the bathroom, she had been going over the picture in her mind. Something had caught her attention when she had seen it earlier but she could not think what it was but then suddenly, she realised what she had seen. All animosity was now long forgotten, they sat down and began to plan how they could retrieve the volumes so that they might find an antidote to their certain death.

Chapter 66

Two into One

Julia Bennett lay awake for much of the night, ploughing through, in her mind, the implications and consequences of Bird being unable to be the host of Morgana's spirit. If he could not, then Emma's spirit may never be free.

As dawn broke, she finally succumbed to the turmoil going through her head and fell asleep but not before convincing herself of the action to be taken.

It seemed only seconds later that, from the scratching on the door by Jake demanding his breakfast, she was reawakened. Her husband was midway through dressing and he knew that his wife had had a disturbed night as he had also been awake for much of it.

"I'll make some tea," he told her and, clipping his trouser belt around his waist, he opened the bedroom door and went down to the kitchen, closely followed by Jake.

With two steaming mugs of tea held in one hand, he opened the bedroom door but found his wife had fallen asleep and so quietly, he reclosed the door and went back into the kitchen. Eager to explore the surroundings of this new house, he waited for Jake to finish his food, which didn't take long, and then, attaching the dog's lead, they went out for a walk.

On his return, he found everyone was up and there was the tempting smell of fried bacon coming from the kitchen. On entering, his wife smiled and handed him a large crusty roll crammed full with rashers of bacon. He sat at the kitchen table and opened the local newspaper, which he spread out before him and started to read.

"Oh. While you were out, Sue from your practice called and asked if you could possibly go in as one of your patients had an emergency and was refusing to see your locum," his wife said as she handed him a mug of tea.

"I bet I know who that is," he replied. "That woman is always moaning but if I don't go in, she will give the staff a hard time."

He left the table and she could hear him talking to his receptionist on his mobile phone.

On re-entering the kitchen, he finished the remains of his bacon sandwich and tea, kissed his wife, telling her that he would return as soon as possible and then left for his work.

She knew that once he arrived there, he would be there for most of the day, "*Attending to problems,*" he would always say.

Shouting to Hugo and Stephanie to hurry up or they'd be late for school, she cleared away the breakfast crockery and put them in the dishwasher. The thumping down the stairs told her that the children were ready. With an explanation to Anne, who was sorting out some washing, she bundled them into her car and drove to their school.

Throughout the journey, she was going through her plan in her mind and since her husband was at work and the children were at school, today was an ideal time put it into practice.

As she stepped back through the door into her house, the silence struck her. It was the first time since they moved in that she had been alone, well except for Anne who seemed constantly worried. In their old house, although there were no near neighbours, there was always the noise of the crashing sea which, while living there, was ignored, but now it was absent, she was aware of the silence. It gave her an overwhelming sense of peace.

Entering back into the kitchen she found Anne leaning over one of her old potion books, while, on the stove, a large saucepan containing her potion bubbled, with small wisps of bluish steam hissing out from under the lid, which rattled with every puff.

"We need to talk," Julia began and indicated that they both sit down. "Dr Goodfellow has told us, that despite how he looks, Bird is in a very bad way and it will take over six months for him to recover and grow a new plumage."

Anne gasped. "But I can't wait that long. At the rate I am ageing I have only a few months, if that." She held her head in her hands and started to sob.

"That's what I thought," Mrs Bennett said, very matter-of-factly. "So I have come up with a solution."

Anne stopped crying, pulled a tissue from the box on the table, wiped her eyes and nose and looked at her with anticipation. Without making eye contact, Julia Bennett went on,

"I have given this matter a great deal of thought and

there is only one other person that you can merge with."
She paused as if frightened to say who this was but then,
collecting herself, she sat up straight and said. "As I was
saying, there is only one other person who can take Bird's
place and that is... me!"

She sat back in her chair and was reluctant to look at
Anne until finally, she turned.

Anne's face was white with shock and she was about to
say something when Hugo's mother put her hand on hers
and explained that, since she was a distant descendant of
Susanna Edwards then she already had 'witches' blood in her
veins and besides, there was no choice. If Anne did not merge
with someone soon then both she and Emma would die.

For several minutes Anne protested but eventually
realised that what Julia was saying made sense.

"When? Where shall we do it?" Anne asked timidly.

"Now! No time like the present, and besides, I am sure
that if any of my family knew what I... sorry, we, are going
to do, then they would try to stop me."

"You mean they don't know!" Anne screamed.

Julia ignored her and pulled from her handbag a white
envelope. "This will explain everything to them, just in
case there are any... problems."

Anne was about to speak but Mrs Bennett slapped the
letter onto the table and announced.

"Right! Let's get on with it. What do I have to do?"

Anne tried to protest again, but Julia was insistent.

Anne gave her one last worried look and walked over to
the stove. After checking and smelling the contents of the
saucepan, she ladled a measure of the liquid into each of
two tumblers which she fetched from the kitchen cabinet.

She passed one of the glasses to Julia and held onto the other.

"Sit beside me and hold my hand." she instructed her companion, then, with a final, "Are you sure you want to do this?" she indicated for Julia to drink the potion and at the same time, drank hers.

The bitter taste of the mixture made both women screw their faces up, and for a moment they looked at each other and laughed as if it were a joke, but then their expression turned to grimaces as the mixture began to take effect. They held hands so tightly that they became white.

Each started to cry out as the effect became more intense. Jake, who had been curled up in his basket, began to bark and dance around them, thinking it was a game. Anne gave an almighty scream and thrashed around on the settee but Julia never let her hand go. Then it was Julia's turn to scream; a very hoarse cry, and her whole body became rigid. Her arms and legs shot out, making her spread-eagled, but still she held onto Anne's hand. The two women writhed and coughed, falling onto the floor in the process. After what seemed minutes the noise stopped and the pair slumped, exhausted on the floor. Only the sound of Jake's excited barking filled the house and even this stopped as he approached his mistress, sniffed her head and gently licked her face.

For over an hour the two lay still, hardly breathing, until, with a choking cough, Julia opened her eyes. She lay still for several more minutes, just gazing at the ceiling. Finally, she turned towards her companion.

She sat up, terrified at what she saw. Before her, was a

limp pile of clothes in disarray, in the middle, a mess of brown hair.

The pile moved and groaned.

"Anne! Are you alright?" Julia spoke, still dazed. A voice that was not hers suddenly came from her throat. "We did it! The potion worked."

Julia was shocked at hearing herself say things which she had not thought. Slowly the dizziness cleared and everything came back. She could feel her heart pounding deep in her chest as she realised that she was now two people in one body.

Kneeling up, she crawled over to the twitching pile of clothes and pulled them aside. A young girl was curled up, sobbing quietly and holding herself as if she would fall apart if she didn't.

Carefully, Julia reached out and gently caressed the young girl's hair. Gasping at the touch, the body twisted herself over to look at, or what had touched her. When she saw it was Julia, she burst into tears and threw her arms around her neck.

"Oh! Mrs Bennett. What's been happening? I've had this terrible dream. A witch took over my body and I could not get her out of my mind."

"Don't worry… Emma. Everything is alright now. The witch has gone and you are quite safe." Julia cooed, trying to sound as calm and reassuring as possible, hoping that the girl did not hear her heart thumping away in her chest.

They each helped one another to stand and it was immediately apparent that Emma had not only returned to her original self but that she had shrunk back down to her original size. So much so that the clothes that she had been wearing before the transfer, now almost fell off. She had to grab hold of them, which made her go red with embarrassment.

"Go upstairs and change your clothes. You may want to take a shower first as I think that it may help you to feel better. When you come down, I will explain everything to you. Now off you go."

Emma nodded, and gripping the sagging clothes around her, trying not to trip on the legs of the jeans, she left and went up to her room. A minute later, the noise of the shower running was heard.

Julia ran her fingers through her hair and, still a little unsteadily, she walked over to a mirror that hung on the wall. With some trepidation, she slowly lifted her eyes and gazed at the reflection. A wave of calm ran through her body as she realised that the person staring back at her was still indeed her. She let out a long breath but it was interrupted by a voice that said,

"My, my. Don't we make a handsome pair?" Which was followed by an uncontrollable laugh…

It was only now that Julia realised the full extent of what she had done, and an overwhelming sense of fear suddenly struck her.

"Don't worry," came the voice again. "I will keep our secret providing you don't do anything… silly."

She was about to ask what was meant by 'anything silly' when Jake, who had been silently watching the whole event, sprang forward and jumped up, putting his paws on her chest.

Tearing herself away from the mirror, she walked over and picked up the dog's bowl, filled it and carefully placed it back down on the floor. Jake's head was in it even before she had time to let it go and it was almost torn from her grip. She smiled and went over to the kettle, filled it and switched it on. *'A cup of tea always helps to solve problems, though I could do with something stronger.'* She grinned to herself and watched the kettle as it sang and began to bubble.

Chapter 67

The Letter

"Quiet, you fool. She'll hear us," Putricia scolded Susanna, as they inched closer to the window through which they could see Julia Bennett filling the kettle.

They silently jostled below the windowsill, each trying to see what was happening in the kitchen and planning the best way to get in unobserved, so that they could fulfil their plan to reclaim the ancient potion books.

"Look! There they are!" Susanna whispered excitedly.

"Where? Where?" Putricia replied, pushing Susanna to one side in an effort to see more clearly.

Julia Bennett thought she heard a noise outside and turned to look out the window, which made the pair of would-be thieves outside duck down.

Although only early afternoon, dusk was descending and Julia switched on the lights. The suddenness of the illumination made the voyeurs shrink further away from the window but slowly, they lifted themselves to look once more through the glass. Putricia could hardly contain herself as she spied the pile of pealing, leather-bound volumes sitting only a few arms lengths away. Yet they might have been miles away unless the two could find a way in, without being spotted and 'repossess their property' as she thought to herself.

Hugo's mother poured out two mugs of tea from a teapot, shaped like a small cottage; a Christmas present from Stephanie from last year. After adding some milk from the fridge, she placed the mugs on a tray, together with a large tumbler of water and a packet of chocolate digestive biscuits. Carefully picking up the loaded tray she went out of the kitchen and Putricia could see her climbing the stairs as the kitchen door swung closed and blocked her view.

"Come on. Now's our chance. She's gone," the witch said, still in a whisper and rubbing the window to remove the misting from her breath, which made a squeaking sound. Susanna shushed her and together they eased themselves down from the ledge on which they'd been standing and tip-toed to the kitchen door. They were delighted to find it unlocked. With a final check to make sure that they were not observed, crept inside.

Suddenly there was a rustle from behind them and both turned in alarm. Jake, his tail wagging furiously, lifted himself out of his basket, hidden in the corner, and nuzzled up to his old friend. Putricia knelt to stroke his head but Susanna poked her and silently indicated to forget the animal and concentrate on getting the books.

The old, yellow-brown volumes were weighty and the pair struggled to carry them all but finally, they had them and began to leave. It was just at this point that Susanna glanced over at the cooker and noticed the large pot resting on the range. There was something familiar about the smell of whatever it contained. Curiosity overcame the need to leave, and she went over to investigate its contents. Putricia, seeing her go over to the cooker, motioned, as best as she could, for her to get back and leave, but Susanna's curiosity got the better of her.

Balancing her burden in one arm, she freed her other and lifted the lid of the saucepan, looked at the contents, put her head close to the pot and sniffed. A broad smile lit up her face and she carefully put down the books on the work surface next to the cooker. Putricia hissed at her to hurry up, or else they would be caught, but her companion ignored her and dipped her finger into the liquid in the pan. She touched the finger to the tip of her tongue and smiled again. She indicated for her friend to put down her load of books and come over and join her. Reluctantly, she did and as she approached the pot and sniffed the aroma of its contents, she realised the reason for her friend's interest and smiling face.

"Is that what I think it is?" Putricia whispered, with almost a laugh in her voice.

Susanna grinned again and excitedly replied that she was sure it was.

"Forget the books, except that one. The one with gold lettering and a broken spine." Susanna mouthed and pointed to the largest of the books in the pile. "We've all we need right here." Silently replacing its lid, she picked up the saucepan and without further ado, they made their way out of the kitchen and fled back to Shore Road as fast as they could. Jake went back to his basket, turned twice and lay back down to doze.

Twenty minutes later a smiling Julia Bennett, carrying the tray with two empty mugs, a half-full tumbler of water and an empty biscuit wrapper, followed by a still subdued Emma and a weather-worn Bird came back into the kitchen from upstairs. Jake roused himself and came and nuzzled Emma, who finally smiled and knelt to stroke him.

"That's strange?" Mrs Bennett said, looking around the kitchen. "I'm sure that I left those potion books by the mixer, and what has happened to the saucepan with the remains of the fusion potion? It was definitely on the cooker when I left. Hugo! Stephanie! Paul! Is anyone there?"

She looked around to see if any of the family had come home without her knowing but despite calling and looking in every room, no-one could be found. Emma and Bird hunched their shoulders, wondering what all the fuss was about. Mrs Bennett crouched down to search under the furniture but found nothing. A second voice in her head said, "They've been here. I know it. I can sense it. They've taken the potion and the master recipe book. If they've got those, then they will be able to reverse the ageing process as well and in doing so will need other subjects into which they can merge. You must stop them before they have the chance to change."

Julia jumped at the intrusion of this voice but she realised that what it said was the only explanation. She wished that her husband was here so that she could ask for his advice and support but she knew that it would be several hours before he returned, by then it may be too late. She looked at Emma and then at Bird wishing that she could ask for their help but she was determined that she would not put her charge in any more danger and, as for Bird… he would be no use either in his present state.

"Bird. Because of your present condition, do you think that it would be safer for you with your friends at the Gnome Reserve?" she asked her guest with a tone in her voice that expected the answer, yes.

The animal looked at her and then himself. "I like staying here with you all," he started, "but I am a little restricted on when and where I go so that you may be correct. I will send a thought message to Chipper to see if it will be alright."

"Oh, I wouldn't bother with that," insisted Hugo's mother, "come on, it's getting dark. I will take you there in the car. No-one will see you."

Bird was a little taken back at the sudden insistence that Mrs Bennett showed in her desire for him to leave and he began to think that he had outstayed his welcome. Reluctantly he agreed.

Grabbing her handbag, she made for the door but then turned and ordered Emma to go up to her room and stay there until either the children or Mr Bennett returned. A minute later, she and Bird were hurtling out of Bideford towards the Gnome Reserve.

It was almost an hour later when Hugo and Stephanie slammed open the front door of the house, both very disgruntled at not being picked up from school by their mother. Instead, they had accepted an offer of a lift from the mother of a classmate of Stephanie.

They called out for their mother as they entered and were surprised that she was not there. They were even more amazed when a much younger looking and more normal-sized Emma came down the stairs.

"What's been happening? You're back to normal!" screamed Hugo and started to walk around her. Stephanie went up to her and touched her face, which made Emma withdraw a little.

"I'm not sure exactly what's been happening myself," she stammered. "One moment I was this ageing version of myself and then I woke up and found myself...well... back to normal."

"That dress looks terrible on you," Stephanie declared. "Come upstairs straight away and I'll find something that's more fashionable.

Emma smiled and together the girls ran up the stairs.

"Where's mum?" Hugo shouted after them.

"She's taken Bird to the Gnome Reserve so that he can recuperate with his friends," Emma shouted back, followed by the slam of his sister's bedroom door.

"I'm his friend as well," sulked Hugo. He threw his school bag into a corner and slouched into the kitchen to see what he could find to eat. He picked up the empty packet of chocolate digestives, hoping that there might be one left but he was disappointed and tossed the wrapper back onto the table.

Jake curled himself around his legs as Hugo opened and closed the various kitchen cupboards, eventually finding a packet of almond nuts which his mother used when she made cakes. He poured himself a handful and then went up to his room, munching them as he went.

He could hear the two girls laughing and giggling in the room next to his and so he turned on his computer, booted up his favourite game of *Minefield* and pushed the volume to maximum to drown out the sounds. He'd been playing for about forty minutes when he heard his father call from downstairs. He paused his computer; he was losing anyway and went down to greet his father.

"Where's everybody?" Paul Bennett asked, looking around. "Where's your mother?"

"Oh. Emma and Steph are upstairs and Emma says that mum has gone to the Gnome Reserve to take Bird back so that he can recuperate with his *friends*." He said the last word with sarcasm, which was noted by his father.

"Oh!" said his father, also noting that Hugo used the name Emma, not Anne or Morgana as he had done up till then, but he gave it no importance. Casually he sauntered into the kitchen to make himself a coffee, which, when poured, he placed on the table and pulled up a chair to read the local paper. As his hand went out to pick up the cup, he noticed an envelope lying beside it. Scrawled on it in his wife's handwriting was his name. Intrigued, he picked it up and read the contents.

He was only halfway through when the colour drained from his face and by the end, he was livid with anger and desperation. He tore up the stairs and burst into Stephanie's bedroom without knocking. His daughter was about to scream at him to get out as both of the girls were only dressed in their underwear, but one look at her father made her realise that this would not be the best idea. Each girl grabbed the first piece of clothing they could find and held it against themselves.

Paul Bennett was about to demand from Emma the whereabouts of his wife when he stopped short and looked at her. "You're back to normal," he sighed almost in a whisper.

"Yes," Emma replied with a beaming smile and was about to explain when Mr Bennett slumped down on the bed and held his head in his hands with the letter gripped between his fingers.

"Then it's true," he mumbled, almost in tears.

"What's true?" demanded Stephanie. "What's wrong, dad? What's wrong?" His daughter was now sounding hysterical and beginning to cry.

The noise brought Hugo to the door and he demanded to know what was happening. Not getting a coherent answer from anybody, almost brought him to tears as well.

At that moment, the front door slammed and Mrs Bennett called up the stairs. Immediately her husband stood up and ordered the children not to move, in such a forceful voice that Stephanie stopped crying and sat, numbed on the bed. Her father closed the door behind him and sprinted down the stairs. The children were unaware of the exact words that were being screamed in the kitchen, but the sheer volume and hostility in them paralysed them all. None of them spoke or moved.

Eventually, the shouting from downstairs calmed down and Mrs Bennett could be heard crying. The three began to stir and it was then that she and Emma realised they were half undressed and that Hugo was in her room. She stood up, pulling a flowery jumper up in front of her and ordered Hugo to get out. He did not hesitate and rushed back into his room, where he smiled and blushed.

Finally, all the noise from the kitchen subsided and the clatter of moving crockery made Hugo realise that it was well-past tea time and he was feeling ravenous. He tapped on his sister's bedroom door and whispered that he was going downstairs. Her door cracked open and two heads appeared and listened. Hearing nothing, all three slowly inched down the stairs, pushing each other to the front so that they would not be first in the kitchen. Emma lost.

Chapter 68

A Third Person

It had been a long walk back from the Bennett's house and the two witches slumped into the armchairs as soon as they had arrived at Shore Road and unlocked the door. On several occasions, Susanna had stumbled, making the liquid in the saucepan splash around. Putricia was glad to be able to put the heavy book down and she rubbed her arms to try to get some life and feeling back into them.

Snatch looked up at the pair, rose from next to the warm radiator and sniffed the saucepan and the book. He did not like the smell of the potion as he backed away quickly as soon as his nose touched the lid.

The whole journey had been made worse in that the two did not wish to meet anyone who may question what they were doing. They frequently had to change the sides of the road on which they were travelling to avoid any confrontation.

Susanna finally arose and shuffled into the kitchen where the light from the still-open white-cupboard door gave the room an eerie glow. While watching Julia Bennett through her window, she had noticed how she had passed her hand over a small white pad on the wall and the room had suddenly become illuminated. Seeing one of these pads on the wall next to the door, she flicked the lever in its centre. The room flooded with light. Such was the shock that she switched it off again. With more control, she lifted the small lever up and down, amazed as the lights came on and went off.

Putricia noticing the flashing from where she sat, came to investigate. After watching Susanna use the switch several times, she had a go and for the next few minutes, they smiled and played with the switch. With the new source of light, Susanna kicked the door of the cold-cupboard shut. She then hunted through the other cupboards pulling out what little remained of the food that they had left and started to prepare a meal. Meanwhile, Putricia went around every room hunting for the small white plaques and flicking the switches in their centres. She was amazed at the fact that she could now see in every room, irrespective of the time of day.

A call from her housemate returned her to the kitchen and in silence, they ate a meagre meal of cornflakes with sour milk and coffee powder sprinkled on top. Half of a somewhat wrinkly apple followed it. The meal finished, Susanna picked up the plates and put them in the sink with several others.

"When shall we do it?" Putricia said, breaking the silence and wiping the remains of her meal from around her mouth with the back of her hand.

"First, we must see what the book says. We don't want

to make any more *mistakes* do we?" Susanna sneered. Putricia felt a little upset at the comment but let it pass, knowing that she was right after all.

By the now brightly illuminated kitchen, they opened the ancient tome and, page by page, flicked through until they found the recipe that they had been searching for. Running her dirt-filled fingernail down the page, she translated the old English script in her mind. She came to an abrupt stop as she neared the bottom of the page and sighed.

"What is it?" questioned her friend.

"We need a third person," she said quietly and then shouted. "We need a third person!"

"What do you mean?" asked Putricia, now beginning to worry.

"To make the potion work, we need someone who we can merge into," she explained with a note of exasperation in her voice.

"Who? Where are we going to find someone?" Putricia demanded, sounding frustrated. They had both hoped that just taking the potion would have stopped the ageing process but now, it seemed that they needed another person's body.

They slumped down on the chairs beside the table in silent, brooding thought.

Several minutes passed until Putricia looked up and asked.

"Does it have to be a person? Could it, say, be an animal… or a *Bird*?

Susanna looked up and smiled and they both rushed back to the brown page.

"Well, it doesn't say that it has to be a person. All it

mentions is that it must be another *being* and that stupid Bird is certainly another *being*.

Each of them smiled and discussed the pros and cons of living in Bird's body. Putricia said that she didn't like the prospect of not having any arms and having to eat worms and insects but Susanna reminded her that she had been living off worms and bugs for centuries. "Think," said Susanna, "he can make himself invisible and walk through walls. If we could do that, then we could walk into that stupid boy's house, take the amulet and kill all of them all at the same time. We could fulfil our vow in one fell swoop and what is more, we could escape without anyone knowing that it was us."

"What about Morgana?" Putricia suddenly thought.

"When she sees our power and what we have achieved, she will come running back to us and if she doesn't, well then…"

Susanna didn't finish her sentence but just smiled.

They each then returned to the potion book, checking and rechecking the instructions so that there were no more mistakes this time. They then sat down and planned how to locate and capture Bird so that they could go forward with their plan.

Chapter 69

Bird's New Home

Chipper was delighted with Bird's return to the reserve and even he was responding to the loving care and attention that the whole gnome community was giving him. His feathers were improving, though they would not return to their colourful previous self until they moulted in the spring. He was putting on weight with all the food he was constantly being given, though he still craved for Mrs Bennett's fairy cakes. His small friend was determined to get him fit again and insisted that they go for long walks each day, though this frequently ended with Bird having to carry the exhausted gnome home on his back.

Oleg had knitted him a pair of brightly-coloured leg-warmers to keep out the winter chills. Bird was a little reticent about wearing them at first but they certainly worked and very soon, he was never seen without them.

At the beginning of his stay, the Bennett's and Emma would frequently visit, but after a while, they thought it best to leave him alone. He had been through a great deal of trouble and whenever Julia Bennett was close to him, she could feel the pent-up animosity of her other-self.

It was February and there had been a hard frost overnight. The ponds around the reserve were frozen. Around their edges, dew-drop icicles hung from the noses and extremities of the artificial gnomes placed there by the owner for the benefit of the visitors. Chipper was playing his favourite game of throwing small stones into the frozen nets of the cobwebs to see if they were strong enough to hold the pebble.

Bird, complete with leg warmers, emerged from the house that the owner had specially built for him. Although it was small by his standards, it was a palace in comparison to the other gnomes' homes.

He stretched his long neck, ruffled his wings and preened himself, straining to get at every accessible spot. Looking up at the sky and sensing a warm day for the time of the year, he asked his diminutive friend if he would like to go for a short walk before breakfast, but Chipper had just found a particularly strong web and already had three pebbles trapped in its fibres. His record up to then had been three and he was desperate to beat it and so he waved hello to his friend, indicating that he wanted to finish his game. Bird lifted his wing, returned the greeting and strode off across the fields that surrounded his new home.

By nightfall, he had still not returned.

Chapter 70

Captured Again

The net covering Bird was cutting in and the more he struggled, the more it hurt until he no longer had the energy, or will, to fight back and made himself as comfortable as he could, under the circumstances.

For weeks the two witches had been planning his capture and were living in a rotting garden shed close to the Reserve to save the long journey to and from their house. The net had been Putricia's idea when she saw it stretched across the inside of the roof, still with the decaying remains of some onions which had been stored on it. The biggest flaw in their plan was, how to manage such a bulky package back to their house without being seen. Susanna had come up with the ideal solution when she noticed the gardener's wheelbarrow lying, forgotten, on its side at the bottom of the lane leading to the owner's house.

It was in this 'carriage' that Bird found himself as it bumped and banged along the road pushed by two very dishevelled characters. Although the two witches tried to avoid as many people as possible, they occasionally had no choice of encounter. The site of an elderly, unkempt man and grey-haired old woman pushing a tatty, loaded wheelbarrow covered in an old sack, made most passers-by move to the other side of the road. The words 'gypsies' and 'travellers' were heard as they passed by; however, one youngish man, walking a small dog, dropped a pound coin into the wheelbarrow as he passed and wished the two a good day. The pair turned and watched him go around a corner, dumbstruck at what he had done. They looked at the coin as it lay glinting in the folds of the sack covering the hapless prisoner. Putricia gathered it up, held it up to show it to her friend and then plunged it deep into one of her pockets.

The journey was exhausting and by the time they re-entered the house on Shore Road, the pair collapsed into their respective chairs. Putricia wiped her mouth, removing the dried saliva and crumbs of the bread rolls that they had bought from a small shop they were passing, with the donated pound. The fresh crusty bread had tasted so good after the stale, mouldy crumbs that they had eaten while living in the shed.

Bird moaned and wriggled under the sack, but neither two made any effort to attend to him. Snatch eased himself from his bed next to the radiator and sniffed at the load in the wheelbarrow. He growled as he recognised the smell and tore the sack away from over the motionless passenger. Bird froze as the large red eyes of the cat drew closer and closer to his.

"Leave him!" snarled Susanna. Still growling, the cat backed away. The witch threw him the last crust of bread roll that she had kept in her pocket for him. He caught the morsel in mid-air and swallowed it without so much as a chew.

Seeing Snatch eating, albeit just a morsel, made Bird realise how hungry and thirsty he was as he hadn't had anything since breakfast. Twisting his head around so that he faced his captors, he asked in a dry husky voice for some water. At first, the two just looked at him as if he had asked for a million pounds, but then Susanna realised that if he was going to be their resident body after the transference, then it would be in their best interests to keep him as healthy as possible. Reluctantly she eased herself out of the chair and went into the kitchen. Returning, she held a bowl of water in one hand and a long-bladed knife in the other. Instinctively Bird recoiled as she approached, the blade held out in front of her. Kneeling, she used it to cut away some of the netting around Bird's head so that, at last, he was able to move it and partially stretch his neck, which was a great relief. The witch, in the old man's body facing him, smiled, sending the smell of its fetid breath over his face. Bird turned away, which made Susanna laugh. She put the bowl on the floor and watched as Bird strained his neck to try to reach the water, but from his position in the wheelbarrow, it was impossible. The witch smiled as she watched him struggle.

Don't worry my pretty thing," she whispered, "Not long now and then we'll be the very best of friends."

Carefully, she moved around and, gripped the handles of the wheelbarrow. In one movement she lifted the handles and tipped its helpless load onto the floor. She pushed the bowl of water towards Bird's head with her foot until, at last, he was able to drink. He was so dry that the first beak-full felt that it was burning his throat as it trickled down, but with each gulp, the pain eased and a great sense of relief came over him.

As he began to calm down, Bird began to wonder what she had meant by *'being the best of friends'*, and the words kept revolving around in his brain. Suddenly he realised that it wasn't just the words swimming around in his head, it was everything else that was swimming as well. All around him, everything was becoming blurred and distorted as the sleeping draft that Susanna had added to the water took its effect. The room was getting darker and vivid colours danced across his vision. Slowly, blackness took over and his head fell to the floor with a gentle bump.

"That should keep him quiet until tomorrow," Susanna muttered, more to herself than her companion. "I'm too tired to transfer tonight and I need to do a final check before we do it, so I'm going to bed."

Putricia got up to protest as she had been eager to get the change done as soon as possible. She had noticed that the ageing process had accelerated and it frightened her that the longer the deed was left, the less chance there would be of success, or at least of reversing the actual ageing. She hated looking progressively older every time she caught sight of her reflection.

A wave of Susanna's hand dismissed her eagerness and she resigned herself to having to wait until the morning. She wished that she could have some of the sleeping potion they had given to that stupid animal in front of her. Slowly she turned and went up to her bed for what, she knew, would be a very long and sleepless night.

Chapter 71

The Gypsies

The loud squawking of a seagull outside his bedroom window woke Hugo. He looked blearily at his bedside clock; 6:18 flashed in front of him. He groaned and pulled the duvet over his head to block out the noise but it persisted until finally, curiosity got the better of him and he pushed back the covers. He knelt upon his bed and pushed the curtains apart.

Flapping and squawking on the other side of the window was a large grey and white seagull with a red mark on its beak. 'Herring Gull'. Its name flashed into Hugo's brain and he was about to close the curtain and return to the warmth of his bed when he noticed the small figure sitting on the back of the bird and directing its flight.

"Chipper!" Hugo screamed and rushed to open the window. A blast of freezing air hit him as the window flew open followed by a flurry of beak and feathers as the large bird flew past him and landed on the end of his bed. Its small passenger slid off its back and before Hugo could react, its taxi had flown back out of the window and escaped as fast as it could.

Hugo, regaining his composure, slammed the window shut. His teeth were already beginning to chatter with the icy cold wind that had accompanied his visitor. He turned and slumped back into his bed, pulling the duvet up over him and holding it around his neck.

"What are you doing here? And at this time in the morning. It's still the middle of the night!" Hugo exclaimed,

The small gnome tried to speak but he was so cold from the journey that his teeth would not stop chattering long enough for him to get a sentence out. Eventually, he managed to blurt out the word, "Bird!"

"What's wrong with Bird?" questioned Hugo, taking the hand of the small gnome and helping him move so that he came to sit next to him under the warm duvet. "He hasn't got himself into more trouble, has he? That animal will never learn."

"He's gone missing!" Chipper finally was able to shout as the warmth of the duvet and Hugo's body next to him thawed him out.

"What do you mean, he's gone missing?"

Chipper related the meeting he had had with Bird the previous day and his invite to go for a walk. "After that, no-one has seen or heard from him," the small gnome said, now almost in tears.

"We'll wait until my mum and dad get up and see what they can suggest," said Hugo as reassuringly as possible, though it was more to reassure himself than Chipper. "In the meantime, you get warm. You feel like an icicle sitting next to me."

Chipper gave a wide grin and snuggled deep into the folds of the duvet.

It was about an hour later when Hugo heard someone stirring from his parents' bedroom, and after pulling on his dressing gown, he waited on the landing for whoever was first to appear. It was his father. He was amazed to see his son up at that time of day but after Hugo had explained everything to him, he understood why. Mr Bennett went into Hugo's room where he sat on the bed and told Chipper to tell him everything he knew.

When he had finished, Mr Bennett explained that there was sure to be some logical reason for their friend's disappearance. He was convinced that nothing untoward had happened, though when he returned to his room and explained the situation to his wife, he did not sound so convincing.

"They've taken him." A gruff voice came from his wife as Morgana made her presence known. "It was they who stole the potion and the master recipe book. That means that they plan to do what I did and merge with someone else to stop the ageing process. They must be getting desperate by now and your Bird friend would make an ideal host, especially with the powers he already has. If they merged with him and could walk invisibly through walls, then they would be undefeatable."

Mr Bennett sat down on the edge of his wife's bed while she held her throat, shocked at what she was saying and having no control over it.

"Let's have breakfast and then we can start a search," she said, but this time in her normal voice. Her husband nodded and went to have a shower. She pulled on her dressing gown and went down to the kitchen. Hugo was hovering outside her bedroom door and he followed her down.

He asked what they were going to do but she just smiled and explained that she and his father would start a search but as for Hugo, he was going to school as usual. Her son groaned and pleaded with her to let him help with the search but she told him firmly that he had already lost too many days from school and if he lost any more, then the authorities would start to investigate the reason why, and that would put them all into serious trouble.

"What about Chipper? Hugo asked.

"We'll take him back to the reserve with us," she explained. "Since that was the last place he was seen, then that's the best place to start. Now get yourself some breakfast and then get dressed for school. Oh! And don't forget to get some for your little friend. I bet he's hungry."

At that point, Stephanie and Emma sauntered through the door, engaged in deep conversation with each other. Hugo was pleased that Emma was back to normal, as since she had returned, his sister was far less grumpy, especially in the mornings.

"My word. You're up early," Stephanie sneered but Hugo ignored her and started to tell them about Bird's disappearance. They were both shocked and pleaded with their mother to allow them to help with the search but she was adamant, citing the same reason that she had given to her son.

When Mr Bennett came down, they pleaded with him as well but all he said was, "Do as your mother tells you." and he sat down and buried his head in the newspaper.

After breakfast, her husband apologised to his wife and asked her if she wouldn't mind searching by herself. He had had so much time off work recently that several of his patients had left as they could not, or were not prepared to wait any longer for treatment. His wife nodded as she realised his predicament and they reassured each other that they were sure the problem wasn't serious and that Bird had gone on one of his fanciful jaunts and got lost. 'He never was good at navigating,' Mr Bennett reminded his wife, who smiled but deep down felt a strong sense of foreboding.

Julia Bennett ushered the children and Chipper into the car, put the heater on at full blast and set off for the children's school. After dropping them off, she sped off to the Gnome Reserve where she was surrounded by concerned Gnomes and the owner, all asking her if she had found their friend. She had to say that she hadn't but then enquired if anyone had seen anything unusual over the last few days.

A loud voice from behind her said. "I don't know about anything unusual but there's been a couple of scruffy old gypsies hanging about for the last few days and I'm sure it was them who nicked me barrow."

Everyone turned to see who had spoken. The gardener had been listening to them and was leaning on his broom. Someone whispered that he looked like a scruffy old gypsy himself, which meant that the pair he saw must have been extremely untidy.

Julia Bennett asked him for a description of the pair and as he gave it, a gruff voice came out of her mouth. "It's them. They have him."

Everyone gasped and looked at her in bewilderment as

they all recognised that voice, or thought they did but Julia coughed.

"I'm sorry, I'm just getting over a cold," she lied and gave another artificial cough.

"What do you mean, '*It's them*'?" spoke up one of the gnomes in front of her.

"Oh. I was just thinking to myself that there is a very small possibility that the two witches might have taken him but it is only a very slight possibility, I'm sure."

"I hope you're right," another of the small people squeaked and many around her murmured their feelings as well.

"Well," Mrs Bennett said, trying to distance herself from what had been said. "Our friend is not here so I will go and see if I can find where he has been hiding and when I find him I will tell him off for causing us all so much worry."

There were several more murmurings of agreement from the crowd around her and, hoping that she had defused the situation, she thanked them all and got into her car. With a final wave, she drove away.

As soon as she was out of earshot, she shouted out loud at her second self. "Don't you ever make your presence known when I am with other people... or gnomes. Do you realise the trouble you would cause if the gnomes knew that Morgana, the cause of all their troubles, and I were the same person?"

A very sheepish course voice erupted from her mouth. "I'm sorry but it isn't easy being trapped in your body."

"I know, and I appreciate the problem as much as you but, until we can find a permanent solution, then try not to make yourself known to strangers."

The rest of the journey back home was in broody silence.

Julia half-hoped that when she opened her front door, Bird would be standing there, beak open, waiting to be fed, but the house was empty.

"I told you, Jane and Susanna have taken him," the coarse voice came again.

"I know." Julia sighed resignedly and slumped down into an armchair. "But where do we begin to look for him?" The other voice was silent.

Wearily prising herself back out of the chair, she went outside to see if there were any signs of him outside but there were none. What she did notice, however, was a large area of trampled ground below the kitchen window with, what looked like, a man's and a woman's shoe prints embedded within it.

The prints confirmed in her mind someone had been spying on them through the window and the only people that could have done that were Putricia and Susanna. A sense of panic came into her chest as she realised the worst; the witches had captured Bird.

She began to feel helpless as the reality of what might happen, no, not *might happen* more like, *what will happen*, to Bird if she cannot rescue him; but how to find him? She knew that the witches had moved from the ruins but she had no idea as to where they were now.

She slumped back down in the easy-chair in the lounge and buried her face in her hands. Jake came up to her and forced his head underneath her arms as if in comfort. She leaned back and stroked his head. Jake whimpered in appreciation.

Suddenly, a thought hit her like a thunderbolt. She did not know where the witches lived but from the scent left behind from beneath the window, she was sure that Jake would be able to track them to where they were living. If that were the case, then all may not be lost after all.

Quickly collecting her heavy coat from the peg by the front door, she gathered Jake's lead and was about to attach it to his collar when she thought again and took from a cupboard his extending leash so that it would give him more freedom to track. As she was about to close the cupboard door, she noticed a stout walking cane that her husband had inherited from his grandfather and which he had used while recuperating from his earlier injuries.

'*That might come in handy*' she thought to herself and pulled it out of the corner, gripping it under her elbow. Thus armed, she fed the lead under Jake's collar and tied it securely. With a new spring in her step, she led the dog outside and coaxed him to sniff around where she had seen the shoe prints. After a few moments, Jake lifted his leg and urinated over the place, which made Julia smile as it made her feel that even Jake had set his seal on the witches' fate. With a shake, he barked and made off. The expanding lead unwound from Julia's hand as she tried to keep up with her guide.

Chapter 72

The Substitute

"Hurry up! I think he's beginning to come round," Putricia called to Susanna who was in the kitchen, giving the potion a final stir as it warmed on top of the stove. She ran her finger down the dirty brown page of the potion book, checking every line to make sure that there were no *mistakes* this time. Taking two large glass tumblers from the cupboard, she filled each one with the foul-smelling liquid. She emptied the dregs from the saucepan into an old teapot, which she thought would be the best way to administer the fluid through Bird's beak and into his throat.

With a final sniff of the tumblers, she carried them, with the teapot, on a small tray, into the lounge area where Putricia had laid out a large duvet from one of the beds, onto the floor.

Bird was lying in the middle, still held tightly by the net, stirring, as if having a nightmare.

"Slacken his ropes," Susanna ordered. Putricia was about to question the order when her friend explained that, if he were still tightly tied after they had made the transition, then they would not be able to escape.

Putricia smiled as the sense of this now seemed obvious and she immediately began to loosen Bird's bonds. He stirred again and twitched, which made her stop but then he settled back and she finished the job.

Susanna knelt beside his body, lifted his head and slowly trickled the potion into his beak through the spout of the teapot. To start with, he coughed and spluttered as the liquid hit the back of his throat and both witches had to hold onto him to stop him moving, but slowly he relaxed as the potion began to take effect and the two relaxed their grip. Finally, the last drop dripped from the spout and Putricia and Susanna grimaced at each other.

Together, they picked up the glass tumblers and started to drink. Each coughed as they swallowed the foul-tasting mixture but persisted. By the time each had consumed half the contents of their glasses, they were unconscious, lying either side of Bird and holding each other's hand as dictated in the recipe.

With a clatter, the two containers fell to the floor, spilling the remains of the potion over it.

Curled up in a corner all this time, Snatch was apparently asleep but, in reality, wide awake and observing what was happening. On seeing the liquid running on the floor and his mistress's unresponsiveness, he decided that he would investigate. The puddles on the floor smelt a little strange but edible. He had not eaten for two days and anything was better than nothing. With a glance at the three bodies on the floor, he began to lap up what was left.

By the time he had lapped up the last drop, he had begun to feel strange but a sudden coughing moan from one of the bodies on the floor made him alert. Bird's body started to shake violently and at the same time, the two either side of him began to thrash about and emit a throaty scream. Snatch could sense that something was not right and fearing that the weird animal that was in the middle of the sandwich was going to hurt them he dived between the two bodies, pushing Bird way from them. The cat lay there waiting for Bird to try to defend his position but the animal's body just rolled from side to side, not attempting to regain his lost territory.

Snatch lay there, now panting, his head swimming as he tried to stand but his legs refused to move. Slowly his focus blurred and strange noises started to stir in his brain. He let out a roar in frustration and, it must be said, fear. Slowly the light seemed to dim and he became unconscious. The last moment he could remember was the sound of a loud banging as if someone or something was pounding at the front door, but then oblivion.

...

Julia Bennett knocked as loudly as she dared on the green front door of 25 Shore Road. It had taken her the best part of two hours to follow Jake's circuitous journey there, having to backtrack on several occasions when the animal had lost the scent, but now she was sure that this was the house and beat on the door to be allowed in. She noticed that several neighbours had pulled their curtains aside to see who was creating such a fuss. Julia was frightened that one of them may phone the police. If that did happen, how would she explain what she was doing? If she told them the truth, then they would lock her up for being insane. She had to get in before that situation arose. Waiting for all the curtains to fall back into their normal folds, she walked around the side of the house. Just as she was giving up hope, she spied a small open window at the rear, which she took to be the window of the toilet as the glass was rippled. Looking around, she found an old wheelbarrow which she dragged over to the bottom of the window. Using it as a ladder, she was able to reach the latch and undo the window enough to squeeze through. She was right, it was the toilet and from the stench rising from under the lid, it hadn't been flushed or cleaned for some time. With a final effort, she landed upside down beside the pan. Ignoring the humiliation and embarrassment, she righted herself and made her way into the house. All the lights were on and it didn't take long to find what she was seeking.

Before her, was the strangest sight that she had ever seen. Four bodies lay before her, all motionless. One, an old man in a pair of denim jeans and a ragged t-shirt, both of which were far too small for his size, a grey-haired old woman, wearing a mismatched skirt and jumper, which again was a very poor fit. Between them, spread-eagled lay the largest cat she had seen, its dark fur ruffled as if in need of a good comb. Almost hidden by its face-down position were two large ivory fangs which were brown and rough looking. Finally, just above their heads lay Bird. Cords of rope lay loosely around his feet, which looked as if they had been tied, judging from the red weals around his ankles.

She ignored the others and rushed up to him, kneeling beside his head and taking it in her hands. He did not stir, but she could feel the pulse beating strongly in his neck. Other than that, he did not appear to be injured any more than he had been when she last saw him.

She was suddenly and uncontrollably pulled away from her action as Morgana took over control of her body. Gruffly a voice came out of her mouth.

"Don't touch them! Any of them. They have taken the transfer potion and if you make any contact with them then you, or rather we, will become involved in the transfer."

Julia dropped Bird's head which made a small bang as it hit the floor and stepped back so that she was pressed against the wall. In silence, she watched as the bodies in front of her began to move and take on new shapes.

The hair of the man began to darken and his curled body became straighter. The old woman's face became less distorted as if the saggy skin was being ironed and filled out. Only the cat with the fangs and Bird seemed to stay the same though the cat's fur did appear to be regaining its sheen, from what had been a very dull coat before.

Julia could feel tears welling up inside her but she realised that they were the tears of Morgana.

"What have we done to ourselves?" Morgana wept through Julia. "After all these centuries, the trials and the hardships we have had to face, it has come to this; me, sharing another's body and them, having to exist as an animal. It would have been better if we had died by the hangman's noose in the first place."

Julia felt remorse at the grief of her other-self. "Is there nothing we can do to stop this or help at all?" she spoke out loud, though this was unnecessary as Morgana could read her thoughts.

"I do not know?" her other voice said. "Susanna was the only real witch… I mean healer, among us and now she is being absorbed into a cat."

Julia was heartbroken at the situation in front of her. She longed for the end of the witches but as Morgana, she was losing her only connection with the past and her true identity.

A loud groan suddenly took her attention from the male body to a small movement from the female. Both of which had now transformed from old, frail, dishevelled people, into young athletic-looking humans in their mid-twenties. Even their clothes seemed to fit as if made for these bodies, although they still looked dirty and creased.

Julia stood, transfixed by what she was seeing, desperately wanting to go forward and help the pair but also knowing that any action by her may destroy any chance of their survival.

For an hour, which seemed only minutes, she just stood and watched as the transformation took its course, until a loud bark from Jake brought her back into reality.

He too had been sitting, silently watching the process taking place in front of him, but nature had the better of him and he needed to go outside to the toilet. He barked and nuzzled up to his mistress, which was his usual way of communicating this message. Julia smiled, almost relieved that her concentration had been broken. Without taking her eyes off the action in front of her, she stooped, picked up Jake's lead and took him outside.

The cold night air brought her instant relief and as she

waited for her pet to run around the small garden finding a suitable place for his needs, she pondered on the distress of her other personality. '*There must be an answer*' she thought to herself. Susanna was able to use the bird potion books to work her spells, well, if she could do it then so could she. A voice inside her told her that she would be wasting her time but Julia, in herself, felt sure that there must be a solution. She just had to find it.

Jake had finished and came back to her side and they both returned to the lounge.

She was surprised to see both humans sitting up but still looking semiconscious and confused. She asked Morgana, in her mind, if it was alright to attend to them but she was told to keep clear, just in case.

Slowly, the two, apparently young people, started to become more aware of their surroundings and, noticing Julia standing there, the young woman lazily asked where she was? Julia swallowed hard, trying to answer and then replied.

"You're in a house in a place called Shore Road. I think. Are you alright?"

"I think so," the girl replied. "What am I doing in Allan's house?" She rubbed her forehead and as she did so, she lifted her arm.

"Arghh! How long have I been here? I need a shower. I smell terrible." She started to get up but slumped back down again as the effort was too much. She looked around and then suddenly saw the body of Snatch still lying prone alongside her and the young man opposite. Ignoring her tiredness, she rolled over, away from the bodies and knelt up. It was at this point she also saw the form of Bird ahead of her. It had begun to twitch a little and the sight of these two *creatures* was too much. She let out a piercing scream, crawling on all fours into a corner and curling her legs up underneath her body.

"Don't be afraid," Julia cooed, trying to calm her down, fully realising the mental and physical stress that she was experiencing.

The scream roused the male body and he tried to jump up in a fight and flight reaction but he collapsed to his knees as he looked around him.

"Wh… at's been going on? Where am I and… who in the world are you?" he demanded, looking at Julia and then at the distraught young woman huddled in the corner. He too then spotted Snatch and Bird lying semiconscious beside him and rapidly moved away, joining the young woman in the corner.

"I will explain everything to you in a moment but first, I must attend to my friends here." Julia pointed to Bird and Snatch.

Bird was still a little drowsy, but he recognised Julia, and as much as he was able, indicated that he was alright and still the old Bird that she had known.

Snatch, however, was not so co-operative. He was rapidly regaining consciousness and his eyes rolled in their sockets as he tried to focus on where he was but more notably, who he was. He roared but then a voice seemed to come from deep in his throat.

"No! No! No!" followed by a loud screeching roar.

The two young people cowered in the corner and held each other in fear.

A deep crackly voice came from Julia aimed at the cat.

"You stupid people. Look what you've done to yourselves. See where your hate and vendetta has led you. I warned you to give it up but you refused and now look at the plight you're in."

"Ha!" the voice of Susanna issued out of Snatch's mouth. "I see that you didn't do much better, trapped in that murderer's wife's body. At least we are free but you are trapped in her and have to do everything she says."

Morgana suddenly became angry and, ignoring Julia's efforts to control her action, she plunged at the cat, trying to hit it in frustration. Snatch sprang away, despite his drowsiness but not before Morgana caught him by an old collar he wore around his neck. The old leather gave way and the collar slipped off his neck and Julia was left holding it, hanging from her hand.

Without any other words, the cat shakily rose to its feet.

"Please help us." The voice of Putricia, somewhat distorted, came from the throat of the cat.

"Silence, you fool!" the stern tones of Susanna followed. "You're in this with me whether you like it or not." With a single bound, Snatch and his uninvited guests jumped at the nearby window. It shattered. For a few moments, he lay motionless on the other side but, rapidly regaining his strength he, and the two witches his body held, raced off into the night.

Julia picked herself up off the floor and remonstrated with her other self at what had happened.

"Will somebody tell me... sorry us, what is going on? Who are you and what was... that thing?" a man's voice boomed from the corner.

Julia brushed herself down and smiled at the duo,

indicating for them to get up and sit on the chairs. When they were seated, she began to explain who she was, who they were and what had been happening. Holding each other's hands, the two sat spell-bound as Julia started her story.

Chapter 73

The Letter

"That's the second time mum hasn't picked us up from school," Hugo moaned as he threw his school bag on the floor in the hall. "It's a good job that Marty's mum was passing; otherwise we'd still be there."

I'm sure that there's a perfectly good reason. She's not normally absent-minded," replied Emma, who had restarted school after her strange growing and shrinking episode. "I'll give her a call to tell her that we are home so that she doesn't worry and go to the school."

Carefully hanging her coat and bag on the coat stand in the hall, she went into the lounge to make the phone call. As she entered the room, her foot kicked against something soft and she looked to see what it was. It was a screwed up piece of paper. Intrigued by this, as Julia was a stickler for picking things up, she bent down and grasped the paper. Unfolding the sheet, she began to read.

My Darling Paul, I know that you will not agree with what I am about to do but I cannot see any alternative. Anne, and Emma, are ageing so fast now that they are on the point of dying. The only way that they can survive and reverse the ageing process is for them to find a new host but this will mean someone else has to be placed in the same predicament as Emma, so I have decided to become the host until Anne can find a more permanent solution. Anne does not want me to do this but if she dies, then so does Emma and I couldn't bear it if that happened.

I know that you will understand and see that we have no other choice. Anne has promised to keep as much in the background as possible so that as far as you and the children are concerned, I will still be Julia and their mother.

Sorry Darling, and please don't be angry with me.

Your ever-loving,

Julia.

Emma sat back on the chair, speechless. She read and re-read the letter, embarrassed that she had read it in the first place and terrified that she had been the reason for Mrs Bennett taking such a risk.

At that moment, Hugo came in and went to switch on the television.

"I think that you had better read this," Emma said almost in tears and held out the letter. Hugo took it and started to read. When he had finished, he sat down in a chair and also re-read it.

"Does this mean my mum's a…witch?" he said quietly.

"I think so," replied Emma, nodding. "But it does say that Anne will stay in the background and not interfere."

She went on, trying to sound as positive as possible and hoping that Hugo would not blame her for it happening in the first place.

"That will explain the big argument that mum and dad had a couple of days ago," Hugo said, more to himself than anyone in particular.

Trying to divert Hugo's attention and the risk of blame, Emma said that she was going to make the phone call to Julia, to tell her they were home but the phone did not answer.

It was at that point that Mr Bennett came home and, after popping his head around the door and saying hello, he looked around and asked where everyone was. Hugo hunched his shoulders. It was then his father realised that something was amiss and asked what was wrong. Sheepishly, Hugo handed his father the creased letter.

"I'm sorry," blurted Hugo, "but it was just lying on the floor, all scrunched up. I didn't know that it was personal and important."

Emma broke in. "It's my fault, really Mr Bennett. I found it on the floor and read it first."

Paul Bennett pulled up a chair and sat down. He was silent for a minute and the children just looked at him.

"Well! I suppose that you should know the truth. I was wondering how to tell you but now it seems that I don't have to." He gave a small grin and opened his arms into which the children ran and they all hugged.

"I tried to ring Mrs Bennett," Emma said, "But there was no reply."

"Where's Jake?" he asked, looking around. The two children also looked around while Emma went into the kitchen to see if he was asleep in his basket but it was empty.

"He's not here." She reported.

"Well. That's it then," Hugo's father said smiling, trying to look reassured. "She's taken him for a walk. She said she might. She'll be home soon. Anyone fancy a cuppa?" Everyone smiled but none of them felt that this was, in fact, the case.

Mr Bennett rose and went into the kitchen. Hugo and Emma could hear the sound of tea being brewed.

Chapter 74

The Inheritance Complete

All three were looking at the window through which Snatch had jumped when a now recovered Bird asked,

"Is there anything to eat? I'm starving."

Everyone turned and laughed at him but then Allan licked his lips and announced.

"You know? I'm starving too."

"Me too," broke in Sue.

"Let's get something to eat," Allan said, getting up to go into the kitchen.

"Oh no, you don't," said Sue firmly. "Before you do anything you're going to take a shower. You smell like you've been rolling in a pigsty...and for that matter, so do I."

Nevertheless, Allan went into the kitchen but within seconds came out again.

"You said that I was untidy but have you seen the mess that those... things have done to my kitchen?" Allan steamed at no-one in particular and strode off into the bathroom. Seconds later, he emerged, holding his hand to his mouth.

"That's it! I'm not staying here. The whole place is a mess and there's no food around anyway."

"May I suggest that you come back home with me and while you're getting cleaned up I will make you some dinner," Julia suggested sympathetically. "Besides, the rest of my family would be very interested in meeting you, now that you are back to normal, as it were."

She rose. As she did so, something fell from the side of the chair on which she had been sitting. It was the old collar that had been torn from around Snatch's neck. She bent down and picked it up. Suddenly, she fell back down into the chair, gazing, wide-eyed at what she held in her hand. The leather was cracked and frayed but in the centre, fastened by a discoloured silver clasp, was a large black stone. Its surface was glass-smooth and reflected the light, almost like a mirror.

"No. No. This can't be real." Morgana's excited voice came out of Julia's mouth.

She turned the stone over and over in her fingers, holding it up to the light and then biting it to see how hard it was.

"What is it?" shrieked Sue, becoming a little unnerved at the sound of Morgana's voice.

"Quick! Come here, both of you!" came an order. "Hold out your hands. Quickly!"

The young pair looked nervously at each other and then did as they were ordered, holding their hands out in front of them.

Roughly, Morgana, for she had now taken over from

Julia, grabbed the right hand of each of them and then smiled. The smile turned to a laugh and then a shout of, "Yes! Yes! Yes!"

The two looked down at their hands. For the first time noticed that each had a ring on the third finger of their right hands. The ring on Allan's finger was crystal clear, like a diamond, while that on Sue's was a brilliant, iridescent blue.

Morgana started to pull the rings off the fingers but Allan and Sue pulled back in pain.

"Careful! That hurt. They're on too tight. We need some soap to help to get them off." screamed Sue.

Julia managed to take back control. "I'm sorry about that," she apologised, "but those rings you are wearing are part of a set."

She reached inside her blouse and pulled out a chain that had been hanging around her neck. Hanging from the end of the chain was a small gold locket and two other rings, one red and one green.

"These are the stones that once adorned the scabbard of Excalibur."

"You mean the real Excalibur? The one from King Arthur?" whispered Sue, gazing at the flashing jewels.

"They were... I mean, are, the inheritance of the three Bideford witches, who I was explaining to you about just now. They each have magical properties but together, their magic is enhanced. Up to now, there have been two parts of the set missing; the black stone and the golden amulet. Together they have unlimited power."

"And now I have them all." Screamed the voice of Morgana, unable to control her excitement from within Julia's body.

"Now *we* have them all," repeated Julia, taking back control.

"But where's the amulet thing?" Allan asked

"Under the protection of my son." Julia smiled, but then hoped that Hugo had not misplaced it again.

Suddenly she remembered that she had walked to the house, or rather, been dragged by Jake who was asleep in the corner and had no transport to get them all back to her home. Fortunately, she had remembered to pick up her mobile phone, which was in the back pocket of her jeans. She pressed it on and, when he answered, asked her husband to come and pick them up. Mr Bennett started to ask a lot of questions about why and where she was and who were the *they* she was talking about but she explained that she would tell him everything when he arrived.

While they were waiting, Julia explained further about the stones, King Arthur, the amulet and how it came into her son's possession and many other answers about the whole story.

Deep inside her, she could feel the excitement of Morgana, as the prospect of reuniting all the elements of the inheritance loomed and the potential that its magic may bring.

Chapter 75

Anne Trembles

Everyone, including Jake, jumped up as they heard the car draw up outside and its door slam.

As the door to the house opened, Mr Bennett was about to bombard his wife with questions and admonish her for making everyone so worried… again, when the sight of the two young people made him stand back. Julia had to quickly reassure him and explain that the two were no longer Susanna and Putricia but Allan Carlisle and Sue Redwell.

Ignoring her husband's plea for information, she ushered them all, including Bird, into the Volvo and seated herself in the driving seat. As the last door closed, she could see her husband take a deep intake of breath as the smell from their passengers hit him. Quickly, despite the cold night air, Julia dropped all the windows and they drove back to the Bennett's house in silence.

As they arrived, Julia showed Sue to the bathroom and shower and directed Allan to the ensuite in her bedroom where there was another one.

She ordered Emma to find some clothes for Sue in Stephanie's room, as her daughter was not due back from her youth club for another hour, while her husband was *asked* if he could find something from his wardrobe that would fit Allan.

As for Hugo, she told him to go and fetch the amulet as fast as he could.

Bird looked around the kitchen for something to eat but saw nothing visible.

While everyone was occupied, she opened a tin of dog food for Jake who was weaving in and out of her legs; his usual way of telling her he was hungry, then she put the kettle on to make a cup of tea, though deep down she wished for something stronger to try to calm her excitement. She smiled to herself as she watched Bird searching for food. She wondered who was the greedier; Bird or Jake. Taking pity on Bird in his sorry state, she threw him a bread roll from the bread bin. He caught it mid-flight and swallowed it whole.

It wasn't long before Sue and Allan came down dressed in dressing gowns and smelling much sweeter than when they had first arrived. They looked at each other and each gave a nod of approval.

Julia warded off all the questions until she had made tea and everyone was seated around the kitchen table, steaming cups in front of them.

Rapidly, she explained to her husband, Hugo and Emma the events of the day, culminating in the discovery of the rings and most importantly, the black stone from the collar.

"Whose ring was that one from then, Mrs Bennett?" Emma asked enthusiastically.

It was Morgana's voice that answered.

"That stone used to belong to Stephen Lloyd, son of Temperance Lloyd, my cousin. He was killed; beaten to death by that foul judge. It was his death, or so we thought, and that of the judge's children, that was the reason we were executed in the first place. Susanna told us that he had survived but died many years later but..." She stopped talking for a moment and then resumed, almost as if she was talking to herself. "But what if Susanna lied and he didn't die but merged with Snatch... then that would explain why Snatch was wearing this stone on his collar?"

She fingered the large black jewel concealed in her hand and then slowly removed from her finger the ring mounted with a large red stone. There was a faint glow as the two stones touched

"Quickly. Come with me," she ordered Sue and Allan and escorted them to the sink.

The rest of the family looked on, totally confused. Their intrigue increased when she covered the couple's hands in washing up liquid. After several minutes and several expletives from the young couple, she held in her hand the blue and the clear rings.

The soapy water had made them sparkle, but when she placed them next to the three stones on the table, the effect was startling as they all seemed to glow and emit beams of light of their respective colour.

"And now, please, Hugo," Julia's voice returned as she held her hand out in front of her son.

He was uncertain whether to hand over his treasure. Although Morgana, or Anne as she insisted on being called, had lived with them for some time and had helped them fight the other witches, he still felt a little distrust. He knew that it was the amulet that all of the witches had wanted in the first place and here he was, being asked to hand it over to one of them, even though she was in the body of his mother.

"Please Hugo. It's alright." His mother's voice came out and she smiled sympathetically.

Slowly he reached into his pocket and carefully, but reluctantly, placed the object in his mother's hands, feeling its warmth growing as he did so.

As all the jewels and the amulet came together, there was a blinding flash and multicolour light beams flashed around the kitchen.

Everyone ducked as low as they could, even Jake, who barked and ran into a corner, whimpering. Only Julia Bennett stayed still. She held all the jewels in her hands and she also then began to glow. Paul Bennett stood up and started to move toward his wife but a loud command in Morgana's voice ordered him to stop. He stood motionless, almost paralysed by fear.

The glow from his wife's body seemed to come to a crescendo and he thought that he was beginning to see double. A second body was slipping sideways out of his wife's. Slowly, the body materialised and a young woman was standing next to her. She was naked and Hugo felt himself go red and looked away.

The glow from both bodies died down and Mrs Bennett slumped down onto her chair. The second body collapsed onto the floor. For a moment no one moved, Emma picked up a towel and rushed forward, covering the nakedness of the girl lying there.

Paul Bennett rushed up to his wife and put his arm around her, checking to see if she was alright. Sue knelt and helped Emma, who was gently stroking the hair of the young woman lying on the floor.

"What's happened?" Hugo called out, half in fear and half in excitement

"I think that Anne has separated from your mother," whispered Emma and looked at the young woman lying in front of her.

Mr Bennett left his wife and went over to take a closer look. He looked at Emma, who up until recently had been the host of the woman. He looked at her questioningly. She nodded gently.

At that moment, the front door burst open and Stephanie came in. She stood at the door and screamed. Her father got up and went over to her, putting his arm around her. He guided her to a chair, sat her down and explained, as best he could, what was going on.

Mrs Bennett was slowly recovering and Sue went over to her to check that she was alright. She nodded and looked up at the girl on the floor.

"Is that who I think it is?" she asked her husband.

The girl moaned and started to move. Julia raised herself and knelt beside her.

"Anne. Anne. Are you alright?"

The body turned herself to look at Julia and she smiled.

Carefully, Sue and Julia helped the girl to her feet and moved her to a chair.

"Steph. Go and see if you can find some clothes for... Anne, here," Mrs Bennett asked her daughter. Still shaking, she seemed reluctant at first to go but a small nod from her mother made her leave the room. A few minutes later she returned with a selection of clothes and a pink, spotted dressing gown.

Mr Bennett said that he had something to do and left the room. Allan also made an excuse and left so that the girl could dress; however, it was not long before Paul Bennett rushed back into the room and started to jump up and down.

"What in the world are you doing?" demanded his wife.

"Look!" he said, smiling broadly and jumping up and down again. "My limp. It's gone. You know, the one I got when I was injured in the tunnel accident." And to prove it, he walked rapidly around the room. Suddenly he stopped again and pointed to Bird.

Everyone turned and looked at the animal. He was sitting on his haunches next to the door.

"Look at him!" Hugo's father almost shouted.

Bird was surprised and seemed stunned for a few moments and then looked down at himself. All of his plumage had regenerated and he looked perfect once more, in fact, better than perfect.

"Did they do all that?" Hugo asked when he had finished gawking at his friend in absolute amazement and pointed to the jewels and amulet lying on the table; a faint glow still coming from them.

Anne finished fastening the dressing gown and sat down. "Yes, Hugo. They did do all this."

Everyone turned and looked at her. Her croaky voice was gone and now it had a sweet feminine tone with a broad west-country accent.

"I'll go and make another cup of tea. These are cold," said Hugo's father, pointing to the untouched mugs on the table. "Give me a hand Hugs."

His son grimaced at the name, saying nothing and leaned over and picked up two of the mugs, doing his best not to spill any, as he still felt quite shaky after all the excitement of the last half hour.

When he and his father returned, all the women were huddled around the table in a loud, excited conversation. They all went quiet as Mr Bennett and Hugo handed round the fresh mugs of tea and a large plateful of hot buttered toast which he had made at his son's request.

The slices disappeared almost as fast as the magic previously, with Bird making the most of the bounty.

"Anymore left?" asked Emma, who had been about to take the last slice when Bird snatched it from her grasp. Mr Bennett smiled and told her that he would see what he could do.

"I'll give you a hand," offered Allan, and the two men left.

When out of earshot and sight of the women, Paul Bennett said that he fancied something *stronger* than tea, a sentiment seconded by Allan. The two went into Mr Bennett's office where he extracted a bottle of Talisker, single malt whisky and two glasses from a drawer in his desk.

"I keep this as my own personal anaesthetic," he said, smiling broadly.

After downing the drink, they returned to the toaster. Ten minutes later, a second plate was placed on the table but Bird was blocked from access to it by Emma until everyone else had had their fill.

Although it was getting late, the conversation continued, as questions and answers went back and forth to and from Anne about her life before her hanging. On several occasions, she broke down in tears as she remembered all the details.

At last, the talking slowed and several of the group started to yawn. Mrs Bennett got up and busied herself making up temporary beds for her new guests until, at last, everyone settled down for the night. Few of them slept, except Bird and Jake, who seemed to be quite enjoying the new visitors and the attention they gave them.

As Julia was walking up the stairs to bed, her husband came up behind her and hugged her waist.

"It's good to have you back... just the one of you. You know, it's very awkward living with two women at the same time. I don't know how some people manage it."

She turned and laughed, kissed him on the forehead and together, they went to bed.

Chapter 76

New Clothes

It seemed to Hugo that he had only been asleep for five minutes when his mother came into his room, waking him to get up and ready for school. After two more calls, each becoming more urgent, he finally made it downstairs for breakfast. Emma and Stephanie had already finished theirs and were in deep conversation on what sort of clothes Anne would like. It appeared to Hugo that a shopping trip was planned for the next day, which was a Saturday and no school.

Bird was sat on his haunches, on a cushion, next to Jake. They appeared to be talking to each other. It was the first time that Hugo had ever seen the two talk. It quite surprised him that they could do it in the first place but, with all that had happened, Hugo was beginning to accept that anything could happen, especially now that all of Excalibur's jewels had been reunited.

Before he left for school, Hugo looked around for his amulet but it was nowhere to be seen. He asked his mother where it was but all she said was that 'it was safe'.

He felt uneasy that the trinket was out of his possession but a hurry-up call from his mother forced him to put his feelings to one side. Two minutes later, they were on their way to school.

Sure enough, the next day, Saturday, all four women were dressed and about to go shopping when Hugo, still bleary-eyed, came down to breakfast.

"Get yourself some cereals," his mother shouted to him as the front door slammed behind them. Seconds later, he heard the deep roar of the Volvo driving off.

"You won't see them for hours," his father's voice muttered from behind a newspaper.

At that point, the back door opened and Allan came in, looking very out of breath and clutching a thick pile of letters.

"I decided that I needed some exercise," he explained, "So I took a bit of a run back to my house. It allowed me to open a few windows to give it an airing and pick up my mail. It's certainly been piling up." He held the thick wad of papers in front of him.

"Make some tea, Hugs," came the voice from behind the paper and after a small moan, Hugo went to put the kettle on. Meanwhile, Allan had sat down by the kitchen table and started sorting out the pile of correspondence in front of him, punctuated by the sound of tearing paper and the frequent word 'Rubbish', at which point the letter was discarded onto the floor. Suddenly he screamed!

"No! I don't believe it. They can't be serious."

Mr Bennett put down his paper and asked what was wrong?

"They've impounded my car. They say that it had been abandoned and if I want to get it back, I will have to pay all the outstanding parking tickets plus a penalty to get it out of the pound. If I don't, then it will be auctioned to pay off the debt. It's over twelve hundred pounds. How in the world am I going to get twelve hundred pounds?"

He swept all the letters off the table in frustration but then realised that he was a guest in the house and sheepishly went on all fours to pick them up.

"Don't worry about the cash," Paul Bennett said sympathetically, "I'll pay the fine. If you wait for a second, I will give you a cheque and then I'll run you down to the council offices, if they're open on the weekend, and we can quickly get everything sorted out. I have to go into Bideford anyway as I need to see an architect friend of mine. I have asked him to draw up plans for turning the old judge's house site into a rest garden, with a memorial to the three Bideford witches. I feel that it's the least I can do to correct the injustice wreaked on them by my ancestors."

Allan beamed and thanked his benefactor for everything. Half an hour later they left in Julia's Smart car.

Hugo sat alone at the kitchen table, slurping the dregs of milk from the bottom of his cereal bowl. Bird came up and joined him and they discussed all the events of the previous few days.

"I know!" shouted Hugo. "Let's go for a walk along the old train track and see if we can find the entrance to Kadavera's cave. Just for old time's sake."

Bird was very reluctant. He did not need reminding of what had occurred in that place but at the mention of 'walk', Jake had jumped up and was brushing around their legs.

"Well OK," said Bird but that's all we're going to do; walk there and walk back. No chasing rabbits down holes. Agreed?"

"Agreed," laughed Hugo. After fastening Jake's lead, firmly, the three set off. It was a cold bright day. Hugo pulled his anorak around him. Bird had become invisible so that no one could see what he was doing, but knew that he must be pleased that he had regained all his feathers.

When they arrived at where Hugo thought that the entrance had been, they looked around for signs of it, but there were none, not even any pebbles with strange wavy lines on the beach.

Hugo sighed. Seeing it as it was now, made it all seem a bit of a dream, except, of course, for Bird standing next to him, or at least somewhere near him for he still could not see him.

His friend spoke. "Well then here we are. I hope that you are satisfied. Now let's get back because I'm getting cold and I'm certainly hungry and if I don't eat something soon then I won't be able to stay invisible."

Hugo smiled and sighed. With a final look around, he, and presumably Bird, turned and ambled back to the house.

As they drew near, there was a throaty roar and the crimson shape of Allan's beloved MG pulled up with a screech of brakes. It looked very dusty but as he alighted, he beamed.

"What do you think of her?" he shouted to Hugo as he approached. "Beautiful, isn't she?"

He rubbed some of the dust from the roof and then looked at his hand in disgust.

"Soon have her cleaned up," he announced and tossed the keys into the air.

As he spoke, the Volvo drew up and parked alongside the MG. All the women got out and Mrs Bennett went to the back and opened the tailgate. One by one and parcel after parcel the boot was emptied until all four women had their arms full.

"Bring that last one will you Hugo and close the boot please." His mother nodded her head at the back of the car. With a small grumble, he did as he was told.

All the parcels and bags were placed on the kitchen table. Mrs Bennett went over to the sink to fill the kettle.

"Where's Bird?" she asked. "I bought some cakes, especially for him.

In a microsecond, Bird materialised and everyone laughed. Julia Bennett pulled out from one bag, another smaller bag, which she tore open, revealing a mix of doughnuts, Chelsea buns and Hugo's favourite, Eccles cakes. Everyone dived in as if they hadn't eaten for a week. Bird had finished three before anyone else had finished one.

With the tea brewed and everyone's hunger satisfied, well except Bird's, the women all started discussing what they had bought and one by one they all disappeared to try on their purchases. Hugo could hear them all upstairs running from room to room as they compared their new attire.

Allan looked at his watch and decided that it was time he left. He explained to Hugo that he was going to take his car down to the car wash and then back to his house to start tidying it up but he did not look too enthusiastic about that idea.

As he left, Hugo's father arrived, carrying a large scroll of papers. He saw his son in the kitchen and the remains of the packaging still strewn over the kitchen table.

"Come and have a look at this," he called to Hugo and indicated for him to follow him into his office. Once there, he enthusiastically laid the papers on the table and rolled them out flat.

The heading at the top of the page announced; 'Proposed plans for the Development of the property known as the 'Old Judge's House'.

Hugo gazed in amazement as his father pointed out all the features that he had asked the architect to incorporate into the drawings, including, in the very centre, a stone memorial to the memory of the Three Bideford Witches; Temperance Lloyd, Mary Trembles and Susanna Edwards.

"But she's not dead," Hugo almost shouted and put his finger on Susanna Edward's name."

"I know that, and we all know that, but everyone else doesn't. They all think that she died on the gallows. It would take a lot of explaining if I left her out, so she is in; and besides, it might make her feel a little bit better about me if she knows that I thought of her."

Hugo nodded, and as he did so, Anne and Stephanie joined them, both sporting new clothes. They twirled in front of them with his daughter asking,

"What do you think then? Doesn't she look great." She pointed to Anne, who nervously turned, showing off the new dress she was wearing. As she turned, she noticed the plans on the table and immediately forgot her clothes. Mr Bennett went over them again with the two girls, finally asking,

"Well, what do *you* think then?" They all laughed and Anne threw her arms around Hugo's father and kissed him. He blushed, the embrace was broken by the appearance of his wife at the door.

"What's all this then? Carrying on behind my back?" She grinned at her husband's embarrassment but then noticed the plans. For the third time, he went over them pointing out the various features, finally looking at Anne.

"I think that the garden would be a wonderful way of remembering my friends and I'm sure that they would approve of your action and lift the curse from you and your family. If only I could contact my sister and Susanna, I'm sure that they would agree." Everyone nodded and with that, Mrs Bennett asked if anyone wanted a cup of tea.

Sue Redwell joined them in the kitchen, carrying a large holdall.

"You've all been very kind to me, especially as I tried to kill you all but it's time I went back to my flat and get on with my own life. I don't know if I still have a job but I will have to see. I suppose I could write about my adventures, they are certainly worth the Pulitzer prize, but I am sure that no one would believe me. Still, I suppose that I could always write a book, a real fairy or rather, gnome story."

Everyone laughed and then hugged the young reporter. Mr Bennett offered to drive her home, which she accepted. After more hugs and tears, the two left; the noise of the Smart car slowly disappearing into the distance.

Anne sat at the table, mug of tea in hand. "Sue was right. It's time to make a life of my own. I have been a burden on you all, in one way or another, for too long and it's time that you lost the responsibility of looking after me. I don't know how I'm going to find a job, my experience of your way of living is very limited but Sue was right again, I do have centuries of memories and experiences. I think that they might make a fascinating book but first I must learn to use one of those things that you have, a *taplock* I think you called it." Everyone laughed and shouted in unison; "Laptop!"

"Well, there's no time like the present," announced Stephanie. "Come with me."

Together they went upstairs to Stephanie's room and they could be heard talking and giggling for several hours.

On his return, Julia explained to her husband about Sue leaving and Anne wanting to go. Between them, they decided to buy her a small flat where she could live but not too far away, so that if she needed any help, then they would be close at hand. When they first suggested this to Anne she refused, but then Mr Bennett pointed out that she was legally dead and had been for over three hundred years so she might have trouble getting a mortgage and all the financial implications that that involved. As for a job, well, he was sure that he could find her one at his dental practice. She hugged and kissed him again but this time, his wife just burst out laughing.

Chapter 77

Hugo's Father's Deception

Time flew by as the Bennett parents organised as much of the legal paperwork that could be done to allow Anne to live as normal a life as possible but they daren't apply for a passport or driving licence, as that would immediately flag her up as effectively being an illegal alien.

They were delighted to hear that the rebuilding of their old house had been completed ahead of schedule, thanks to a spell of warm, dry weather. Much of their efforts were taken up packing, ready to move back in. Finally, the day came and the removal lorries parked in the drive. Up to this point, Mr Bennett had not allowed Hugo or Stephanie to visit the house so that when they did, it would be a great surprise as he had explained that he had made a few… changes.

As they entered the new house, Hugo was awestruck. It seemed so much roomier. Walls had been taken down and the whole lower floor made open-plan.

"Close your eyes, you two," he said to the children, "and come with me."

They closed their eyes and held his hands, Hugo was excited as he did not know what to expect and after what seemed an epic journey, they stopped. There was a funny smell in the air.

"OK kids. Open your eyes."

When they did so, they both screamed with excitement. In front of them was an indoor swimming pool.

"It's heated!" screamed Stephanie as she bent down to feel the water.

"Well you kept moaning about the sea always being too cold to swim in, so I thought that you might like this," their father joked. "After all, what's the point of having an inheritance if you don't use it." He looked at Anne as he said this and she blushed.

The rest of the day they explored the house, organising the rooms, telling the removal men where to put this or that. Hugo was delighted that his bedroom was now twice the size but his enthusiasm was curtailed when his mother warned him that, now he had more room, if he didn't keep it tidy, then he would be in trouble.

Christmas was fast approaching and Julia Bennett wanted to make this one very special, as it would be the first one Anne had had for centuries. For the actual day, she decided to organise a surprise party. However, she wanted to invite all the gnomes, as well as Sue, Allan, Peter Goodfellow, Puchy and of course Bird. It was then that she realised that if she held the party at their own house, then it may create problems if anyone happened to see their *unusual* guests. A quick phone call to the delighted owner of the Gnome Reserve solved that problem and arranged everything for it to be held there.

Everyone was awake early when the day finally arrived and Hugo was itching to open his presents but his mother insisted that he, like everyone else, must wait until they were all assembled at the Gnome Reserve.

When they arrived, the accumulated guests were already in full party mode and cheered as the Bennett's walked through the doors. Everyone wondered who the young woman that was with them was as they didn't recognise her. Several were on the verge of running back to the protection of their houses when they found out that she was the witch Morgana. To avert any misunderstandings, Paul Bennett decided that he would give a little speech to explain her presence and to wish everyone a happy Christmas. This suggestion satisfied most of the guests but several, mostly gnomes, kept their distance, just in case.

At last, it was the time to open their presents, much to Hugo's relief and for almost half an hour, there was the sound of tearing paper and excited screams. Hugo got the electric hoverboard that he had been dropping hints that he wanted for several weeks before. All the women, Anne included, seemed to have been given wardrobes of clothes. Bird was enjoying several of the cakes and goodies when Anne came up to him and gave him a small parcel.

"This is for your brother," she said, almost blushing.

Bird tore off the wrappings and found within them a small bottle, with a blood-red liquid inside. He looked at Anne and, after thanking her, looked puzzled. She smiled and whispered that it was the antidote to reverse the original potion and to stop Bird's brother from growing.

Bird was absolutely overjoyed and wrapped his wings around her in appreciation.

Mrs Bennett grinned when she saw this, as she had secretly helped Anne make the potion when everyone was out of the house.

It was quite late in the evening when the Bennett's finally arrived back at their house. As they all sat down in the lounge before going to bed, Hugo's father went into his office and returned with a large roll of paper, which he spread out on the table in front of them.

On the paper was an artist drawing of, what looked like a very elegant garden, with statues and fountains. He looked at Anne and said,

"Well. What do you think of the memorial garden for your ancestors.?"

Anne looked at the picture and then at everyone standing around who were all smiling.

"It's beautiful," she sobbed. "I think that they would be very proud to be remembered in this way."

"Right then," announced Mr Bennett. "All we need to do is get the confirmation from the planning people and we can make a start on it as soon as possible."

Everyone cheered and then relaxed into a cacophony of chatter, interspersed with the odd yawn as the events of the day finally took their toll.

One by one, they drifted off to bed until Paul Bennett was the last man standing. He finished off the glass of his favourite single malt whiskey, Talisker, from the Isle of Skye, rolled up the picture of the garden and went to bed himself.

The next day Bird announced that he was going to Australia so that he could give his brother the present which Anne had given him.

"How will you get there?" Stephanie asked.

"Your father is going to drive me to Heathrow airport, and after making myself invisible, I will get on a plane to Australia," replied the animal.

"But you can't stay invisible for that long," interrupted Hugo.

"Ah! We've thought of that," Bird joked. "Your mother has made me a big box of her fairy cakes which she is going to package up and send them by airmail to Australia. I will board the same flight and hide in the baggage area. During the flight, when I get hungry, I can find the package, open it and eat the cakes. That way, I can stay invisible. Simple."

Everyone laughed and patted him on the neck.

"You're going to need a big package knowing how hungry he gets," joked Hugo, and everyone laughed again.

Over the next two weeks, before school started back, the house was a hive of activity, what with the process of still settling into the new home and getting everything prepared for Bird's journey.

The cakes were baked and packaged and a few days after New Year, the Bennett parents, with Bird in his invisible form, drove him up to Heathrow. There was one worrying moment when Bird's body heat set off an alarm from a scanner as he passed through but it was put down to a glitch and all went well.

As they were driving home, they gazed out of the car window as the Qantas 747 carrying their friend, thundered overhead as it climbed into the twilight of the sky.

The next day, Paul Bennett decided to have a lie-in, as they had not arrived home till the early hours due to a road accident on the M4 which had delayed them for several hours. Julia Bennett had forced herself out of bed to make sure that her children and Emma were not late for the beginning of the new term at school. On her return from the school-run, she slumped down on a chair in the kitchen and clutched the hot mug of coffee which she had just made herself. Her husband joined her a few minutes later, saying that he could not sleep so he would get on with some paperwork after he'd read the local newspaper.

Emblazoned across its front page was the headline; *Beast of Exmoor strikes again. Farmers demand action.*

The report read that farmers on Exmoor had organised a petition to their local MP, asking that action be taken to control the devastation that was being wreaked on that part of the county by, what was known as *The Beast of Exmoor.*

The farmers were concerned over the increasing number of stock, both sheep and cattle, that were discovered across Exmoor with their throats torn out by, what can only be described as, a ferocious animal. The report continued that on several occasions a large, cat-like animal, had been spotted in the same vicinity as the killings.

As they finished their drinks, they heard footsteps coming down the stairs. Paul Bennett put down his paper and Anne joined them. She wished them a good morning and pulled up a chair close beside them.

"I've been thinking," she said, somewhat awkwardly. "You've all been very kind to me but I think that it is time for me to go and make a life for myself. I like living with you all but I think that if I do not make the break, then eventually I would get in the way."

Julia started to protest but Anne silenced her and

explained that she had thought very hard about it and had made up her mind.

"In all my centuries of existence I have never ventured more than a handful of miles from Bideford and, since I am no longer able to increase my lifespan without more body changing, I would like to see more of the world. You have very kindly given me a large sum of money," she said, nodding to Mr Bennett, "and I would like to use some of it to see what I have been missing."

Julia wanted to argue but realised that the girl was right. If she were in her position, then she would do the same.

"When do you intend to leave?" she asked.

I thought that now would be the best time because if I wait until everyone is here, then they may persuade me to stay and that would not be right."

Julia felt a lump growing inside her throat as she tried to choke back the tears that were forming.

"One thing before I go?" said Anne. "I feel very guilty about my sister and Susanne who are trapped in Snatch's body."

Mr Bennett moved his newspaper away from Anne's vision.

"I am sure that when I tell them how kind you all are and what you have planned for the memorial garden, I feel convinced that they will see how wrong they have been. If they do, then, if I have the jewels and the amulet that make up our inheritance, I can separate them from Snatch and we can all live together, happily."

"I'm not so sure that is a good idea," said Mr Bennett, pushing the newspaper further underneath the chair where he had thrown it and looking at his wife sternly.

"Well. I'm not so sure either but, after all, technically the jewels and amulet do belong to Anne."

Anne nodded. "I promise that if they do not agree to return to normal, then I will not separate them from Snatch."

For almost an hour the two Bennett's discussed the pros and cons of handing over the *inheritance*, especially on how they would explain its loss to Hugo, until finally Mr Bennett agreed but not before he had an idea.

Going into his office, he unlocked his safe and withdrew a small plastic box. Inside, surrounded by cotton wool, lay the jewels. In a second similar box, the amulet glowed faintly.

Taking the amulet out of its box, using a paper tissue to prevent direct contact with it, Mr Bennett took it to his shed in the garden. From one of the drawers, in an old dressing table, he withdrew two round containers. Taking out a wad of what seemed like a yellow putty from one pot and a similar amount from the other, he started to mix them. When it was even, he rolled it into a ball and then flattened it into a disc. Picking the amulet from the bench, he pressed it into the putty and then waited for it to set. When he was sure it was hard, he made a similar disc of putty and moulded it over the first, encasing the amulet. When this had set, he pulled the two pieces of putty apart and removed the charm. Inside the discs, was an exact imprint of the amulet.

Hugo's father carefully inspected his work and smiled at its result. He replaced the trophy into his pocket and placed the impression into a plastic bag. With bag and amulet, he returned to the women.

His wife asked where he had been but all he would tell her was that he was, *fixing things,* and winked.

After a final plea for her to change her mind, the Bennett's reluctantly handed over the jewels and amulet to Anne. She smiled and rubbed her treasure between her fingers. A look of utter delight crept over her face, which made Mr Bennett feel that he had made the wrong decision but now it was too late.

Carefully, she threaded all the coloured jewels, still in their rings, onto the chain which held the small locket, and fastened it around her neck. She placed the black stone from Snatch's collar into her coat pocket and the amulet into the inside pocket.

As she did this, she noticed Julia's questioning look.

"All the elements must be kept separate," she explained, "until they are needed. Otherwise, they will become useless and lose their power."

Paul Bennett then realised why she had insisted to him not to put everything in one box when he put them in his safe.

With a flood of tears from the women, Anne picked up her rucksack, walked out of the house and out of their lives, or so the Bennett's thought.

"I hope that we have done the right thing," sobbed Julia and hugged her husband for a long time.

When she had calmed down, Mr Bennett said that he had to make a call at his surgery to send something over to the dental laboratory. He waved the plastic bag from the shed in the air.

Julia was confused by this but told him not to be long and if he could remember to collect her dry cleaning from the shop in the supermarket.

When he had left, she tried to busy herself with chores, but the thought of Anne being alone frequently moved her to tears. She kept asking herself if she had made the right decision in letting her leave.

It was a week later when Hugo came home looking and feeling very dejected. His mother asked him what was wrong. She thought that he was still upset about Anne leaving without saying goodbye, but when she asked him, he told her that he had been dropped from the football team as he had scored an own goal, twice in one match, at school and the captain had been livid because up to that point they were winning but Hugo had made them lose.

"Can I have my amulet back?" he pleaded with his mother. "Whenever I have it on me, I feel much more confident and have always scored."

She lied to him that it was in his father's safe for safe-keeping and he would have to ask him when he returned from work. Immediately she said it she regretted it, knowing full well that it wasn't in the safe and it would now be even more difficult for her husband to explain its absence.

As soon as her husband came in from work, she took him to one side and explained her lie, expecting him to be furious. Instead, he smiled, kissed her on the cheek and took out from his pocket, the amulet.

"But I thought that you gave Anne the amulet?" she gasped and reached out to touch it.

"I did," her husband replied. "But before I gave it to her, I took an impression of it with the stuff that I use to make models to allow the boys at the dental lab to make crowns for teeth. I asked them to make a duplicate amulet and they did a pretty good job, don't you think?"

Julia smiled and gave him a big hug which was interrupted by Hugo coming into the room. He still looked sad as he told his father why he wanted to have the amulet back. His father explained that putting your faith in good-luck charms was not the best way forward but Hugo was insistent. Finally, his father appeared to give in, though the look he gave his wife was one of humour, as he had made his son grovel. He strode into his office and made a point of opening his safe as loudly as he could. He took the new amulet from his pocket and made it appear that he had taken it from the safe. Holding it up between his tissue-covered fingers, he presented it to Hugo, who joyfully tossed it into the air without giving it a second look and ran up to his room muttering, "Yes. Yes. Yes. You wait, Barry Jones. You'll wish you never dropped me now that I've got this." And he tossed it into the air again.

Chapter 78

Call to Friends

The cold wind tore around Anne's face and legs. Her ski jacket, which Stephanie had bought her for Christmas flapped around her body. The sun was just about to set, though it was impossible to see it through the driving drizzle that occurs on the top of Exmoor.

Fingering the black stone in her pocket and stoking the jewels around her neck, she ignored the weather. She felt the warmth of the amulet flowing into her body as it lay in the pocket next to her heart. She smiled as she gazed out intently at the barren hills and valleys in front of her. The words of Mr Bennett kept rolling through her mind; *'What's the point of having an inheritance if you don't use it?'*

Throwing her head backwards, she laughed and shouted.

"Come my friend's! Come to Morgana! Come and see what I've got for you!"

In the far distance, close to the horizon, two bright red eyes looked up from the bloody, still-warm carcass of a sheep. A loud howl came from between two large yellow fangs as the beast of Exmoor pounded towards the cry.

The end